The Ca

a Henrietta Allen West

Going Home

Henrietta Alten West

LLOURETTIA GATES BOOKS • MARYLAND

Llourettia Gates Books, LLC
P.O. Box #411
Fruitland, Maryland 21826

Hardcover ISBN: 978-1-953082-30-5
Paperback ISBN: 978-1-953082-31-2
eBook ISBN: 978-1-953082-32-9
Library of Congress Control Number: 2024912852

Photography by Andrea Lōpez Burns
Cover and interior design by Jamie Tipton, Open Heart Designs

This book is dedicated to my friend
Grace Ann Durden.
She was beautiful, smart, and kind.
Everybody loved her. She introduced me to the
17th century Italian artist, Artemisia Gentileschi.
I miss you Grace Ann.

Contents

CAST OF CHARACTERS

Elizabeth and Richard Carpenter
Elizabeth and Richard live in a small town on the Eastern Shore of Maryland. Richard is a retired pathologist who did some work for the Philadelphia Medical Examiner's office many years ago. Elizabeth is a former college professor and CIA analyst. She began writing mystery novels after she had her 70th birthday. They spend the winters at their home in Tucson, Arizona.

Gretchen and Bailey MacDermott
Gretchen and Bailey live in Dallas, Texas. Bailey is a former IBM salesman, oil company executive, and Department of Defense intelligence agent. He currently is making another fortune selling commercial real estate. Gretchen works in the corporate world as the head of an HR department. Because she is so competent at everything she does, she actually runs the company she works for. She says she is going to retire this year. Her friends have heard this before.

Tyler Merriman
Tyler has recently moved to Fayetteville, Arkansas. Everyone suspects that Tyler flew the SR-71 Blackbird for the U.S. Air Force during his younger years. After he retired from the military, he made millions in commercial real estate. He flew his own plane around the country. He is an avid skier and hiker

and rides his bicycle everywhere. He's had a series of surgeries in the past year and has finally become the Bionic Man.

Sidney and Cameron Richardson

Sidney and Cameron have several homes and their own private plane. Cameron is a former IBM wunderkind who went out on his own to start several globally-known computer companies. Sidney is a retired profiling consultant who owned an innovative, successful, and very profitable home organization business before she married Cameron. The Richardsons are currently building a world-class resort in Arkansas.

Isabelle and Matthew Ritter

Isabelle and Matthew live in Palm Springs, California. Matthew is a retired urologist, an avid quail hunter, and a movie buff. Isabelle has retired from her career as a clinical psychologist and now owns a popular high-end interior furnishings store and design business. Her creative skills are in great demand, and she works way too hard to please her demanding clientele.

J.D. Steele

J.D. lives in Saint Louis. He is a lawyer who gave up his job as a prosecuting attorney to found his own extremely successful trucking company. He is a logistics expert. Olivia, the love of his life, died in November of the previous year. J.D. has been inconsolable over Olivia's death, but his friends are thrilled he is attending the reunion this year.

Juanita de Cabo

Juanita is the Richardson's long-time friend and helper. She hails from Cabo San Lucas, Mexico and now has a house at the River Springs resort in Arkansas. She is a fabulous cook. Her daughter is visiting to help out with the work of feeding the reunion group.

Ginny Randolph/Virginia Delacroix

Virginia Delacroix is a talented local artist who lives in River Springs, Arkansas and creates her artwork out of found objects. She has been unhappily married to Bubba Randolph. Bubba is a chicken farmer, drug dealer, and drug addict who beats her up on a regular basis. Virginia is desperate to have a new life away from Bubba.

Rebecca Sells

Becky is Sidney Richardson's best friend. Together they can do anything. Becky is a very successful New York City real estate mogul. She is rich and resourceful. She goes to great lengths to protect Virginia Delacroix and to promote the artist's extraordinary talent.

Raymond Barstow

Raymond "Bart" Barstow is Cameron Richardson's friend and a retired FBI special agent. Cameron asks Bart to come to River Springs to help with a situation that involves fentanyl trafficking and to find a friend of Sidney's who has gone missing. Bart finds that doing the right thing sometimes involves making a different choice than doing what the law dictates.

Maximillian Sobrille

Max is an art forger who was born in Gibraltar. He has a unique gift that allows him to paint perfect copies of famous paintings. He has used many names and has copied artwork in museums all over the world. He has made a fortune selling his forgeries and has finally retired to Shadowlawn in Franklin, Louisiana. A lucky find in a New Orleans antique store offers him the opportunity to do something he never imagined he would have a chance to do.

Roy George and Leonard DeNunzio

Roy and Leonard are burglars. They dress up in uniforms that belong to the Boston police. Even with their obviously fake mustaches, they are able to talk their way into the Isabella Stewart Gardner Museum in the early morning of March 18, 1990. They ransack and rob the place and get away with the heist of a lifetime. They are bumblers, and their adventures are chaotic. They don't know what to do with the masterpieces they have stolen.

Prologue

The Camp Shoemaker reunion group was making a special effort to have fun at this year's gathering. Olivia Steele had passed away in November of the previous year after an incredibly courageous fight to live. Her friends had known, the last time they'd been together, that Olivia was gravely ill. Everyone who knew her had loved this special woman. She was beautiful, brilliant, brave, kind, fun, and funny. She personified every good thing you could imagine in a human being. J.D. was inconsolable. Olivia had died less than a year ago, and he was making a valiant attempt to keep on keeping on. He was planning to attend the reunion. His friends were thrilled that he was coming and were looking forward to seeing him.

The good news was that two of their own, Cameron and Sidney Richardson, were in the process of building a world-class resort in the middle of nowhere. Bucolic and quiet with the best views of nature one could dream about, River Springs Refuge was the perfect place to get away from it all and relax.

The Richardsons had bought the hundreds of magnificent wooded acres and designed the resort themselves. It was a work in progress. What had already been built was a delight. Sidney's good taste and gift for interior design were to be found in every one of the individual cottages. The resort was close to a river and a lake...both famous for their fly casting and trout fishing. Some of the Shoemaker boys might decide to try their hand at fishing, but most forays close to the water would be sightseeing events only for the majority of the reunion goers.

Some of their crowd had been able to attend Olivia's funeral. Those who could not make it had spent a long weekend with J.D. at a historic hotel in Winslow, Arizona. Olivia had been toasted and celebrated in Winslow, and there would be more celebrations of her exceptional life during the reunion this fall. Olivia would have loved the Richardson's resort, and the weekend's participants were certain that Olivia would be there with them in spirit.

The Reunion

ARKANSAS

2023

*A**ll of the men in the group had celebrated their* 80th birthdays that year. They had met at Camp Shoemaker when they were eight years old. They'd all been assigned to Cabin #1, and even when they'd moved on to other cabins when they were older, they always maintained that they were #1. They had never stopped believing that they were. They'd lost touch over the middle years of their lives, but Matthew Ritter had brought them back together for a reunion fourteen years earlier. The group had enjoyed each other and had such a good time, they'd decided to continue the fun year after year in some exceptional places all over the Western Hemisphere. All of these reunion locations, of course, had to have outstanding food.

Because they were celebrating in a more remote location this year, there were fewer restaurants to choose from in the local towns. In spite of protests that she not do so, Sidney had graciously volunteered to cook several of the meals. She was an excellent cook. She knew how to make three kinds of gravy. But cooking for a crowd was not supposed to be required on these special weekends. Good food was of paramount importance to these octogenarians and their partners, but no one would be happy if Sidney slaved away at the stove. There were a few restaurant options in the area. One of these restaurants was owned by the Richardsons and run by the chef Cameron had hired from New Orleans.

Fortunately Cameron and Sidney had their best helper, Juanita, to assist in the kitchen at their home. Juanita was like family to the Richardsons, and she had her own house on the resort's property. Juanita's daughter was visiting, and the two women would help Sidney with the cooking and the cleaning up.

River Springs Refuge was low-key and informal. The cabins were well-appointed and beautifully decorated. They were, in fact, downright luxurious. The views of nature were everywhere, and they were inspirational. It promised to be a restful and soothing weekend. Some of the recent reunions had involved adventures that were not entirely appropriate for people in their seventies. But try to tell that to this group as they'd hopped on motorcycles and speed boats to rescue the good guys and go after the bad guys. The group *said* they really did want to "lay back and be cool." But they had seemed to thrive on the challenges of previous years. Would they be content to rest, relax, and drink a glass of wine... without the excitement of their past get-togethers?

Several of the Camp Shoemaker crowd happened to arrive at the same time. There was an impromptu welcome fest in the driveway of the Richardson's river house. These yearly reunions and the chance to spend time together had become more precious to the Camp Shoemaker crowd as the years went by. Sidney gave everyone their housing assignments and reminded them that cocktails would begin at the Richardson's home at 5:00 that evening. Individual cabins were strategically placed in the woods. Each cabin fit perfectly into its rustic surroundings on the outside and was beautifully decorated and appointed with all the modern conveniences on the inside. There would be enough time to unpack, get settled, and have a little bit of a rest before they would get together again at the Richardson's.

River Springs Refuge had become Cameron's latest project, and he was all in. He loved every aspect of creating his resort in the woods. He loved moving dirt. He loved putting in bulkheads. He loved building roads. Cameron was overseeing the construction of several new cabins and the renovation of the enormous log house and its garage that were going to become a lodge and high-tech conference center. Cameron was in his element. He had made his fortune in data processing and computers, but that was then. This was now, and he had never been happier than working to make River Springs Refuge a first-class retreat for companies from all over the world. Retirement was a word and a concept that was not in Cameron Richardson's repertoire.

Cameron had purchased a fleet of electric golf carts to make it easy for guests to get around at the resort. Everyone in the Camp Shoemaker group loved the golf carts and much preferred driving them to trying to maneuver their big, noisy cars and trucks in the pastoral surroundings. Tyler Merriman had grown tired of the Colorado winters and had moved to Fayetteville, Arkansas so he'd been able to drive to River Springs. Bailey had flown to Little Rock from Dallas, and Gretchen was driving to the resort the next day. She was still working and had a job to do. The Ritters were arriving late for dinner that night. Their plane from California had been delayed…as it always was. J.D. Steele had arrived with Bailey from the Little Rock airport, and the Carpenters had driven to the reunion from the East Coast in Richard's pickup truck. They were on their way to Arizona for the winter.

The Richardson's river house was ideal for the setting. On its own private road, it was sited perfectly beside the Little Red River. It was constructed of natural materials and used natural colors. The rustic stacked stone of the exterior fit beautifully with its surroundings. The interior was elegant and comfortable. Sidney and Cameron were superb hosts who had created a modern but warm and welcoming home in the wilderness.

As an appetizer, Sidney served a beautiful charcuterie platter that was almost too lovely to disturb. But the crowd that gathered was hungry from their travels, and it was not long before they attacked the artful arrangement of cheeses and other savories. It seemed that age and various medical issues among the reunion goers had drastically reduced the demand for alcoholic beverages. Sidney had been worried she would not have enough beer on hand, but there was more than enough of everything to satisfy the crowd this year.

Elizabeth was drinking Coca-Cola and ice water almost exclusively but would drink a glass of red wine if she was also eating food. Richard was laying low because he didn't want to drive the unfamiliar golf cart into a ditch. He also didn't want to get lost in the woods. Bailey had been told by his cardiologist that he could not drink alcohol with the medication he was taking. He was having a drink anyway… but only one? Sidney had always been a teetotaler, and Cameron was cutting back because of his blood pressure. Only J.D. and Tyler were seriously surveying the bottles on the bar. The wild and wooly days of youth had morphed into the more careful drinking habits that accommodated doctors' orders and the demands of aging. This group could have fun without imbibing, and the stories and the laughter were in full swing when the Ritters arrived.

Sidney's chili and her homemade beef vegetable soup were fabulous, and almost everyone had a bowl of each. The homemade cornbread went perfectly with the chili and with the soup. Everyone oohed and aahed when Juanita put a basket of her hot and crispy homemade corn chips on the table. The peach cobbler with vanilla ice cream was to die for. This down-home cooking had been exactly right for their first meal together. Nobody wanted the evening to end. The first night together was all about seeing each other again and catching up. If too much time was spent talking about the side effects of blood pressure medication and how many days one had been required to wear a heart monitor, that was the price to be paid for having had the audacity to live to the age of 80.

Everyone loved their cabins. Sidney's magic had been brought to bear in the building and in the decorating and furnishing. Every cabin had its own kitchen…complete with a dishwasher and a full-size refrigerator and all the dishes and pots and pans one could possibly need. Each cabin was relaxing and beautiful. It was going to be the best weekend.

Cameron had planned a tour of the resort's building sites for the next morning. The parade of golf carts made its way around and through the construction vehicles that were scattered in the woods. Priority had been given to removing as few trees as possible. Cameron's workmen's jobs had been made more difficult because it was important to save the vegetation. But the results and the heavily wooded surroundings of the cabins were testimony that the "save the trees" crusade had been worth it.

Many developers routinely level a building site and roll their bulldozers and other vehicles in to construct the houses. It is more efficient to be able to build without having to work around existing trees and other vegetation. After the new buildings are completed, builders plant new trees and bushes. That was the easy way, but that was not the way things were being done at River Springs Refuge. It would be more difficult and therefore more costly to build the cabins among the trees, but it would be so much better when it was all completed.

Cameron and Sidney had also purchased a large log house and matching log garage that had been built on a property contiguous to theirs. The previous owners of the log house and garage had collected antique cars...hence the six-car garage. The car collectors had built the log house and the log garage in the 1970s. Cameron's plan was to join the enormous garage and the enormous house into one enormous rustic lodge. Conferences would be held there. An almost full-time chef and his staff would run the kitchen, and gourmet meals would be served. It would be the ultimate high-tech center for meetings...here in the middle of the woods. The work was already underway to make the former log home and garage into a twenty-first century retreat and conference center. Cameron's unique vision was apparent to all his Camp Shoemaker friends. They were looking forward to coming back to visit the lodge when it was finished. Cameron said it would be ready by the following fall.

After the tour of the cabins and the present and future River Springs Refuge Conference Center, the group transferred from the golf carts to highway-worthy vehicles and traveled to the famous Red Apple Inn for lunch. The restaurant and country club was set on an island in the middle of a large lake. The delightful bistro was open to the public.

Cameron had been coming here for decades and was good friends with the management. Everyone's lunch was delicious, but Elizabeth thought her plate of chicken salad made with grapes and slivered almonds, Bing cherry salad on the side, and strawberry bread was the most unusual. She had not seen Bing cherry salad on a menu in many, many decades. It had been one of her mother's specialties. When Elizabeth saw it on the menu at the Red Apple Inn, she had to order it. And the Red Apple Inn's version was the real thing. She savored every bite. It tasted exactly like her mother's recipe had tasted.

While Cameron had been moving dirt, putting bulkheads in along the river, building roads, building cabins, and creating his resort and high-tech conference center, Sidney had also been making the adjustment to "country living." Their life in the city was work for Cameron, although he was making some attempts to pull back and train others to take over the leadership role in his computer company. Sidney was involved in philanthropic work and fundraising for worthy causes. She was very good at this and enjoyed it. At first she had been reluctant to neglect her responsibilities in the city. Sidney never neglected anything, but she felt as if she was being a little bit lazy when she spent too much time at her river house in the woods.

Sidney had run several successful businesses before she married Cameron, and she could not pretend to be lazy for long. Truth be told…she was never lazy. Her epiphany about the secrets of this rural area had taken place, more than a year earlier, at the farmer's market near River Springs when she was buying homemade bread at one of the stands. The woman who wrapped Sidney's loaves of whole wheat, sourdough, and carrot cake bread was wearing a stunning jacket. Sidney knew about a lot of things, and she was quite accoplished at many things. One of her greatest talents was her eye for design. She could instantly recognize what was beautiful, creative, and unusual. It wasn't the style of the jacket so much as it was the fabric that caught her eye. The cloth of the jacket had obviously been hand woven. It was a combination of colors in an entirely original pattern. Sidney had to ask where in the world the woman who was selling bread had bought such a jacket.

"I made it. I made the jacket. I like to sew."

"But the fabric. I've ever seen anything like it before. Is it wool?"

"Yes, it's all wool. My aunt is a weaver. She weaves these wonderful fabrics. She uses only natural fibers, and she dyes her own. In fact she grows her own sheep for the wool. This fabric is made from the wool of her sheep. She makes the dyes out of natural fruits and vegetables that she grows in her garden. She weaves fabrics made of cotton and linen, too."

"The colors are so rich, so intense. Does she sell her cloth, the fabrics she weaves?"

"No, she just does it for fun. She sometimes gives me pieces she's woven, and if I have time, I turn them into gifts for friends and family. She has stacks and stacks of the beautiful pieces she's created. She has closets full of fabric, and she has this room in her house that's entirely filled up with her loom."

"Do you think she would be willing to sell any of her work?"

"Sure, but who would want to buy it?"

Sidney realized there was a woman living somewhere in this very rural place, and nearby, who was an incredibly gifted weaver. What a shame she didn't have a place where she could sell her wares and make some money.

Sidney was almost always in a hurry when she went shopping at the farmers' market. She had certain stalls where she bought the things she needed…vegetables, bread, and homemade pies. It dawned on her that she should spend more time here and look at some of the other things that were for sale at the market. She came back the next week when she could take a more leisurely look at the non-food items that were for sale. She got the things on her list that she needed, and then she spent some time exploring. At the back of the market, close to the parking lot, she saw a young woman who was struggling to set up a stall and get her goods displayed. Sidney was curious and stopped to see what was going on.

"Do you need some help?" Sidney was always willing to help out.

"Thanks, I appreciate the offer. But I think this is the last of it. We share a stall here at the market. None of us can afford to rent the stall every week. This wasn't supposed to be my week. The truth is, I've never sold anything here before. My friend Dani, that's Danielle Sorensen, called me and said she was sick and couldn't come today. I'm late, but it seemed a shame to waste the rental. It isn't cheap, you know, and they don't give us a good spot anyway. But here I am, and I haven't brought the right things to display my work. I'll know next time…if there is a next time."

Sidney wasn't sure she followed everything this woman was saying. "I'm Sidney. What's your name, and what are you selling?"

"I'm Ginny and I sell creations made from found objects." Ginny giggled a little bit when she told Sidney what she was selling. "I love what I do. It's a hobby really. It doesn't cost me much, and probably nobody will want to buy any of it. Dani tells me my creations are beautiful and that if I promoted them, they would sell. My husband says my creations are 'junk made out of junk,' but what does he know? He's a chicken farmer."

Sidney had to laugh at that one. "Let me see what you make." Sidney wasn't expecting much and was stunned when Ginny unpacked the first beautiful objet d'art. It was an intricately crafted miniature house... or something similar to that. It was not easy to say exactly what it was, but Sidney had never seen anything quite like it before. It was painted red and silver, but the paint did not obscure the craftsmanship of the small building. The minute Sidney saw it, she wanted to buy it. She picked up the object and examined it more closely. It was made entirely from plastic forks. Plastic forks! Really? The little house had been constructed using only the handles of the forks. Ginny had cut off the prong ends, and these were perfectly made into the roof and perfectly placed as windows and to decorate "the house." Ginny had painted this exquisite little gem of plastic forks and glue to enhance its charm.

"Ginny, this is absolutely phenomenal. I've never seen anything quite like it. Your work is unique and uniquely fabulous."

Ginny blushed bright red, all the way down to the roots of her naturally curly bright red hair. Sidney wondered if anyone had ever before in her entire life complimented Ginny about anything. Made shy by the praise she had received; Ginny removed the newspaper wrappings from two more items and put them on the counter of the stall. One item was a sculpture of a tree made from buttons. You wouldn't know it was made of buttons if you didn't look closely. It was another amazing work of art. The next item GInny unwrapped was the sculpture of a girl's head, made entirely out of strips of Styrofoam. Ginny had painted this one so it resembled marble. It was light as a feather, but you would never know it was made out of anything but marble until you picked it up.

"You have an incredible talent, Ginny. I can't believe you have never tried to sell your work anywhere before."

Ginny's face fell. "I have to hide what I do. I have my own small flock of hens, and my husband lets me keep the money I make from selling the eggs. I don't make much money on the eggs, but what I do make goes towards buying my share of this stall. I've just bought in although it's a stretch for me to be able to afford it. I can display and sell my creations once every six weeks. There are six of us who share the stall. None of us can afford it on our own, but together we can rent it and share the cost. My husband hates my hobby. He says it's stupid. He says all I'm doing is making junk into more junk. I don't work on it until after he's gone to bed at night. He gets up early and goes to bed real early. Then I have time to work on what I love to do. He doesn't know what I'm doing…after he's asleep."

Sidney knew that this shy, almost scared young woman had an amazing gift. She knew that this highly original work would sell for really big bucks in New York City. It made her sad that this woman's talent was "hidden under a bushel" and being put down and ridiculed by a chicken farmer husband who didn't know what he was talking about. An idea began to form in Sidney's head.

"These friends of yours who share the stall…the other five women. What do they sell?"

"We all sell different things. Chelsea sells scarves that she makes and decorates with her own vegetable dyes. They are the most beautiful colors, and she grows all the things she uses for colors and designs in her own garden. Danielle, that's my best friend Dani, paints bisque ware. She's a wonderful artist, but she may have to drop out. She has a kiln, but it's an old one. It costs her a fortune to fire it up. She can't really afford to fire her work anymore. She needs a new kiln, but she can't afford one. Darla makes baskets out of the natural grasses you find growing everywhere around here... along the side of the highway and everywhere. She makes picnic baskets and bread baskets and toy chests and everything else you can imagine... all out of the grass she cuts for free from beside the road. She has some special secret process she does with the grass so it stays flexible and doesn't dry out and break. I don't know what she does to it, but her baskets are really beautiful. You'd be amazed with what she can make with only a bundle of grass."

Sidney was sure she would be amazed. She'd had no idea this amount of talent and creativity existed out here in River Springs. These women deserved a showcase for their talents. Sidney thought she had an idea that could provide that showcase.

Ginny was still talking about the women who shared her stall. "Eileen makes jewelry out of colored wire. It's quite elegant. She makes earrings and necklaces and bracelets. Her kids' jewelry is really cute. Helen makes storage boxes out of leftover roofing materials. Her uncle owns the metal roofing business in Pangburn. He's really successful, and he's a super-duper salesman. He's put a roof on almost every house in the area... for miles around. And he uses metal roofs of every color you can think of. He gives the leftover pieces, and there are lots of those, to Helen, and she makes storage boxes of all sizes and shapes, every one of them made out of leftovers. There are pieces that are too small for her to use for her boxes, and she gives those really small pieces to me for my creations." Ginny stopped talking. "You don't really want to hear about all of this, do you?"

"Oh, yes I do." Sidney was adamant. "Oh, yes, I certainly do. I want to hear everything."

Sidney was elated. She felt she had stumbled on a treasure trove of creativity and originality... here in the backwoods of Arkansas, a place where she'd least expected to find it. How had she not known about any of this before? The people Sidney was used to working with in the city were focused on different things. These artists and crafters who lived in the area of River Springs were not highly educated or professional women. Sidney had never thought to look for talent here in this remote farming country, but in the environs of River Springs was where she had found it.

Sidney had already been looking for quilts. She wanted a beautiful quilt for each of the king-sized beds that every cabin at the resort would have in its bedroom. She'd bought a few and had contracted for others in specific colors. But these latest discoveries went far beyond quilts.

Sidney was more than curious and even baffled about what motivated these country women to turn their considerable creative talents to the unique and unusual. Because their aspirations for selling their crafts were limited to once every six weeks at the farmer's market, the motivation could not be financial gain. Sidney wondered if the isolation, on a chicken farm for example, and the lack of employment opportunities for these women had caused them to dig deep inside themselves to tap their inner artistic souls. Had living without conventional outlets and jobs inspired them to develop their own imaginations and originality? Whatever the reason, Sidney was delighted to find these talented women in her midst.

Sidney wanted to give these women an outlet for their remarkable work. She wanted them to have a place to sell their wares…on a full-time basis, not just every few weeks at the farmer's market. Sidney wasn't interested in making money for herself. She had founded, run, and sold several lucrative businesses before she'd decided to travel the world with Cameron. She didn't need the money, but she could see that these country artists' lives would be greatly enhanced if they were able to make some extra money by selling the things they made. Their self-confidence would soar when they realized how wonderful their efforts really were and how much in demand the fruits of their labors would be.

Sidney noticed that Ginny had never said what her own last name was. She'd only told her Danielle's last name. When she had described the work of the women who shared the stall, Ginny had used only the women's first names and had never mentioned the last names of any of the other women who sold their work at the farmer's market. Sidney wondered about this and found it puzzling and interesting.

Cameron had bought the old grist mill that was close to the lake in River Springs. When the river was dammed up in the 1960s, many older homes had been sacrificed and were now at the bottom of the lake. But someone, or maybe it was pure good luck, had made certain the mill survived. The building had been empty for more than ten years. It had been a run-down wooden structure with a ton of charm that needed a ton of work and a ton of money to make it functional and presentable. The building still had its original mill wheel on the side of the building, the wheel that had turned to grind the local farmers' grain in times gone by. The wheel had needed a major reconstruction to save it from collapsing.

Cameron provided that necessary ton of money and made sure that the mill was transformed into an attractive and comfortable restaurant. He was determined that the original mill wheel would one day turn again as it welcomed customers for an outstanding meal. When he'd bought the old mill, it was full of mice and overgrown with vegetation. But underneath the many years' worth of neglect, there had been a ton of potential.

Cameron had hired a chef away from a famous restaurant in New Orleans. Cameron had convinced the chef, who was tired of the congestion in the French Quarter and tired of the rat race of running a high-end restaurant in New Orleans, to leave his job and come home to Arkansas. Georgio had promised to run the kitchen at the lodge that Cameron was renovating, but he also wanted something of his own. Georgio was eager to leave the very high profile and very high-priced restaurant where every tourist who came to New Orleans wanted to eat. There were late hours and too much pressure that came with his job at the famous eatery. Georgio had been mugged twice. His French Quarter apartment had been burglarized and ransacked. He could never find a place to park his car on the street. He was tired of the city and needed a change. Cameron had offered him the chance to have that change.

Cameron had purchased the property that held the mill, and he was working with Georgio to make it into a first-rate restaurant with a first-rate kitchen. Cameron had many irons in the fire right now, but he had promised his chef from the Big Easy that the mill would be ready when he arrived. There had been many emails and Zoom calls while the renovations were in progress. The chef wanted input into every detail of the kitchen that was being built in the old mill. Sidney had been more help in this process than Cameron would ever know. The mill would be ready when Georgio arrived. Sidney and Georgio were already working on menus.

Georgio had trained at the Cornell Hotel School and at Le Cordon Bleu in France. He knew his way around all kinds of food. The mill would be his own special place, and in that kitchen, he would allow his creativity to soar. The menu offerings would be his alone. When Cameron's lodge was ready, the menus there would be more conventional and designed to please a variety of palates. But at the Old Mill Restaurant, it would be whatever Georgio wanted to serve.

There was another building on the property, close to the structure that was in the process of becoming the Old Mill Restaurant. Cameron had suggested that Sidney might want to do something with this former shirt factory building. It was not as picturesque as the original old mill, but it was not as old as the mill either. The former shirt factory building was a sturdy, long, narrow, one-story structure. It was large and had wide plank wooden floors that would be magnificent after they were refinished. The building was covered in its original gray, weathered shingles. It was in good shape. In addition to a new roof and a larger bathroom, it needed a reincarnation to become something other than the exclusively functional space it had been in the past.

The location of the shirt factory, next door to the mill, would be the perfect spot for Sidney's "Women's Work

Collective." Those who came to the mill for an extraordinary meal would be invited and tempted and encouraged to meander into the building beside the mill. Sidney was excited about gathering the work of her country artists, and she had big plans to refurbish the shirt factory. She intended to work with each artist and crafter to get their input about the best way to display each one's work. Did they want a table? Round? Rectangular? Did they prefer shelves? A hanging rack? Sidney had a definite vision for how her Collective would look...on the inside and on the outside.

When Sidney learned that the woman who wove the magically beautiful cloth was in a wheelchair, she immediately began to imagine how she could make the required accessibility of the building into something unusually attractive and special, as well as handicap friendly. Who had ever decreed that steps were nicer to look at than were ramps? Ramps took up more space than stairs, but Sidney had all the space she could possibly want. She would show the world how accessibility could also be beautiful.

All the women who shared the farmer's market stall made beautiful things and wanted to participate in the Women's Work Collective. These talented craftswomen and artists also knew other women whose goods might be appropriate for Sidney's project. The renovation of the shirt factory was progressing. Workmen had completed the improvements to the exterior and installed a new HVAC system before the weather got too cold. Skylights had been added to the new roof. The construction crew would be able to work comfortably on the interior during cold winter days. Sidney hoped to be ready to open when the Old Mill Restaurant opened…on the first day of May.

The floors were refinished, and the walls were painted. A new and larger bathroom, complete with a changing table, had been completed. Sidney was already using her small office at the rear of the building. The shed behind the shirt factory had been cleaned up and made into a waterproof storage room. It now sported gray shingle siding that matched the main building and also matched the nearby restaurant. Sidney had hunted long and hard for exactly the right tables and other ways to display the creations of the women who were going to sell their products in the Women's Work Collective. She'd had comfortable couches and chairs reupholstered and slipcovered. A coffee and tea station was an essential spot in the design of the space at the newly reinvented store.

Sidney worked closely with the women and encouraged them to use the long winter months to get ahead on building their inventories, making the things they would be selling at the grand opening and during the summer months. They discussed how the women would take turns manning the craft stations for each other. No one could be expected to spend all day every day at the Collective, and that was not necessary. A schedule was worked out. Sidney was furnishing the building. The women would each contribute, depending on the proceeds from their sales, to paying for the utilities. The old shirt factory had been transformed into a contemporary space that was light and bright and welcoming.

As Sidney's project had been evolving, the Old Mill Restaurant had also undergone a major renovation. Georgio had arrived in February…as soon as Mardi Gras was over in New Orleans. He had put the finishing touches on the sleek and modern kitchen, the dining room that would have tables covered with white tablecloths, and an old-fashioned wood and brass bar Georgio had created. The restaurant's sign said, "The Old Mill," but its renovation had been designed and accomplished with an updated twist. Sidney and Georgio often ate lunch together. The chef was trying out recipes he thought might earn a place on his final menu, and he wanted Sidney's input on his dishes. Sidney had decided that country living might be interesting and fun after all.

She still kept up with her meetings and her fundraising in the city, but her women's project and the natural attractions of the country were convincing her to spend more and more time in River Springs.

Opening day, May 1st, was an enormous success. In fact, because May 1st occurred on a Thursday, the opening festivities had turned into a weekend-long event. Thursday, Friday, Saturday, and Sunday were all opening days. The curious had driven from Little Rock out into the country, and they'd scrambled to make reservations to eat at The Old Mill Restaurant.

Georgio planned to serve a special version of meat loaf every week. Each week there would be a different and creative offering of the comfort food favorite on the menu. For opening day weekend, Georgio offered a meat loaf sampler that included a small portion of each of the upcoming weekly specials. One was a traditional meat loaf with a tomato sauce topping. There was a ham loaf with a sweet and sour mustard glaze. There was a turkey meat loaf flavored with sage and thyme and topped with a cranberry compote. This one was similar to having a Thanksgiving dinner all on one fork. The cheeseburger meat loaf was popular with its cheesy stuffing and bacon topping, but the sellout favorite of the weekend was the "Not Really A Meat Loaf" meat loaf. The fresh salmon, shrimp, and scallop combination loaf with onion, dill, and a few breadcrumbs was topped by a lemony glaze that included lemon zest. Georgio's homemade tartar sauce was served on the side. Customers begged their waiters and waitresses to convince the chef to keep the seafood one on the menu every week. The chef's level of creativity that the meat loaf choices had demonstrated was presented in every offering on the menu.

Georgio was shocked at the response to his new restaurant. It had been a hectic opening weekend. Georgio knew the traffic would eventually slack off, but he wondered if he had been kidding himself when he'd made the decision to move to Arkansas with the idea of having a less busy life. It didn't look as if things were going to be less busy, even here in River Springs.

At the Women's Work Collective, Sidney had been ready with tables and shelves fully stocked, and she had been amazed at the volume of sales that had been totaled up in one long weekend. She knew there would not always be so many customers coming through, but the initial response to her Collective had far exceeded her expectations. She was thrilled, and the enthusiasm and delight of success showed on the face of each of her extraordinary craftswomen.

Every one of Ginny's creations had sold, and she'd taken orders for several pieces in custom colors. Chelsea, who made scarves, had also sold out, but she hadn't brought enough stock to sell. She'd underestimated how wonderful her customers would find her neckwear. And she hadn't charged enough. Sidney suggested she raise her prices and get busy making more scarves. They were clearly quite popular.

Sidney was exhausted but thrilled with the success of her new venture. Her shop and The Old Mill Restaurant would be closed Monday through Thursday during the rest of May and June. Sidney and Cameron usually spent four days a week in the city, but that was probably going to change. During the peak months of summer and until the leaf peepers had viewed their last fall day, the restaurant and the Collective would be open Tuesday through Sunday. After the first of

November, shorter hours would again give everyone a chance to rest and rebuild inventory.

Sidney knew the Camp Shoemaker crowd would be arriving for the reunion in late October. She wanted to participate in the events that she and Cameron had planned for the group. To have the free time she wanted, Sidney would have to have someone take over for her at the Collective while their guests were visiting. She knew she needed to train an assistant anyway. The Women's Work Collective was going to be a success, and Sidney realized she was going to need help. She felt that Ginny, of all the women who sold their work at the Collective, had the most potential for being able to run things when she was away. Sidney's only reservation about Ginny was that the woman seemed to be afraid of her husband's disapproval. She was not only afraid of doing something to displease him. She seemed terrified of the man himself.

Sidney had met several of the spouses and partners of the women who sold their work in her store, but she had never met Bubba Randolph, Ginny's husband. The spouses and partners of her artists, if they had them, were mostly farmers and construction workers. Eileen's husband worked at the pharmacy in River Springs. Sidney purposely didn't pry into her women's private lives. She wanted the collective to be about the women, not about their male companions or the lack thereof.

Sidney suspected that Bubba, or whatever his real name was, was an abusive husband, but she had never seen any outward evidence of this. Sidney was certain Bubba had another name, but she was not going to ask Ginny anything about him. Ginny never mentioned Bubba. It was almost as if he didn't exist for Ginny. Ginny had decided to sell her work under her maiden name, Virginia Delacroix, but she used her married name for everything else.

Sidney decided she would talk to Ginny about becoming her assistant. She wanted someone in the group to be able to take over the Collective when she and Cameron traveled. She knew she would need someone to cover for her during the long weekend when the Camp Shoemaker group of friends were in River Springs. If Ginny was enthusiastic about the position, Sidney would train her. She knew Ginny was somewhat computer savvy. She'd mentioned searching online using her phone to buy special glues for her pieces. If Ginny didn't already have a laptop, Sidney would buy one for her.

Two members of the reunion group had opted to go
trout fishing on the morning of their second day. They'd
caught a few and released them. But they had stories about
who had almost upset the fishing boat and who had been
the one who'd fallen asleep with his rod in the water. Sidney
had ordered deli sandwiches delivered to the Richardson's
house, and the long-time friends were enjoying the October
breeze while they ate their lunch on the large screened in
porch at the back of the house. The porch overlooked the
Little Red River.

The big story the fishermen had to tell at lunch was about
the magnificent views along the water. Tyler Merriman had
participated in the fishing trip and was curious about a
cottage he had seen on a bluff beside the lake. The cottage
was made of stone and had what looked like a thatched
roof. It was a cottage straight out of the Cotswolds in
England. Tyler was widely traveled. He had ridden his bike
over many of the roads in the British Isles as well as on the

roads of many European countries. He knew a Cotswold cottage when he saw one, and he had not expected to see one beside a lake in rural Arkansas.

Sidney and Cameron knew exactly which cottage he was referring to. They had, just weeks earlier, bought the Cotswold cottage from the River Springs women's shelter. Quite unexpectedly, the property had been left to the shelter in the will of the previous owner. The English cottage was a curiosity for everyone who came to River Springs. There was quite a story about the cottage, its ownership, and its interesting roof.

Cameron wanted to tell the story. "The house was built in the 1930s, and it originally had a genuine Cotswold-style thatched roof. The woman who built the cottage was from England. She had married a rich American, a man considerably older than herself, and they'd lived in New York City for years. When the rich guy died, she wanted to leave the city. She picked River Springs, Arkansas as her new home. She said it reminded her of England. She'd never warmed up to the brownstone she'd lived in during her years in New York, and she went all out to recreate a piece of the British Isles here on the Little Red River. She was determined to have her cottage and had all that gorgeous yellow stone brought over here from some quarry in England. We have beautiful stone here in Arkansas, but she had to have English stone for her English cottage." Cameron had been intrigued by the fact that anyone would pay so much money to import special stone from across the Atlantic.

Sidney picked up the story. "But the stone for the exterior was only the beginning. Even more expensive was the thatched roof she had to have. Cottages in the Cotswolds still have thatched roofs, but they cost a lot to keep up...even in England. Back in the 1930s, nobody in Arkansas knew how to put on a thatched roof. Most people who lived in this area probably didn't even have any idea what a thatched roof was. Our Englishwoman brought over boatloads of thatch, and she brought over a professional roofer who specialized in putting on thatched roofs. Apparently he was very good at what he did. But he was also young and handsome, and he stayed and stayed and stayed…at the cottage — for much longer than it took to put on the roof."

Cameron wanted to tell the rest of the story. "It didn't take a genius to figure out that he was never going to leave. He became the Englishwoman's live-in lover. They weren't married. They were foreigners. And he was twenty years younger than she was. It was a scandal, as you can imagine, in this small town in Arkansas in the 1930s. The English couple kept to themselves for the most part, and of course the thatched roof was repaired regularly. It always looked perfect…even during the war when thatch had to be difficult to come by in the USA." Cameron chuckled to himself. He enjoyed telling about the scandal of an older woman marrying a much younger man. Sidney was only fifteen years younger than he was. "When they dammed up the river in the 1960s, the cottage was high enough up on the bluff that it wasn't flooded and left underwater as so many other houses were. There was plenty of property around the cottage, and there still is. The English people spent a lot of time planting and taking care of the garden. Whoever planned the landscaping spared no expense. There was a rose garden, a perennial garden, a cutting garden, an herb garden, a kitchen garden… every sort of garden you could think of. Some of the property that goes with the cottage is cliffs and bluffs. The gardeners who lived in the cottage were able to put gardens only on the flatter places. There's still quite a bit of unimproved property around the house. Plenty of protection for any recluse.

"The Englishwoman lived to be ninety-four years old and died in the mid-1980s. She left the cottage and the rest of her fortune to her young man, who by this time, of course, was no longer young. He must have really loved her as he never remarried. In fact, he became even more of a recluse, a hermit really, and died in the house in the late 1990s. But the thatched roof, as well as the magnificent gardens, had been maintained in excellent condition for almost seventy years. After the live-in Englishman who knew how to make and maintain thatched roofs died, nobody in the whole state knew how to repair that roof. The house was sold to a couple from Chicago, and they had no idea what to do about the roof. They finally ended up putting an asphalt shingle roof on the place. It looked horrible. They only came to River Springs part-time, and eventually they stopped coming at all. The house stood vacant for almost ten years."

Sidney had clearly taken an interest in this cottage and was eager to share her information about it. "Several years ago, another recluse bought the cottage. The place was a mess. It was full of rodents and bugs. A family of red foxes had taken up residence inside. They were living in an old couch the Chicago people had left behind. You can imagine the smell. The shingle roof was in total disrepair by this time, and water had leaked into the upstairs rooms of the cottage and caused a lot of damage."

Sidney continued. "Nobody is really quite sure about the name of the man who's owned the cottage most recently. He lived there for more than five years, and he died just a few months ago. Juanita and I cleaned out his house. He had been an enormously mysterious guy. The cottage was owned by an LLC, and of course that doesn't tell you anything. No one, that I've heard about, ever met him to have a conversation with him. But whoever he is, whoever he was, he had totally fixed up the cottage. It's in perfect condition, inside and outside. And he worked his magic on the gardens. He did all that outside work himself, supposedly. But the real story is about the roof."

"The recluse brought another roofer over from England? And he married that roof thatcher? It's whole new world out there." J.D. was being silly.

"No! Better than that. It's so much better than that." Sidney smiled. She obviously loved to tell this part of the story. "That roof is made of metal. It looks exactly like it's made of thatch. Especially from a distance, you'd never dream it was anything but thatch. But in fact, it is an indestructible and long-lasting metal roof. There's a big metal roofing business in Pangburn. Some of you drove by it on your way here from Memphis. The ugly asphalt shingle roof the couple from Chicago had put on the Cotswold cottage was coming apart and had to be replaced. Apparently, the new reclusive owner of the cottage talked to the owner of the metal roofing company. The recluse paid to have the Pangburn roofing people make a roof out of metal that looks exactly like thatch. I guess he paid them a lot of money and kept working with the company until they came up with a roof that looked authentic. I've heard via the 'country grapevine' that the roofing people think the man who owned the cottage was an artist of some kind. I guess he painted a picture for the roofing people, to show them exactly the way he wanted the roof to look. After several tries, they were able to make a metal roof that suited this guy. And it's to their credit that they were able to make a roof that looks like that. It's quite an amazing thing."

Cameron was good at identifying trends that were coming in the future, and he was making a prediction. "Now everybody is going to want a Cotswold cottage with a metal thatched roof. This roofing guy in Pangburn is so successful. He's an extraordinary salesman. Have you seen any roofs in the area that are anything but metal? And you won't."

"So you guys own the Cotswold cottage now? Who inherited it from the recluse?" Tyler was curious about the cottage and what was going to happen to it.

"That's another interesting part of the story. He left the cottage to the women's shelter in River Springs. No one was expecting that, particularly the director of the women's shelter. A lawyer called her and told her the owner had left the English cottage to the shelter. They don't really have a use for the cottage. They sold it to Cameron and me. We paid full price." Sidney laughed when she said that. "But the women's shelter is how I happened to get involved…even before we bought the place. I volunteer and give some money to the women's shelter. The director of the shelter knows I have wonderful Juanita to help me, so she asked if we could clear out the house and get it ready to put on the market. I jumped at the chance as I'd been dying to see the inside of the cottage. Oddly enough, the cottage was almost cleared out. There were only a few clothes and few pieces of furniture left in the bedroom. There were some things in the kitchen, but it was mostly empty. It's almost as if the recluse knew he was going to die and got rid of everything."

Sidney continued. "After I saw what excellent shape it was in and rather than put it on the market, we bought it from the women's shelter. I've always loved that cottage. It's not on our side of the lake or very convenient to Cameron's resort, but it is an incredibly charming place with a magnificent garden. We will rent it out or think of something to do with it."

The reunion group met again for pre-dinner drinks at the Richardson's. Elizabeth Carpenter didn't come to the house with Richard. He was going to have to bungee cord the wheelchair onto the golf cart. When they arrived at the Richardson's he was going to have to undo the wheelchair so Elizabeth could use it inside the house. But the real stumbling block was the step up into the Richardson's house. It was quite a small step, but the step was too much for the wheelchair. Elizabeth had to get out of the wheelchair, step into the house, and get back into the wheelchair. This was not a problem for her. But this evening, Richard was going to have to do all of that with the wheelchair, and then after an hour, he was going to have to do it all over again. If Elizabeth had attended the happy hour, the Carpenters would have had to drive the golf cart back to their cabin, undo the bungee cord to get the wheelchair out of the golf cart, and load the wheelchair into the truck to drive to the restaurant. Elizabeth decided it wasn't worth the trouble for her to attend the cocktail hour. She would be drinking Coca-Cola anyway. So she stayed back at the cottage and sent Richard on without her.

Of course everyone wanted to know why Elizabeth hadn't shown up for happy hour. Richard said it was because it was too difficult to get the wheelchair into the house. That was only part of the story, but Sidney and Cameron jumped right on the problem. Cameron was primarily an engineer, and he was able to easily resolve the obstacle of the step and the wheelchair. By the next morning, he had designed and built the perfect small ramp that enabled the wheelchair to effortlessly and easily get up into the house without Elizabeth's having to walk anywhere. Bravo to Sidney and Cameron. Elizabeth was touched by how quickly these two outstanding hosts had rallied around to solve her problem.

After the cocktail hour that Elizabeth did not attend, the group was going into town for dinner. They had a reservation at a Cajun restaurant. The cafe was fairly new, and those who loved Louisiana food were enthusiastic in their praise of the authenticity as well as the deliciousness of the menu offerings. But the Cajun Kitchen didn't have a liquor license. Years earlier, that would have prompted the Camp Shoemaker boys to BYO bottles of wine or a six-pack. Now that they were in their ninth decade of life, only a couple of them bothered to bring any wine. One six-pack of beer was brought in, but sweet tea and soft drinks were the preferred beverages of the evening.

The shrimp tasted as if they'd come out of the Gulf of Mexico that day, and maybe they had. A platter of shrimp remoulade was ordered for the table. When that platter was demolished, another platter was ordered. Richard ordered the crawfish etouffee and declared it was as delicious as any he'd eaten in New Iberia, Louisiana, the heart of Cajun country. Several people ordered the gumbo. Matthew and Isabelle Ritter split the seafood plate of lightly fried shrimp and catfish. An enormous family style bowl of red beans and rice made the rounds of the table. Oyster and shrimp po'boys were popular, and no one went away hungry.

Sidney joined in the fun and enjoyed the seafood, but she was preoccupied. Her assistant, Virginia Delacroix, had not come to work for several days. Ginny knew that Sidney had duties at home for most of the long weekend and especially needed her help in the store during that time. Ginny was a responsible person, and it was not like her to fail to be where she had promised she would be. The group was scheduled to shop and have cocktails at the Women's Work Collective on Saturday night before they went to the Old Mill Restaurant for dinner. Sidney especially wanted Ginny to be at the shop for that event.

Sidney had texted Ginny repeatedly, asking where she was and if she was all right. Sidney had not had any answers to any of her texts, and she was becoming more and more concerned. She knew that Ginny had a difficult husband. Sidney didn't know any details, but she always worried about asking too much of Ginny. Ginny had told her that Bubba wanted a big breakfast and his dinner on time. Ginny had to work the rest of her schedule around his demands. Bubba had his lunch every day at the diner in Rosewell with his cousin Gene Randolph. Bubba said it was his 'social time,' but Ginny knew there had to be another reason he went to Rosewell every day at noon. She hadn't yet been able to figure out exactly what Bubba was up to, but she knew he was up to something.

The Robbery

BOSTON

1990

"*I already have the cops' uniforms, complete with* hats. They're the real thing. None of this fake costume stuff for us this time. Mr. M got them for us. And I have the fake mustaches and badges." Roy George knew he'd gone over these things before, but his partner in this job needed a great deal of reminding. "Just be sure you have the truck and the van I told you to steal. They both have to have stolen out-of-state license plates. You're to park the van a half-mile from the museum…exactly at the place where I showed you. We have to park there so we've got some cover to transfer the loot from the truck to the van. It's gonna be quite a few pieces, so that's why we need a truck. And that's why we need a good place to transfer the art to the van, a place where we can't be seen. It'll take some time to transfer all of it. Then I drive the van to meet up with Mr. M. I know the meeting place. You'll follow me in the truck. We turn the van over to Mr. M. He promised to give us our money as soon as he's got his hands on the artwork. Mr. M will drive the van away, and you and I will drive away in the truck. We will change out of the cop uniforms in the truck, so don't forget to bring other clothes. I'll drop you close to your house, but you'll have to walk the rest of the way. We'll have been wearing gloves the whole time, so we won't have to take time to wipe down the truck. I'll leave the truck on the street…somewhere the real cops will find it. Then I have to get home. I've borrowed my cousin's car, and I'll park it in the neighborhood of where I'm going to drop off the truck." Roy George knew that his partner in crime, Leonard DeNunzio, was very good at stealing cars and pretty good at following directions. He wasn't the smartest tool in the shed, but Roy had worked with him on many jobs.

"You've already told me this stuff a hundred times. I know what to do. I know when to do it. I've never let you down. And I won't let you down this time." Leonard was irritated that Roy was telling him the same thing over and over again.

Roy knew he would have to tell Leonard the plans a few more times. It never hurt to imprint every step over and over into Leonard's pea brain. Roy was nervous about this job. It was the biggest one they'd ever done for Mr. M. Part of Roy's nervousness was because he'd sensed that this burglary was super important to Mr. M. Mr. M was nervous about whether or not it would be successful. Roy had never seen Mr. M be nervous before, and that made Roy nervous.

This burglary was more complicated than any of their previous jobs had been. This heist had to do with stealing artwork. Neither Roy nor Leonard had stolen artwork before, and according to Mr. M, this stuff was really valuable — more valuable than anything they'd ever stolen. Mr. M had very specific instructions about everything they were supposed to do once they got inside the museum. It seemed to Roy that Mr. M had serious doubts as to whether or not they would actually get into the museum in the first place.

"If we can get inside the museum, you follow my lead. I know what to do. Just follow my directions exactly."

"Yeah, yeah, I know. You know everything. I just do what you tell me to do. Like always."

Roy had a floor plan that showed all the floors of the museum. He had a booklet with the photos and the names of the pieces of artwork in the museum. Mr. M had marked the pieces of artwork he wanted them to steal. Roy had studied both the floor plans and the booklet many times. He thought he knew which pieces of art they had to steal and where each one of them was located in the museum. He thought he knew pretty much how long it would take to steal everything on the list.

A year earlier, Mr. M had put one of his own men inside the Isabella Stewart Gardner Museum in Boston. That guy had been employed as a janitor at the museum for almost six months. Mr. M's man was smarter than somebody who would usually work as a janitor. He was there, not really to clean the floors, but to find out everything about where certain paintings were hung and what security systems were in place. He learned the guards' routines and everything else a burglar might need to know about a location they were going to rob.

"The janitor" was able to steal a copy of the floor plans of the museum. He realized that to take away a certain piece of sculpture, a special tool would have to be used to remove it from the table to which it had been attached. Most importantly, he learned every detail about the security system that was in the museum. When he'd found out everything Mr. M wanted to know, the guy quit his job as a janitor. There was a lot of turnover in those menial jobs anyway. Mr. M planned to wait six months after his man quit working at the Gardner before he tried to rob it.

Mr. M. had given all of his information to Roy George. Roy knew that the men who would be the guards at the museum at the time the heist was planned to take place were part-timers. They were both musicians and were not professional security people. They were not very well-trained as security guards. Supposedly at least one of them liked to smoke dope and sleep on the job. The other guard liked to practice his trombone while he was guarding the museum. Roy felt it would be easy to fool these poorly trained amateurs and get into and out of the museum.

The robbery was planned for the weekend. It would happen the night after the Saint Patrick's Day parade. That year, the parade was to be held on the Boston streets on Saturday, March 17th. When Roy and Leonard, dressed in their police uniforms, knocked on the side door of the museum, it would actually be early on Sunday morning following the parade. Nobody liked to work on weekends, and the security A-team would not be working at the museum that night. Roy knew exactly what to do to neutralize these nonprofessional guards. There were only two of them. Roy knew exactly where the alarm button was located…on the security desk. The alarm button would allow the guards to notify the police station. Roy knew what to do to keep the guards from pushing the button to call the real cops.

Mr. M had told Roy about the computer printouts. Roy knew where the surveillance tape could be found. He knew everything he needed to know to cover their tracks after the robbery was completed. It would take some time to get everything from the museum that Mr. M wanted them to get, but Roy felt he had it covered. He didn't think Mr. M needed to be so nervous about it.

"Where's the truck? You were supposed to have a truck. We are stealing some pieces of art that are large. This is a hatchback. The stuff we're lifting from the museum won't fit into a hatchback. What were you thinking?" Roy was furious and could scarcely speak. This was the biggest job of his life, and he realized he'd been a fool to trust Leonard, the pea brain, to do what he was supposed to do.

"This is the only car I could find to steal. You wanted a pickup truck, but people in Boston don't drive pickups. And it's a weekend, so there aren't delivery trucks and box trucks out on the street. They're all locked up and put in a garage until Monday. I couldn't find a truck to steal. This is the best I could do, and I was lucky to be able to steal this. But I got the van, and it's parked where you showed me to park it. And I got the license plates. Two are on the van, and two are on the hatchback." Leonard knew Roy was angry with him. He didn't seem to grasp why Roy was so angry or why the hatchback had not been a good choice to transport the stolen goods from this job.

"You just don't get it, do you? We are not going to be able to load everything Mr. M wants into this little car. And if anyone stops us or looks in the back, they will see right away exactly what we have inside. A hatchback could not have been a worse choice. A station wagon or even a big sedan with a big trunk would have been better than this piece of shit hatchback."

"I did the best I could. It's all I could find that was available. It will have to do. It's too late to find anything else... even if I thought I could find something else...which I can't. You wouldn't believe what I had to do to get the van. I'm not going to tell you what I had to do either."

Roy was at his wits end. Even though the hatchback was a horrible choice, the timetable was set. The job had to go ahead on this night...for so many reasons. This heist could not be postponed. Roy had studied the sizes of the paintings they'd been told to steal. He didn't think at least a couple of them would fit into the hatchback if they were still in their frames. Roy realized that they were going to have to cut the larger paintings out of their frames. Mr. M had specifically said he didn't want Roy to do that. It significantly diminished the value of the artwork to cut it out of the frame. If they were unable to get a painting out of its frame, Roy had planned to bring the frame with the painting still in it. That would not be possible with the hatchback. Mr. M. had said these paintings were top of the line artwork and had to be handled with care. He would not be at all pleased to find that some of the paintings had been cut.

Mr. M had specified they needed two vehicles. Someone might see the vehicle they used to drive the artwork away from the museum, so that car or truck would have to be abandoned on the street as soon as possible after the robbery. A van parked near the museum would be noticed and remembered. Mr. M and Roy had decided a truck of some kind would be all right to use at the museum. Mr. M then wanted the stolen goods transferred to a white utility van. He would drive the artwork away in the van. There were so many white vans everywhere. Electricians, plumbers, landscapers, and lots of other tradespeople used them. The only thing about the van Leonard was to steal was that it could not have a logo or any writing on the side. It had to be anonymous.

Roy almost decided to call off the whole thing and re-schedule it for another night. But he knew it had to happen this weekend and on this night. Things would not be right at another time. Certain guards, that were not very good at their jobs, were on duty at the museum that night. Mr. M and Roy had both done their homework. It had to happen now. The burglary at the Isabella Stewart Gardner Museum had to happen as scheduled. It would all happen early in the morning on Sunday, March 18, 1990. Roy was not at all happy about it, but he decided that the show had to go on.

"Get into your uniform and put on the mustache. I'm ready to go, and we are already behind schedule. At best, this job is going to take more than an hour, and who knows what complications we might run into with the guards. We have to meet Mr. M before the sun comes up. Your failing to get the truck has already put us way behind, so hurry up with yourself." Roy was angry, and now he was also nervous. He'd thought he was prepared for this job, but things were not turning out as he had planned.

They knocked on the door at the Palace Street entrance, the employee's entrance. Roy did the talking. He told the museum's security guard who came to the door that there had been a report of a disturbance at the museum and that the police had been called. He explained to the guard that he was required to investigate the report about the disturbance and had to be allowed into the museum to check out that possibility. Roy was able to convince the guard to let both himself and Leonard, the other phony policemen, into the museum. They went immediately to the security office.

Although Leonard already knew there was only one other guard on site at the museum, Roy asked the guard who else was in the museum. Roy knew that one guard was assigned to stay in the security office while the other guard made the rounds of the various rooms of the museum. Then they traded jobs. Roy knew the one other guard on duty that night was making his rounds of the museum. Roy was able to convince the guard in the security office to call the second security guard away from his rounds to return to the security office.

While they were waiting for the second security guard to return, Roy asked the security guard who was in the office for his identification. When the guard produced his ID, Roy told the guy that there was a warrant out for his arrest. The guard protested that this had to be a mistake. He swore there was no warrant out for his arrest. The guard knew he was being unjustly accused, and he was upset by the false accusations. In the confusion about the arrest warrant, Roy was able to get the guard to move away from the desk where he was sitting and where the alarm button, connected to the Boston police station, was located. Roy and Leonard subdued and handcuffed the unhappy guard.

When the guard who had been doing rounds entered the security office, Roy told him to "get up against the wall." The second guard was also handcuffed. At this point, Roy informed the guards that this was a burglary. Roy and Leonard put duct tape over the eyes and mouths of the two guards. They led the two men to the basement of the museum. Roy knew exactly where the door to the basement was located because of the previous surveillance of the property that had been done by Mr. M's "janitor." The two guards were left handcuffed, duct taped, and unable to free themselves in the basement of the museum while Roy and Leonard went about stealing millions of dollars' worth of art from the Isabella Stewart Gardner Museum of Art.

*S*ure enough, when Roy saw two of the paintings in the Dutch Room that were on his list of pieces to steal, he was almost certain they were too large to fit into the hatch-back if they were left in their frames. Both of these painting by Rembrandt van Rijn, *Christ in the Storm on the Sea Of Galilee* and *A Lady and Gentleman in Black*, would have to be cut out and the frames left behind. Roy and Leonard removed the Rembrandt paintings from the wall and threw them on the floor. The glass of the frames shattered, and they made no attempt to collect the pieces from the floor of the Dutch Room. There was no time for clean-up. Roy used a knife to cut the paintings from their frames. The damage they had done was all too obvious.

They removed another large Rembrandt from the wall but left it behind on the floor of the Dutch Room. Instead they helped themselves to a small postage stamp-sized etch-ing, a self-portrait by Rembrandt. The miniature portrait by Rembrandt was tiny. Time was short. The large painting would not fit into the hatchback, but the little self-portrait definitely would. Roy slipped the valuable but easily over-looked miniature painting into his pocket.

Roy knew nothing about art, but Mr. M had told him that the painting of the storm was one of the two most important pieces in the robbery. This was Rembrandt's only seascape. *The Concert* by Johannes Vermeer was the other most important painting that was to be stolen. If they got nothing else, the burglars were to be sure they got these two paintings. While Roy was busy cutting the two Rembrandts out of their frames, Leonard had removed the painting by Vermeer from its frame. He had not had to cut the Vermeer out of the frame, but he had taken the frame apart. The frame was in pieces on the floor. When Roy saw what Leonard had done, he screamed at him. "It wasn't necessary to take that one out of its frame. That frame would have fit into the back of our little car, you idiot. You wasted all that time, and you destroyed the frame. If nothing else, leaving it in the frame would have protected the painting. Now it's out of the frame and can't be put back."

Roy also took a Govaert Flinck, *Landscape with Obelisk*, from the Dutch Room. Some years earlier this painting had been attributed to Rembrandt, but more recently it had been reevaluated. Experts had decided that the piece had in fact been painted by Flinck.

When Roy saw what Leonard was doing, he began yelling at Leonard because he was taking too long trying to free one bronze vase that was attached to a table. Leonard had a special tool that fascinated him. He was spending way much too much time with the tool…trying to unscrew the piece from the table. He finally freed the ancient Chinese gu.

When they tried to roll up the famous and incredibly valuable pieces of art they had removed from their frames, the paintings were so heavily coated with lacquer and varnish they wouldn't roll. They cracked, and some of the pieces of the paint broke off and fell to the floor. So instead of rolling them, the robbers decided to fold the artworks. There wasn't time to worry about the flakes of paint that were coming off the paintings.

Having made a mess with their first pieces of art, they were both now stressed. Roy, who usually was able to keep his cool even when Leonard panicked, was also very upset about the way the burglary had progressed so far. Things were not going well. They'd made a terrible mistake with the two largest paintings when they'd cut them from their frames. And they were running out of time.

They hurried to gather the other pieces that were on Mr. M's list. In the Short Gallery there was a flag and a finial that was especially important to Mr. M. The flag had belonged to Napoleon. They were not able to get the flag out of its display case and left broken glass and the fractured frame behind on the floor. They were only able to dislodge and take the bronze eagle that was the finial on the flag pole. The finial looked like gold, but it was not gold and not worth very much.

Roy consulted his floor plans frequently to be sure they were on the right floor and in the right room. He consulted the booklet to be certain they were taking the paintings that Mr. M had specified. They were not efficient in their movements around the museum. Roy had lost his cool, and they doubled back and had to retrace their steps to locate all the pieces marked on the booklet.

Both men were beginning to panic as they had already spent more than an hour inside the museum. In the end, they scrambled to round up the rest of the items on the list...

dashing from one room to the next, hoping they were picking up the right pieces. They grabbed a few wrong ones, and if and when they realized they had the wrong things, they left them on the floor among the broken frames and broken glass. There wasn't time to worry about all the things they'd broken or about the frayed edges of the canvases that they were stealing from the Gardner Museum.

The two left and then doubled back to the Short Gallery and grabbed five sketches by Degas. Roy didn't think these were the sketches he was supposed to take, but he was so stressed by this time, he took them anyway.

They needed to leave the museum. They'd already been there longer than Mr. M had told them to stay. He had specifically told them not to stay inside for more than one hour. They were behind schedule and had to wrap things up and get on their way to the rendezvous. They gathered up their loot and went downstairs to the Blue Room.

Mr. M had given very specific instructions about a certain painting in this room. He said this painting by Manet, the one of the man in the top hat entitled *Chez Tortoni,* was to be removed from its frame. The empty frame was to be left on the chair behind the desk of the museum's security director. The burglars were to take the painting with them. Roy took care of this project. Mr. M liked to leave a calling card behind sometimes when he did a job. The frame from this last painting seemed as if it was the calling card for the heist at the Isabella Stewart Gardner Museum of Art.

They made their way to the museum's office for one last task spelled out by Mr. M. Roy tore the printout that the computer had sent to the printer in the security office. This printout showed the movements of the burglars as they made their way from room to room and floor to floor inside the museum. Roy crumpled the printout and stuffed in in his pocket. He would get rid of it later. Roy did not realize that of course the information from the printout was still securely preserved on the museum's computer. Roy needn't have bothered taking the printout, but Mr. M had told him to tear up whatever was in the printer.

Roy also took the surveillance tape. He knew that his face and Leonard's would be on that tape. Even with their fake mustaches and their disguises, they worried that they might be recognized. Mr. M had told him about that and told him to make sure the security tape was not left behind. The guards had seen their faces in person. Stealing the surveillance tape and the printout from the computer would slow down and make the inevitable and ensuing investigation more difficult. Roy had been told to be sure to do these things, and he took the extra time to do them.

Finally they thought they had the things that were on the list. They had been told not to harm the security guards. This was to be an art heist and did not include shooting or killing anyone. The burglars were on a timetable. They had to find the artwork, get it all out of the museum, and reach their rendezvous point with the specified pieces. They thought they would be meeting the man who was bankrolling this operation. Mr. M was their contact, and they had to meet him and turn the goods over to him before 4:00 a.m. in the morning. This all had to happen before they were paid anything.

They made two trips from the museum to the hatchback with their loot. They were pressed for time and knew they'd been sloppy and left a mess behind. They stuffed their treasures into the hatchback. The door almost wouldn't close because the car was so full. No one had interrupted their chaotic robbery of the art treasures, and they didn't think anyone was watching them as they hurriedly and roughly packed their vehicle full of the precious and priceless artwork. They were tired but exhilarated as they left the Isabella Stewart Gardner Museum behind and drove through the streets of Boston early on that Sunday morning. Neither Roy nor Leonard had any idea of the value of the artwork they had just stolen. They had not treated it with the care and respect it deserved. They were a couple of two-bit burglars who had been entrusted with the heist of the century.

They drove the hatchback to the spot where the van was parked. Their plan was to transfer the artwork to the van. If anyone had seen the hatchback parked in the area of the Gardner Museum, moving everything to a van and abandoning the hatchback was an important step in the escape. The van was also stolen and had stolen license plates. It was fairly well-concealed where no one would see the two men as they transferred their booty from the hatchback to the van.

After they'd handed the artwork off to Mr. M and been paid, their plan was to drive away in the hatchback and leave it on the street with the keys in the ignition. The hatchback was their getaway car. Leonard had stolen the car, and by leaving it on the street, someone would find it or steal it again. They had worn gloves the entire time they'd handled the artwork and driven the hatchback. There would not be any telltale fingerprints left behind.

They made the transfer of the artwork to the van in record time, but they were a couple of minutes late arriving at the rendezvous location where Mr. M had told Roy to meet him with the van. Or at least, they'd arrived at the place where Roy thought Mr. M had told them to meet him. Even though they arrived a few minutes late, Mr. M wasn't there when they pulled up in the van. They waited. And then they waited some more. Roy was momentarily struck with a terrible fear that he had misunderstood where the meeting place was supposed to be. He knew he had not made a mistake. But why had Mr. M not shown up as planned?

Roy was getting very nervous. He knew they could not turn the van over to Mr. M once it was no longer dark. Roy knew that he and Leonard had to be far away from this meeting place by dawn. He had to get rid of the van somehow. Roy knew that sunrise would be at 6:30 that Sunday morning. He didn't know what to do. They could not wait much longer. Where in the world was Mr. M, and what was Roy going to do with a van full of paintings if Mr. M didn't show?

And he didn't show. Had he been warned off from picking up the artwork? Had he been in a car accident? Had Mr. M doubted Roy's ability to talk his way into the museum? Had Mr. M not believed that Roy could pull off the theft of the artwork? What had gone wrong? Roy was now desperate. They had to get away from Boston and the scene of the robbery before the sun came up. Roy did not fully grasp what a huge crime he and Leonard had committed, but he did know that law enforcement would be all over the place when someone came to the museum and found the guards tied up in the basement. He figured the story about the robbery at the Gardner Museum would be big news on the radio and on TV. He knew that many officers of the law would be looking for the paintings that had been stolen and for the people who had stolen them.

Roy had not counted on having to make a run for it with the stolen goods. But he made the decision that they had to get out of Boston and out of Massachusetts as quickly as possible. Time was not on their side. They grabbed their changes of clothes from the hatchback and left the car on the street. The two thieves headed west in the van to get to the Massachusetts Turnpike. Roy did not have a plan at this point for what to do with the paintings, with the van, or with himself and Leonard. He never found out why Mr. M had not shown up at their meeting spot as planned. Their big heist had gone to poop.

Roy vaguely remembered overhearing a discussion about states and countries and other places that had a lenient statute of limitations on stolen art. He thought that Mr. M had been planning to somehow get the stolen artwork to one of those places. But Roy could not remember where any of those places were. He thought France might be one of them, but he had no way to get to France. Scuttlebutt among thieves had yielded the information that Louisiana had a kind of justice system that was different from the justice systems of the other states in the United States. Louisiana supposedly had laws that were like those of France. Roy, who was now stressed and confused and not thinking clearly, put these two pieces of unsubstantiated information together in his over-loaded and muddled brain. He decided that he and Leonard would drive to New Orleans, Louisiana and try to sell the van load of artwork there.

At this point they both were still wearing their Boston Police Department uniforms. Because the original plan had been for Roy and Leonard to walk away after they had turned over the van to Mr. M, they'd brough along a change of clothes. A real Boston cop might stop them while they were walking on the street and wonder why they were wearing police uniforms. Their intention had been to change into civilian clothes after they'd transferred the artwork from the truck to the van. They would change in the truck. But the truck had not materialized. They'd been left with a hatchback. When Mr. M had failed to meet them to take the van and the paintings off their hands, the burglars had at least had the foresight to grab their changes of clothes from the hatchback.

Because they had been running late when they'd transferred the artwork to the van, they had not changed their clothes while they were in Boston. They stopped along their getaway route and took off the police uniforms. Roy realized that wearing their Boston PD uniforms while buying gasoline at a service station in Pennsylvania would not have been a smart thing to do. They dropped the cop uniforms into a dumpster.

The radio was broken in the older van they were driving. Leonard had stolen the van off the street in Manchester, New Hampshire. He'd put stolen Connecticut license plates on it. Leonard was good at that kind of thing. It seemed as if the van was in fairly decent shape. It would probably hold up and would probably make it to New Orleans. But because they could not listen to the radio, the two were basically cut off from the news that was being reported about the robbery in Boston. It was probably for the best that they didn't know they were being hunted by law enforcement throughout the country.

They slept in the van. Roy had an Exxon gas credit card, so they could charge their gas. But they didn't want to spend the money to get a motel room on the way to New Orleans. They knew they would have to get a place to stay once they arrived in the Big Easy, but one of them would have to find a way to get some cash or steal somebody's credit card before they could get a room.

The two were basically without a plan. They were on the run. Roy knew what they had in the van was worth a lot of money. He thought he could find a buyer for the stolen artwork. He was used to working with a fence, but he knew this artwork was special. He would have to take more care with how he tried to sell it. He and Leonard were supposed to have been paid when Mr. M met them with the van and took possession of the goods. But Mr. M had never turned up to get his precious artwork. So, of course, they'd not been paid for their part in the robbery. They both needed their money. Roy figured they would have to sell the artwork on their own in order to come out ahead on the job.

They'd taken turns driving, but Leonard wasn't very good with the map. When one man was driving the other was navigating and sleeping. Roy knew Leonard was better at sleeping than keeping them on the right road, so he didn't sleep very much when he wasn't driving. They'd been lost a few times, so the trip had taken longer than it should have. Neither Roy nor Leonard had ever been to New Orleans or to Louisiana. They arrived before dawn and were surprised how warm it was in March. In Boston, there might still have been several snow storms on the horizon. That was not going to happen in New Orleans. It was already spring there, and even though it was very early in the morning, it was humid. They were not going to need their coats while they were in "The City That Care Forgot."

The first thing they had to do was to get some money. Leonard was a pretty good pickpocket, so when the sun came up, they drove the van around in downtown New Orleans, looking for the fanciest and most expensive hotel they could find. Leonard was also pretty good at picking out a good mark, in this case a rich guy with a fat wallet who was probably a tourist and probably wouldn't notice when his pocket was picked. It took twenty-five minutes before Leonard found the guy he was looking for and made the score.

They knew from past experience that it would be a while before the man, Thomas Loper, was able to notify all of his credit card companies that his wallet had been stolen. There was over $800 in cash in the wallet. Roy and Leonard hurried to a Holiday Inn in downtown New Orleans to get a room. They got a room in the name of Thomas Loper and paid for a week with one of Loper's stolen credit cards. Fingers crossed they'd be able to stay at the motel for the full week before the card bounced. To stay close to downtown in this popular tourist town, they'd had to pay more for the room than they'd thought they should. The room had two double beds, and they decided it was okay, especially since they weren't really paying for it anyway. Thomas Loper was paying.

They hadn't had much sleep on the road and were both exhausted after the long drive. After taking showers, they collapsed and slept until late in the afternoon. When they woke up they knew they needed food, and they needed clean clothes. They'd had to pay to park the van in the parking lot of the motel. To pay for parking seemed another unnecessary expense, but then again, they weren't actually paying for it themselves. They would walk to wherever they had to go. They didn't want to drive the van around town with the stolen and valuable artwork in the back.

They walked to a department store called Maison Blanche that was just outside the French Quarter. They bought the new clothes they needed and charged their purchases on the stolen credit card. It seemed that the card had not yet been reported as stolen. While they were in the dressing rooms at Maison Blanche, they each put on an outfit from the new clothes they'd bought. They threw away the clothes they'd worn on the long drive from Boston.

Then they went looking for something to eat. Roy knew that New Orleans was famous for good food. He also had heard that the French Quarter was where it was happening in New Orleans. They walked across Canal Street into the French Quarter and found a café that advertised "Authentic Cajun Cooking." Neither Roy nor Leonard knew what Cajun cooking was, but if it was authentic, they figured it was probably worth a try. Roy knew what authentic meant.

Roy ordered a shrimp po'boy. He didn't really know what a po'boy was, but from the description on the menu, it sounded like a big sandwich made with fried shrimp. Roy knew he liked fried shrimp, so he ordered that. Leonard ordered the Cajun catfish po'boy. He knew he liked fish and thought he'd had catfish before. Roy loved his shrimp po'boy. But Leonard couldn't eat the Cajun catfish because the sauce that was on it was way too spicy for his New England taste buds. So he ordered red beans and rice with sausage, and he liked that. There had been a long list of drink options on the menu, most of which neither man had ever heard of. They each ordered a Budweiser.

Music poured out of several of the bars and joints on Bourbon Street. The warm, sultry weather and the jazz music were exotic and seductive. Neither Roy nor Leonard had ever been to a place quite like New Orleans. There were strip joints and t-shirt shops next to each other. And there were a lot of both of these, one after another. Leonard wanted to go into every one of the strip joints, but Roy told him they were supposed to be looking for art galleries. He'd read in a brochure he'd picked up at the Holiday Inn that there were quite a few art galleries in the French Quarter. Roy thought he might find a buyer for the stolen artwork at one of the galleries.

Roy said they needed to be one block over from Bourbon Street. The art galleries seemed to be mostly located on Royal Street. Royal Street was not as loud and crowded as Bourbon Street had been, and there were quite a few galleries on Royal. At ten o'clock at night, many of the galleries had already closed. The art thieves would come back the next day to try to find a buyer for their spoils.

The next morning, they were back on Royal Street looking for a gallery that seemed like it might be in the market for what they had to sell. So many of the galleries sold ultra-modern pieces of art. Neither Roy nor Leonard knew anything about art, but much of what they were looking at as they perused the places on Royal Street looked to them like kids' finger paintings. Much of it was nonrepresentational.

"This stuff doesn't look like anything. It looks like somebody spilled the paint bucket and then walked in the paint. And that one looks like somebody just threw the paint at the wall." Leonard was way out of his element with the avant-garde galleries of New Orleans. Roy tried to be more optimistic and act like he knew what he was doing. The reality was that he didn't have a clue what to do with the stolen artwork. He had no idea how to go about finding someone to buy it.

They were discouraged. They went into a few of the galleries and quickly realized they were in the completely wrong places. The other customers in the galleries had come there to buy art, not to try to sell something. Roy didn't have any idea how to begin a conversation with the people who were in charge at these art stores. How does anyone begin a conversation when one is trying to unload a van full of stolen artwork?

They stopped in one gallery that had a painting in the window that they could understand. The painting on display was called *Red Dog Harry*. It was a painting of a blue cat sitting at a table in front of a plate of crabs. There was a Red Dog brand beer sitting beside the plate. The two men liked the colorful cat painting. They didn't know it was a take-off on the "blue dog paintings" that had become so popular in New Orleans. There was no price tag on the cat painting, and Roy stuck his head in the door of the gallery to ask how much the painting in the window was selling for. Roy had no intentions of buying the "Red Dog Harry" painting. He didn't have any money. But he thought this gallery might be interested in the kind of art he had to sell. Roy was rudely informed by a snotty gallery director that the painting in the window was not for sale at any price. Roy and Leonard moved on down the street.

Getting money for the job they'd pulled off in Boston was going to be more difficult than Roy had imagined. He decided to visit a pawn shop. He was familiar with pawn shops and how they operated. Maybe he could get some pointers from the owner of a pawn shop. A pawn broker might be able to give him the name of someone who would be interested in buying Roy's stolen goods.

Both Roy and Leonard were getting nervous about the van. Leonard had stolen it in New Hampshire more than a week earlier. He didn't like to hang onto the vehicles he'd stolen for that long. Usually it was just a one-night getaway job, and then the vehicle was abandoned on the street. That was what this van had been stolen for...a one-night break-in job. The van should have been back on the street days ago so someone else could steal it or the police could find it. And then there were the license plates. Those were stolen, too, and they'd been on the van for too long. Leonard wanted to turn the van over to a chop shop. In order to do that, they were going to have to unload the artwork from the van and find a place to store it. Leonard was going to have to steal another car for them to drive around town.

They gave up the gallery search for the day and went back to eat lunch at the same café they'd been to the day before. Roy had another shrimp po'boy, and Leonard had red beans and rice again. They returned to the Holiday Inn. Roy looked in the phone book in the lobby for a self-storage place. They would unload the artwork into one of the self-storage units, and then they could take the van to a chop shop. Roy intended to find a pawn shop and talk to somebody about how to fence his stolen artwork. Disposing of the art was going to take more time than he'd thought it would take and much more time than he'd hoped it would take. Every day they worried that the credit cards they were using would be reported as stolen. When that happened, the cards would be denied when they tried to use them.

Roy found "Bargain U Storage Units" which was not far from the Holiday Inn and sounded as if it wouldn't cost too much to rent a small unit. It was down by the river and looked a little sketchy… even to Roy. But he hoped they wouldn't have to rent the unit for very long. They paid for one month because that was the minimum amount of time allowed to be able to rent a unit. They used one of Thomas Loper's credit cards to pay the rental fee.

Because Roy was not supposed to have had the masterpieces from the Gardner in his possession for any extended length of time and because he knew nothing about preserving the artwork he had stolen, he did not understand the importance of storing the paintings in a climate-controlled environment. He opted for the smallest and cheapest storage unit that Bargain U Storage Units had to offer. It was not climate controlled. New Orleans was hot and humid…even in April.

Roy had to buy a lock, and he and Leonard unloaded the contents of the van into the unheated and unair-conditioned storage space. It was a 5 X 5 unit and it smelled like mildew. There was a little bit of water on the floor of the unit, but they were able to wipe up the water with a rag they found in the van. They propped the artwork up on the jack and the spare tire they also found in the van. The jack and the tire would keep the artwork up off the floor of the small rental unit. Because they were planning to get rid of the van, they figured nobody would miss the jack or the spare tire.

Leonard had located a chop shop in Gretna, Louisiana that looked like the kind of place where he could get a few bucks for the van. He stole another car for them to use to get back to New Orleans after they'd dropped the van at the chop shop across the river in Gretna. Leonard found out-of-state license plates in the parking garage of the Royal Orleans Hotel. He took the license plates off the van and dropped them in a dumpster. He put the stolen license plates on the car he'd just stolen. He put the license plates from the car on the van. That ought to confuse everybody who might be looking for any of the stolen vehicles. Roy drove the van to the chop shop. Leonard followed him in the car he'd stolen. The back of the van had paint chips and chips of lacquer from the artwork all over the floor. Using his hand, Roy swept these out into the grass at the chop shop. They got $300 for the van.

Roy drove the stolen car back to New Orleans from the chop shop and dropped Leonard at the Holiday Inn. Then he drove to the pawn shop he'd looked up in the phone book. He thought he might be able to sell the stolen artwork, that was now getting wet and mildewed in the storage unit near the river, to the pawn shop guy. Roy knew he would have to be cagey about the fact that the artwork was stolen. But he was sure it wouldn't be the first time a pawn shop had purchased stolen goods. What he didn't realize was how infamous these particular stolen goods that he had to sell had become.

"I've got some paintings and some other artwork I'd like to sell. It's first-rate quality, and you will be able to sell it for a lot of money. I had a buyer here in New Orleans, but the sale fell through at the last minute. I've got to leave the city, so I'm looking for a quick sale here. You will get a bargain price on this lot." Roy had several lies lined up to tell the pawn broker.

"I'll have to see what you are selling before I can give you a price, let alone pay you anything. I don't buy anything sight unseen."

Roy had folded up one of the Degas etchings and stuffed it in his pocket. He brought it out to show the pawn broker. The man behind the counter looked carefully at the drawing. He looked at the drawing for a long time. Then a lightbulb seemed to go off in his head. His eyes grew large with surprise, and then they filled with fear. He pulled his hands away from the drawing as if it might bite him.

"I don't want to do business with you. I don't want you in my shop. Leave now. If this drawing is part of what I think it is, you are in so much trouble. You will get me killed." The pawn shop owner looked terrified. He was totally serious when he warned Roy. "You will never be able to get anybody to fence this stuff for you. Get out of here right this minute. You were never here. I never saw that drawing. You don't know me." He pulled a small handgun from underneath the counter and pointed it at Roy.

Roy grabbed the drawing and ran out of the pawn shop. He wasn't going to mess with the handgun the pawn shop owner had looked ready to use. Roy had worried the artwork he wanted to unload was just too hot and too famous to take to an ordinary pawn shop. After his encounter with this guy, he knew he had a big problem. It was going to be a lot of work to find someone to take this load of goods off his hands. He didn't have the skills or the contacts to make a deal like this one was going to have to be. But he kept telling himself that surely somebody wanted these paintings and these drawings. Roy returned the drawing to the storage unit and drove back to the Holiday Inn.

Leonard was standing in the parking lot waving his arms in the air when Roy arrived at the motel. Leonard was holding two trash bags full of something as he rushed to the car he'd stolen for Roy to drive to the pawn shop. He pulled open the door on the passenger side, threw the two garbage bags in the back seat, jumped into the car, and pulled the door closed. "Just drive. Just get out of here. The card we used to rent the rooms here bounced. It must have finally been reported stolen. The motel's manager came to the room and demanded that I give him another credit card. He said the one we'd given him when we checked in had been denied. I told him we didn't have another card. He got real angry and told me to get out. He started shouting at me and said he was going to call the police. I found these trash bags in the cleaning cart that was sitting outside the room next door. I put our stuff in them.

I'm not sure I got it all, but it's the best I could do. We've got to get out of town...now!"

Roy had decided on his way back from the pawn shop that they were going to have to give up trying to sell the stolen artwork. It just was not going to be possible to find a buyer who was willing to pay them anything. They were probably going to have to go back to Boston. And if they went back to Boston, they were going to have to come up with a story to tell Mr. M about what had happened to the artwork.

"Get the car away from the motel before anybody sees us." Leonard was scared. Roy drove the car away from the Holiday Inn and in the direction of the bus station. "I agree we need to get out of town now. But where are we going to go?" Roy had a cheap apartment that he rented in Boston, but because for all intents and purposes they'd lost the artwork, he was terrified of seeing Mr. M again. He wracked his brain to come up with a story that he and Leonard could tell to Mr. M about what had happened to the goods from the Gardner Museum.

The pair barely had enough cash left to buy two bus tickets to Boston. They needed to save some of the $300 they'd made from selling the van for food to eat on the bus during the trip back to Boston. The trip would take almost two days. It wasn't easy to travel from the deep south to New England on the bus. They climbed on board the bus, each carrying a dark green garbage bag that held their clothes. They wondered if they could possibly hide from Mr. M for any length of time. Maybe they shouldn't go back to Boston at all? They knew Mr. M would be all over them about what had happened to his artwork.

Leonard insisted they had to go back to Boston. He lived with his aunt there. She didn't charge him any rent for staying with her, and she fed him for free. She also did his laundry. He had a good thing going in Boston and didn't want to give it up. As the Trailways bus made its way north and east, the two travelers came up with a story they thought might shift the blame and keep them out of trouble…for a little while anyway.

"So, here's what we're going to do. When we get back to Boston we are going to act as if nothing unusual has happened. We will go to our houses and carry on doing our usual things. If Mr. M comes around and wonders where we have been for the past couple of weeks, we will tell him we took a little vacation to Atlantic City after our successful art heist. He will be furious because he never got his art. He will demand to know where it is. We will tell him that we delivered the van with the artwork inside…on time and at the specified location to his man…the morning of the robbery. We will tell him we turned over the artwork as planned. We'll tell him we got paid and decided to go to Atlantic City to celebrate our success. We've both been to Atlantic City before, so we can easily talk about what we did there."

"But we didn't get paid, and we didn't hand off the artwork to Mr. M's man. Why would we have done that anyway? We would never have handed the van and the artwork off to anyone but Mr. M." Leonard knew the story they were going to tell had lots of holes in it.

Roy was making it up as he went along. "What if Mr. M couldn't make the meet at the last minute. Who would he have sent in his place? He knew we had to hand over the take. It was hotter than hot. He would have wanted to get it off the street and into a hiding place as soon as possible. I'll always wonder why he didn't show up to get his artwork.

"Mr. M might have sent Jimmy Marks. Who else might have known about the heist and might have wanted to take the stuff for themselves? Let's tell Mr. M we turned over the van and the artwork to Jimmy, and he paid us. That shifts the blame to Jimmy and gets us off the hook. Jimmy won't know anything about the heist or the artwork, but he'll have to talk his way out of it if we both say we turned the art over to him."

Roy continued. "I think we're in danger, Leonard. At first, Mr. M will believe what I tell him. He trusts me. But Jimmy is going to say he doesn't know anything about any van or any artwork. And he doesn't. When Mr. M has figured out that Jimmy really doesn't know anything, he will be back on us. I don't think this is going to work out in the long run. If worst comes to worst, I'll tell Mr. M the truth…that we hid the artwork in a self-storage place in New Orleans. This really was all his fault anyway because he didn't show up at the meet."

"I'm really worried about this, too. Mr. M is on our side as long as we do what he wants. He's going to be very unhappy about not having his artwork. He planned this job for a long time — for over a year at least. It was important to him. I think he's going to come after us…no matter what we tell him." Leonard understood the gravity of the situation.

"We just have to act as if the transfer of the goods came off as we'd expected it would. Mr. M will believe that somebody paid us since we're not complaining about not getting paid. He'll believe somebody paid us, but he won't know who that was. Then he'll be spinning his wheels trying to figure it out and find whoever it was. He'll think somebody in his organization betrayed him, met us and got the artwork, and paid us off. He could spend months or years hunting them down. Eventually he will sort through it all and find out we lied to him. Then he will probably want to kill us. That's when I'll tell him about New Orleans."

James Marks was murdered in Lynn, Massachusetts
in February of 1991. The killing was a classic mob-style
hit, and Marks was known to have ties to the Boston mafia.
He was shot in the back of the head, and his murder was
never solved. Law enforcement doesn't spend many resources
investigating mob hits.

Among the characters of the underworld, every burglar
and mob guy in New England was taking credit for the
heist at the Isabella Stewart Gardner Museum. Everyone,
criminals and non-criminals, had known for years that the
Gardner had terrible security. It had only been a matter of
time until it was hit by somebody hoping to make a big score.
Law enforcement was running around in circles…doing a
lot of speculating and interviewing many, many people they
thought might have some connection to the robbery. But
the FBI, who had taken over the case from the local law
enforcement people, in reality had very few actual facts to
work with. In spite of interviewing every mobster they could

get their hands on, especially those with ties to Boston, the FBI struck out. They had nothing.

Eventually Mr. M caught up with Roy and Leonard. He tortured both of them until Roy finally gave him the truth. Roy gave him the paperwork for the storage unit in New Orleans where they had left the artwork they'd stolen from the Isabella Stewart Gardner Museum. Roy had paid for one month's rental on the unit. He did not seem to understand or he didn't care that when the rent wasn't paid on a storage unit, the contents of the unit were disposed of in one way or another. In the case of Roy's storage unit, he'd failed to pay any rent beyond the first month. Because he was using Thomas Loper's credit card, the unit was rented, of course, in the name of Thomas Loper. This complicated things when Mr. M sent his representative to New Orleans to try to recover the contents of Mr. Loper's storage unit.

The problem was that it had been more than a year since the robbery before Mr. M sent his man to New Orleans to try to locate the artwork from the Gardner Museum. A few weeks after Roy and Leonard had left their treasures at the self-storage unit, Bargain U Storage Units had gone bankrupt. It had subsequently been sold at auction. It took more than six months for the new owners to sort out who had paid rent on the units and who hadn't paid. The new owners of the self-storage facility eventually realized that Thomas Loper's unit was several months in arrears, and they cut off the lock to clean it out.

It rains a lot in New Orleans, and some of the self-storage units leaked when it rained. All the units that were not climate-controlled were damp and smelled like mildew. When the new owners opened up Thomas Loper's 5 X 5, it was full of mold. There was water on the floor. Whoever was deciding what to do with the contents of the abandoned units apparently saw something in the Loper unit that piqued his interest. The bronze eagle finial was encrusted with dirt, but it was an eagle. The guy who was in charge of getting rid of stuff was a patriotic guy, and he liked eagles. There wasn't much in the unit, and he decided he would keep the finial along with the rest of the contents of the unit. He would put it all in the utility closet in the rental office and sort it out later.

He forgot all about the finial and the artwork he'd put in the utility closet. Then the business was sold, and he lost his job. In the spring of 1991, the self-storage business was sold again. It became Broussard's Bargain Self Storage. When Mr. M's man brought the paperwork from the previous year to find the unit that a Mr. Thomas Loper had rented in the spring of 1990, the current owner, Mr. Broussard, knew nothing about the contents of the 5 X 5 or about any artwork. He did find out that the credit card which had been used to rent that unit had been reported stolen. He never connected the moldy junk in the utility closet with Thomas Loper or the stolen credit card. In fact, Mr. Broussard did not even know the moldy junk in the utility closet was there.

Mr. M believed that Roy and Leonard had lied to him again. The biggest score of his life had slipped through his fingers. He had used these two men to do his jobs for years, but now he was enraged that they had lost his artwork. He had nowhere else to look. It was a dead end for everyone.

Roy George was found dead from an overdose of cocaine in his Quincy, Massachusetts apartment in March of 1991. Although he had never been known to use cocaine and he certainly did not have the money to buy any cocaine, his death was ruled an accidental overdose. Many believe that Roy George's death was murder.

Leonard DeNunzio disappeared on March 17, 1991, almost exactly a year after the Gardner Museum robbery. His body was found three months later on June 11, 1991, in the trunk of his car. His car was parked in East Boston across the street from a pizza parlor known to be frequented by the mob.

None of the artwork from the Isabella Stewart Gardner Museum heist has ever been found. It remains missing as of the summer of 2024.

The Reunion

ARKANSAS

2023

9

Isabelle had a thriving store and business in Palm Springs. Gretchen was all about women's issues and supported many causes that promoted success and good health for women. Elizabeth was thrilled that Sidney had embraced the talents of the women she'd discovered in the communities around River Springs. All three applauded Sidney for having made a significant commitment to encourage the women in her community by establishing the Women's Work Collective. The three friends had wanted to visit the Collective as soon as they'd heard about it, and they could not wait any longer. There was nothing planned for Friday morning, so they convinced Sidney to take them to her store.

Elizabeth considered not going because she knew it was difficult for anyone to get her wheelchair in and out of a vehicle and in and out of most buildings. She didn't want to cause a ruckus at the Collective. She felt as if she'd already caused a bit of a ruckus at the Richardson's house, but Cameron had solved that with his perfect mini-ramp. One ruckus was enough. But the women insisted that Elizabeth come along.

Sidney said she wanted Elizabeth to see how she had made the building accessible for one of her artists who was also in a wheelchair. Elizabeth was delighted and quite impressed when she saw what Sidney had done with landscaping and the ramps. Everyone used the ramp to get into the Collective, and it was all so attractively and artfully done nobody ever imagined that it had been achieved with the handicapped in mind. Accessibility could be beautiful. Elizabeth told Sidney she should write a book about how she had been able to make this happen at her store. All owners of businesses everywhere could take a lesson from Sidney's creative inspiration about how to make a building look good and at the same time make it accessible.

The women were impressed with everything about the Collective. They looked at all the merchandise and bought quite a few items. Isabelle was in serious discussions with several of Sidney's artists about the possibility of carrying their work in her own store in Palm Springs. California customers in Palm Springs would pay big bucks for the unusual and the unique. It was a productive morning for many reasons, and when their shopping was completed, the women were ready to go next door and enjoy their lunch at the Old Mill Restaurant.

Gretchen was remembering that there had been a Nancy Drew book from her youth that she thought had "Old Mill" in the title. All four women had read the series many decades earlier, and they were trying to remember the title. Finally Gretchen Googled it, and it was settled. They discovered that *The Secret of the Old Mill* had in fact been a Hardy Boys book. The women admitted that they'd also read those books which had been intended to be read by boys. Nancy Drew had starred in *The Secret of the Old Clock* and *The Mystery at Lilac Inn*. All of these older women confessed that they'd always wanted to be Nancy Drew. The entire lunch discussion was about each woman's reasons why she had wanted to be Nancy Drew and why each one had loved the series about the young woman amateur detective who had a boyfriend named Ned and drove a blue roadster.

Chef Georgio was too young to have known about or read the Hardy Boys books, but after listening in on the discussion, he decided he might offer a Hearty Boys' Special on the menu every day during colder weather. He also wondered if he should include a Nancy Drew Stew daily special on the fall menu. Georgio was currently offering sandwiches, salads, and cold soups for lunch. In the heat of the summer, no one wanted anything more. As of the first of November when there was a chill in the air, he was going to add hot soup and hot sandwiches to the lunch menu.

Currently, the Moroccan chicken salad was the most popular offering. There were two other imaginative chicken salad entrees. There was a triple seafood salad platter that featured a scoop of each…lobster salad, shrimp salad, and tuna salad. It was the most expensive item on the lunch menu, but it was more than worth it. The salads came with a basket of Georgio's special homemade yeast rolls of all kinds. There was a fresh fruit salad, served with ham salad and tuna salad finger sandwiches on the side. Georgio offered an entrée that was entirely made up of various kinds of delicious tea sandwiches.

The women all ordered the seafood salad platters for their lunches. They also ordered the platter of tea sandwiches for the group to share. Georgio comped this part of their order. He wanted their opinions on his tea sandwiches. He was thinking of offering an afternoon tea on Saturday and Sunday afternoons. His tomato and cheese tea sandwiches and the watercress and butter tea sandwiches received the most votes. Georgio had done something remarkable and secret to the butter on both sandwiches. No one really had room for dessert, but they split an order of the trio of homemade gelatos. Today's offerings were pistachio, dark chocolate, and tangerine...Yum!

Sidney stayed behind after the others had gone back to their cabins for an afternoon nap. She was becoming more and more concerned about Ginny. She asked Georgio. "Have you seen Ginny anywhere around in the past few days? I can't get in touch with her. She was supposed to be running the store for me while my friends are here visiting, but she's not been to work for several days. It's not at all like her to fail to turn up when she's promised to help me out. And she's not returned any of my texts or phone calls. I'm getting really worried."

Georgio answered with a worried look on his face. "I haven't seen Ginny since last weekend. She was at the Collective. But that husband of hers, that Bubba, was here one morning this week banging on my door. It was Wednesday morning, I think. He was high on something or he might have been just plain drunk. He was looking for Ginny, too. He said she hadn't come home the night before, or he might have said she'd not been home for several nights. He was slurring his words, so it was almost impossible to understand what he was saying. He said he'd tried to get into the Collective, but it was all locked up. He was pretty angry about that. I guess he thought Ginny might be in the Collective building. But thank goodness he couldn't get in there. He must have seen the light in my office. I was in the kitchen early that day.

He was rude and belligerent and insisted that I had to know something about where Ginny was. I told him I hadn't seen her. He said he didn't believe me. I finally slammed the door in his face. He stumbled around outside for a while and then got into his pickup and left. He was so drunk or so drugged up on something, he never should have been driving. Bubba could become a real problem for you. It's obvious he's already a real problem for Ginny, but if he comes around here high and acting crazy, he could be a problem for you and for me. Nobody wants a guy like that in their face when they go out for a nice dinner...or really, anytime."

Sidney was worried, too. "I'm afraid you're right about Bubba. I think he's into drugs, and I wonder how that affects his behavior towards Ginny. There's no way it can be good. She seems terrified of her husband, and I don't blame her. He sounds like he's a very scary person. And if he's on drugs, I can't have him anywhere around the store. I don't want him anywhere around the restaurant either."

"Good luck keeping him away. I think Bubba is used to doing whatever he damn well pleases. He's a bully and an asshole. And that's before he even gets into the drinking or the drugs." It was clear that Georgio did not like Bubba.

"I'm sorry he bothered you. You should call the police or the sheriff the next time he comes around. I will sign something that says he's trespassing...a restraining order." Sidney was not going to put up with Bubba harassing Georgio at the restaurant.

"That won't endear you to him."

"I don't care. I can't have him around here. He's got to stay away...whatever that takes." Sidney was clearly troubled about Ginny's well-being and wondered if her husband had found her. She prayed he hadn't. "Let me know if you see Ginny. Tell her I've been trying to reach her."

Sidney didn't have the time right now to look for Ginny, but she was very worried, especially after hearing about Bubba coming to the restaurant. She decided to send texts to a couple of women she knew cared about Ginny. Someone had to know something about where she was. Sidney didn't think Ginny had any family in the area, but she knew Ginny had several good friends who would want to help her out if she were in trouble. She would send the first text to Dani, who was Ginny's best friend.

Sidney was surprised to immediately receive a text back from Ginny's friend Dani. The text asked Sidney to call her immediately. Sidney was in her car when she received the text, and she called Dani back right away. Sidney could talk on the phone hands free from her car. "Dani, it's Sidney. I'm trying to find Ginny. She's disappeared, and I'm really worried about her. Have you seen her?"

"Oh, Sidney, thanks so much for calling back right away. Ginny's in real trouble. It's Bubba." Dani was silent on the other end of the line, as if she didn't know where to begin to tell Sidney about Ginny's situation. "Bubba has always been a problem. I'll tell you more about that later. But right now, I need your help to find Ginny. She was here at my house, hiding from Bubba, until last night. Bubba beat her something terrible. She was bleeding and all cut up when she arrived at my house last Monday night. She needed to go to the hospital but wouldn't go. She said Bubba would find her if she went to the hospital. I told her she had to report the beating to the authorities. She said Bubba has connections at the sheriff's office. She said they'd never arrest Bubba or do anything about any domestic abuse. Law enforcement hates domestic abuse cases anyway, and apparently Bubba has a relative of his, a cousin or a nephew or somebody who works at the sheriff's office and will do whatever it takes to protect him."

"So where is Ginny now? Why did she leave your house?"

"I argued with her because she really did need to go to the ER. Her wounds were that serious. Bubba has never been a prince or a prize, but apparently he's gotten involved in drugs the past few months. People think drugs are an urban problem, but that's not true anymore. Bubba has escalated his abusive behavior to a level no one ever expected. If Ginny runs into Bubba again, he's going to kill her. He's that angry and that insane."

"Where is she, Dani, what's happened to her?" Sidney wanted to hear the background of what had happened with Bubba and Ginny's marriage and the whole drug thing, but not right now. At this moment, Sidney wanted to know where Ginny was and how she could help her.

"I bandaged up Ginny's wounds as best I could. Some of the places where he attacked her with a knife really needed stitches. She stayed here for a few days…until last night—Thursday. Bubba came to the house last night. He was high and drunk and who knows what all…acting crazy as a coot and loaded for bear. He almost destroyed my front door banging on it. He knocked out the glass at the sides of the door. Ginny was terrified, and I was terrified. I locked my son, Jimbo, in his room and told him not to come out under any circumstances. He's only eight years old, and of course, he was terrified, too. Bubba said he knew Ginny was here at my house, and he was coming back with an axe and a gun and tear my house apart until he found her. I told him she wasn't here. But of course she was here. But then she ran away."

"Did you call the sheriff? Somebody has to involve law enforcement to get this Bubba maniac off the streets. He can't be allowed to go around beating up Ginny and terrorizing everybody else in the county."

"When Bubba was banging on the front door, Ginny grabbed her backpack and ran out the back door of my house. I wouldn't open the door for Bubba, but I'll tell you, I was worried that he was going to tear the door down with his bare hands. I don't know what kinds of drugs he's on, but whatever it is, they have made him into a super-strong madman. If he gets hold of Ginny, she'll be dead. But Ginny refused to let me call the law."

"Do you know where she went when she left your house?"

"After she left, she sent me a text and said it was too dangerous for her to stay at my place. She said she couldn't put Jimbo and me in the line of fire. She said she had to disappear someplace where Bubba would never find her."

"But she didn't say where that was?"

"She didn't say. When she left, all she took was this old backpack she'd brought with her. She ran out of here as fast as she could. She didn't have a coat or her purse or any clothes or anything. At least she had on shoes. She had her cell phone in her pocket, so thankfully she could text me. But the charger for her phone is beside her bed in the guest room where she was sleeping. She doesn't have any way to charge her phone, so she will be incommunicado by now."

"Where do you think she ran to…if she didn't have any money or her purse or even a coat?"

"I think she ran into the woods. There's national forest land behind my house. It's not quite a wildlife preserve, but almost. It's pretty much only woods and animals…no houses or any signs of civilization. It's a beautiful place, but it isn't a place where anyone would want to spend the night. I hate to say it, but I think Ginny is probably hiding out in that woods."

Dani continued. "I texted her back that I wanted her to stay at my house. I told her I wouldn't let Bubba hurt her. I told her I have a gun and would use it to protect her. I sent her several messages asking her to come back to the house, but I never heard from her again. I'm very worried. I'm afraid something terrible has happened to her out there in the national forest. There are black bears there and coyotes and other wild animals. And it gets real cold at night. She doesn't have a coat. She's already spent one night sleeping in the woods. She can't spend another night out there. We have to find her."

*S*idney was frightened for Ginny and for Dani and her son, Jimbo. She was also feeling like she was under a lot of pressure. She'd needed Ginny to take over running the Collective while the reunion group was visiting. They had a full schedule of activities and meals and wanted Sidney to participate in all of it. Cameron was always supportive of whatever Sidney wanted to do, but he was also occupied with entertaining his old friends who were in town for the long weekend. That night was going to be "cook your own steak night." Sidney had bought sides at the farmer's market and had made a salad and some other things to go with the steaks. The group was getting together early that afternoon because Matthew Ritter was showing a full program of movie montages. The group was scheduled to gather at the Richardson's house for Matthew's show at 3:30.

Sidney was torn between entertaining her guests and going to search for Ginny. She was already stressed and worn out, trying to keep the Collective going without Ginny's help and trying to cook for the reunion group. She finally found a few minutes to take Cameron aside and tell him what was going on. Cameron immediately wanted to call the authorities to look for Ginny and to take Bubba into custody. Sidney told Cameron about the close connection, the "friend" Bubba supposedly had inside the sheriff's department.

Sidney was worried that if law enforcement found Ginny, they would either take her to a hospital or send her back to her home. Sidney knew Ginny did not want to be sent to either of those places. Sidney told Cameron he could not involve the sheriff's office at this time. He didn't want to comply with Sidney's wishes, but in the end he agreed to give her some time to find Ginny on her own before he called in the help of the authorities. He did, however, call his own contact inside the sheriff's office. He learned that law enforcement was already looking for Ginny. Bubba had been into the sheriff's office and filed a formal missing person's report. Apparently, it had not been a pretty scene with Bubba.

When Cameron reported to Sidney that the sheriff was already looking for Ginny because Bubba wanted to find her, Sidney was even more anxious to find Ginny as soon as possible. If Ginny went to the hospital, the authorities would be notified. Sidney was frantic to find her before the sheriff did. Sidney knew if Bubba found Ginny, he would kill her. If the sheriff found her, she would be sent home and reunited with Bubba. Sidney knew this was the last thing in the world that could be allowed to happen to Ginny.

Sidney decided to skip Matthew Ritter's movie clips. She desperately wanted to search for Ginny but knew she would have to be back in the kitchen in time to get dinner on the table. With all the things she knew she would have to do that night and before she could set out to look for Ginny, Sidney had to rest. She was worn out and headed for her bedroom to lie down for a while. She intended to rest for an hour and then go to the woods to begin her search for Ginny in earnest.

Sidney fell asleep and didn't wake up until her phone buzzed at four in the afternoon. It was a text from Georgio. He asked Sidney to come to the restaurant. He said it was of the utmost importance that she come immediately. Sidney was groggy from her nap but was able to rally. She slipped out of the house, hurried to her car, and broke the speed limit as she raced to the Old Mill Restaurant. She was not even out of the driver's seat when Georgio rushed out to meet her.

"Ginny is here, and she's in terrible shape. I just now found her. There's that storage room at the back of the restaurant that isn't heated. I keep food in there that doesn't have to be refrigerated but needs to be kept cool…onions, potatoes, apples, vegetables. I call it the larder. Ginny was hiding in there…under the table and behind some boxes of pasta. She'd fallen sleep. Even though there isn't any heat in that room, I guess it's warmer there than it is in the woods. I probably wouldn't have found her, except she knocked over a stack of boxes. I heard the commotion and went to see what had made the noise. I was afraid a critter, like a raccoon or a fox, had got into my store room. I couldn't figure out how an animal could possibly be in there, but you never know. What I found was Ginny hiding under an old table I keep there. She was terrified and tried to run when I found her, but I stopped her. She collapsed. She's bleeding and dirty. She has leaves and pine shats in her hair, and she looks as if she's been sleeping in the mud all night. Poor thing. The first thing she said to me was to beg me not to tell anyone she was here…in the restaurant. She said that whatever I did, I couldn't call the sheriff. She said she would end up dead if I told anyone at the sheriff's office where she was. So I called you."

"Thanks, Georgio. It's true what Ginny says about the sheriff. Bubba has the sheriff's office looking for her... officially... with a formal missing person's report, and all of that. If Bubba gets his hands on her, he will kill her. His cousin or somebody related to him is a sheriff's deputy, and I think he knows all about the way Bubba treats Ginny. This deputy protects Bubba. My suspicion is that this law enforcement guy probably beats up his own wife, if he has one, and he thinks that's okay." Sidney paused and felt sick to her stomach with the realization that a law enforcement person thought it was okay to beat up your wife. "Whatever we do, we absolutely cannot notify the sheriff. We can't let anybody know she's here. And I mean anybody! I'm not even going to tell Cameron she's here. I don't know what we're going to do about any of this in the long run, but in the short run we have to keep her alive. Does she seem ill or is she mostly cold and dirty?"

"She's got terrible wounds on her body. I think Bubba must have attacked her with a knife as well as with his fists. I think some of the wounds might be infected. They look really nasty. The dressings haven't been changed in days. She's so dirty it's hard to tell about the wounds. She seems disoriented. She probably didn't get much sleep in the woods, and she may be suffering from hypothermia because she was outside all night. She's not eaten anything in more than thirty-six hours. Whatever is wrong with her, she needs to be in a hospital. I understand why that can't happen, but she needs care in the worst way. I finally convinced her to at least go upstairs to the guest room where it's warm. We need to do something."

"I know it's Friday night, and this is a big night for the restaurant. You go ahead and do what you need to do to get ready for Friday night and get the food out. I'll take care of Ginny and get her cleaned up. I know someone I think will be willing to come and take a look at her and keep quiet about what he sees and what he does. I'm going to try to do this on my own. Cameron is such a straight arrow. He never steps outside the law. I can't tell him we have found Ginny. I hate to keep things from him, and I won't lie to him. Long ago we promised never to lie to each other. But I don't think he understands the extent to which Ginny's life is in danger." Sidney wished she'd brought bandages and a bunch of other things from her house. "I'll do what I can, and I will call in my retired doctor friend who I hope can keep his mouth shut."

Sidney made her call to Dr. Alex Caruthers. He had a house near Cameron and Sidney's resort, and Sidney had run into him a number of times when she'd been out walking. Caruthers' wife had died the year before, and he always seemed lonely and wanted to talk. Sidney had his cell phone number and called him as she made her way into the restaurant. She got his voicemail and asked the doctor to call her back immediately.

Georgio, the chef, had chosen to live above his restaurant. Cameron had offered to buy him his own house nearby in the neighborhood, but Georgio wanted to live as close as possible to his creation, his baby, his own eatery. The mill was a big building, and the rooms of the restaurant—dining rooms, bar, and kitchen and larder—were all on the first floor. Georgio had the entire second floor as his living space. He only used about half of it, and he'd never taken the time to unpack all of his boxes. Cooking and food were more important to Georgio than getting settled into his apartment above the restaurant.

Georgio never thought he'd have any guests visit him, but when the mill had been renovated, Cameron had insisted on making provisions for a guest room with an en suite. The mill had plenty of room on the second floor for a guest suite, and it seemed like the sensible thing to do. Georgio had given Sidney carte blanche to furnish the guest room and to put sheets and towels and toiletries in the bathroom of the guest suite.

Sidney found Ginny lying on the top of the bed in the guest room. There were boxes stacked against the walls, but Ginny was beyond caring about the aesthetics of the room in which she was sleeping. Sidney didn't want to frighten Ginny. The young woman was already scared to death, and Sidney tried to be gentle as she roused Ginny from her sleep. When Ginny woke up, she saw Sidney and opened her mouth to start screaming. Sidney grabbed Ginny's hand. Sidney put her finger in front of Ginny's mouth. She made the classic shushing sound to keep Ginny from crying out.

"Don't worry. You are safe. I'm not going to call the sheriff or anybody who can hurt you. Dani told me all about Bubba's connection to the sheriff's department. I'm going to take care of you and make sure Bubba doesn't find you." Sidney paused to see if Ginny was listening and understanding what she'd said. "We need to get you cleaned up. I know you slept in the woods last night, and I understand why you felt you had to hide out there. We are going to get you well, and you won't have to go to a hospital. I know why you don't want anything to do with the hospital." While Sidney was reassuring Ginny, she was also carefully peeling away the torn and dirty bandages from Ginny's wounds. Some places looked infected to Sidney, but she wasn't a medical person and didn't trust her diagnoses.

As Sidney was helping Ginny into the shower, Sidney's phone rang. "Can you wash your own hair, or do you need help? You need to make sure you don't leave any dirt in any of these wounds. I have to take this phone call, but I'll be back to help you get out of the shower." Sidney left the bathroom to talk on her phone.

"Thanks so much for calling back right away, Dr. Caruthers."

"Call me Alex, please."

"Alex. I have a situation on my hands and need your help. It's an 'off the books' situation, in a way, so I don't know if you will be comfortable helping me." Sidney paused to give the doctor a chance to say something. When there was only silence, she felt she could continue. "My assistant at the Collective has been severely beaten and attacked with a knife by her abusive husband, who is also into some serious drug use. She desperately needs medical care. Her husband, the abuser, has a relative who is a deputy sheriff. My assistant can't call law enforcement for this reason, and she doesn't feel safe going to a hospital because of her husband's influence and connections with the sheriff's department. This woman is in hiding. If her husband finds her, I am convinced that he will kill her. He has already filed a formal missing person's report with the sheriff's department, and he is looking for her everywhere. I know you are a retired physician, and I'd like for you to look at my assistant's wounds. They may need stitching up, and they may already be infected. I am concerned she may be suffering from hypothermia. She spent last night sleeping in the woods. That's how desperate she is."

"What can I do to help?"

"I want you to see her and treat her wounds. She needs bandages and will have to have them changed at least every day. If she has an infection, I'd like for you to prescribe whatever antibiotics she needs. I will pay you. I don't know if she has insurance or how good it is, but whatever it is, she can't use it."

"Let me see what I have around the house. I assume you want me to come right away. Can you pick me up at that bench where you sit when you are taking your walks? I can be there in ten minutes."

"Thank you Alex. I appreciate your being willing to help me out with this. And you seem to have grasped completely the importance of keeping everything between the two of us and not involving the authorities. I will pick you up at the bench in ten minutes."

Sidney helped Ginny out of the shower. Ginny's clothes were torn and covered with blood and dirt. They would have to be washed repeatedly or thrown away. Ginny had nothing at all to wear to keep her warm. Sidney found a t-shirt in one of Georgio's still-packed boxes. It looked clean enough. Sidney didn't want Ginny to put anything on over open wounds that would expose her to more germs. Ginny pulled the t-shirt over her head, and Sidney found a clean sheet in the linen closet so Ginny could wrap something around herself like a skirt.

Sidney explained to Ginny about Dr. Alex Caruthers. She trusted Caruthers and promised Ginny that she could also trust him. Ginny was smart and knew she needed help. She was thankful that Sidney had taken things in hand and was bringing the doctor. Ginny was too defeated and wounded and exhausted to fight her anyway. Sidney made sure Ginny was warm enough in the guest bed and left to pick up Alex Caruthers.

When the renovation had been done on the restaurant building, Georgio had insisted on having a back staircase so he could escape to his private living quarters without traipsing through the main part of the restaurant. Sidney and Dr. Alex Caruthers came through the kitchen's rear entrance and quickly and quietly went up to the second floor using the back stairway. Ginny was sound asleep when they reached the room where she was hiding. Dr. Caruthers had brought his medical bag and a supply of sterile bandages.

Sidney again woke Ginny gently and introduced her to Dr. Caruthers. Even before he saw the extent of the wounds on her body, it was obvious to the doctor and to anyone that Ginny had been terribly traumatized. Alex paled when he saw how badly the young woman had been beaten and stabbed. He immediately got to work tending to her wounds. Sidney wanted to stay to take care of Ginny, but she had to get back to her own house where the steak barbecue was about to start. Ginny tried to offer a weak smile, but it was a half-hearted effort. Sidney promised she would be back later that night to check on Ginny.

It was difficult for Sidney to return to the hilarity of the reunion crowd. The rest of the group was enjoying the montages Matthew Ritter had prepared. They were starting happy hour…in the toned-down form it had taken this year. Sidney was preoccupied with Ginny and wondered what was happening on the second floor of the Old Mill Restaurant. Ginny's condition was all she could think about as she put the steaks out for Cameron to cook on the grill and heated up the side dishes she'd bought at the farmer's market. Sidney was in a daze when she went to the refrigerator and brought out the huge salad that she and Juanita had made. The salad was full of homegrown tomatoes, arugula, marinated artichoke hearts, and other wonderful things. Sidney and Juanita had made three kinds of homemade salad dressing, including Sidney's special recipe for Thousand Island dressing. Sidney was operating on automatic and didn't even realize what she was doing as she put the food on the counter.

Matthew Ritter had made up his own version of "Name That Tune." He had a series of songs that had been written especially for movies. Many of these songs had become famous. Matthew had prepared a mix of the famous songs. When they heard the tune, he wanted his friends to guess the name of the movie the song was from and the name of the song. There were no words to give any hints, and everyone had to guess based only on the music. The Camp Shoemaker crowd had an enormously fun time guessing the songs and the movies. Even though everyone was supposed to cook their own steak, Cameron ended up cooking most of the steaks. Cameron cooked everyone's steak perfectly, and the dinner was a huge success. Sidney had guessed several of the songs and movies, but her mind was really miles away.

Elizabeth loved the twice baked potatoes that Sidney had served and wondered aloud if whoever had made them would deliver to Maryland or to Arizona. Preparing twice-baked potatoes is a lot of work, and the ones Sidney had found were exceptionally delicious. Everyone was having fun, but Sidney's heart wasn't in it. All she could think about was Ginny. She couldn't wait for everyone to leave her house so she could get into her car and drive to the restaurant. Cameron would object to her going out so late at night, and she couldn't tell him that Ginny had been found. Ginny was officially a missing person. Sidney was afraid Cameron would feel he had to go to the sheriff's department with the news that Ginny was no longer missing.

Finally their friends went back to their cabins for the night. Cameron headed for the master bedroom, thinking Sidney would be following him. He thought she'd looked really tired that evening. But Sidney was out the door, in her car, and on the road as soon as Cameron headed for the bedroom. When she reached the Old Mill Restaurant, there was only one group of four people still seated in the dining room. Georgio was busy in the kitchen, and Sidney ran up the back stairs to check on Ginny.

Ginny was sound asleep in the guest room, and Dr. Alex Caruthers was sound asleep in a chair beside her bed. Sidney hated to wake either one of them, but she knew Dr. Caruthers probably wanted to go home and spend the night in his own bed, rather than sit up in a chair all night. She gently shook Caruthers to wake him.

"How is she?"

Being a doctor and old habits die hard, Caruthers was instantly awake. "She's resting comfortably. I've got her on some big doses of antibiotics, and I'm hoping that will do the trick to keep the infection at bay. If the oral antibiotics don't take care of it, I'll have to put in an IV. Georgio brought up some soup for her, but she wouldn't eat it. She was able to drink some Gatorade. I told her she had to stay hydrated, or I would have to put in the IV. She doesn't want that so she's trying to drink plenty of liquids. She told me a little bit about this Bubba she's married to. She's got to get away from that man…for good. He's never treated her well, but she says he is now involved with drugs. I guess he has been dealing for some time, but a couple of months ago, he began to sample the wares. Now he is out of control and apparently addicted. You have a problem on your hands with Bubba. Ginny told me his cousin is a deputy sheriff, so nobody can go to the authorities about Bubba. But somebody is going to have to do something."

Sidney was also stumped about what she was going to do to help Ginny. It seemed as if Bubba held all the cards in this situation. That was so, so wrong and couldn't be allowed to continue. Bubba was such a loser. It made Sidney angry to think that Bubba was in control of this situation. "If you feel you can leave her, I'll drive you home so you can get some sleep."

"I'll be back in the morning. I can drive my own car tomorrow, now that I know what the setup is here. I'll park behind the Women's Collective, if that's all right. I don't think Bubba will recognize my car, but better safe and all of that. Georgio told me that Bubba has been here threatening him, wanting to know where Ginny is. Georgio expects him to come back. Of course, Ginny wasn't here when Bubba came before, but now she is here. The stakes are much higher. I am certain Bubba will kill her if he finds her. So, he absolutely must not find her."

The doctor grabbed his bag. Sidney and Alex Caruthers quietly left the bedroom and went down the back stairway. They went out the rear door of the restaurant, and Sidney drove Caruthers home.

On the way to his house, Sidney had to ask him a couple of questions. "Alex, I'm curious about why you agreed so readily to help Ginny…under the radar and without involving a hospital or law enforcement. My husband thinks I should go to the authorities, but I've told him I won't do that. He doesn't know Ginny has been found, and I'm not going to tell him. I hate to keep things from him." Sidney's face told it all. She was agonizing over not being completely upfront with Cameron. "I really appreciate your understanding and your grasp of the situation. You realize we can't involve anybody official…either anybody in the hospital ER or in law enforcement. So, thank you. I am forever grateful."

"To answer your question, you may or may not know that I am a retired OB-GYN specialist. I had a practice in Tulsa, Oklahoma for many years. During those years I delivered many babies and dealt with many couples who were infertile. Most of my patients and their partners were delighted to hear the news that they were expecting a child, but there were a very few who were not happy to learn they were going to have a baby. Most of the people who came to me were thrilled when they received the news that a baby was on the way, and that was one of the things that made my profession so rewarding. Giving a couple the good news brought me much happiness. However, once in a while, I felt that the husband or the male partner of the couple was less than delighted to find out that his wife or girlfriend was pregnant. I practiced medicine for fifty years. Two of my patients were murdered while they were pregnant, and the person who committed the murder was never brought to justice in either of those cases. I am certain, as certain as I have ever been of anything, that in those two cases, the father of the baby was the person who killed the mother and the unborn child. I would never be able to prove any of it in a court of law. I have only my own instincts and reasons for believing as I do. In both cases the father of the child got away with a double murder. One of these was a married couple, and the other couple had lived together for years. I suspected something was wrong in their relationships, but there was nothing I could do to stop those killings. I feel terrible that I was not able to keep these tragedies from happening. I know women are at risk from abusers, and if I possibly can, I will always go the extra mile to keep them from being hurt."

Sidney was listening with enormous interest. "Of course the Laci Peterson case immediately comes to my mind. That perpetrator, her husband, was caught and is being punished. But I don't really understand why these men, and thank goodness there are so few of them, are motivated to commit murder when their wives or girlfriends become pregnant. I have never been able to understand that."

The doctor hesitated and sighed. "I have spent many hours of my life pondering that question. I have talked with a number of my colleagues who are psychiatrists. My understanding is that these murderers are basically malignant narcissists. They feel threatened when it appears that a child is going to come into the picture to share the love and attention that the wife or girlfriend has previous showered exclusively on him, the male partner. Of course there are many, many narcissists who don't go so far as to kill their pregnant wives or girlfriends. Why one narcissist goes over the edge and kills…that gets into the field of the psychiatrist who understands the criminal mind. But you may be surprised to learn that homicide is a leading cause of death among pregnant women. Almost all of these homicides are committed by the male partner—a husband or a boyfriend. She wants the baby, but he does not."

"I've heard that statistic quoted but always found it hard to believe. There have been several high-profile cases on the news, of course, but I have a feeling there are many more of these murders that do not make it to television."

"This was one of the most disturbing aspects of my practice as an OB-GYN specialist, and thank God I only had two women who were murdered in this way. But I saw too many other women who were covered with bruises and who had broken limbs and black eyes. Of course they always said they'd fallen or run into a door or some such excuse. But I knew better. That's why I realize how important it is that I help Ginny in every way possible and why I realize no one can report any of this to the authorities. I'm sorry to say that sometimes a partner who works in law enforcement is also a perpetrator. She can't go to the hospital for the help she needs. I get it. You can count on my discretion—completely."

"Thanks again, Alex. Please keep me in the loop. I know I can count on you to do everything possible for Ginny. It's the long run I am most worried about."

"Yes, you are right to be worried about the long run. She can't go back to living with Bubba. The man needs to be in jail, but it doesn't sound as if that's going to happen. I'll be in touch."

Sidney was wiped out and had to concentrate on making herself stay awake as she drove home. She was as quiet as she could be as she parked her car and entered the house. She didn't want to wake Cameron. She hated keeping anything from him, but she felt she had to protect Ginny. Sidney took a shower in the guest suite and slipped into bed without rousing Cameron. She felt like a thief in the night. Something had to happen to resolve this situation, but Sidney had no idea what that resolution would look like. A long-run solution was illusive. Ginny could not go back to living with Bubba, but where would she go? Sidney's mind was racing. Her brain had to stop trying to figure everything out that night. Even though she'd had a nap that day, exhaustion finally took precedence, and she slept.

"Where did you go last night, and what's going on?" Cameron knew Sidney had been late coming to bed. He knew she'd driven someplace in her car.

"I can't tell you, Cameron, and I won't lie to you. So don't ask me."

"This has something to do with Ginny, doesn't it?"

"I told you not to ask me."

"Why won't you talk to me?"

"Because you are such a straight arrow, and you always trust law enforcement and want to call them...even when they don't deserve to be trusted."

The Restoration

LOUISIANA

The Past

Maximillian Sobrille purchased Shadowlawn in Franklin, Louisiana in 1998. He had made his fortune forging art and selling both the originals (replacing the originals with his excellent forgeries), in some cases, and the forgeries (successfully fooling the buyer and selling the copies as originals), in others. His work was so fine and his attention to detail was so precise that he was able to fool even the most skeptical expert and all of the art auction houses. He loved what he did, and he had made an enormous amount of money doing it.

He had purchased the antebellum mansion in Franklin from an estate at a bargain price. The last remaining family member to live in the house had died. There were only distant heirs, and none of them wanted to buy the magnificent but antiquated money pit. It stood empty for five years. The beautiful but neglected home was going to require extensive work to rehabilitate and modernize it. Maximillian's skills as an artist and the vast fortune he had amassed made him the perfect buyer for the pre-Civil War mansion.

Maximillian was a recluse. It might even be said that he was a hermit. He nodded to his neighbors but never got into a conversation with any of them. He had his groceries delivered. In fact, he had everything delivered that he possibly could have delivered. When he occasionally had to go to the grocery store or the pharmacy, he was polite but did not chat. He somehow managed to interact and communicate sufficiently with the workmen he was paying to bring Shadowlawn back to the magnificent home it had been in the past. He preferred to communicate via Zoom…even if he was close by, and he always wore a disguise. He did not want any of his workmen to know what he looked like. He paid well, so the people who worked for him were willing to put up with their eccentric and taciturn client.

Shadowlawn looked like an antebellum plantation house, and indeed the gracious mansion had been built prior to the Civil War. But it had never been a plantation house. The man who had built Shadowlawn was a businessman. He was a shipowner and had made his fortune in the import and export business. He was never a planter. He had never had a plantation. He did not grow the cotton that was the agricultural king of the era. He did, however, load the cotton that was grown by others onto his ships and deliver it all over the world. And he owned a dry goods store in Franklin. He had built Shadowlawn as a town house.

Initially the house had been built on a sizeable parcel of land. Through the years, that parcel had become smaller and smaller. From time to time, Shadowlawn's owners, strapped for funds, had sold off some of the surrounding acres. The road that ran through town and in front of Shadowlawn was widened several times. The demands of the municipality for more and more of Shadowlawn's front yard had also eaten away at the size of the mansion's grounds. The bayou had protected Shadowlawn's rear boundaries from encroachment, but by the time Maxamillian Sobrille bought the property, the size of the grounds had been significantly reduced. Maxamillian planted a thick bamboo break along one property line and trees and bushes on another. He built an expensive and substantial fence around the entire place and installed a beautiful but impenetrable gate to keep out unwanted visitors. Maximillian valued his privacy and wanted to be left alone.

Behind the main house, there was a substantial building that had once served as the kitchen when Shadowlawn had servants and the lady of the house never cooked. Maximillian lived in this outbuilding while the big house was being restored and rebuilt. He'd had a nice bathroom and a tiny kitchen put into the one-room structure. He was interested to learn that the former kitchen building where he was now living had also been where the Smith family had lived for more than two years while the mansion was being built. That had been more than one hundred and fifty years earlier.

Maximillian had decided he wanted to live in the mansion for the rest of his life, so he combined two rooms at the rear of the main house into a large master bedroom and bathroom suite. He thought one of these rooms might have been where the servants ate their meals and the other might have been a playroom for the owner's children. The other bedrooms were all upstairs, and even though he would probably never have a guest visit Shadowlawn, let along stay overnight with him, he had all of the upstairs bathrooms made into en suites with modern bathrooms. All the rooms in the mansion were large. After the renovation was completed and the kitchen inside the house had been completely updated, Max intended to use the former kitchen building behind the main house as his art studio.

Because Maximillian was an artist, he wanted to do everything right for this impressive pre-Civil War home. His artistic sensibilities demanded that he pay attention to every detail. He was meticulous in his restoration and in the colors he choose for the two parlors, the library, the dining room, the morning room, and the office. He brought an expert plasterer from New Orleans to repair the walls. He hired a carpenter from Monroe, Louisiana who specialized in reproducing the woodwork of historic buildings. He spared no expense, and the result was truly a work of art, a feast for the eyes…a home befitting an artist of Maximillian's caliber.

Some of the original furniture had endured and was still in the house. Maximillian kept as many of these antiques as he could, and he had them cleaned and repaired. Maximillian made trips to New Orleans to search for the perfect pieces to finish furnishing his mansion. The antique dealers on Royal Street were always happy to see Max coming. They knew he had money to spend. It was on one of these trips to Royal Street that he stumbled on the treasure that both broke his heart and provided him with the project of a lifetime.

Maximillian didn't engage his neighbors in conversation, and he rarely went anywhere outside his own home in Franklin. When he shopped for furniture in New Orleans, he said only what he had to say to learn about a piece he thought he might like to buy. If he decided to make a purchase, he said only what he needed to say to complete the transaction. Once and only once, he gave himself away in a furniture emporium because this particular business also sold artwork.

Maximillian was intrigued by the pieces that hung on the walls of one store where he shopped. It was an eclectic place…part furniture store and part art gallery. In addition to paintings and furniture, it also sold sculpture, old books, and manuscripts. In addition to looking at the furniture, Max could not help but also spend time looking at the artwork on the walls. The shop's owner could not help but notice Max's interest in the paintings.

The owner of the gallery was also the person who managed the business day to day. Remy Boucher loved what he did and was always looking for something unusual to display and sell. The only time he was away from the gallery was when he was traveling and searching for the treasure that no one else on Royal Street would ever find. Remy tried to engage Maximillian in conversation whenever the recluse came to Remy's place of business. Trying to talk to Max was like pulling teeth. It became a challenge for Remy to see if he could say anything that would capture Maximillian's interest and entice the man to speak more than a few words.

Remy had connections all over New Orleans and all over Louisiana. He knew there were treasures that could be found in abandoned storage units, and he occasionally spoke with the people who owned and ran these places in the New Orleans area. One such establishment was being closed down for good. Those who had their belongings stored in the units were given a year to retrieve and move their things. Anything that was still left in the units at the end of the year would be auctioned off or sold to a junk dealer. Remy knew there might be something worthwhile left behind He asked the owner, who was selling the business to a developer who intended to tear down the storage facility and build houses on the land, if he could look over what remained after the owners of the units had moved the contents.

Remy's contact didn't have anything much to show him from the abandoned storage units, but the owner was also cleaning out the office of the storage facility. The office would be torn down along with the storage units to make way for the ranch houses the developer was going to build. A previous owner had stuffed some artwork into a closet in the office. It had been years since anyone had paid attention to what was in the closet or cleaned it out, but when it came time to tear down the building, the owner decided he should at least get rid of whatever was in there.

When the owner finally got around to tackling this long-delayed and onerous task, he found broken furniture, stacks of paper files that had been left on the floor, an eagle finial that looked as if it had once belonged with a flag or on a flagpole, a giant package of toilet paper, some dried up banana peels, a lot of spiders and dead cockroaches, a nice toolbox from Sears, one desiccated mouse, two boxes full of unopened junk mail, a bronze vase that was covered with mold, two bags of trash that should have been put in the garbage can decades earlier, and some long-ago discarded artwork that was folded up and covered with mildew and stuffed into a plastic bag. Except for the Craftsman toolbox, the owner decided he didn't have time to fool with the rest of it. Something about the artwork made him hesitate before he threw it all away. He called Remy Boucher to come and have a look at the paintings and drawings. The owner of the storage facility felt it was pretty much all ruined by mold and mildew. If it was worthless or if Remy didn't want to make the trip to look at the artwork, he would send it to the dump with the rest of the contents of the closet.

Remy almost didn't go to look at the artwork. What could possibly be worth anything that had been forgotten for more than ten years in a closet in the office of a self-storage facility? He didn't have the time to drive across town to look at something he knew ahead of time wasn't worth it. But the owner of the facility was an old friend, so Remy decided to make the time to look at what his friend said he thought was artwork. He procrastinated about this chore, and finally two days before the facility was sold, he arrived to look at what had been left in the closet. He didn't really look at the artwork very carefully. It had been more than ten years since the art heist in Boston. Most people who were not from New England or who were not interested in art had forgotten about the paintings that had disappeared in 1990. Remy was interested in contemporary art, and he had forgotten about the robbery in Boston that had occurred in the previous century.

However, Remy was drawn to the flagpole finial. It was a bronze eagle, and it had a certain panache that Remy liked.

He thought he could hang it on the wall in his gallery. "I'll take the paintings and other pieces if you'll throw in the eagle. Box it all up, and I'll take it with me."

Remy knew his friend wanted to make a few bucks from the transaction, and this was fine with Remy. "I'll have to charge you for the eagle, and for the box." The owner told him, and then he laughed.

"How much for the eagle?"

"Ten bucks...plus two bucks for the box. It's a nice big box. It's new."

"It's a deal."

They folded the artwork into the box as best they could and put the finial on top. The canvases were stiff with paint and lacquer. Two of them were frayed and too large to fold easily. Pieces of paint fell from the canvas as they folded the paintings. Remy didn't pay much attention to the artwork that was going into the box. He was focused on the bronze finial in the shape of an eagle. Remy put a strip of duct tape on the box to keep it closed while he drove it back to his gallery.

When they'd moved the box out of the closet, Remy saw a small something on the floor. He bent down to pick it up. Something about the face on the miniature portrait looked familiar to him, but he couldn't put his finger on what it was. It was a tiny little piece, measuring less than two inches by two inches. The man whose face was pictured in the portrait was a scruffy looking guy in a cap. He had a mustache and a lot of hair. Remy stuck the small piece into the pocket of his jacket and loaded the box into his van. He gave his friend twelve dollars in cash and drove back to Royal Street.

Remy didn't think that anything in the box was worth much except for the finial. It was on top of the other things packed into the box, so it was easy to retrieve. He didn't take anything else out of the box which he put in his upstairs storage room with the rest of his junk. Remy hung the finial on the wall of his gallery. Nobody paid much attention to it. There were many more interesting things in Remy's elegant store to capture the attention of serious buyers with money to spend. Nobody showed any real interest in the finial until Maximillian Sobrille came in a few months later.

Max always noticed when there was something new in Remy's gallery. Remy had decided the man had a photographic memory, as he was always immediately drawn to the items that had not been in the gallery the last time he'd been there. Max spent a long time looking at the finial that was hanging on the wall. Remy attempted to engage his customer in a conversation about the finial. "It's a beauty, isn't it? It's bronze, and I like the way the eagle is positioned. Not the usual bald bird icon in flight that's poised on most flagpoles." Remy was trying out a little humor on his very serious buyer.

Max turned to Remy with wide eyes. Remy had never seen Max look like this. Max looked like he was almost in shock, and at the same time, he appeared to be almost angry. "Where did you get this bronze finial? I want to know everything about where you found it."

Max was quiet but listening to every word as Remy told him the story of the self-storage facility that was being sold to a developer. Max didn't say a word. He just listened. Remy almost forgot to mention the box of worthless and moldy paintings and drawings he had boxed up and brought back and left in his storage space in the attic above the gallery. He remembered the tiny portrait he'd put in his coat pocket, but he couldn't immediately put his hands on the jacket he'd been wearing that day. Max continued to stare at the finial, and Remy scrambled around to find the missing jacket which was hanging on a hook in the back hall of the gallery underneath a bunch of other coats.

The tiny painting of the scruffy young man was still in the pocket. It was an intriguing little piece because it was so small. Remy brought it out and handed it to Max. Max almost dropped the miniature portrait. He stared at it as it lay in his hand, and he just kept staring at it. Remy was afraid his customer was going to faint. Or maybe he was having a stroke or a heart attack. None of those things would be good.

Finally Max spoke. "Did you find both of these pieces, the miniature and the finial, at the same storage place?" This was one of the longest sentences Remy had ever heard come out of the mouth of Max Sobrille.

Remy nodded that indeed he had found both pieces at the storage facility. Max was silent for a long time before he spoke again. It was almost as if he was afraid to ask his next question.

"Was there anything else there…where you found these two items?"

"Just a bunch of old paintings covered with mildew. The paint and the lacquer were coming off the paintings in chunks. They're dark and not really worth looking at. In fact I haven't actually taken the paintings out of the box, so I haven't seen all of them. The ones I have seen are in terrible shape. The large ones were cut out of their frames at some point, and the edges are all raggedy. They're a mess and not worth your time. I know you like quality, and the artwork from the storage unit is not quality."

"I want to see this box of artwork."

"Trust me, it's not worth your time or my effort to bring it down from the attic."

"I want to see it." Almost subconsciously and completely focused on what else Remy had to show him, Max slipped the tiny portrait into the pocket of his pants.

Remy knew that Max was an odd duck. But this was ridiculous. He almost told Max he wasn't going to go up to his attic storage space and bring down the box. It was kind of a big box. "Okay, I'll show it to you, if you really want to see it. But you'll have to climb up into the attic with me. I'm not dragging that box down here. Too much mold. I'm allergic to mold."

Max didn't say anything but walked to the lift at the back of the store. Remy had a primitive lift so he could move furniture from floor to floor. The lift was not an elevator, and Remy didn't maintain it very well. He didn't use it very often. The lift creaked and groaned when it moved up and down. It was old and needed work. Remy led Max to the stairs. Looking at a box full of mildew didn't rate a ride up in the lift.

Once they reached the attic, Remy had to scrounge around to find the box he was looking for. There were hundreds of boxes of stuff in his attic. None of it was organized or labeled. Finally Remy located the one with the moldy artwork. Max had not uttered another word during their trek up the stairs or during the hunt for the right box. Remy pulled the box in front of Max. Just at that moment, the bell on the front door of the gallery sounded. A customer had probably just walked in. Remy left Max with the box. "Knock yourself out," Remy said as he hurried back down the stairs, shaking his head and wondering about the eccentricities of some of the people who came into his shop.

Max was almost certain he knew what he would find in the box, but he was not prepared for the condition of the artwork. It was so much worse than he had imagined it would be. No one had treated these paintings with the respect they deserved. He could not even begin to guess what had happened to the priceless masterpieces on their journey from Boston to this sweltering attic above a gallery in New Orleans. Max pulled out the pieces one by one. He was almost sick to his stomach as he unfolded each work of art. He was devastated to see the shambles he'd uncovered. He lay the pieces of art out on the floor of the attic. Remy's upstairs storeroom was air-conditioned, but the AC in the attic did not work well enough to cool anything.

Max broke down and wept when he had finally brought out every piece from the cardboard box. He was confronting a tragedy of unimaginable proportions. This was an affront, not only to the world of art, but to the world as a whole. These works of art were completely ruined. They would never again be able to be displayed anywhere. The fact that he had finally found these missing treasures and the fact that they had been destroyed by time and mistreatment overwhelmed Max.

He could not rejoice that the lost had been found. He could only grieve that something wonderful had been lost forever. It would have been better if he had never found these paintings and these drawings. It would have been better if no one had ever known what had happened to them. The whereabouts of the artwork stolen from the Isabella Stewart Gardener Museum should have remained a mystery for the ages. If they'd never been found, hope would still be alive that one day they would be recovered. Now all hope was gone, gone for all time.

Maximillian Sobrille was hardly ever at a loss about what to do. He almost always knew exactly what should be done in any situation. But he was completely stumped now, as he surveyed this catastrophic destruction of beauty. He had no idea what he should do about his horrible discovery. He sat on the floor staring at these treasures that had been found but were now lost forever. After a while he came to the decision that he had to become the caretaker of this disaster. He would become the guardian of these once magnificent works of creative genius. It broke his heart, and he knew he had to keep all knowledge about this destruction from becoming known to anyone but himself. He had to hide these pitiful remnants of something that once was wonderful. He had to get them out of Remy's gallery and take them to a place where they would never be seen again.

Max was in another world as he packed the paintings and the drawings and the bronze gu back into the cardboard box. He pushed the box towards the lift and loaded it onto the rickety platform. He rode down in the lift with his box. They arrived on the main floor of the gallery, and he pushed the box in the direction of the door that went to the street. Remy was engaged with another customer and gave Max a puzzled look as he maneuvered the large box out of the lift.

"I want to buy the box of artwork. How much will you charge me?"

"I assume you also want the finial. Right?" Max nodded his head yes. "You can have it for one hundred." Remy was always ready to put a few dollars in his pocket. "But you can have the stuff in the box for free."

Max took a hundred-dollar bill from his wallet and handed it to Remy. Remy was busy and didn't bother to give him a receipt for the payment. That was fine with Max. He was in a daze and not thinking about much of anything. Both men had forgotten all about the tiny painting that was now in Max's pocket. *Portrait of the Artist as a Young Man* by Rembrandt van Rijn would be a bonus for Max.

Max removed the eagle from the wall of the gallery and added it to the box. He left the box by the gallery's front door while he went to find his van. Parking is always impossible in the French Quarter, so he had to walk a ways to where he had parked. He drove back and stopped in front of the gallery. He struggled to load the box into his vehicle. Remy was still engaged with a customer who had potential. He vaguely noticed Max struggling with the box full of junk as he pushed and pulled it out the door. Remy had slipped the $100 bill into his own pants pocket, and then he forgot all about weird Max and the finial and Max's trip to the gallery attic.

All the way back to Franklin in the van, Max's mind was going a million miles an hour. It was a two-hour drive, but Max remembered almost nothing about being on the road and driving back home to his mansion that backed up on Bayou Teche in Franklin, Louisiana. He was almost surprised when he found himself at his house. He had not yet figured out what to do about the box he had in the back of the van. He was still at the stage of cursing whoever had stolen the famous artwork and who had not bothered to take care of the treasures they'd had in their hands. Max did not understand how anyone could have treated the paintings and the drawings in such a derelict way. He had to assume they'd not had any idea what they'd possessed. And then they'd abandoned their cache or forgotten about it.

Max had made his fortune by breaking the law, but he had his standards. He felt sick to his stomach when he thought of the box of ruined artwork in his van. What in the world would he ever do with it? He couldn't destroy it.

That would be another tragedy on top of a tragedy. But he could not allow the world to know, let alone see, what had in fact happened to these masterpieces. His own heart was crushed by the desecration. He could not inflict such pain on the art world as a whole. He knew that many still held out hope that the works which had been taken in the Gardner heist would one day be found.

And in fact they had turned up, but Max did not want to reveal the find to either the art world or to the wider public. He felt as if he had something in his possession that was toxic or radioactive. He couldn't live with something this valuable on his hands, and he couldn't bring himself to get rid of it. This hot potato that he had brought from New Orleans was burning a hole in his van and a hole in his heart. Max left the box in the van for weeks. Weeks became months. Months became a year.

They say that one year is an appropriate period for grieving. Maybe that was what Maximillian Sobrille had been observing when he'd left the box of artwork in the van for a year. Maybe it had been necessary to leave the paintings and the drawings in the van for a year so that he could appropriately grieve what had happened to these irreplaceable pieces that would never again be seen by anyone but himself. He wished a hundred times he'd never found them. He wished he'd never brought them from New Orleans. He wished he'd not decided he had to be the caretaker of this secret debacle. There was no way to make this right.

It was as if Max had forgotten what he did best. He was an art forger. He had amassed his fortune by forging masterpieces. Somehow, in his shock and dismay about the Isabella Stewart Gardner Museum heist, he had been afraid to think about the superb skill he had at his disposal. It was not until he'd brought the box from his van into his artist's studio, the old kitchen which had served Shadowlawn in a previous century, that he was able to think about what to do with his find going forward. It was an awesome responsibility. He was almost afraid to consider the options. Could he possibly handle this opportunity? Was it within his scope and was it something he even dared to undertake?

Maximillian Sobrille had intended to retire. He'd made his fortune. He did not plan to copy any more paintings...ever. He was going legit. He had been lucky and smart to avoid being caught so far. He was not sure he wanted to get back into the game again. He had planned to do something different with his artist's palate and his brushes. He was out of practice. But it was tempting. Max agonized over his dilemma as he wondered if he would be giving the art world a gift or doing it a disservice.

It had taken more than a year for Max to bring himself to confront the artwork he'd acquired from Remy's gallery. He reluctantly brought the box of ruined paintings and drawings into his studio. The box that had been sitting in his van for a year now sat in the mansion's former kitchen which had become his studio. Finally, Max was ready to open the box and make an assessment of the condition of the artwork. There was a small closet in the studio. When Max had lived in the kitchen, during the months when Shadowlawn had been undergoing its restoration, Max had used the closet as a place to keep his clothes. The door didn't lock, but Max could remedy that. He decided he would hang the drawings and the paintings inside the closet.

Max brought out each piece that had been stuffed into the box. He treated each work of art with the respect and reverence he felt it deserved, even in its ruined state. The five sketches by Degas were in terrible shape. They were torn and water stained and covered with mildew. Large pieces were missing from these etchings on paper. Max felt they would not be difficult to reproduce. He had copied works by Degas before. He hung the drawings in his closet and moved on to the other pieces in the box. The Manet portrait, *Chez Tortoni*, was relatively small. It had been removed from its frame, not cut out of the frame. This painting had not been cruelly folded like the others had been, probably due to its smaller size. This was the one painting from the heist that might be able to be saved. But it had suffered from many temperature fluctuations and was now covered with mold. It was presumptuous of Max to attempt to copy a Manet, but he knew his capabilities. He hung the Manet in the closet.

Max handled the Vermeer with particular reverence. Max idolized Vermeer. He loved Vermeer's use of light. It was even more difficult to copy the way Vermeer used light than it was to copy the way Caravaggio used chiaroscuro. Copying a Vermeer was the art forger's greatest challenge. Max had never copied a painting by the Dutch artist. Early in his career he he'd had an opportunity to copy a Vermeer, and he'd been tempted. At that time, Max had not felt like he was ready to take on the forgery of a Vermeer. Now Max felt as if he was good enough to undertake such a challenge. Max knew he could do this now, but it would take special care and skill.

Vermeer died when he was only forty-three years old, and the number of paintings in his body of work was limited because he had not lived longer. Vermeer had not been a starving artist. In fact he had not been primarily an artist at all. He had followed in his father's footsteps as an art dealer. It has been suggested that Vermeer's painting was in fact a much-loved hobby. He sold his paintings to a small circle of patrons in the town of Delft in Holland where he lived with his wife and family. During their marriage, his wife gave birth to fifteen children, eleven of whom survived. It is really quite astonishing that Vermeer was able to complete as many paintings as he did in his short life. It is not any wonder that several of his paintings that depict middle-class domestic life include the figure of a pregnant woman. One must wonder how many children he might have sired if he had lived to be eighty years old.

Art experts throughout the years have found Vermeer's perspectives puzzling and intriguing. It has been suggested that he might have used the camera obscura to develop and enhance his paintings. The camera obscura was a predecessor of the photographic camera which was invented in 1816. Whether or not Vermeer used the camera obscura, his work is remarkable and cherished.

Vermeer's paintings have gained in popularity and value in recent years. The loss of the Vermeer from the Gardner was a much-lamented tragedy. When Max found *The Concert* in New Orleans, the painting had been pierced through the center by some kind of a sharp object with which it had come into contact after leaving the museum. It was ripped almost in half as a result of its encounter with whatever had torn the canvas. Max's heart physically hurt when he looked at the damage that had been inflicted on this masterpiece. Max felt that it was even more presumptuous of him to attempt to copy a Vermeer than it was for him to copy the Manet.

The Govaert Flinck painting had been an odd choice for the burglars who had stolen the paintings in 1990. Why had this one been chosen, or had it been removed by mistake? The painting, *Landscape with Obelisk*, had originally been attributed to Rembrandt. Was that why it had been on the list of paintings to steal? Had the list been out of date? *Landscape with Obelisk* had been displayed in the museum back-to-back with Vermeer's, *The Concert.* Perhaps this was why it had been taken. This piece had been painted, not on canvas, but on a wooden board. It might have survived and been repaired enough to be rehung in the Gardner, but something had spilled over the front of the painting. Whatever had been spilled on this masterpiece had contained alcohol and had taken the paint entirely off its wooden foundation in several places. The paint had run, and the piece of art was badly streaked. It did not look like anything now, except maybe an old board that had been used as a doormat on which to wipe ones feet. If he could be certain that the wooden board on which the Flinck had been painted was not irretrievably damaged by whatever substance had removed the pigment, he might be able to reuse this original foundation for the new painting.

The two paintings which had been the most severely damaged were the two by Rembrandt. Both *A Lady and Gentleman in Black* and *Christ in the Storm on the Sea of Galilee were* large paintings. They had both been cut from their frames. Whatever instrument had been used to cut them free had not been one that had been intended for that purpose. It had not been sharp enough and had not done a good job of cutting through the canvas thick with paint and varnish. Inevitably whenever a painting is cut out of its frame, some of the painting is lost. It might be a fraction of an inch, but the painting is diminished nonetheless. Max speculated that these two had been cut from their frames because they were large paintings. It would have taken more time to carefully remove each one from its frame. It had been a robbery, after all, and the thieves had wanted to get their paintings and make their way out of the museum as quickly as possible.

The two Rembrandts had been folded, which is a completely forbidden way to treat an oil painting. This is well-known to anyone who has worked with paintings. But apparently this absolutely taboo way of handling artwork had not been a part of the burglars' repertoire. They had done the unimaginable, the unthinkable, the unforgiveable. They might have tried to roll the paintings, but these two were so thick with paint and varnish, it would not have been possible to roll them. When they had been folded, the paint and the varnish had actually fallen off the paintings where the creases were. The edges of both of these paintings were terribly frayed. It looked as if a mouse or a rat had chewed at one of the edges of the smaller masterpiece. But the worst damage had been done to the large Rembrandt seascape. It was more than 5 feet X 4 feet in size. As it had been moved and folded and unfolded and refolded over the years, it had been significantly ripped where the frayed edges were. More flecks of paint had been lost when the painting had been almost ripped in half. These two Rembrandt canvases would never see the light of day again. Max was shattered when he saw the way the Rembrandts had been treated. Both were totally destroyed.

The Rembrandt's storm painting was important because it was the artist's only painting of a seascape. The artist specialized in portraits and had done relatively few outdoor paintings. The cost of the loss of this painting was incalculable because of its uniqueness. The dark painting of the couple was a tragedy because of the artist who had painted it. It was an interesting painting, but not unique in its subject matter.

The ancient Chinese gu was intact, as was the bronze eagle finial. The tiny self-portrait etching of Rembrandt as a young man was precious to Max. It was in relatively good shape. He did not have to copy the miniature and was going to have a difficult time giving that one back.

Max hung the ten masterpieces and left the two metal sculptures in the closet. He bought an imposing padlock and did his best to secure what was left of the Isabella Stewart Gardner Museum treasures.

*I*t had taken several days for Max to go through the box of paintings and drawings and hang each one in the closet. It was more a matter of an emotional journey, and the damage done to the paintings felt like damage done to Max's own psyche. Now that he knew the condition of each piece of art, he had confronted the reality of what he had to work with. He was better able to make an assessment of what there was to do and what he would have to undertake if he was willing to try to restore some of the pieces and copy some of the others. He reached the difficult decision that only the small miniature etching and the two metal pieces were salvageable. The other pieces were irretrievably lost. It took some time for Max to admit this to himself and to decide where he was going to go from there.

If he was going to do something with his own artistic gift and with this serendipitous find, he needed to prepare. He realized that the best way to prepare and perhaps the best way for him to make a good decision was to do a stint in a museum. Did he still have the skills he used to have? Could he still produce a copy that would fool the experts? In order to prove to himself that he still had his abilities, Max would have to be surreptitious with his work at the museum. And of course he would have to successfully hide what he was doing from the other people he worked with. The true test would be if and when he was able to sell the paintings he produced. Would his copies sell? In the past, his work had always fooled the art dealers. Could he still paint well enough that his forgeries would be accepted as the real thing? Could he still fool a sophisticated and wealthy buyer?

He changed his name a little bit and made applications for low-level watchman and security guard positions at several museums all over the country. He visited each museum to see if he could do what he had to do in each location. A few of the museums seemed as if they could work for him. He crossed others off his list. He created a fake story about his past work experience and counted on the fact that no one would check his references. He would have preferred something farther away from the East Coast and something very far away from New England, but in the end he took the position as a nighttime guard at the Philadelphia Museum of Art. It would only be a temporary job, and after checking it out, Max decided it would probably be an easy place to get away with what he wanted to get away with.

It was a difficult decision and involved leaving his retirement and his solitude and his beautiful home in Louisiana. He loved how much of a recluse he could be there, and he hated to think of sacrificing the comfortable existence he had been able to create for himself. But in the end, the lure of the artwork that he had almost accidentally acquired and the mission he felt compelled to undertake won the day. He had found the treasures. He knew they were forever lost to the world. He knew he had the skills to do something to make things better. It was not possible to rescue or restore the paintings. It was not going to be possible to make things right the way he had hoped. Too much had been destroyed. But Maximillian Sobrille was going to prove he could still fool anybody and everybody with his forgeries. His solution was second best to being able to restore the original paintings, but it was something.

The job Max had set for himself would require a prodigious amount of work. It might take many months just to acquire the authentic canvases and papers and to mix the right paints. It would take years to copy all the artwork. He would have to be better at what he did than he had ever been before. This project would be the true test of his genius. He would have to outdo himself with every stroke of his paint brush. When the time came, he would have to become Rembrandt. He would have to become Degas and Manet. He would have to be Vermeer when he presumed to copy and paint *The Concert*.

Max temporarily relocated to Philadelphia. He changed his name to Sobril Macharene. He was afraid his new name might be too close to his old name, but he finally decided to go with it. He found a place to rent in North Philadelphia that was a short bus ride from the museum. He didn't want to live too close to where he worked, but he didn't want to be so far away that he had a long commute. His rented apartment was a far cry from the mansion he lived in when he was in

Louisiana. When he had days off, he made occasional trips back to Franklin while he worked in Philadelphia.

When he had reassured himself that his skills had been brought up to date, he would try to sell the copies he'd made. This would be the true test of whether or not his forgeries would be able to pass as the original artwork. When he had finally decided whether or not he felt as if he was going to be able to follow through with his plan, he would disappear quietly from the Philadelphia Museum of Art, as he had disappeared from so many other museums in the past. He knew how to fade into the woodwork and become a ghost.

Max Sobrille knew he would have to find a way to sell the copies he made of famous works of art. This was the most difficult part of forging a masterpiece, but it was the ultimate and most important part of the process. Being able to sell one's work was the only true test of whether or not it was worthy and was able to fool the experts. Max didn't need the money. He had become very wealthy over the years... selling the originals as well as the copies of the masterpieces he forged. He had made his fortune several times over. He had a beautiful house. He had the time and the money to do whatever he wanted to do.

Even though he realized he was putting everything he had at risk, he had decided that he had to go back into a museum and once again copy the famous art that was preserved there. He felt he needed to hone his skills and see if he still had the gift that had enabled him to make his millions from forged artwork. He had chosen the Philadelphia Museum of Art, and he had a job as a night security guard there. He worked on developing his cover story. He was ready to go, but he had not yet found anyone to whom he could sell his forgeries. If he couldn't sell his work and thereby prove that he still had the skills to paint flawless copies, it might be a waste of time to go to Philadelphia.

He didn't know anybody who lived in Philadelphia. He'd never worked at the art museum there. Even though he had not yet found a buyer for his copies, he began his work as a guard on the night shift and his work as an art forger. It wasn't long before he realized he still had it, whatever it was that enabled him to copy a work of art exactly. It was a gift. Max knew this and was thankful for it.

Max had given a great deal of thought to his gift over the years. It was as if his eyes were directly connected to his incredibly accurate hands. He was able to paint exactly what his eye was looking at. He could reproduce anything perfectly. He had known of autistic savants who could listen to a piece of music one time, sit down at the piano, and reproduce the music perfectly...playing a piece with all its intricacies and elaborate chords. Max decided he was like one of these savants, only his gift was not in reproducing musical works. Max's gift was the ability to perfectly reproduce visual works of art.

However, Max found that with the passing years, it had become more difficult to sell his forgeries. He didn't know exactly why this was true and wondered if he had become unwilling to take the risks he had been willing to take when he was younger. In Philadelphia, he eventually found someone who was willing to buy his artwork in exchange for diamonds. Max didn't need the diamonds, and he didn't want the diamonds. He felt having diamonds in his possession put him in some kind of danger.

At last he found someone who lived in his neighborhood who would buy his diamonds for cash. Max knew the shady and suspicious guy who bought his diamonds was cheating him, but he didn't care about that. He mostly cared that he had found a way to sell his copies. Then he found a way to unload the payments that had been made in diamonds, and he made a little money. The little bit of money he made in the diamond transactions with his sleazy neighbor, Damon, he donated anonymously to the Philadelphia Museum of Art.

Max had always been and always would be a recluse. He couldn't change that part of who he was. He had his groceries delivered and his dry cleaning picked up from and delivered back to his North Philadelphia rental. He kept to himself. He was polite to the people he worked with, but he didn't chat and didn't make friends. He kept his job at the Philadelphia Museum of Art for several months, enough time so that his leaving wouldn't arouse suspicion. When he felt as if he had stayed long enough, he packed the few things he'd brought with him from Louisiana and left town. He mailed his guard's uniforms back to the museum.

He was delighted that he had been able to prove to himself that he still "had it." He now felt confident that he could copy the Gardner Museum masterpieces. He still was not completely certain he was willing to make the enormous commitment the project he had in front of him would require.

He had loved making the copies he'd completed while working at the Philadelphia museum. He realized that in the past he had used his gift to make money, and he'd made a great deal of it. Not keeping any of the money he'd made for the work he'd done in Philadelphia was proof enough for Max that he also genuinely loved what he did. It was not just about the money. He had made a fortune from his painting, but in Philadelphia, he'd been delighted to give away the little bit of money he'd earned trading his paintings for diamonds. He still loved doing the paintings. Max had always known that painting was who he was in his very soul.

He would make no money on the Gardner project. In fact, it would cost him a considerable amount of money to find the authentic materials with which to recreate the 17th, 18th, and 19th Century masterpieces. And it would take years to complete the forgeries. It would be his best work, and he wanted to devote to the project all the time and the energy it would require. He realized he could not possibly turn away from this opportunity. He admitted to himself that he wanted to pursue the years-long project that he had ahead of him. It was indeed a gift, and he embraced with enthusiasm the massive effort it would require to replace the works that had been stolen from the Isabella Stewart Gardner Museum in 1990. The Isabella Stewart Gardner Museum paintings and drawings and Max's commitment to them took on the quality of a religious crusade, a sacred trust.

Max knew how to find the materials he needed. He had done this many times before. He would need to acquire old canvases of the right sizes from the correct time periods. He would have to correctly duplicate the pigments and the medium and the binders each artist would have used. To recreate a convincing copy, he could use only materials that would have been available during the century in which each masterpiece had been painted. He had made these concoctions before, so he knew how much of which pigments to add to the egg yolk. He knew how much and what kind of turpentine to use as he precisely prepared his paints.

He already owned some of the correct period brushes, but he would have to acquire more. Different artists used different kinds of brushes. He decided he would need a larger

and better oven. He already had an oven to bake his paintings to make the oil paints dry more quickly, but he could
afford to buy a new oven that would be perfectly calibrat-
ed. To help the aging process along, he baked the paintings
in his oversized oven. The turpentine he used in creating
his paints also helped to dry and age the paintings. There
would be no mistakes. He would be able to age his copies
perfectly. Each painting would be dried in such a way that
it would appear to have been created centuries earlier. The
craquelure of each would appear in exactly the correct form
and depth to accurately reflect the time period in which the
original work of art had been painted. After a painting was
completed, he used the proper varnish and aged it with the
correct medium. Only then would every masterpiece Max
created become indistinguishable from the original.

Max also wanted to have in front of him several excellent
reproductions and photos of each piece of the artwork he intended to copy. He was used to working with the originals that
resided in museums. He had the originals from the Gardner
in his possession, but they were tragically degraded. It would
be difficult if not impossible, using only the originals in their
current horrible condition, to reproduce exactly what the
originals had looked like before they'd been destroyed. Max
would have to have photographs and prints of the original
masterpieces in order to make his copies.

Max needed places where the things he ordered could
be sent to him covertly. Max could not have either the necessary materials, or the reproductions he needed to work
from, sent to his home in Louisiana. It was his hideout, his
refuge. It could not be compromised. Texas was not too far
away from Louisiana. Living in Franklin, Max could reach
the panhandle of Florida by driving a few hours. He set up

post office boxes in random towns in random places in these two nearby states. Nothing would be sent to Louisiana.

Max even took a vacation in Maine and had prints and photographs sent to a post office box in Rockland. The Farnsworth Art Museum that featured many Wyeth paintings was there, and Max had always admired the work of all three generations of Wyeth artists. He had copied one painting by Andrew Wyeth, and the exhibits in Rockland were tempting. But Max resisted, collected what he needed from his post office box, and went home to Louisiana.

Max enjoyed this part of the process. He enjoyed searching for the perfect canvases that he could clean and age and make even more perfect. He liked the intrigue of acquiring his materials from far and wide. But it was paramount that he protect his home and not have anything delivered there that might give him away.

Acquiring and preparing the canvases for his copies was the greatest challenge Max faced. To obtain the canvases he needed, he bought relatively inexpensive paintings from the period he intended to copy. The sizes of the canvases had to be exact. The age and size of each canvas was critical in fooling the critics. Max had developed his own process for transforming these canvases. He knew how to completely remove all of the paint from a less important painting of the period. He was able to completely wipe the canvas clean of the previous artist's work down to its sizing. He knew how the artists he was going to imitate treated the sizing on their canvases. Max was meticulous in his preparation of the canvases so there would be no questions raised when the experts examined his copies.

When Max began each painting, he used an appropriately aged but empty canvas that had the perfect dimensions on which to forge his masterpiece. Each canvas was so carefully prepared it would have exactly resembled the canvas that was used by the original artist. Max paid an extraordinary amount of attention to every aspect of painting his copies. Because of his diligence and attention to detail as well as the genius of his eye and painter's brush, not one of his completed works had ever been suspected of being anything but the original.

When he had everything he needed, Max settled in to devote his time and efforts to bringing the stolen masterpieces back to the world. He occasionally took a break and drove to New Orleans for a visit to Galatoire's or to have a shrimp or oyster po' boy from his favorite café in the French Quarter. He never returned to Remy Boucher's gallery.

Max gave himself completely to the biggest and most demanding project of his life. He had in years past studied the works of every artist whose paintings he intended to copy. For the current project, he again studied in depth the works of each of the artists whose work he was going to paint. He knew well what pigments and colors he would use for the underpainting of the masterpieces he would copy for Rembrandt, Manet, and Flinck. He had painted copies of these artists' works before. Vermeer, however, had produced relatively few paintings during his short lifetime, and Max had never copied a Vermeer. Max had to do some extra research on the texture and colors of Vermeer's underpainting. He wanted to be sure he copied the Vermeer painting, *The Concert*, perfectly.

Max set up his three easels side by side. He put the remnants of the ruined masterpiece on one easel to the left. He put the best reproduction he had of the work of art on the easel to the right. He placed his perfectly prepared, empty canvas on the easel in the center. He knew very well that every artist, no matter who they were and no matter when they created their work, painted with unique brush strokes. Mac respected this and had learned to imitate the brush strokes of the old masters. Because he had never painted a Vermeer, before he began to paint the Vermeer, he practiced for weeks to learn to duplicate Vermeer's brush strokes.

Max painted at the same times of day as Rembrandt supposedly had painted. He ate the same food as biographers said Rembrandt would have eaten in the 17th century. Max wondered if these biographies had got it right. He grew tired of bread and herring. He felt the cheese and butter that comprised much of the diet of the Dutch Golden Age was overdone. Sometimes he had to stop being Rembrandt and revert to consuming delicious Louisiana seafood. When he was painting, Max dressed in clothes similar to those that Rembrandt would have worn. In effect, he tried to become the artist whose work he was copying. When he had finished painting the Rembrandts, he became Vermeer and tried to live as Vermeer had lived. In turn, he became Degas and Manet and Flinck.

Max was in his element. He loved reproducing the ruined treasures from the Gardner Museum. He took his time and made certain every stroke of his brush was perfectly done. He had become obsessed. Sometimes, he found himself unable to do the work for days at a time. He wondered if he was succumbing to old age. Or maybe this was his brain's way of taking a rest? He finally decided that he was experiencing what writers call "writers' block." Max diagnosed his problem as "painter's block." He knew he had sometimes become too intense about attempting to actually become the artist whose work he was reproducing.

He had long ago stopped regarding the work he had undertaken as forgery. He thought of what he was doing as a restoration. He was taking something that had been completely destroyed, and he intended to recreate it. His mission was to bring this artwork back from the ruins. He felt he was doing a community service. He had thought a lot about how he was going to return the masterpieces to the museum from which they'd been stolen, but he'd not yet figured out exactly how he was going to do that.

To overcome his painter's block and regain his momentum, Max took up gardening. He had a wonderful piece of property in Franklin. The Louisiana weather was hot in the summer, but it was also extremely plant friendly. Louisiana always had plenty of rain. The brief downpours that semi-tropical Louisiana experienced almost daily kept his plants healthy. Max took on his landscaping chores as an artistic challenge. He made the yard and gardens that surrounded his Louisiana mansion, Shadowlawn, into another work of art. This time he had helpers—Mother Nature and the Almighty—with contributions of sun and rain, helping him grow his organic work of art. He also grew vegetables and herbs in his garden and learned to be a better cook as well as a very fine landscape architect.

Max spent years doing his "restoration" on the Isabella Stewart Gardner Museum masterpieces. As his work on the Gardner Museum pieces was drawing to a close, he realized how much he wanted to do one last "in person museum job." He knew that most art museums in urban areas now did extensive security checks on those who applied to work for them. Even the lowly nighttime security guards and museum cleaning people were carefully screened. He looked long and hard to find a position where he would be able to temporarily borrow a painting, copy it, and return it without anyone becoming suspicious. He knew he would be putting himself in danger, and he knew he probably shouldn't undertake another job like this one. But the danger was part of the fun for him. It would be his last hurrah.

Although selling his copies off as originals had given him tremendous psychic satisfaction, part of the fun in the past had been the money he had earned selling these copies. He was done with stealing anything, and he certainly didn't need the money. He was getting older, and he wanted one last chance to be in the game. It was a huge risk he didn't have to take, but he was going to go for it. He had a nagging feeling in the back of his mind that this last attempt to "borrow" artwork was foolhardy, and he should not do it. After this gig, he promised himself that he was definitely going to retire once and for all.

He took a job as a member of the cleaning staff at the Penmoor Resort in Colorado Springs, Colorado. There was an extensive private collection of Western art at the Penmoor. The Penmoor was a hotel and resort and did not vet their cleaning people as carefully as larger and better-known art museums did. The resort kept their paintings that were not on display and the paintings that needed work in their subterranean workroom. Max managed to secure an assignment as a nighttime janitor in this somewhat secret basement location. He thought this would be the perfect place for his last undercover foray into the formal art world.

He changed his name again, and he probably made a mistake by not changing his name to something very different than the false names he had used in the past. The name he chose for Colorado Springs, Machs Sobrille, was too similar to his own name and the names he had used at other museums. Over the years, he'd grown complacent about obscuring his identity. He packed up a few things, moved temporarily to Colorado Springs, and rented a modest house. He didn't plan to be there very long. He worked unnoticed for a few weeks, but then, all of a sudden it seemed to Machs, the resort decided to experiment with a new security system.

This became Machs' downfall. He was caught as he tried to smuggle one of the resort's artworks, that he had "borrowed" for a few days, back into the Penmoor's basement artwork room. Machs took pieces home that he could roll up and fit into his special cane. His special cane was wider in diameter than most canes. The tip of the cane came off easily, and Machs could insert the painting. He always used his special cane, whether or not it contained a painting, when he arrived at and went home from his work at the Penmoor. When he brought each painting back to return it to the collection, he used his special cane to smuggle the painting back into the resort. The painting he was trying to return to the Penmoor art collection was hidden inside his cane. It was during one of these returns that Machs got into trouble.

His system had worked well for several weeks, until one night when was caught in the parking lot. Somehow, he had given himself away. A woman had become suspicious of him and began to chase him. He'd tried to run but realized he'd become too old to run, especially from this somewhat younger woman. He couldn't remember the last time he'd tried to run anywhere. The woman chased him a few hundred yards, tackled him, and sat on him. She'd taken him down in the parking lot of the resort. Machs would never know how she had learned about his special, non-standard cane. She easily removed the tip of the cane. She found the painting.

Machs, which was the name he was using in Colorado, was arrested and stayed in jail for two nights. It was not a good experience for this very reclusive and private person.

He worried that whoever was prosecuting his case would somehow find out about his previous activities. He'd always tried to be circumspect, but he'd never before been caught, let alone put in jail. When he was arrested, he'd had his fingerprints taken. When that happened, he was very concerned that he might have left his fingerprints or other unknown clues behind in other museums in other places.

He was lucky when the judge allowed him to post bail and stay at his house until he was formally charged and went to trial. Machs had no intentions of staying at his house or sticking around in town to go to trial. It was easy for Machs to slip away from Colorado Springs and return to Louisiana. Max Sobrille was good at escaping and existing below the radar. Colorado Springs would never again see hide nor hair of the art forger. Max's days of taking silly chances were finished.

Because he was now in the database of law enforcement and had been arrested and fingerprinted, Max knew he was going to have to reinvent himself once again. He'd finished the Gardner Museum project. He'd had his one last go at sneaking around and copying masterpieces, and that hadn't gone at all well for him. In fact it had been a disaster. He knew he was still skilled at painting copies. But he had to admit to himself that he was no longer good at trying to be inconspicuous, borrowing paintings to copy, and returning them. Security around artwork had changed. His employment at the Penmoor in Colorado Springs had been a big mistake.

Max had always thought he would live out his life and die an old man at Shadowlawn, his mansion in Franklin, Louisiana. He had renovated the house with his old age in mind. But after his misadventure in Colorado Springs, he realized he was going to have to rethink his situation. He was going to have to move away from Shadowlawn and find a new place to live. He was going to have to take on a new identity that included a new name that was very different from any of the names he had used in the past. He hated to give up his one last connection to his birthplace in Gibraltar, but to save himself in the long run, it had to be done.

He would have to find a new home, preferably a place that was in the middle of nowhere, a place where no one he had ever worked with or known before would be able to find him. He had to pick a place to live where no one from his past life would accidentally run across him. He would have to relocate to somewhere that was remote enough such that no one who lived in any town nearby would have ever seen his face. He would have to become more reclusive than ever. He looked at islands in Maine. He looked at remote locations on Michigan's Upper Peninsula, in the Arizona desert, and in Montana's vast expanses of wooded territory.

He realized that choosing to live in a place with very cold weather would work on his arthritic joints to make him much more uncomfortable. Louisiana didn't get very cold, but it was terribly damp all the time. As he grew older, the dampness had caused his arthritis to bring him more and more pain. He would have to find a place that was neither terribly cold in the winter nor terribly hot in the summer. After an extensive search, he finally found a place he liked that was exceedingly remote. He would be safe there. He found a wonderful house that was for sale and determined that the English cottage was perfect for him. His new home would be in River Springs, Arkansas.

He still had not decided how he was going to return the stolen artwork to the Gardner Museum. He would have to take his masterpieces with him when he moved to River Springs. He bought his cottage and planned the renovations that had to be done on the place. This would be his last home, and Max wanted it to be exactly the way he wanted it. The renovation included adding a stunning new roof to the cottage. The roof was made of metal but looked exactly like thatch. Max drew up plans, hired a contractor, and accomplished the renovations to the cottage all long distance via Zoom. His contractor did the work, was paid, and never once met with Max in person. Max always wore a beard and a disguise when he spoke with the contractor on their Zoom calls. The man would never recognize the owner of the cottage if he met him on the streets of River Springs. Max considered his renovation to have been successful for that reason alone.

With all the work Max had done to restore Shadowlawn, he was able to sell it for a substantial price. The woman who bought the property from Max wanted most of the furniture, along with the house itself. Max set aside the things he thought he could use in his new home and marked these to take with him to the cottage in Arkansas. He cleaned out his studio behind the main house. Wearing protective gloves, he carefully built crates for each painting and each drawing he had created. He would, at some time in the future, give them all to the Isabella Stewart Gardner Museum. He packed up the few pieces of furniture he wanted to keep, his painting gear, his clothes and personal items, and the crates of artwork. He drove his rental truck north to River Springs. The woman who had bought Shadowlawn never laid eyes on the previous owner. When she moved in, any and all clues about the person who had owned the mansion before she bought it were long gone.

Max had taken particular care crating the masterpieces he had spent so many years perfecting in his art studio. He wanted to be the only person to touch the artwork until it was handed over to the Gardner Museum. He put wheels and handles on the wooden crates that protected the master-pieces. The wheels and handles enabled Max to easily push and pull the crates up and down the ramp that led from his art studio. He just as easily was able to push the crates up a ramp into the U-Haul truck he had rented.

He had prepared a special "hidden room" at the River Springs cottage in Arkansas. This space was at the back of his detached garage. This special hiding place was climate controlled with a back-up generator. Without help from any-one, Max would be able to push the crates of artwork off the rental truck and store them in their special climate-controlled space at the back of his garage. His treasures would be secure in their hiding place until he decided how he was going to deliver them to their rightful owner.

Max had mixed feelings about leaving his home in Louisiana. He realized that Shadowlawn was too large for one man, especially for a man who was getting older. He needed more and more help to keep the place clean and do repairs. He realized he was going to need a lot of help with the yard. When he turned seventy years old, he was able to admit to himself that his mansion in Franklin had become too much for him. The mansion was large, and the yard was large. Max knew that to maintain the place, he was going to require more and more help as the years when by. It was time to leave. His new cottage in Arkansas had a yard with tremendous potential, and the property was smaller and more manageable. The cottage was just the right size for his needs. Max would be able to bring the gardens at his new home in

River Springs back to life, and he would enjoy doing it. It would be just the right project for his later years.

As he drove his U-Haul away from Franklin, Louisiana, Simon Maxwell decided he was looking forward to living in Arkansas. The masterpieces were crated and ready to send back to the Gardner. Simon still had not determined exactly how he was going to deliver the stolen masterpieces to the museum, but once he had decided what to do with them and because of the way he had crated the artwork, it would be easy to again load the crates into a U-Haul truck.

*S*imon Maxwell *waited until all the renovations* on his cottage were completed before he left Louisiana in the rented truck full of his belongings. The crated paintings were at the back of the truck so they could be unloaded first. Simon had bought an SUV in his new name and had it delivered to the garage of his new home outside River Springs, Arkansas. He had purchased an SUV because he had observed that most of the neighbors who lived around his cottage drove either SUVs or pickup trucks.

Simon had never wanted to stand out, wherever he had lived, and he did not want to stand out in River Springs. He knew the local inhabitants would be curious about who had purchased and spent a great deal of money to renovate the cottage. This was the price he had to pay for moving to a new home and hiring a local contractor to make it into the place he wanted it to be. But he wanted to fit in with the local customs as much as he was able to do that, so he bought an SUV. His real intention was that no one would ever see him actually driving the SUV, but he bought it anyway.

The trip from Franklin, Louisiana to River Springs, Arkansas was a long one-day drive. Simon stopped midway in his journey overnight to rest because he was tired. He wanted to arrive at his new home after dark. He planned to unload the crated artwork at night and store it in its specially constructed hiding spot in his garage. No nosy neighbors could be allowed to witness the unloading and hiding of the crates. He would leave the U-Haul truck that held the rest of his furniture and boxes parked outside the house.

Simon had arranged for a crew to unload everything that remained in the U-Haul and move his furniture and personal belongings into the cottage. He knew he was not able to do this for himself. He had sent detailed drawings to the moving crew, floor plans that designated exactly where each piece of furniture was to be placed in each room. His boxes were carefully marked, and hopefully the crew would deliver each one to the room where it was supposed to go and where Simon would eventually unpack it. Simon had also arranged for the U-Haul to be picked up and returned. He had plenty of money. All of these services could be arranged at arm's length…for a price.

After successfully unloading and storing the crated masterpieces in his garage, Simon drove away from his new home in his new SUV. He was going to explore his new locale while the moving crew unloaded the rental truck and organized his cottage. He would return only after his furniture and boxes had been unloaded into the house and the U Haul had been returned.

Simon Maxwell settled into his cottage and decided he had made an excellent decision to give up his mansion in Franklin, Louisiana. He loved living in a smaller space. He painted sometimes, but mostly he worked in his garden. He'd decided that one way to remain below the radar was to grow most of his own food. He planted extensive gardens of all kinds... mostly decorative. But he also planted a large vegetable garden and a beautiful herb garden. He was an artist and enjoyed looking at his creations as well as being able to pick fresh vegetables and herbs to feed himself from the bounty of his labors. He learned to preserve the plentiful harvest and taught himself to can his tomatoes and green beans in glass jars. He bought a freezer for the squash, new peas, asparagus, and other vegetables that were better when frozen.

Simon learned to order his groceries online and had his meat, dairy products, eggs, bread, and anything else he couldn't grow himself delivered to his home. He ordered everything else from Amazon. No one ever saw the mysterious Simon Maxwell when they made deliveries to his cottage. He remained a recluse who had become famous for his beautiful gardens. No one in the area had ever actually met the man in person. Rumors and anecdotes ran rampant in the absence of reality.

The years flew by, and Simon was happy in River Springs. He had never needed other people in his life, and he didn't need them now. His life's routine was interrupted when he realized he was ill. He ignored the pain and the other symptoms, as so many people tend to do, until he finally realized he had to see a doctor. He had never applied for Social Security or

Medicare, and he had never had any health insurance. He made an appointment to see a specialist in Dallas, Texas, and he paid the doctor in cash.

The news was not good, and Simon made an appointment to see a doctor at the Ochsner Clinic in New Orleans to receive a second opinion. The diagnosis was confirmed. Palliative treatments were offered and declined. Simon had decided that he would allow nature to take its course. He wanted no prolonging of his pain. Simon drove back to River Springs to put his affairs in order. The time had finally come for him to decide how he was going to transfer the Isabella Stewart Gardner Museum's works of art to where they had come from.

Simon had become attached to the artwork he had copied and created. He had expended considerable time and energy, years in fact, to reinvent the masterpieces that had been stolen from the Gardner. They were his pride and joy. He decided he would put the paintings, the drawings, and the other artifacts into a climate-controlled storage unit in Boston. He would try to find one that was as close as possible to the Gardner Museum. He absolutely did not want to have to answer any questions about how he had acquired the masterpieces. He was going to claim that he had restored, not forged, the paintings and the drawings. He didn't want to answer any questions about the alleged restorations either. He did not want his name or any name at all associated with the return of the stolen works of art. He wanted to remain totally anonymous, even after his death.

Simon began composing a letter to the director of the Isabella Stewart Gardner Museum. His letter would explain that he had accidentally found the artwork in New Orleans. He would say only that he had worked to restore the paintings. He would say he was an expert who specialized in art restoration and that he had worked his magic on the masterpieces. The Gardner Museum would find their artwork returned in much better shape than it had been when it was stolen. The layers of old lacquer and varnish and the remains of previous bad restorations had been removed. Because Simon had so meticulously cut his copies from their frames to mimic exactly the way the thieves had treated the paintings when they were taken from the Boston museum back in 1990, he hoped there would be no question as to whether or not these were the originals that were being returned.

Max knew from past experience that his canvases and his paints would hold up to the most intense scrutiny by chemical analyses and other kinds of tests and scans. He was confident that his skill at reproducing the original artists' work would more than convince even the most rigorous examinations by art experts. Simon also would put in storage the other original artifacts that he was "returning" to the Gardner Museum. He decided he would explain some things in his letter that would go to the museum. Most of the details would be known to himself alone. No one would ever know exactly what had occurred in the journey that the stolen masterpieces had endured. His letter to the museum would be unsigned. He would wear gloves so that not a single fingerprint would be on the letter or on the envelope.

Simon extensively researched and finally hired a Boston lawyer to carry out his wishes after he was dead. He would entrust his lawyer with the letter he was composing to the Gardner. In addition to the restorer's explanation about how the masterpieces had been saved, Simon would give the Gardner Museum the address of the storage unit where the paintings and other artifacts could be found. He would put the keys to the climate-controlled storage unit in the envelope with the letter, and the letter to the museum would be sealed.

Simon did not want the paintings and drawings with his accompanying letter of explanation to be sent to the museum until after he had been dead for at least a year. He'd laid out all of this with the lawyer who would handle the transaction according to his wishes. After his death, the lawyer would be instructed to wait one year. Then the attorney would be instructed to mail the letter addressed to the director of the Gardner Museum so that it would arrive on March 17th of that year. The paintings had been stolen in the early morning of March 18, 1990, and there seemed a certain full circle symmetry that pleased Simon about announcing the return of the masterpieces on March 17th.

Simon had amassed a fortune from his years of copying famous works of art. He had a wonderful property in the cottage and gardens where he'd lived during his years in River Springs. He'd given serious thought about what to do with his fortune. He had researched the various local charities and organizations to determine which ones would be the most worthy of his gift.

He had decided he would leave his cottage and his fortune to the local women's shelter in River Springs. The women's shelter seemed like a good cause and certainly needed the money. Simon knew they struggled to stay afloat and were always short of funds. They would be shocked and over-whelmed by his generous bequest. He hoped that his wealth would be able to save some lives.

Simon had never been married and had never actually been in a relationship of any kind with another human being. He didn't have and had never had any friends. He was totally a loner and a very odd duck. Naïve about relationships, and especially about marriage, he was also a passive and peace-loving kind of person. He could not understand domestic violence. He was puzzled by it but decided to support the local women's shelter. He knew it must be difficult to hide anyone in a very small town such as River Springs. Maybe his financial support would allow the shelter to send the women who were at risk out of state to save them.

Simon began to think of himself as Maximillian Sobrille again. He had invented many names for himself throughout the years and had lived his many different lives in many different places. For almost all of his life, he had done what he loved doing most, and he had accumulated considerable wealth doing what he was destined to do. Many people cannot, at the end of their lives, conclude that they had lived their lives doing mostly what they loved and entirely on their own terms. Max could make that claim. He had lived most of his life outside the conventions of the legal system, but he had always had his own set of standards. He believed he had delivered copies that were just as good if not better than the originals of the masterpieces he had chosen to imitate. He had done his best with every job he had undertaken.

And he had relished the risks he'd taken. Even though he had always been a recluse, he had taken tremendous risks with his profession. He had smuggled some paintings out of museums, copied them, and returned them. This had involved his taking some hair-raising chances. At other museums, he had been able to find secret places on site where he could paint in hiding while he was supposedly doing his job as a night watchman or a janitor. He would take the painting off the wall at night and spend hours working on the copy. By morning, the real masterpiece would be back on the wall where it had always been. No one would ever suspect that the painting had ever been off the wall for even a few minutes.

But Simon Maxwell, aka Maximillian Sobrille, had two secrets. These secrets were a result of his weaknesses. He loved the work of Johannes Vermeer more than he loved the work of any other artist. He worshipped the few masterpieces that Vermeer had created. He thought Vermeer was a genius. He'd had one other chance to copy a Vermeer before he had stumbled across the stolen works from the Gardner Museum. When presented with that previous opportunity earlier in his career, Max had determined he was not really ready to copy a Vermeer at that time in his life. He had decided against attempting it. To have this second chance to copy one of Vermeer's paintings was the greatest opportunity of Max's artistic life. He decided that this time he was ready.

Max's first secret was that he had made not one, but two, copies of the Vermeer painting, *The Concert*. One of these copies was crated and stored in the special hiding place at the back of the garage at his cottage...along with the other works of art Max intended to "return" to the Gardner. The second Vermeer copy hung on the wall directly across from his bed in Max's cottage. The only difference between the two copies was that Max had not been quite as careful with the preparation of the canvas for his own copy of the painting. Because he was not trying to fool anybody with the copy that hung in his bedroom, he had not gone to as much effort to make the surface of the ancient canvas as pristine as he had done with the canvas he had used to make the copy he was giving to the Gardner Museum. He was the only person who would ever see the copy he was keeping for himself.

However, he had been as meticulous in the care and skill he'd taken painting the copy for his own pleasure as he'd taken with the copy he made to give to the Gardner. The

Vermeer copy was the first thing Max saw when he woke up in the morning and the last thing he saw before he went to sleep at night. Because no one ever came into Max's house, he hadn't worried about whether or not anyone would ever discover this second copy of the Vermeer masterpiece.

As his death approached and he realized, as Hamlet said in Shakespeare's tragedy, that he would soon be "shuffling off this mortal coil," Max began to wonder what he was going to do about the Vermeer he loved so much, the Vermeer he had chosen to keep as his own to look at every day. He knew he had taken a huge risk by making a second copy and hanging it on his wall. It was his weakness. What to do with "his" Vermeer when he died was a dilemma that dovetailed with Max's other secret.

Max's second secret was that he had never disposed of the destroyed paintings and drawings he'd found at Remy's gallery in New Orleans. These were, of course, the originals of the Isabella Stewart Gardner masterpieces. He had not been able to bring himself to destroy them, even though they were completely unfit to be viewed by anyone. To make his ruse convincing when he returned the "stolen paintings" to the Gardner Museum and to have the museum director and the experts who would examine the paintings believe that he was returning the originals, he had to be certain no one ever again saw the ruined originals. He had to get rid of these wrecks where no one would ever find them, and he likewise had to have a plan to get rid of his second copy of Vermeer's painting of *The Concert*.

The ruined original paintings of the great masters deserved a proper burial. Max had delayed getting rid of these originals because at some level, in his own mind, he felt it was somehow oddly sacrilegious to destroy something which had been painted by these brilliant, long-dead artists. At the same time he felt it would be more of a disgrace for the art world and the public at large to view these once-adored paintings in the condition in which he had found them. He decided it would be a disservice to everyone if these destroyed and moldy remnants of the once wonderful paintings were ever allowed to see the light of day. He had to get rid of them. But even in their destruction, they deserved to be treated with special care.

Max's cottage was on a beautiful lake. When he thought of the ruined paintings, the originals, he thought of them as wrecks. He decided that a fitting end would be for them to find their final resting place at the bottom of the lake. These were the wrecks of the art world, destroyed by evil thieves and left to deteriorate. Max would give them a proper burial in the lake he looked at every day. In that way, as long as he lived, they would always be a part of him.

He knew that in time the canvases would become part of the detritus at the bottom of the lake. But he did not want to take a chance that an identifiable piece of one of the paintings would float to the top of the lake and be discovered. He carefully shredded each of the paintings and drawings that had been rendered useless. He gathered the tiny slivers into fine mesh nets. He added some heavy stones to the nets so that the corpses of these masterpieces would be sure to sink to the bottom of the lake. He hoped the fish and the water and time would destroy all of it. Even if one tiny piece happened to float to the surface of the lake, no one would be able to identify what it had been once upon a long time ago.

He made his pilgrimage to the lake at night. His property had come with a boat dock which he had never used. The dock was made of wood and had not been maintained. It was collapsing into the lake. Max had never walked onto the decrepit dock, but he walked out to the end of it this one time to drop his nets of remnants and rocks. He watched as they sank down to what he hoped was the lake's bottom and their final resting place.

Max knew he had to drive the crated paintings that were stored in his garage to Boston and secure them in a safe and climate-controlled storage unit before he became too weak. He was well aware of how his illness would progress and knew that at some point he would no longer be able to drive or move his crated artwork into a storage facility. He rented a small U-Haul truck using one of his alternate identities and drove it to his property at night. He loaded the crates on wheels into the truck. The ramp that had come with the truck made this a relatively easy chore, but Max realized he was losing his strength. He hoped he had not put off the transfer of the masterpieces for too long. It would be a journey of almost 1,500 miles to deliver the artwork to Boston.

Max hated to stay in hotels and motels. He felt exposed when he was in any public place. He didn't want to be seen. He also worried that something would happen to him along the way, and someone else would take possession of his masterpieces. The drive to Boston would take him three days. When he was younger and healthier, he might have driven straight through to Boston. But he was old now, and he was sick. He was not able to drive for twenty-four hours without sleeping. He considered renting an RV so he could sleep without going into a hotel, but he determined it would be too difficult to load the crated artwork into an RV, even a large one. He considered sleeping in the U-Haul truck to avoid staying overnight in a place where other people would see him.

In the end, he realized he was going to have to stay in a hotel. He chose to stop in Knoxville, Tennessee and Harrisburg, Pennsylvania on his way to Boston. He made reservations at the largest motel he could find that was just off the interstate highway. It would be a long and arduous journey, but Max had taken on this project as a crusade. He would be able to bear up and get through it by drawing on the commitment and almost religious fervor with which he regarded his task. It was a holy ritual, a mystical journey.

He was exhausted when he arrived in Boston. He had rented an Airbnb there where he would stay for four nights. Renting a house and staying in the city for four nights was a big risk for him to take. Max had never been to Boston, and he did not know his way around the city. He hated to leave the U-Haul truck parked outside the Airbnb, but he was near the end of his mission and decided it would be all right to take the chance. He had rented a car to drive around the city and to drive home. The U-Haul truck was too cumbersome and too noticeable to drive any more than he had to drive it.

Max used the car to drive to the storage facility where he had rented a unit for the paintings. He'd paid to rent the space for ten years but knew he would have died well before this period had elapsed. He knew he could access his rental unit twenty-four hours a day. He planned to unload the artwork that night and get rid of the U-Haul truck as soon as possible. His age and his illness were getting to him. He was exhausted from the long drive, and he spent several hours resting until it was dark. He drove the truck to the storage facility. Hoping that he would be able to unload the crates into his unit without any witnesses, he'd driven to the storage facility in the middle of the night so no one else would be there when he arrived with the U-Haul. Another truck was leaving as he arrived, but as far as Max could tell, no one else was there.

Unloading the crates from the truck was the easiest part of the trip. He wheeled the paintings down the ramp from the rear of the rental truck and rolled them into the storage unit. He secured the lock and took special care not to lose the keys. The lock had come with two keys, and he wanted to send both keys with the letter he had written to the Gardner Museum. Max had been meticulously careful to wear gloves whenever he handled the artwork he was copying. He had been just as careful when he constructed the crates to protect and move his paintings and drawings. Whenever he moved the crates from place to place, he was likewise always wearing gloves. This had become second nature to him, and he was compulsive about always protecting against leaving any fingerprints. His fingerprints would never be found anywhere on any of the crates or on any of the paintings.

Max drove his U-Haul to a shopping mall parking lot, put the key under the driver's side floor mat, and left the truck to be picked up. He made a phone call to the local U-Haul people and told them where to find the truck. He had rented the U-Haul and made all of his hotel and motel reservations using alternative identities. The storage facility was rented under the name of a bogus LLC which did not exist. He had paid for the rental unit at the storage facility with a cashier's check. No one would ever know that Maximillian Sobrille had participated in this Boston operation. Mission accomplished. Max had been able to maintain his anonymity.

Max was exhausted and could barely make the walk from the shopping center parking lot where he had left the rented U-Haul truck to the Airbnb where he was staying. He was on the point of collapse. He realized that he had left the delivery of the artwork for too late in his illness. He did not know if he would be able to get himself back to his cottage in Arkansas. He was afraid he might die here in Boston. He fell into bed and slept for thirteen hours. When he woke up, he was surprised and thankful that he was still alive. He had pushed himself too hard, but he had done what he had set out to do. He had been thinking about this final step in his plan for almost a decade. And now it was done.

Max realized he probably would not be alive on March 18th to send his yearly text to his lawyer. He had a prepaid phone that he used only to communicate with the lawyer once a year. Max removed the SIM card from the cell phone he used to send the text that let his attorney know he was still alive. Max flushed the SIM card down the toilet. He found a rock in the yard of the house where he was staying and smashed the rest of the phone to bits. He put the pieces of the phone in a Ziploc bag and put the plastic bag on the seat of his rental car. He would drop the pieces of the phone in various trash cans and dumpsters on his way back to River Springs. This last link between himself and the Gardner Museum would disappear.

Max slept again. When he woke at noon the next day, he took the final steps necessary to complete his mission. His final task was to put the two keys to the padlock from the storage unit in the envelope with the letter he had written to the Gardner Museum. He wrapped both keys in tissue paper and sealed them with the letter. He put that letter into another envelope which held his final instructions for the lawyer who would take care of his affairs after Max had died. He put these envelopes into a third envelope that said in large letters on the outside that it was not to be opened until a year after his death. He sealed it all into a mailing envelope addressed to his attorney who had his office in Boston.

Max had put years of thought into exactly what he would say to the Gardner Museum about the treasure trove he was leaving to them. He had also planned carefully how he would leave the letter for his attorney to send. He reviewed it all to be certain he had it exactly right. He did not want to overlook any detail. It was paramount that he never be linked to the artwork in the storage facility. When he'd reassured himself one last time that he had covered his tracks completely, he set out for the post office. He finally sent it all to his attorney, certified mail, just before the post office closed for the day. Max had arranged everything with the attorney via email. The attorney had already been paid and was now just waiting to receive the envelopes and final instructions from his anonymous client. Max had to trust. Everything was now completely out of his hands.

After he'd sent his mailing envelope from the post office, Max was hungry and thirsty and anxious to get on the road. He'd already packed his few belongings and left the Airbnb. He drove to a nearby diner for a meal. He ordered the baked scrod dinner and had two lobster rolls wrapped to go. He bought three bottles of iced tea and put these in his cooler with the lobster rolls. He would leave Boston forever and drive until he could not drive any more. Along with his exhaustion, he was experiencing a sense of relief and satisfaction that he had done what he'd intended to do. He had at last accomplished his goal.

Max realized he'd left the delivery of the artwork for too late in his illness. He had not realized until this last road trip to Boston and back to Arkansas how debilitated he had become. But he had done it. He had followed through with his plan, in spite of being old and in spite of being ill. This sense of accomplishment kept him going as he made his way to Roanoke, Virginia. He had driven more than eleven hours. He stopped at a Marriott Courtyard and slept for sixteen hours. He ate a large breakfast at a diner in Roanoke and set out to drive the rest of the way home to his cottage in River Springs.

What happened after this trip did not matter to Max. He had left his holy grail that was to be returned to the Isabella Stewart Gardner Museum in a storage unit in Boston. His instructions and a letter and two keys had been left anonymously with a lawyer. It was done. He had completed his crusade. He hoped he might have atoned in some small way for the numerous illegal activities he had engaged in during his life. He drove and drove. It seemed like an endless journey to reach River Springs. It was more than a twelve-hour drive from Roanoke, but he finally arrived at his cottage. He was beyond being exhausted, but he drove the rental car into his garage and parked it beside his SUV. He did not want anyone to see the rental and wonder why this man of mystery was driving a car with New Hampshire license plates.

He fell into his bed at the cottage. His life was almost at an end. He had lived it his way and had spent most of it doing what he loved. No man could ask for more than that. When he woke, it was dark outside. There were still a few details to be taken care of.

In his younger, healthier days, Max had bought a bicycle. He hadn't ridden it very much, preferring to have his exercise in his garden rather than on the rough roads that surrounded the cottage. He put the old bicycle in the trunk of his rental car and pulled out of his garage. He would leave his rental in a parking lot in River Springs for the car rental company to pick it up. He had already notified them where they could find it. Max planned to ride the bike back to his home.

As he was about to pull away from the cottage, he remembered that the second copy of the Vermeer still hung on the wall in his bedroom. He went back into the house and removed the painting from the wall. He put the painting in his garbage can temporarily. He promised himself that when he returned from leaving his rental car to be picked up, he would decide on a more ceremonious and fitting way to get rid of this last piece of incriminating evidence. Max had already disposed of most of his household goods and most of his personal possessions. He knew his life was at its end, and he had cleaned out his cottage accordingly. Delivering the paintings to Boston had been his most important final act.

He drove the rental car to the town of River Springs where he left it in a parking lot. He took the bicycle from the trunk and gingerly mounted the bike to ride back to his cottage. It had been years since he'd ridden the bike, and although he hadn't forgotten how to ride it...something one never forgets... he was very unsteady and unsure as he peddled away from town. He was out of breath and in considerable pain. He knew he should not have tried to ride the bike back to his cottage. Max's heart finally gave out as he drove off the road and into a field. Maximillian Sobrille, citizen of Gibraltar, brilliant art forger, and recluse extraordinaire, passed away alongside the road in rural Arkansas. Max we hardly knew you.

The Reunion

ARKANSAS

2023

*S*idney and *Cameron were hosting a brunch for the* Camp Shoemaker group, and of course, everyone sat around afterwards talking and reminiscing. Juanita had made her own special recipe of huevos rancheros and was doing most of the clean-up. Matthew had a couple of montages they'd not had time to view the day before, so he was anxious to show them to his friends.

Matthew's second montage was about the masterpieces that had been stolen in the famous heist at the Isabella Stewart Gardner Museum in March of 1990. Several books had been written, and a number of documentaries had been made about the audacious robbery. Matthew had some excellent slides of the paintings and drawings and other pieces that had been stolen. He'd prepared a montage of the slides, the documentaries, and the movies. The story he had to tell was intriguing and exciting.

The Richardson's river house was open concept, and one could see the enormous television flat screen from anywhere in the room, even from the kitchen. Juanita was intrigued by the burglary and the artwork, and she was watching from the kitchen as she cleaned up after the brunch. When Matthew showed the montage about the heist and came to the slides he had of the pieces that had been stolen from the Gardner Museum, Juanita could not help but utter an audible gasp. It was almost a cry. Sidney was standing next to her in the kitchen and was shocked to hear Juanita's outburst. Juanita's eyes were wide, and she looked as if she had seen a ghost. She dropped her dish towel and ran outside. Sidney followed her to try to find out what was wrong.

"Juanita, what in the world is the matter? You're white as a sheet. Are you hurt?"

"I've seen one of those paintings, one of those paintings that was stolen." Juanita was clearly shaken by having viewed Matthew's slide show and montage.

Sidney figured that Juanita must have seen a print or a copy or a picture of one of the paintings in a magazine or in a book. She knew Juanita hadn't seen any of the actual paintings that had been stolen. No one had seen any of those paintings or drawings or artifacts for more than thirty-five years. Sidney did her best to explain to Juanita that she hadn't really seen the painting but merely a picture of it or a print. Juanita was terribly upset. She looked as if she felt guilty about something.

Sidney cared a great deal about Juanita and wanted to do something to reassure her. But at this moment, Sidney was preoccupied with what was happening with Ginny Randolph. Sidney told Juanita not to worry about it, and they would talk about it later. Juanita did not seem satisfied with Sidney's explanations. She looked as if she was scared to death about something. Sidney's conversation with Juanita was interrupted when her phone rang and it was Alex Caruthers. She excused herself from trying to comfort Juanita to take the doctor's call in private.

"Sidney, you need to get over here. Ginny is talking, and there is more to this than we had figured on. The drug thing is big, and Ginny is really in the crosshairs. And not only in Bubba's crosshairs. I don't want to talk about it over the phone, but you need to hear this from Ginny herself. I'm old, and I'm not prepared to hear everything that Ginny wants to tell me. I'm afraid she is in real danger from several different directions. I'm concerned that she's put you and Cameron and Georgio in danger, too, because you are helping her. She really needs some sort of official protection, but I have no idea how to provide her with that. I don't think we amateurs can do this."

"I know Ginny, and I don't think she would become involved in something criminal. I hear what you are saying, and I don't know what to do about it either."

"I don't think she's really done anything criminal. I think she tried to do something good and consequently has got herself into a lot of trouble. There is much more to this than Bubba and his drug problem. Ginny has stepped in it big time. Please come to the restaurant and hear about it directly from her. I know you'll know what to do when you've heard her story."

Juanita had gone back to the kitchen, and Sidney was trying to slip away without anyone noticing her departure. She hated to leave Juanita when she was so upset, but she didn't know what she could possibly do right now to help her. Dr. Caruthers had called her for help with Ginny, and Sidney decided that today, Ginny was her first priority. Cameron frowned when he saw Sidney leaving. She ignored him and went to her car.

The reunion group was going to the Old Mill Restaurant for dinner that night. It would be their last night together. Sidney wanted Georgio to be able to focus on presenting a fabulous meal for the Richardson's friends. Sidney also wanted to have Ginny, who was staying upstairs at the restaurant, resting in a calm and quiet state while she and Cameron joined their friends downstairs at the restaurant for dinner.

Sidney slipped into the kitchen and up the back stairway while Georgio was busy at the stove. Dr. Caruthers looked frazzled when Sidney entered the guest bedroom. Ginny had gone to sleep. Sidney knew something was brewing, and it wasn't something good.

"Thanks for coming right away. Ginny has been talking. She's doing okay physically, but she seems confused. She has been talking in her sleep and talking when she is awake. I'm quite concerned for her mental health. Of course, she's terribly afraid of Bubba, but she has also revealed some information about other things she's become involved in. These revelations, which I'm not certain she even intended to make to me, are such that I think she needs to be afraid of a number of people besides Bubba. I wish she had not told me all that she's told me, but she has. I don't feel as if I am in any real danger, but I'm afraid that you and Cameron as well as Georgio might be drawn into Ginny's mess."

"What is all this, Alex? I have no idea what you're talking about."

"One of the reasons Bubba is so desperate to find Ginny is not only to beat her up...although I'm quite sure he wants to follow through with that agenda, too. The new information

Ginny had to share is that he's also desperate to find her because she took his drug stash. I guess she found where he was keeping the packages of fentanyl he was dealing. He didn't know that she'd already found his drugs when he beat her so horribly this last time. He's addicted now that he has started using, and he's out of control angry and acting stupid a lot of the time. Bubba beat Ginny badly. But Bubba also put his fentanyl in a backpack and hid it under the bathroom sink in their house at the farm. We know he's not too bright. Of course she found the backpack full of drugs and hid it in a different place. After he beat her up this last time, she managed to get away from their house. When she left, she took Bubba's drug stash, which was in the backpack, with her. Apparently she's now hidden the drugs somewhere. I guess it's a whole lot of drugs and worth a whole lot of money. Bubba is into the fentanyl business big time. If Ginny got away with an entire backpack full of fentanyl, that will be worth a lot of money. It also could kill a lot of people. One reason Bubba has been so anxious to find her is because he wants his drugs back. And I don't think she is going to tell him where they are. If he finds her, he will kill her trying to get her to tell him where she's hidden the backpack with the drugs."

Sidney felt sick to her stomach. This was worse than she had imagined. She'd accepted that Ginny was an abused wife, and Sidney was willing to protect her from Bubba, even if it meant sending her far away someplace to make sure she was safe. But this was another thing altogether. Sidney was not prepared to protect Ginny from whoever was trying to find the drugs she'd taken from Bubba and now had hidden who knows where. Sidney needed help with the situation as she understood it. She needed Cameron to call in somebody from law enforcement who didn't have anything to do with the local sheriff's department. Sidney was panicked and trying not to show it.

"Did Ginny tell you where she's hidden the drugs?"

"Not exactly. And that's another problem. I think she hid the backpack somewhere in the woods, and now she doesn't remember exactly where it is."

Sidney was not prepared to deal with fentanyl that had been stolen from a major drug consortium or from the mafia, and that's what it seemed as if Ginny had inadvertently become involved with. And now Ginny couldn't remember exactly where she'd hidden nearly a million dollars' worth of drugs? No wonder she was out of her mind with fear. Sidney was headed in that direction herself. She wondered if she should try to move Ginny, if for no other reason than to protect Georgio and the restaurant. She decided to leave things as they were for the moment, mostly because she didn't know what else to do.

Sidney had no reason to believe that anyone except the doctor and Georgio suspected she was hiding Ginny above the restaurant's dining rooms. It seemed safe to leave her where she was, at least for a day or two. Alex Caruthers, on the other hand, was clearly uncomfortable knowing about the big drug stash that Ginny had taken and hidden and lost. He wanted out, and Sidney couldn't blame him for that.

Sidney had so much on her mind and was feeling so much pressure, she struggled to think clearly and make good decisions about what to do. She knew she needed Cameron's help with this, but she wanted to get Ginny safely out of harm's way before she involved any more levels of law enforcement. She wanted Alex Caruthers to stay with Ginny until after the reunion group's dinner at the Old Mill that night. Sidney was worried that, if she didn't have someone watching over Ginny, she might wander down the stairs into the restaurant while people were eating. She knew Caruthers wanted to be off the case, but Sidney was going to do her best to convince him to stay…just for this one last evening.

Sidney was unsure of Ginny's mental state and didn't want her to accidentally stumble out of her currently secure hiding place without realizing what she was doing. Ginny was going to recover, but she needed time to heal and time for the antibiotics to run their course. Sidney was able to prevail on the doctor to stay at the restaurant with Ginny until after the group's dinner that night. She told him he was free to end his responsibility to Ginny after the dinner. Sidney would have to trust that Ginny wouldn't try to make a break for it and run away once Alex was no longer staying by her bedside.

They got dressed up…or somewhat dressed up. Isabelle wore her best all-white outfit with a scarf made of knitted solid gold threads. She called it her Rapunzel scarf because it was made out of real spun gold. She wore metallic gold flats and looked ravishing. Elizabeth wore a pair of black cashmere pants and a long black cashmere turtleneck tunic. She wore two strands of her exquisite pearls…inherited from her mother. Gretchen wore a blue ankle-length silk dress that clung to her curvaceous but trim and extremely fit body. The dress matched her eyes, and she looked almost magical in royal blue. Sidney wore a red cashmere pants and top outfit that stunned even Cameron. The men tried but could not come close to looking as good as their wives looked.

It was the last night of their reunion. When one has reached the age of eighty years, no one is absolutely certain that they will be available and able to attend the reunion the following year. They'd tossed around a few ideas about where to meet next fall, but no decisions had been made. Everyone was determined to have a festive time tonight. Olivia had already been lost to them, and most painfully lost to J.D. It was important to grab hold of every minute they had together.

Their large round table was covered with a white tablecloth, and the champagne flowed. Georgio had outdone himself as he prepared a special meal for the group. The restaurant was open for other customers on this Saturday night, but Georgio was focused on Sidney and Cameron's friends. He had created two soups to choose from. It was a chilly night outside, and everyone wanted to warm up with soup. One soup was a stroganoff soup which included thinly sliced strips of filet of beef, onions, mushrooms, and tiny egg noodles. The rich clear beef broth was flavorful and served with a dollop of sour cream on top. The other soup was a seafood soup, almost like a bouillabaisse. It was a tomato-based clear seafood broth with chunks of lobster, shrimp, scallops, crabmeat, and solid white fish. Besides the seafood, colorful miniature vegetables in the soup plate added to the beauty of the presentation.

The soups were so delicious, Richard suggested that Georgio serve another round of soup and skip the rest of the dinner. Georgio assured his audience that they would be happy with their entrees, too. One entrée was a favorite from the regular menu. It was a cross between salmon Oscar and salmon Florentine. The grilled salmon was served on a bed of sautéed spinach and topped with Maryland jumbo lump crabmeat and Hollandaise sauce. Tiny roasted potatoes were served on the side. The meat entrée was a lamb shank that had cooked all day in a gravy of herbs and vegetables and wine. It was served with mashed potatoes that had cream cheese added to them. French green beans sautéed in butter were served with the lamb. The vegetarian plate was probably the most dramatic. It was an enormous beefsteak tomato that had been hollowed out and stuffed with seasoned and well-sauced spaghetti squash. The room temperature spaghetti squash overflowed the tomato. The sauce served with the squash was a combination of what had been scooped out of the tomato minus the seeds, chopped parsley, chopped mint, chopped cucumber, lemon juice and lemon zest, olive oil, and feta cheese.

Gretchen ordered the vegetarian option and groaned with delight when she tasted it. It was so delicious, she passed it around the table for everyone to have a bite. Because it was such a crowd pleaser, the group insisted that Georgio bring two orders of the beefsteak tomato for the table to share in place of a salad course. Where in the world had he found these beautiful, enormous, and flavorful tomatoes so late in the season? Georgio was a wonder.

They were all so full, the Chantilly cake with fruit might have been ignored as dessert if it hadn't looked so beautiful and so delectable. It was made with three layers of sponge cake that had been flavored with vanilla beans and a touch of Galliano. The icing was whipped cream and crème fraîche instead of the usual cake frosting. Raspberries, blackberries, blueberries, and strawberries filled the whipped cream between the layers of vanilla cake and were arranged in artistic profusion on the top of the cake. It was a dessert to bring tears to one's eyes. Even those who did not normally eat dessert were unable to resist the call of the Chantilly cake.

Georgio was summoned from the kitchen to receive a standing ovation for his culinary performance. His admirers clapped and shouted "Bravo." He smiled and laughed and almost cried. Cameron was beaming. Georgio sat down beside Sidney to have a glass of champagne with the group. Sidney's mind was never far away from what was going on with Ginny. She knew that Georgio had been trying to tempt Ginny into eating something. So far she had refused to eat. Sidney whispered in Georgio's ear, "Give her a piece of this cake. She won't be able to resist it."

Elizabeth and Richard were leaving early the next morning to continue their drive to Arizona. Gretchen had to go to work on Monday, and Isabelle was anxious to return to her store in Palm Springs. But J.D., Bailey, Tyler, and Matthew intended to hang around at the River Springs resort for a few extra days. They didn't want the reunion to end and would stay in their cottages for a while longer. This was fine with Cameron. He was happy to have them stay, but he told them there would be no more meals provided by Sidney. The four were on their own for that. Sidney had worked hard to cook for the group over the long weekend, and she was leaving to drive to Little Rock on Monday morning for a meeting of one of the charities she raised money for.

Before she left for Little Rock, Sidney wanted to have some time alone with Cameron to tell him what was going on at the restaurant and to try to convince him to help without compromising Ginny's whereabouts. When she was able to get him alone, Sidney told him everything. Although he wanted to help any woman who was being abused, he was furious that Ginny had put Sidney in such a terrible position by getting involved with Bubba's drugs. Cameron was worried that whoever was expecting to take possession of the fentanyl or expecting to be paid for handing over the stash to Bubba would eventually realize that Ginny had taken it. Bubba would blame the disappearance of the drugs on his wife, but he always blamed everything that went wrong in his life on Ginny. In this case however, it really was Ginny who had taken his drugs. And now she had forgotten where she'd hidden them.

Everyone knew that Sidney and Ginny worked together at the collective and had become friends. Cameron was afraid that whoever might come after Ginny would turn their attention to Sidney when they were unable to find Ginny. This was not an unreasonable thing to fear. Things were a mess. Cameron was happy when he watched Sidney drive away from River Springs that morning. He'd urged her to stay at their house in Little Rock until everything had been resolved, but he knew she would not be willing to do that. He knew she would be back in River Springs as soon as she could possibly return. He knew she would rush back to help Ginny.

From time to time, Cameron had done favors for various people who worked for the federal government. Most of these favors had to do with resolving computer issues. He intended to call in some payback for those favors now. He contacted a friend who was a retired FBI special agent. Cameron told Raymond Barstow, whom everyone called Bart, that he had to drop whatever he was doing and drive down to River Springs from Fayetteville that day. Cameron let his FBI friend know it was an emergency that needed special handling, discretion, and immediate attention. Cameron was not often worried or frightened by anything. But involvement with drug dealers and a missing backpack full of fentanyl were worth being worried about.

The Old Mill Restaurant was usually closed on Mondays, but the four men from the reunion group who were staying in River Springs had prevailed on Georgio to make his "variety of meatloaves" special for their dinner that night. Cameron was going to join them for meat loaf, mashed potatoes, and green beans. He'd decided his friends could be helpful to him in terms of searching for the missing drugs. The four mostly wanted to be together a little longer and hang out with each other. They didn't have a fixed agenda or much of anything else to do.

Cameron sent a text to each of them. They'd driven to the Red Apple Inn to have lunch. Cameron asked them to meet him at the Richardson's house before they went to the Old Mill for dinner. He told them he had an assignment for them and needed them to help him out with something of the utmost importance. He would explain it all to them when they arrived at his house that evening.

After Cameron had dispensed soft drinks and beer to his friends, he made his pitch to enlist their help in his search. "Thanks for coming. I have an outdoor scavenger hunt for you that has a real prize at the end of it. I can't tell you what that prize is. And, at the risk of sounding ridiculously mysterious, if you find the prize, you can't keep it. But I will have a surprise reward for the person who finds it." He had their attention.

They'd enjoyed scavenger hunts as boys at Camp Shoemaker. He knew his friends loved scavenger hunts, or at least they had when they were young. He assumed that these friends, in their older years, would go along with his game that was really not at all a game. Everyone loves a scavenger hunt.

No one said a word. They were waiting for further instructions from Cameron. "Someone Sidney and I know has lost a backpack in the woods. In fact, this person has purposely hidden that backpack in the woods. Now they can't remember where they've hidden it. We know approximately where in the woods the backpack was hidden, but always remember that it is hidden. It might be in a hole in the ground. It might be under a pile of leaves or pine needles. It might be inside a hollow place in a tree trunk or a log. Who knows? You will need all of the tracking skills you learned years ago at Camp Shoemaker to find the prize. I suggest you work in teams of two for safety's sake. We have to find it. It's worth a lot of money, and it is absolutely critical that the backpack be found. We will begin our search tomorrow morning early. I would love it if you could find it tomorrow, but you probably won't be able to find it that fast. But please do your best. I will drive you all to the woods where the person who lost the backpack says they think they hid it. Are you in?" They all agreed that they were in and were looking forward to the excitement of the search. They left for dinner and Cameron urged them all to go to bed early and get a good night's sleep.

Cameron wanted to protect Ginny as much as he possibly could. He knew it was important to Sidney. He didn't tell his searchers that the person who had hidden the backpack was a woman. He purposely didn't tell them what was in the backpack. He wasn't certain that withholding this information was the right decision, but he was concerned that one or more of them might freak out of they knew exactly what they were looking for.

The next morning the four scavenger hunters were eager to begin their search. Sidney had told Cameron exactly where she thought Ginny might have hidden the backpack. When Ginny had left Dani's, she'd run into the national forest that was behind Dani's house. That was where Sidney thought Ginny must have hidden the backpack and spent the night. That was where Cameron was going to tell his friends to begin looking. He shared with them that the person who had hidden the backpack had also spent the night in the woods. Any signs they found that indicated a human being had been walking or living or sleeping in the woods might be a clue as to where the backpack had been left.

Matthew teamed up with Bailey who had to take it easy because of the defibrillator vest he was wearing. Having a doctor nearby might come in handy. J.D. and Tyler were the other team. Cameron made sure each pair of his buddies had a satellite phone and could call for help and communicate with each other. Sometimes regular cell phone service was not available in the national forest. The scavenger hunters had set up a search grid and were to call or text Cameron if they found anything. Cameron hunted in the woods with them until it was time for him to meet his FBI friend, Raymond "Bart" Barstow.

Cameron told Bart almost everything. He told him about Ginny and Bubba and the backpack and the fact that he had his friends searching the woods for the drugs. Cameron did not tell Bart where Ginny was hiding or that anyone knew where she was. Bart, of course, wanted to find Ginny and bring her in for questioning. He said the obvious...that she had to turn herself in and talk to the FBI. He wanted her to tell the authorities everything she knew about Bubba's involvement with the fentanyl. Bart also said it was critical that she be in touch with law enforcement to insure her safety. Cameron explained that Bubba abused Ginny and had threatened to kill her. He told Bart about Bubba's cousin who worked as a deputy sheriff. Cameron knew that involving local law enforcement was out of the question. That was the reason he had called on Bart.

The two men knew that finding the backpack full of drugs was the first order of business. If they had the backpack, they thought they could use it as bait to draw out Bubba and others involved. They both realized that somebody out there had to be desperate to get their hands on the missing drugs.

They didn't know what to do about Ginny. Even though Cameron now knew she was hiding at the Old Mill, he realized this was only a short-term solution. She was only there with Georgio until her wounds were sufficiently healed and she had recovered her strength. Ginny was in danger, and Cameron hoped Sidney could come up with a plan for how to help her in the long run.

Sidney's attention was not on the agenda of the meeting she was attending in Little Rock that Monday morning. Her mind was going a million miles an hour on other things. She could not make herself think about anything except what was going to happen to Ginny. Even though Sidney was angry with Ginny about taking the drugs and then losing the backpack, she was fond of Ginny and wanted to help her. Sidney felt Ginny was incredibly talented and was committed to encouraging her work. And, truth be told, Sidney wondered what she herself would have done if she had been in Ginny's shoes. Given a rotten and abusive husband who was now addicted to the drugs he was dealing, Ginny had taken the backpack and run with it. Sidney thought she also might have done the same thing, given Ginny's circumstances. If Sidney had found Bubba's stash, she thought she might have done exactly what Ginny had done and hidden it in the woods.

Sidney's best friend from high school lived in New York City. She was a successful real estate agent and dealt with wealthy clients who wanted to buy and sell expensive Manhattan properties. Rebecca Sells had the perfect last name to deal in real estate, and she used her name as a marketing tool. Becky and Sidney had been best friends for many years. Sidney always said Rebecca was the person she would call if she was in trouble. She said Becky would show up with a car and plenty of cash and not ask any questions. Sidney said she would absolutely do the same for Becky if her friend called her for help.

Sidney called on Becky for help with Ginny. Sidney knew that Ginny needed to be relocated someplace far away from River Springs. If the right venue for selling her pieces could be found and the right strategy for marketing could be arranged, Sidney felt that Ginny could earn more than a decent living by selling her artwork made out of found objects. Sidney respected Ginny's abilities and was certain there would be more demand for her extraordinary gift in the New York City area than there was in River Springs. Ginny Randolph, who would be known as Virginia Delacroix after she had left Arkansas, could make it in New York City. Sidney was sure of it. She knew Becky would be able to find a place for Virginia Delacroix to live. Sidney knew Becky had connections with people in the New York area who were involved with the arts, including quite a few people who owned and managed galleries of all kinds.

As soon as her fund-raiser meeting ended, Sidney drove to her Little Rock residence and called her friend Becky. She told Becky everything that had happened, including all about the situation with the lost backpack full of fentanyl. By the end of the phone conversation, Becky was well aware of the risks she would be taking by agreeing to help Sidney help Ginny. Becky was a fierce advocate for women, and she was a brave person. In spite of the risks, she was all in to help with Ginny's relocation. The two best friends put their heads together over the phone and came up with what they felt was close to being a foolproof plan.

Becky already had a place in mind where Ginny could live. The rental was not in Manhattan; it was across the Hudson River in Hoboken, New Jersey. Someone had paid to rent the warehouse, that also contained an almost-new condo, for a year, and for some reason, they had abandoned their already-paid-for warehouse and condo after two months. Becky was about to put the place back on the rental market when Sidney called her. The property was a two-bedroom, two-bathroom condo that had been built inside part of a converted warehouse. The condo had its own front entrance onto an alleyway, but the back door opened directly into the warehouse. It would provide Ginny with a place to live as well as plenty of warehouse space to work on her projects. Becky had been suspicious of the previous renters. Something had been going on with them that was not quite right. And then they had disappeared.

The space was unusual because it consisted of a condo built inside a warehouse. Not everyone would be happy with this unconventional living arrangement. Becky had worried that the previous renters had been doing something illegal in the warehouse. She suspected they might have been involved with printing counterfeit money. She was quite relieved when they disappeared without a word. They'd been gone for more than a month, and Becky didn't think they were coming back. They had taken everything from the warehouse and had left behind only the two walls of built-in wooden shelves they'd added. It had not been possible for them to take the shelves with them. The shelves were completely empty. The tenants who had disappeared in the night had stripped the warehouse bare of everything that they could take with them. These sketchy renters had also left behind some interesting and unusual paper in a box that they'd leaned up against a trash can. Becky had rescued the paper.

One additional thing the previous renters had not been able to take with them from the warehouse was the deep industrial stainless-steel sink they'd installed. Becky knew it must have cost them a significant amount of money to put in the sink, and it was there to stay. Sidney was delighted to learn that running water was available in the warehouse. She knew that Ginny, who often found many of her work materials in dumpsters, needed a place to scrub and dry her "finds." The industrial sink would be perfect for Ginny, and she would not have to take the Styrofoam containers and used coffee cups and other articles of flotsam and jetsam into the condo's kitchen to wash them.

The condo had been rented furnished with the minimum of essential furnishings. Whatever the previous tenants had brought to the condo, if they had actually ever lived in it which Becky doubted they had, was now gone. The condo had been wiped down. Becky thought it had probably been scrubbed to remove the fingerprints of the previous occupants. She would have it scrubbed down again before Ginny moved in…this time for cleanliness.

Becky did not think Ginny would be in any danger living in the warehouse and condo combination. As a responsible real estate agent, she had already had all the locks changed and had reprogrammed the automatic door openers. The warehouse was leased under the previous renter's name which was an innocuous and probably bogus LLC. The previous tenant had already paid the rent on the property for the next eight months. Virginia's name would not have to appear on any paperwork, and she would not have to pay any rent for eight months. Ginny Randolph would become a ghost, and she would be able to spend her time creating art to sell. No more chicken farming for Virginia Delacroix.

Becky scheduled the cleaning team to arrive the next afternoon. Finding the right gallery to handle Virginia's work would take more time, but Becky was on it. Sidney would handle getting Ginny safely to the warehouse in Hoboken, New Jersey. Using the Richardson's private plane to transport Ginny was one possibility, but Sidney decided it would be better if she drove Ginny to her new location. Cameron was uncomfortable with having Ginny at the restaurant. Even though Raymond Barstow was on the case, Cameron still talked about wanting to call the local authorities. The sooner Sidney could get the woman out of Arkansas, the better.

Sidney knew she would not be able to use her own car to make the drive halfway across the country. She also didn't want there to be any record of her renting a car. She would need to buy another vehicle to get Ginny to Hoboken. An older pickup truck with an extended cab would not attract attention in Arkansas or while they were on the road driving east. A pickup would be one of hundreds on the highways as she drove through rural Tennessee, North Carolina, Virginia, and the Eastern Shore of Maryland. Sidney had never spent any time in New Jersey so she didn't know what type of vehicle would be inconspicuous there.

Sidney called Georgio at the restaurant and told him what he had to do to get Ginny ready to move out. Then she called Ginny and told her what was going to happen. Ginny was to be ready to leave the Old Mill the next morning before dawn. Sidney would be there to pick her up at the rear of the restaurant. Ginny was worried about what would happen to all the things she had left behind in the house she'd shared with Bubba. Sidney assured her that at some point, when she felt it was safe to return to the farmhouse, she would pack up the things Ginny wanted and send them to her in New Jersey. Sidney asked Ginny to text her a list of things she needed right away and for their road trip.

The warehouse condo had some furniture, and Becky was going to be sure Ginny had everything she needed to live there comfortably. Becky didn't think the previous tenants had ever slept in the condo, but she bought all new mattresses for the beds anyway. The mattresses would be delivered the next morning. When the cleaning service arrived to get the place in good shape for Ginny, Becky would have them put new mattress pads, blankets, and bedspreads, as well as clean sheets on the beds. Becky would stock the refrigerator and the pantry.

Sidney realized when she spoke with Ginny over the phone that the young woman was still in shock. She didn't want to make things worse for her by moving too quickly, but she felt she had to get Ginny out of harm's way as soon as possible. There was no time to lose, and Ginny was in danger from more people than Bubba. Because she had taken the drug stash, she was also in danger from whoever those drugs belonged to. Ginny had to disappear quickly and without a trace.

First Sidney took an Uber to shop for the truck. She knew where to go for what she wanted. She found an anonymous gray F-150 that had some dents in the side and a little rust around the edges. It was perfect. She signed the papers, wrote a check for the truck, and drove it off the used car lot.

Ginny had left everything behind when she'd run from Bubba and gone to Dani's house. Sidney was going to buy a few clothes for Ginny to wear on the trip to New Jersey and to tide her over in Hoboken until Sidney could send her things from the farm. Sidney went shopping for the clothes and for a few other things Ginny said she needed. Sidney purchased two duffle bags to hold it all. In addition to what she'd bought at the store, she found some nice things for Ginny in her own closet that she didn't wear any more.

Sidney called Georgio again and asked him if he would pack a cooler of food for the next day's trip from Arkansas to New Jersey. Sidney would have to stop for gas, but she didn't want to waste time sitting in restaurants or diners along the way. And she wanted as little evidence as possible that she and Ginny had ever made the trip. Eating in restaurants risked exposure. The fewer surveillance cameras they encountered, the safer they would be. The fewer surveillance cameras that recorded their faces, the less likely it would be that anyone would know where Ginny had gone. Sidney didn't want her own face on the cameras either. They would eat in the truck while they drove.

The Relocation

HOBOKEN

2023

*S*idney *made the drive from Little Rock to River* Springs in a little over an hour. She had driven way too fast and arrived at the back door of the Old Mill Restaurant at 5:00 in the morning. It was still dark. Georgio helped Ginny walk down the stairs to the back door from the guest room on the second floor. She was still hurting from her wounds and the beating she had received from Bubba. After Georgio had loaded Ginny into the passenger seat of the truck, he went back into the restaurant's kitchen for two coolers. One held drinks, water, and ice, and the other one held food. He went back to the kitchen again for a large box that contained snacks and food that didn't need to be kept cool. The chef loaded everything into the second seat of the truck's cab. Sidney was very grateful for Georgio's help. The truck had been parked behind the restaurant for only about ten minutes. No one noticed the old Ford pickup when it headed to the highway to drive to Memphis. The truck was one of many on the road. Ginny was on her way to safety in Hoboken.

The trip would take more than twenty hours, even if they didn't stop for anything. Ginny had not fully recovered from her injuries, but Sidney felt it was imperative to get her out of Arkansas in spite of her not being in good physical or mental condition. Sidney had decided she would drive until she couldn't drive any more. Then they would stop and find a motel room for the night. Ginny slept most of the way the first day, only getting out of the truck to use the bathroom when they stopped to fill the truck with gas. It wasn't easy to get Ginny in and out of the truck. She was still seriously debilitated, and Sidney was worried, every time they stopped and Ginny had to climb out of the truck, that Ginny would fall and hurt herself. That absolutely could not be allowed to happen. Ginny's appetite had not returned, and in spite of the delicious food Georgio had packed for the trip, Ginny was only able to nibble at a sandwich. More than once Sidney wondered if she had made the right decision to drive Ginny to the East Coast. She worried that she might have rushed things with Ginny.

Sidney stayed in touch with Cameron during the long drive. Before she left, she had told him what she planned to do to help Ginny and about driving her to New Jersey. Cameron didn't really want Sidney to undertake such a difficult drive, especially with Ginny who was not behaving entirely rationally. At the same time he was glad Sidney would be out of River Springs and out of the state for a while. He hoped the situation with Bubba and the drugs could be resolved before Sidney came home.

Sidney and Ginny had driven for more than ten hours and finally stopped to spend their first night in a motel outside Asheville, North Carolina. Both women were exhausted, and they slept late the next day. Sidney thought she could drive the rest of the way to Hoboken in one stretch if she was rested. Sidney knew she would be pushing things if she tried to make it from Asheville to Hoboken in one long day. She decided they would spend a second night at the motel in Asheville. It was a good decision to take an extra night to rest. They would sleep late a second day and then leave for the long drive. Sidney and Becky had decided it would be best if the two women in the truck arrived in Hoboken after dark.

Sidney was taking a somewhat indirect and convoluted route to their final destination. It took a little longer, and Sidney was certain no one was following them. They would cross the mouth of the Chesapeake Bay via the Bridge Tunnel in Norfolk and drive north on the Delmarva Peninsula to Lewes, Delaware. The Cape May Lewes Ferry would take them to New Jersey. Once they were in the Garden State, it would be less than a three-hour drive to their rendezvous with Becky.

Cameron and his friends had searched the woods all that first day and found nothing. No backpack and no drugs had been discovered. They would set out again the next day to finish the grid search in the national forest. Serendipitously, before they set out to hunt for Bubba's backpack again the next morning, Sidney sent Cameron a text. She had more information that she thought would help them find the missing drugs. She was contacting Cameron to let him know that Ginny had remembered something about where she had hidden the backpack in the woods.

Ginny told Sidney she'd climbed up into a maple tree with the backpack and left it securely tied to a tree branch. The reason she'd climbed into a tree to hide the drugs was because she didn't want to leave the backpack lying on the ground or buried in the ground. Ginny had been worried that animals would try to get into the backpack if it was buried or hidden at ground level. If the backpack was torn or broken, fentanyl could be scattered on the floor of the forest. If fentanyl was scattered in the woods, Ginny had been afraid a lot of animals might die. She knew how deadly the drug was to humans and figured it must also mean sudden death to animals.

Cameron was glad to have this information, but it meant the team of searchers would have to go back over the territory they had already covered. No one had been looking up into the trees during the previous search. They'd been looking for holes in the ground and under piles of leaves and pine needles. Knowing that Ginny remembered she'd secured the backpack in a maple tree was some help, but it was not a lot of help. There must be tens of thousands of maple trees in the forest behind Dani's house.

Sidney asked Ginny a few more questions and texted Cameron that Ginny remembered she'd hidden the backpack in a sugar maple tree. The leaves of the sugar maple had begun to turn red when Ginny had hidden the backpack. The tree should be easy to find a week later because the tree would be in full color this late in October. Cameron was excited to hear this news and hurried to pass it along to his team of scavenger hunters. There were plenty of maple trees in the national forest, but only a few had leaves that were red.

Ginny apparently knew her trees, and she had chosen the sugar maple because she knew its leaves would continue to turn red. It would be easy for her to find the tree again. As she started to recall her wild flight into the woods, more details of what she had done began to come back to her.

Sidney had not given Ginny much of a choice about leaving River Springs. After they'd spent two nights in Asheville, Ginny was more rested. They left Asheville early the next morning. Ginny slept less and was awake more during the second leg of the trip. She began to eat, and the rise in her blood sugar helped both her mood and her energy level. She began to talk. She shared with Sidney that she was tremendously relieved to be leaving Arkansas and the entire region. Ginny had never been to New Jersey and didn't know if she would be able to adjust to living in an urban area. She'd almost always lived in rural Arkansas, but she admitted to Sidney that she had dreamed for many years of leaving her farm life behind and going to live in a city.

During their long day in the truck and when Ginny was able to stay awake for more of the day, she began to tell Sidney about her life. It was as if she felt safe talking about her past once she found herself far enough away from her old life. The farther away from River Springs they drove, the safer and the more confident Ginny felt. She wanted to talk and had decided it would be all right to share her story with Sidney.

Ginny and Bubba had dated a couple of times when they were in high school. It wasn't a big thing, and certainly there was nothing serious about their relationship. Ginny had gone to the University of Arkansas in Fayetteville and double majored in business and fine arts. She was an excellent student and made good grades. She'd come home for vacation the summer before her senior year and gone on a date with Bubba. She didn't really like him much, but their parents were friends. The parents mistakenly thought they might be able to make a match between Ginny and Bubba. Bubba was not into drugs back then, and he was a fairly good-looking guy. Bubba wasn't going to college. He didn't like to read or study or take tests.

Their date didn't go well. Bubba got drunk, and when he was driving Ginny home, he stopped the car and tried to take off Ginny's clothes. She fought back, but Bubba had his way and raped her. After the attack, Ginny beat him with an umbrella she found in the car. Ginny told her parents about the rape, but they didn't believe her. They were friends with Bubba's parents and continued to regard him as a possible future son-in-law. Ginny had not gone to the hospital or reported the rape to law enforcement. She had hated herself every day for years afterwards for failing to do these things.

As much as she tried to deny it, Ginny finally had to admit to herself that she was pregnant. By Christmas, her pregnancy had begun to show, and in January, when she told her parents, they were furious with her. They demanded to know who the father was, and they seemed relieved when she told them it was Bubba. A quick marriage was arranged for Valentine's Day. Ginny was only twenty years old, and Bubba was nineteen. Neither was ready for marriage, and neither one was happy about the union. But a hurry-up wedding was what was expected under the circumstances. Sidney was angry with herself because she felt she had been weak and had agreed to go along with what her parents wanted her to do.

Bubba wanted Ginny to immediately quit school and move onto his farm to take care of him. He thought he was a catch because he had a farm with six chicken houses on it. Ginny lost the baby less than a month after she'd married Bubba. She ended up feeling as if she'd married him for no reason, and she was horribly depressed. Bubba was constantly on her to quit school. Bubba said she'd never need a college degree as a chicken farmer's wife. They fought constantly. Ginny continued to attend her college classes. Bubba began to beat her. Ginny snuck away from the farm to take her final exams at the end of the school year.

Ginny never told Bubba she'd received her degree. She hid her diploma from everyone. She was too depressed to think of leaving Bubba. She didn't have the energy, and she was afraid of him. She knew if she asked him for a divorce, he would kill her rather than let her go. She was his prize. He had his fragile pride, his fragile ego, to protect. Ginny was miserably unhappy, and it made her feel sick to even look at Bubba. She sought refuge in her art, making things out of found objects. Ginny and Bubba had no money to spend on anything. Ginny began creating her art because found objects were all she could afford. This outlet for her imagination became her passion and her reason to keep on living.

Armed with the information about the sugar maple tree, the searchers set out with renewed enthusiasm to find the object of their scavenger hunt. It was in fact just a hunt, with the few scarce clues coming in bits and pieces from Ginny's memory as she rode east in the pickup truck. There was a lot of ground to cover in the national forest, but by mid-afternoon of the second day, they thought they had located the backpack in the sugar maple.

The problem was that these four searchers were all eighty years old, and their tree-climbing days were a long time be-hind them, way someplace in the past to be sure. Ginny was decades younger than these guys, and it had not been too difficult for her to climb the tree and secure the backpack. Cameron and Bart arrived on the scene. Bart found it difficult to believe that this whole scenario had played out as it had. He'd had his doubts from the beginning, but there was the backpack…up in the tree. Bart finally became a believer in this bizarre and convoluted world of Cameron's friends and acquaintances.

Neither Cameron nor Bart was about to climb up into the maple tree to rescue the backpack. But Camerson had workmen at the resort, and he asked one he trusted to climb the tree for him. The backpack was recovered, and Raymond Barstow took possession of the many pounds and many dollars' worth of fentanyl.

Raymond Barstow said he had a plan to try to lure Bubba and the other drug dealers Bubba was working with into coming after the backpack. But Bart was no longer a special agent with the FBI. He had retired years earlier. Things could get complicated. Bart left River Springs late that afternoon with the backpack and the drugs in his custody. He promised he would return the next day. Cameron confessed to his four friends that the backpack they had searched for so diligently had been full of the drug fentanyl.

Everyone was glad the backpack had been found and that the drugs were on their way *away* from River Springs. Now they only had to worry about Bubba and company who would be frantically looking for their stash and furious when they couldn't find it. Cameron was tremendously relieved that Ginny and Sidney were no longer in the area, but he was worried about what would happen when Bubba couldn't get the fix he needed and couldn't find his fortune's worth of fentanyl.

Cameron let Sidney know the backpack had been found and was being sent to the FBI or the DEA or someplace that would know what to do with it. Sidney and Ginny were both relieved about the drugs, but Ginny was still worried that someone would come after her to punish her for stealing the drugs from Bubba. She didn't think Bubba's influence could reach her in New Jersey, but she wasn't as sure about the drug people Bubba had been dealing with. Ginny had no idea who they were or if they had a nationwide network. Could she still be in danger?

Sidney had planned Ginny's rescue and relocation primarily with Bubba in mind. Sidney knew Bubba would never be able to find his wife in Hoboken. He'd probably never heard of Hoboken and probably didn't really know where New Jersey was. But the people with whom Bubba had been doing business were another story. Sidney didn't know anything about who these people were. She didn't know much about the drug trade or about how drugs were distributed and sold. She knew what she had seen on the television news and on cop shows and what she'd read about. But the monetary value of the drugs in the backpack spoke to a much more powerful drug connection than she wanted to know about.

Sidney was second-guessing herself about the decision to move Ginny to New Jersey. She was asking herself the same questions Ginny was wondering about. Did the drug dealers that Bubba had become involved with have a national presence? Did these people operate in New Jersey? Could the people who Bubba had been doing business with find Ginny? Did Ginny need to change her name? Did she need an entirely new identity? How much danger was Sidney herself in because she was hiding Ginny?

Sidney didn't share her concerns with Ginny, but she knew Ginny also feared retribution from Bubba's drug dealer connections. "You will be completely safe from Bubba in Hoboken. He doesn't have the mental wherewithal to be able to search for you and find you. But I understand your being worried about the people Bubba has associated himself with. They will never get their drugs back, and that's a lot of money to have slip through their fingers because of Bubba's stupidity. I'm sure they will go after Bubba first. He will blame the disappearance of the drugs on you. But who knows if his suppliers, whoever they are, will believe his story."

"I'm worried that they, whoever 'they' are, will believe him and try to track me down. I really am the one who stole the drugs from Bubba and hid them. Now the drugs are in the hands of the FBI or somebody else in law enforcement. I am the one they ought to come after. It isn't that hard to fool Bubba, but how can I protect myself from these unknown drug dealers?"

"I have some ideas about that, and we will work it out with my friend Becky. One of the reasons I wanted you to relocate so far away from River Springs is partly because of the unknown threat. One of the reasons I'm not driving my own car to Hoboken is for the same reason. I tried to take every possible precaution to keep your disappearance a secret so *no one* would know where you are or where you are going to be. I hope it will be some time before anyone realizes that you've left the area of River Springs. I have not told Dani that you are safe. I will eventually tell her you are all right, so she doesn't worry about you. But that's all I intend to tell her. If Bubba goes to her house again looking for you, she won't be able to tell him anything because she won't know anything."

"What about the threat from the people whose drugs Bubba had, the drugs I took? Will they be able to find me in Hoboken?"

"I told my friend Becky, when she was looking for a place for you to live, that you needed an extremely low-profile location. She knows you are in hiding. Mostly she thinks you are in hiding from Bubba, but she also knows about the drug dealers who supply Bubba. She selected the condo in the warehouse for a reason. We didn't want you to be in a high-rise apartment building where you would run into your neighbors and lots of other people every day. Your new place is almost completely isolated. You won't run into anybody unless you want to. The condo doesn't even have an address. You will have to get a post office box. I suggest you form an LLC and do all of your business, pay all of your bills, take care of all of your snail mail correspondence, and receive all packages through this LLC. It will provide you with the anonymity you need to have. Do you think you can live that way?"

"I can live that way for now. I don't want to know my neighbors, and I don't want anybody to know me or even see me. But what will I do about grocery shopping and going to the drug store? I can order stuff I need from Amazon and have it sent to my post office box. But I can't shop for bread and milk and fresh fruit and vegetables through Amazon."

"I think Becky has a solution for that problem. We talked about it briefly. My understanding is that there is a pizza restaurant directly in front of the warehouse where your condo is located. That pizza restaurant faces on a main street, and of course it has an address. It's owned and managed by someone in Becky's family or by someone she knows really well. That's how she happened to know about and became the real estate agent for the warehouse rental. Whoever owns the pizza place also owns the warehouse property. I think you will be able to order your groceries online and have them delivered to the pizza restaurant. They are always receiving deliveries of food, so a few more bags of groceries won't be noticed. We can probably arrange for Becky's friend to leave your grocery order outside the garage door of the warehouse. I have seen photos of the warehouse and the neighborhood, but we will have a better idea of the possibilities when we get to Hoboken and can see the place in person."

"It seems you have thought of everything. I will welcome the chance to have some time alone to work on my art. When I was living on the farm and with Bubba always around, I never had enough time to devote to my passion. I had to hide everything from him. I'm so glad to leave that life behind me. You have no idea. I am no longer Ginny Randolph. I will never be that person again. I am now Virginia Delacroix."

Every place has traffic problems, but Sidney and Virginia arrived in Hoboken at rush hour. Sidney decided that everybody who worked in New York City had chosen to live in Hoboken, and they were all on the road driving home that night. It was Thursday night. She couldn't even imagine what the traffic must be like on Friday night. It was dark when Becky met them at the entrance to the warehouse. She raised the door with an automatic opener, and Sidney drove the truck directly into the building. At least there would not be an issue with parking on the street.

The truck was parked in the middle of the warehouse. Becky's Mercedes was parked there, too. The warehouse was a big and empty space. Sidney hoped Virginia would be able to fashion an adequate work area from the cavernous warehouse. It looked pretty forlorn right now with its concrete floor and old brick walls. Becky hugged Sidney and also hugged Virginia . Becky helped Sidney get Virginia out of the truck and headed in the direction of the condo. The condo had two entrances. One entrance opened directly into the warehouse from the back door of the condo's kitchen. The other entrance, which was the front door of the condo, opened onto a paved alleyway that ran behind a block of stores. Virginia was completely worn out from the long trip, so when they brought her in through the condo's back door, she collapsed on a chair at the table in the kitchen.

The condominium was a one-floor open concept arrangement. It was dark outside, and although they could not tell how light the space would be during daylight hours, Sidney could see that there were several skylights in the ceiling and a wall of windows in the apartment that faced the alleyway. Because of all this glass, both the warehouse and the living quarters would be much lighter and airier than Sidney had expected they would be.

Sidney and Virginia had purposely arrived after dark, so no one in the area would see them. Neither woman could appreciate the view of the park on the other side of the alleyway that Becky said they would love. The previous tenants had been unusually conscious of security and had installed, at their own expense, an iron fence around the front of the condo. The fence was tall, and its gate was well secured. No one was at all welcome to come and go through the front door of the condo.

Becky had brought takeout from a Greek restaurant she liked, and they opened the cartons and dug into the delicious food. As exhausted as the travelers were, Sidney hoped that she and Virginia would be revived by the hot meal. Sidney helped Virginia take a shower and settle into the bed in the main bedroom. Virginia thanked Sidney and Becky profusely for all they had done and fell asleep immediately. Plans for the future would have to be discussed another day. Everyone was too tired to think about or do anything that night. Becky had wanted Sidney to stay with her at her apartment in Manhattan, but that would have to happen on another visit. They'd already decided that it was important for Sidney to also lay low. Sidney would stay in the guest room of the condo. It was essential that no one suspect that she had ever been to Hoboken. As far as almost anyone knew, Sidney had never left Arkansas.

There were two bathrooms in the condo, and Sidney was glad to have her own space. She would be able to take a long shower and not wake Virginia. Virginia was still fragile, and Sidney was not sure how much of that was emotional and how much was physical. Maybe it didn't matter which it was, and she hoped that time and rest would take care of both sources of Virginia's fragility. Sidney was able to make herself stay awake long enough to send a text to Cameron to let him know they had arrived safely in Hoboken. She took a shower, washed her hair, and climbed into the bed in the guest room that was inside the condo that was inside a warehouse.

Becky had thoughtfully stocked the pantry and the refrigerator, so there was breakfast food available. An expensive and fancy coffeemaker had been left behind by the previous tenants who had disappeared in the night. Becky had scrubbed it, so Sidney was able to make coffee the next morning. Sidney began to feel better about leaving Virginia in this place. There were quite a few details still to be worked out, but Sidney was almost convinced that Virginia would be safe and could work on her art here.

Sidney made herself breakfast and gave some thought to how Virginia might turn the large warehouse into a suitable work space. Thankfully, the warehouse was heated and air conditioned, so Virginia would be able to use it all year around. Sidney had told Virginia she would stay with her in Hoboken for a few days to help her get settled. She intended to help Virginia get the warehouse set up as a studio where she could work. Sidney could see that strategically placed skylights would provide the warehouse with natural sunlight for much of the day.

Another surprising feature of the warehouse was that some parts of it had excellent lighting. Becky had shared with Sidney her suspicions about the previous occupants of the warehouse—that she'd been afraid they were into printing counterfeit money or something equally nefarious. When they'd abandoned their project, whatever it was, they had cleaned out everything and left precipitously. The excellent and costly task lighting over parts of the warehouse bolstered Becky's suspicions about the activities of the former occupants.

Sidney made some sketches of floorplans and some lists about what furniture she thought might work for Virginia. Virginia slept until past noon, but after she'd had some lunch, she seemed in better shape and said she was eager to help plan her new work area. Becky's cleaning team had scrubbed down the condo and the warehouse, including the walls of built-in shelves the suspected counterfeiters had not been able to take with them. Virginia would have all the storage she needed.

Sidney and Virginia discussed the other things Virginia thought would work for her. They ordered tables, some of them on wheels, shelves on wheels, and wheeled carts from

Amazon. They ordered seating. They ordered Virginia's supplies that she needed to begin working on her art. Most of the deliveries from Amazon would be delivered to the pizza place…the next day! The order from Amazon was large and contained a few large pieces of furniture. Sidney was thankful that they would be able to get the warehouse set up for Virginia right away.

Becky promised to be at the pizza restaurant to receive the Amazon deliveries and direct the delivery people where everything was to be unloaded. She was excited about Virginia's new lease on life and was eager to help get the warehouse ready for the young artist. There would be many things arriving from Amazon that would have to be assembled. Although Virginia had not been able to bring any of her creations with her, she and Sidney both had photos on their cell phones of many of Virginia's masterpieces. They forwarded these pictures to Becky who would be able to show them at various galleries where she thought Virginia could sell her work.

Virginia was worn out from the planning and the ordering they'd done. She was still recovering her stamina. They had an early dinner of Chinese takeout, again brought by Becky, and everyone went to bed early. Many of the Amazon deliveries were scheduled to arrive the next day before noon, and all three women wanted to be rested and ready to tackle the work when the furniture arrived.

They worked hard the next afternoon. Virginia had taken a nap in the middle of the day, but Sidney and Becky had soldiered on. Becky had brought the toolbox she kept in the trunk of her car. There was always something that needed to be fixed at the last minute when one was a real estate agent.

When Virginia appeared in the warehouse after her nap, her eyes lit up, and she smiled for the first time in weeks.

Sidney and Becky had arranged the tables and the carts and everything else according to the space plan that Virginia had helped design. Everything was ready for her. Boxes of plastic forks, glues, paints, pounds of buttons, and other materials were stowed on the shelves. There would be plenty of room to store the rest of the things Sidney had promised to send from Virginia's Arkansas home.

Virginia was clearly delighted. She told Sidney and Becky that her new work area was a hundred times better than the secret closet she'd been using for her base of operations, work area, and storage back in River Springs. Seeing her new workspace had energized her, and she couldn't wait to begin working on her found-objects art again. Sidney had decided she would leave Hoboken the next day or the day after. When she saw the smile on Virginia's face, she was finally reassured that things were going to be all right for the young woman.

Becky worked with Virginia to set up an LLC over the internet. It took no time at all. Becky rented a post office box for the LLC and opened a local bank account for the LLC. Sidney was indebted to her life-long friend for her willingness to take care of everything for Virginia. Sidney was worn out from worrying about Virginia, and although she would miss Virginia at the Women's Collective, she knew Virginia was safe now. Becky had contacted several galleries that were interested in carrying Virginia's work. Virginia would be financially secure once she got her products on the market. Sidney was happy to leave Virginia in Becky's extremely capable hands.

Sidney let Cameron know she was ready to come home. She told her husband that she wasn't up to driving the truck all the way back to Arkansas, and she proposed selling it in Hoboken. Cameron told her he wanted the truck to use at the resort. If Sidney could drive it to the Philadelphia airport, she was to park the truck in the long-term parking lot there. Cameron would send their private jet to Philadelphia to fly Sidney home. He would send a driver on the plane who would pick up the truck at the airport and drive it back to Arkansas. Sidney was tough, but she had worn herself down worrying about what to do to relocate Ginny Randolph. Sidney had kept pushing herself until she was convinced she had found a solution that guaranteed Virginia Delacroix was out of harm's way, settled in a new place to live, and had a job that would support her.

All of that had now been accomplished, and Sidney finally allowed herself to relax and unburden herself from her worries. She realized how tired she was and welcomed Cameron's offer of the private flight home and the driver to deal with the truck. The drive from Hoboken to the Philadelphia airport was less than two hours, depending on the traffic. Sidney could do that. She and Virginia and Becky ordered pizza from the restaurant in front of the warehouse. Becky brought a bottle of champagne. They ate at one of the tables in the warehouse and toasted Virginia's new life.

Sidney left Hoboken the next morning before five a.m. She hoped to beat the rush hour and arrive at the airport before dawn. Her plan was to be on their private plane before the sun came up, before almost anyone was awake at the private air terminal to see her board the plane. Sidney wanted everyone to think she had never left her home in Little Rock. She would tell anyone who asked that she'd had a two-day virus of some kind but was fine now. She'd say she had stayed at home, wrapped herself in blankets, and eaten chicken noodle soup.

After Sidney boarded the plane in Philadelphia, she immediately fell asleep. She'd been awake since four that morning, and she slept all the way to Little Rock. Cameron had a car waiting for her on the tarmac when the plane arrived. She didn't have to go through the terminal at the airport so she wouldn't have to take the chance that anyone she knew would see her or recognize her. She slipped back into town unobserved. She'd done a good deed for a woman she admired. Now she needed to take a break and get some rest.

Ginny Randolph had disappeared. She'd run away from Dani's house into the woods of the national forest, and the story was that no one had seen her since. Maybe she had kept on running and had successfully made her way out of River Springs? Maybe she had died in the woods? Everyone knew Ginny had been badly hurt in her last fight with Bubba. But everyone also knew that Ginny was smart and resourceful. She was a survivor. No one claimed to know anything for sure about what had happened to her.

Sidney would let Dani know that Ginny was okay. But Sidney would not let anyone know that she knew where Ginny was or what name she was using. No one would ever suspect that Sidney had helped Ginny Randolph disappear. It was essential for Virginia's safety and for Sidney's safety that no one know Sidney had helped her relocate. The whole town knew that Ginny worked with Sidney at the Women's Collective, so it was important to Sidney that no one realize she knew where Virginia Delacroix was.

Sidney and Cameron still had to deal with the fallout from the backpack full of drugs that Ginny had taken from Bubba. An angry Bubba would be harassing them sooner or later, but they could handle Bubba. The unknown was whoever had supplied Bubba with the drugs and wanted their money or their drugs returned to them. Bubba was caught in the middle, but the Richardsons were quite concerned that whoever was supplying Bubba would come to their door eventually. It had been Cameron who had turned the fentanyl over to the feds. The four friends who had managed to find the backpack in the sugar maple tree would never breathe a word of what they had done or what they had found in the red maple tree in the national forest. Sidney and Cameron felt they had covered as many of the bases as they could. Now all they could do was wait to see if there would be further consequences.

The Reunion

ARKANSAS

2023

*A*s promised, Raymond Barstow returned to River Springs the next day. He brought the derelict backpack with him. It had been tested for DNA and fingerprints and everything else law enforcement could test it for. Fortunately, it looked as if it was the same old, scruffy, dirty backpack that Bubba had used to hold his drugs. It weighed the same as it had weighed when the fentanyl was inside. What was different was that in place of the fentanyl, the DEA or somebody had put sealed plastic bags of powdered sugar in the backpack. The contents of the bags looked exactly like fentanyl. No one would know about the substitution until they had unsealed one of the plastic bags and tasted what was inside.

The former FBI agent hoped the ruse would hold up for a while. Barstow had a plan to draw out Bubba and the bad guys who were supplying the chicken farmer turned drug dealer. Cameron was relieved that Ginny was no longer in town, and he wanted Sidney to stay in Little Rock until things were back to normal in River Springs — whatever normal was going to be for them going forward. Sidney, on the other hand, was anxious to get into Virginia's house at the farm to pack up her clothes and other belongings, especially the things Virginia needed to continue producing her artwork. But Sidney knew all that would have to wait until the Bubba factor had been taken care of. She was not going anywhere near Virginia's house as long as there was any chance that Bubba would find her there. Sidney was afraid of Bubba, as she absolutely should have been.

Although Cameron loved having his old friends around, he told them it was time for them to leave. He didn't want them to be in any danger when Raymond Barstow put his operation into play to trap Bubba. The Camp Shoemaker boys hated to miss the excitement but knew they would be in the way once the fentanyl hit the fan. They made their plans to leave the Richardson's resort the following day and had one last wonderful meal of prime rib with all the trimmings at the Old Mill Restaurant. The octogenarians were sad to say goodbye to Chef Georgio and each other.

At least two of the group were bachelors who cooked for themselves or ate out. Bailey cooked for himself when Gretchen was out of town, which was often. Matthew and Isabelle had dinner at restaurants almost every night because of the demands of her job. All of them had loved having home-cooked meals, especially meals that were home cooked by someone other than themselves. Georgio would be sorely missed.

No one knew for sure what Bubba would do or where he would go when he got desperate for his next fix. No one knew how much of a supply he already had on hand to feed his habit. If he had reserves, he might not have to search for more drugs for a week. Or he might need to resupply himself the following day. Sooner or later, he would be in withdrawal and need to find more. When that time came, Raymond Barstow wanted to be ready.

Drug users manage their addictions in different ways. Bubba was always short on drugs and short on money. He had scored a huge coup with the backpack full of fentanyl. He knew he had to get the bulk of that stash to dealers who would distribute it on the street. Bubba also knew that, before he turned the fentanyl over to the as yet nonexistent network of people who would distribute the drugs, he would skim off some of the fentanyl for his own personal use. The dealers would pay for whatever Bubba gave them to sell, and Bubba would be flush with cash after that transaction had taken place. Most of the cash he made from that deal had to go to pay back his suppliers. When he first acquired a large supply of drugs, like a backpack full, for a short period of time Bubba felt as if he were rich beyond his wildest dreams.

Bubba usually tended to put off using his last fix until he was sure he had secured a solid supply of future fixes. As his addiction progressed, he probably would not be that careful about using his last existing hit of drugs. But at this stage of his addiction, when he'd scored the backpack full of fentanyl, he knew he had a good supply. He still had a few hits left from his current stash. Because he thought he had plenty of drugs on hand for the future, he began to use his existing drugs more freely.

Then his backpack disappeared. He couldn't find it. He was sure he had hidden it under the sink in the bathroom, but when he went to retrieve it, it wasn't there. He had panicked and decided that Ginny had taken it. He blamed Ginny for everything that went wrong with his life. But his brain was so messed up with the fentanyl he'd been using, he was not absolutely certain what he'd done with the backpack. Had Ginny really stolen it, or had he hidden it someplace else? He couldn't be certain of anything in his drugged condition. Blaming the loss of his drugs on Ginny gave Bubba the chance to beat her up, and he never neglected an opportunity to do that.

Sidney knew, and she had mentioned it to Cameron, that indeed Bubba had stored the backpack under the bathroom sink. That's where Ginny had found it. She'd remarked to Sidney about what an idiot Bubba was. Ginny had wondered who would think their drugs were really hidden if they put them under the bathroom sink? Ginny had felt compelled to take the backpack and hide it in a better place. After Bubba had beaten her so badly, she had grabbed the backpack of drugs from where she'd hidden it and run from the farmhouse to Dani's. Then she'd escaped into the woods.

Because Raymond Barstow knew where Bubba thought he had hidden his backpack full of drugs, Bart knew what to do. He returned the backpack that was now loaded with powdered sugar to the cabinet underneath the bathroom sink in Bubba's house. Barstow had attached an exceptionally tiny tracker to one of the seams in the backpack. He would be able to track the backpack full of powdered sugar when Bubba or someone else discovered the backpack under the sink.

Bubba would eventually find the backpack there, and Barstow felt when that happened, they would have Bubba. If Bubba didn't find the backpack, Barstow was certain someone else would. Whoever had the backpack would be in Barstow's sights. The DEA agents on call would follow the tracker in the backpack. The hope was that following the backpack would lead to the people who had supplied Bubba.

In addition to catching Bubba and his suppliers, Cameron had stressed that Bart's plan, whatever it was, must also be designed to exonerate Ginny. Cameron wanted whoever was supplying Bubba to believe that Bubba alone had been responsible for losing the drugs and that his wife Ginny had nothing to do with any of it. That was one reason Barstow had decided to return the backpack to the bathroom. Cameron had insisted on a foolproof plan that would insure Bubba's suppliers did not come after Ginny…for the drugs, for the money, or for revenge.

Raymond Barstow had a man who was an expert at breaking into houses without leaving any traces behind. This operative was given the task of returning the backpack to Bubba's hiding place under the bathroom sink. The operative was also charged with installing surveillance cameras throughout the inside of Bubba's house. Surveillance cameras were tiny now and would not be detected. When Bubba was at home, Barstow would be able to monitor his every move. Law enforcement knew they could catch Bubba. They hoped if they watched Bubba long enough and followed his backpack wherever it went, that they could also catch his suppliers.

There will always be customers who want to buy the opium that is produced in the poppy fields of Afghanistan and Myanmar. Opium is the basis for many kinds of legal and illegal drugs, a list that includes morphine, codeine, heroin, and oxycodone. The Taliban, now in control of Afghanistan, derive most of their financial resources from the almighty poppy. But poppies require soil and water and sunshine to thrive and produce their product. The illegal drug trade is turning to less expensive sources that do not require land or water or good weather or harvesting by machines or people to produce their doses of painkillers and doses of death.

Fentanyl is sweeping the United States as the cheap replacement for oxycodone which has become increasingly difficult to get either by prescription or on the street. Heroin is frequently laced with the less expensive fentanyl. Fentanyl is also added to cocaine. Fentanyl is a product that is made in the laboratory. If one has all the ingredients, it is easy to make and does not require large poppy fields.

Quality control over illegal drug manufacturing is by definition nonexistent. There is no quality control over the production of the fentanyl that is sold on the streets. Whoever buys and uses the drug is buying and using a "pig in a poke." The strength of the dose is entirely variable from one batch of fentanyl to the next. All illegal drugs kill users and addicts. But fentanyl, for a number of reasons, is a particularly dangerous killer. It is the latest scourge on the street for users and addicts.

Memphis, Tennessee is a major center for the distribution of all kinds of products in the United States. Its location, on the Mississippi River and roughly at the geographic center of the U.S., gives the city an ideal location for commerce of all kinds. FedEx has its largest hub in Memphis. Trucking and railroad transport routes branch out from Memphis to everywhere. Most of the business in the rapidly growing metropolitan area of Memphis is legitimate and provides the country with the machinery and pharmaceuticals and other products it needs.

It would not be surprising that, along with the growth of its legitimate and legal business transactions and transport, Memphis has also become a center for the distribution of illegal drugs. Drug use is no longer exclusively an urban activity…if it ever was. Drug use is now rampant in small towns and rural areas throughout the United States. Networks of middlemen and dealers have appeared in areas not previously overwhelmed by illegal drugs. The epidemic is everywhere… even in rural Arkansas.

Bubba Randolph, looking for a way to get rich quick and perhaps as a way out of the hard work and day-to-day grind of raising chickens, became a worker in the drug trade. Bubba was naïve about how to recruit dealers and distribute drugs on the street. He talked a big game, and that was how he had stumbled into being a middleman for the growing fentanyl business that was sweeping the country, including the area of River Springs.

Bubba was a blowhard and a braggart, but he was also fairly handsome. If he made the effort, he could make himself presentable. That was how he had been able to convince those higher up in the drug business that he could put together an effective network to distribute the fentanyl in his area of rural Arkansas. In fact, Bubba didn't have a clue about how to accomplish this. He had no idea how to begin to build a drug distribution network. Eventually he also became a victim of the product he was trying to sell.

Bubba's suppliers had been patient with him. But eventually they reached the point of no return. Their patience had run out, and they wanted their money. They realized Bubba was not only a big talker but also a big loser when it came to actually performing. Bubba had always been disorganized about everything he did. Then Bubba became a user. And now he had become an addict. Many dealers were users and addicts, but middlemen and suppliers were not supposed to dip into the product they were selling. Those who had initially gone into business with Bubba felt there was a huge untapped market in this part of Arkansas. They saw potential and millions of dollars that were as yet unrealized. Bubba had not been able to do what he'd said he would do. Bubba had failed to deliver. Bubba had to go.

But before Bubba had to go, he had to either return the unsold drugs he had in his possession or turn over the money he had made from running the fentanyl through his distribution network. The truth was that Bubba had lost the drugs, and he had not received any money for what he had never distributed. He had appropriated some of the product for his own personal use, but the rest of it had disappeared. He had no idea where it was. He was in big trouble, and he knew it.

Bubba was frantically looking for his backpack full of drugs and looking for Ginny because he had decided she'd stolen the drugs from him. He was also trying to lay low where his suppliers couldn't find him. And he was always trying to feed his habit. As is true with all addicts, feeding the habit takes priority over everything else in one's life. Finding the next fix takes precedence over doing one's regular job and maintaining relationships with one's family. All efforts and energy are focused on getting high. That's just the way life is for any addict. That was just the way life was for Bubba.

Maybe Bubba was unusually stressed that day. Maybe he had finally realized in what a very bad situation he'd found himself. Maybe he was frightened. Maybe he just wanted to get an extra special high on board. Maybe he'd forgotten how many hits he'd already had. He hadn't yet found the backpack that Raymond Barstow had returned to the cabinet under his bathroom sink. For whatever reason, Bubba chose to finish up his current stash of fentanyl that day. Maybe the fentanyl he took for this final fix was stronger than his usual dose. No one would ever really know all the reasons why Bubba was much, much higher than he usually was and much, much higher than he should have been.

He'd already called the contact who supplied him with drugs and told him that his wife Ginny had stolen the drugs from him. Bubba thought he knew where she was. He said he was going after her to get the drugs back. Bubba's supplier had heard this song and dance before. Middlemen and dealers who became addicts often blamed wives, girlfriends, other friends, and whoever they could think of for the loss of their stashes. Bubba's supplier didn't pay too much attention to the fact that Bubba was blaming his troubles on his wife. The drug network that operated above Bubba and supplied him had his number by now.

Bubba made his way to Sidney and Cameron Richardson's resort by the Little Red River. He'd stayed away from their property until now, but he knew that Ginny worked with Mrs. Richardson at that stupid store where she sold her crap. In his stoned and confused state, he had decided that Ginny was probably hiding out at the Richardson's house. He had looked everywhere else for her and hadn't been able to find her. He figured she had to be hiding at their home. It was his last chance to find her…the only place he'd not already looked. He drove his jalopy truck to the resort and parked about a half mile away from the house. The Richardson's residence was on its own private road that was a dead end. It was purposely apart from the rest of the resort. The Richarson's privacy was guaranteed because everyone had to drive through a complicated construction area and some confusing roads to find the house.

Bubba parked his old truck where he thought nobody could see it. He walked the rest of the way and stood at the front door of the Richardson's house. He banged on the door and started shouting. He demanded to be let inside to search the place. He was shouting that he knew the Richardsons were hiding Ginny there, and he was coming in to get her.

Juanita was the only person at the Richardson's home when Bubba came to the door. She was frightened by the pounding and the shouting. She was busy making lunch for Cameron and Bart who were working at the lodge and discussing its transformation. They would be back soon and ready to eat. Juanita liked to cook and missed Cameron's friends who had left a few days earlier. Juanita hoped Sidney would return soon because she had something very important that she needed to discuss with her. She was glad that Sidney wasn't at the house when all the pounding and shouting started.

There was a surveillance camera focused on the front door, and Juanita was able to access the camera on her cell phone. When she saw who was pounding on the door and shouting outside, she hid herself in one of the bedroom closets and called 911. There was a deranged man at the door. He was wearing dirty clothes and his hair was standing straight up on his head. Juanita had never seen the man before, but it wasn't hard to figure out that he was big trouble and hadn't been invited. Juanita of course didn't know that Bubba had a cousin working in the sheriff's department who protected him from getting mixed up with law enforcement. Juanita didn't know the name of the man who was attacking the Richardson's front door, so she never mentioned Bubba's name when she called for help.

Bubba smashed the glass that was in the top of the front door of the house. But he couldn't reach the lock or the door handle from the outside. He pounded the door again in frustration, and then he wandered around the side of the house in his drugged state. He was out of control and didn't remember where he was or why he was where he was. He stumbled through the yard to the back of the house. He thought he might be able to get inside that way.

What had started out to be a beautiful crisp and clear November day had turned dark and cloudy. The sun had disappeared, and the rain had begun. The sudden thunderstorm soaked the ground and made the grass in the Richardson's yard a slippery mess. Visibility was poor. The property sloped down away from the road and towards the water. There was a magical view of the Little Red River at the back of the Richardson's house.

Bubba was looking at the screened porch that stretched along the back of the house as a possible way to break in, and he was not watching where he was walking. He wandered through the trees and stumbled down a steep incline. He tripped over the roots of a tree and fell on his face. He was too out of it to be able to catch himself and stop his descent down the hill. He rolled over and over, down, down, down towards the river.

As he reached the bottom of the hill, he tried to grab hold of some bushes. He was able to stop his downward progress. He was at the edge of the water, and he attempted to stand up before he fell into the river. But when he tried to stand, he hit his head on a low-lying tree limb. His encounter with the tree knocked him out cold, and he ended up face down in the water. The water was fairly shallow where Bubba landed, but he was unconscious and had never learned to swim. He couldn't save himself. Even if he had been an excellent swimmer, he was so far gone with the drugs he'd taken that no amount of aquatic skill could have saved his life.

Bubba drowned in the shallow water at the edge of the river, face down in the plant life that lived by the shore. No one knew he was there. He died alone, a victim of his own bad choices. The current of the Little Red eventually broke Bubba's body free from the plants in which he was entangled and carried him away down the river.

Bubba's suppliers had known he was on the edge of falling apart. They had seen his ilk before. They wanted their drugs back. They'd put a man on Bubba to follow him to try to discover what he'd done with their fentanyl. Bubba had no idea he was being followed. He was being followed because his drug suppliers hoped he would lead them to the stash he'd said was in a backpack, a backpack that he'd told everyone his wife Ginny had stolen.

The man who was assigned to follow Bubba should not have been surprised when his mark approached the Richardson's house. The watcher kept his distance. Bubba was too close to the house, and the watcher had been warned not to go near this particular residence. It was well known that the Richardsons had the latest in electronic security all around their house. The watcher had been told to maintain as low a profile as possible. He knew his face could not be recorded on any surveillance cameras.

The watcher was able to see when Bubba stumbled down the embankment behind the house, hit his head on the tree limb, and fell into the river. The watcher was afraid to try to rescue him. Bubba had hit his head hard, and the watcher wondered if he had broken his neck when he'd fallen into the water. Bubba was too still as he lay at the shallow edges of the river. The watcher could see that Bubba was dead and knew the current would eventually carry him downriver. He knew the river and thought he knew where Bubba's body would end up. The watcher planned to get there first.

The watcher notified his bosses that Bubba was dead. He needed help disposing of the body where no one would ever find it. The watcher also needed to get rid of Bubba's old truck. He didn't want the Richardsons to find the truck on their property and call the sheriff to begin looking for

Bubba. The watcher knew his bosses also wanted to search Bubba's house for the drugs he said he'd lost. No one wanted to go into Bubba's house while there was any chance that he would find them there. Bubba was a loose cannon and a wild and violent man. No one wanted to mess with him, especially when he was high. Now that Bubba was dead, it would be safe to search his house. The coast was clear.

Two men went to Bubba's house. They immediately found the backpack underneath the bathroom sink. They actually laughed at Bubba's choice of a hiding place. Who would ever hide their stash under the bathroom sink? They could scarcely believe their luck. No one tested the drugs when they were first discovered, so no one knew yet that the backpack was full of powdered sugar with not a hint of fentanyl in sight.

One of the men who had found the backpack knew Bubba was not very smart. "He said his wife stole his backpack and ran away with his drugs. Don't they all say that? They always try to blame their mistakes and their stupidity on somebody else. This one didn't even try to find a decent place to hide the stuff. What a loser he was."

Bubba's body was chained to a couple of cement blocks and dropped into the lake. With any luck, he would be a bag of bones by the time anyone found him, if in fact anyone ever did. As far as his friends and family or anybody knew, he'd disappeared into thin air. Bubba's truck also disappeared. Bubba and all traces of his demise were gone.

By the time the sheriff's department responded to Juanita's 911 call, Bubba had fallen into the river and floated away. The deputy who came in response to Juanita's call for help thoroughly checked the inside of the house. Then he checked the grounds. The deputy was able to reassure Juanita that no one was anywhere around the house, in the house, or on the property. The deputy and his men were certain that there was no longer any threat. They saw the broken glass by the front door, so they knew that someone had been at the house and had tried to get in. The crisis had been resolved. The excitement was over.

Raymond Barstow knew there was significant electronic surveillance in place around the outside of the Richardson's house, and when he heard the description of the man who'd tried to get inside, Barstow was certain it had been Bubba who'd frightened Juanita. When Raymond Barstow checked the footage from the surveillance camera by the front door, he saw that it was indeed Bubba who had come to the door. The Richardsons had surveillance cameras all over their property, including several in the rear by the screened porch and by the river.

Raymond Barstow checked all the cameras around the outside of the house. He watched as Bubba stumbled down the riverbank and hit his head. He saw that Bubba had fallen into the river at the rear of the house and had not been able to save himself from drowning. Bart was quite certain that Bubba was dead, and he informed Cameron of that fact. Because the body was no longer lying at the edge of the river where he had fallen, Bart assumed that Bubba's body had floated downstream. Barstow figured Bubba's body would surface at some point. Bodies usually did. But Bart didn't discover until later everything that had been done to Bubba's corpse to keep it submerged.

Cameron informed Sidney that Bubba had without question drowned in the river but that his corpse had never been found. His death could not be confirmed with a body or with an autopsy. Sidney would have to take his death on faith and on the evidence provided by the surveillance cameras around her home.

Bart had observed, by watching the cameras he had installed inside Bubba's house, that two men had gone to the house within a few hours of Bubba's disappearance. They'd immediately found the backpack under the bathroom sink. Bart activated the app on his phone that followed the tracking device he'd had sewn into the seam of the backpack. He hoped to find Bubba's suppliers by following Bubba's backpack. But he had gained something else that was almost as valuable. He had video surveillance of the two men who had picked up the backpack from Bubba's house. He had photos of their faces, and he had the evidence that they had picked up the backpack they thought was full of drugs.

Bart knew Bubba's suppliers would become enraged again when they discovered that the contents of the backpack had been switched. No more fentanyl. They would not know who had replaced the drugs with sugar, but they would for sure have Bubba at the top of their list for who had done it. Had Bubba sold the drugs and replaced the fentanyl with powdered sugar? Had he hidden the drugs someplace else, and left the backpack full of sugar for his suppliers to find? Those who had the backpack now would only know for sure that they were out almost a million dollars. But could they blame anyone? Bubba was dead. They had found Bubba's backpack but could only speculate what might have happened to the drugs they'd thought they would find inside. It was a complete and total bust.

Retired special agent Barstow was closely tracking the location of the backpack, and he had high hopes of finding out who had been supplying Bubba with drugs. Bart and Cameron could only hope that whoever had found the drugs in their not very good hiding place, would be convinced that Bubba alone had been in control of the drugs. He had tried to shift the blame to his wife, but they hoped those with the backpack believed that Bubba was the one who'd had the drugs all along. But what had happened to all that fentanyl? It had been replaced with sugar.

In addition to being able to track the backpack that the suppliers believed was full of fentanyl, Raymond Barstow also knew what two of the people looked like who'd searched Bubba's house. Barstow had hoped to follow Bubba when and if he made contact with either his suppliers or with his distributors. That had not happened and was not going to happen now that Bubba was dead. But the two men who'd searched the house after Bubba died had their faces in the FBI database. Facial recognition software might identify them as drug dealers who were already known to law enforcement. Or these might be new dealers whose faces had now been added to the record. Raymond Barstow hoped his electronic tracker would lead him to Bubba's suppliers, but at least there were two additional drug dealer's faces to add to the roster of those wanted by the FBI. They were officially entered into the database of bad guys.

Barstow had promised Cameron that whatever happened, Ginny would be exonerated as having had anything to do with the drugs. Barstow felt confident that the way things had played out, no one would go looking for Ginny. He crossed his fingers that this was true. No one knew, of course, what would happen when the suppliers realized that their packages of fentanyl had turned into packages of powdered sugar. Anything could happen then. The suppliers might return to

Bubba's house to search for their drugs, or they might decide that Ginny had something to do with the substitution. But they couldn't fish Bubba out of the lake and bring him back to life to ask him about anything.

When Sidney found out that Bubba had drowned, she immediately let Virginia know the news. Sidney Richardson informed her that the drug-dealing, abusive husband that Ginny Randolph, who was now Virginia Delacroix, had left behind in Arkansas was dead. Sidney told Virginia only that Bubba Randolph had drowned in the river and that the abused wife did not need to worry about Bubba ever coming after her again. Virginia admitted that she felt a tremendous sense of relief that Bubba was no longer a threat to her, but, in spite of the fact that she had never loved the man she was married to, she was sorry that his life had ended in such a desultory and depressing way. Drugs do that to people. They die in chaos and misery.

Sidney returned to River Springs and made plans to clean out the Randolph's house. Sidney had volunteered to send to New Jersey whatever belongings Virginia wanted from her Arkansas farm. Ginny had left Arkansas in fear of her life and with only the clothes on her back. Ginny Randolph had made herself over into Virginia Delacroix. She vowed that she would never go back to the chicken farm she had shared with her spouse, and she was grateful that Sidney was willing to pack up and send her things.

Sidney had a key to the house and wasted no time gathering together the few items Virginia wanted sent to Hoboken. Virginia wanted very little from the house. She wanted her artwork and art supplies, some of her clothes, a few specific personal items, and one or two pieces of furniture. She'd made a list for Sidney. She told Sidney to get rid of everything else that was not on the list. This included most of her clothes and most of the furniture in the house, as well as everything that had once belonged to her now-deceased husband. Virginia didn't want to keep anything that reminded her of Bubba, the house they had shared, or the life she'd had with the loser she'd been married to.

Sidney was to donate everything that was left in the house to the Goodwill, to the women's shelter in River Springs, or to the local landfill. Virginia did not want to ever put on any of the clothes again that she had worn as Bubba's wife. She'd always hated being his wife, and the clothes she'd worn reminded her of those unhappy years. Virginia wanted a few pieces of furniture that had belonged to her family, but she hated everything else in the house. It had to go!

With not much on the list, Sidney had been able to quickly pack up the things Virginia wanted from the house and rent a truck. Sidney was careful, and she drove more than a hundred miles into Tennessee with the truckload of boxes and furniture to ship to Hoboken. Sidney wanted to be certain that no one in River Springs, or in Arkansas, knew where Ginny Randolph was living or where Virginia Delacroix had gone to begin her new life. Because Sidney had sent it all from a town in Tennessee, no one would ever have any idea where the boxes and the furniture were headed. Sidney had gone to a great deal of effort to keep Virginia's new location a secret.

Sidney asked Virginia to send her a power of attorney so she could act for her to sell the chicken farm. When Bubba had died, Ginny inherited the farm. The farm had been owned in both of their names. Ginny had insisted on that when she'd married Bubba. Sidney hired a lawyer who went to court to have Bubba declared deceased. Because there was no body and no death certificate, it had been necessary to show the judge the videos of Bubba lying in the Little Red River. Only after the judge had declared Bubba dead could the farm be sold.

Virginia wanted nothing to do with the chickens or the farm. Because Bubba had neglected the chickens after he'd become addicted to fentanyl, many of the birds had died, Sidney sold the few that had managed to survive and hired someone to clean up the mess that was left of the farm and the house.

She got rid of everything else in the house and the barns that Virginia didn't want. Whatever wasn't worth donating went to the landfill. Sidney hired people to do the necessary repairs to the house and to have some painting done. She staged the house and hired a real estate agent to sell the place. The proceeds from the sale of the farm would be a big help to Virginia Delacroix's bottom line until she began to sell her artwork.

Sidney had been so busy, and she'd had so much on her mind in recent weeks. She knew she had neglected Juanita.

Juanita was upset about something and wanted to talk to Sidney about it. After dealing with the drama of Ginny and Bubba, Sidney wanted some time without any drama, but she knew Juanita needed to talk. Sidney was devoted to Juanita, and when Sidney had completed dealing with the Randolph house and farm, she made time for Juanita to tell her what was bothering her.

"I know you have been worried about something since Cameron's friends were here. I'm sorry I didn't have the time or the energy to listen to what you had to say back then when you first told me you were troubled about something you saw in one of Dr. Ritter's montages. Please tell me all about it now, Juanita. You are such a good person. You don't have to worry about anything you have done. We will work it out. I promise."

The tears began to roll down Juanita's face. She had held inside what was troubling her for so long, she could barely bring herself to tell Sidney about it. Juanita choked out a few words through her tears. "I took something. I kept something I found in the trash. I didn't think it would matter. Then I saw the slide show that Cameron's friend put on for your group. It was Dr. Matthew Ritter's montage. I realized I had one of those paintings he had in his slides. I took one of those paintings, and I still have it. I don't know what to do with it."

"Where did you get this painting from the trash? If you took something from the trash, that means somebody threw it away and didn't want it any more. You didn't steal anything, if that's what you are worried about. Where did you find this painting?"

"Do you remember when we cleaned out the house of the man who died on the side of the road? The one who died riding his bike. He left his cottage to the women's shelter.

You and I went to the English Cottage, and we sorted out the few things he'd left in the house. We got rid of everything that was still at the house. When I took a load of things out to the trash can, I found a painting there. It was sitting right on top of the rest of the trash, framed and everything. I really liked the painting. I didn't think it would matter if I took it. It reminded me of my grandmother's home in Mexico. She had a music room with a piano. When I was a child, the family used to gather in that room, and someone would play the piano. We would all sing and have a wonderful time. The painting I found in the trash can brought all of that back to me. I thought of the old days, of my childhood, and how wonderful it had been to have everyone together, singing and making music. My uncle played the violin. There is something that looks like a violin in the painting. I know this painting isn't of Mexico, and I know there is no piano. I know it was painted in a different country hundreds of years in the past and that the people don't look anything like my relatives in Mexico. But it reminded me of when I was young and my family was all around me. I stole the painting from the trash and took it to my house. It's a beautiful painting. Then I saw Dr. Ritter's slide show, and I realized I had one of those works of art that had been stolen many years ago in Boston. What I have is a real painting, not a print or a reproduction. It is painted on a canvas and painted with real oil paints. I thought maybe I had something I shouldn't have, something that didn't really belong to me."

"Oh, Juanita. I'm so sorry I didn't talk to you sooner about this. You tried to tell to me about it, and I brushed you off. You have been worrying and suffering guilt about this…needlessly. I could have reassured you and saved you so much grief. I am so, so sorry. I had too many things on my mind. That's the truth, but it's no excuse for ignoring your concerns. First of all, you didn't steal anything. You took something from the trash, something someone had thrown away. So promise me you won't blame yourself for having stolen anything. You didn't! So mark that off your list of things to be worried about. Let me take a look at the painting. Do you still have it at your house? We will figure this out together. It will be fine."

Juanita nodded that yes she had the painting at her house. She didn't say much, and she was clearly still worried. They walked to Juanita's house which was just through the woods. Juanita had the painting in her bedroom closet. She'd had it hanging over the bed in her bedroom until she'd seen the slide show several weeks earlier. After the montage about the art heist at the Isabella Stewart Gardner Museum, Juanita had been afraid to keep her rescued painting out in the open until she'd found out more about where it had come from. Sidney was not an expert on evaluating the authenticity of artwork, but she recognized the painting at once. She assumed it was a very excellent copy of *The Concert* that had been missing for almost thirty-five years.

"You are right, Juanita. This is a real oil painting. And it is a very good one. I would be fooled, too, if I didn't know this painting had been stolen and has not been seen for decades. I also don't blame you for rescuing it from the trash can. I would have rescued it, too, if I'd found it. It is certainly worth hanging on your wall." Sidney paused and looked at Juanita who did not look like she was feeling any better about the painting she had "rescued."

"Why don't I have this painting authenticated? An expert in old masters' oil paintings will be able to tell us that this is just an excellent copy of the stolen art. Is it okay if I send it to an expert? They will return it to you, and you can hang it up wherever you want to hang it. It's yours. So whatever you want me to do with it, I'll do it."

"I want to be sure it's not the stolen painting. So yes. Send it to your expert. I want to know everything the expert says."

"Will you promise me you won't worry about this anymore?"

"After I have heard from your expert, I won't worry about it anymore after that."

Sidney took the painting and sent a quick text to Becky. As if Becky wasn't already dealing with enough…trying to run her real estate business, take care of Virginia, and have a life of her own. After wrapping it securely in bubble wrap, Sidney boxed up the painting and took it to the post office the next day. Who knew how long it would be before Becky was able to have her contact at the Metropolitan Museum of Art in New York City take a look at the painting?

The Renaissance

HOBOKEN

2023

Ginny Randolph had disappeared. She was no longer anywhere at all. A woman named Virginia Delacroix had moved into a warehouse condominium in Hoboken, New Jersey and was beginning a new life. She made art from found objects and hoped to be able to make a living selling her work at a gallery in New York City. Becky Sells, a friend of Virginia's and a successful New York City real estate agent, had found the best New York gallery to handle Virginia's artwork. Becky negotiated an exclusive contract for Virginia that included an introductory gallery showing of Virginia's objets d'art. The gallery promised to pull out all the stops and invite their wealthiest and most famous patrons to the opening. The opening would introduce Virginia Delacroix's work to the world and hopefully would launch the young woman's successful new career.

Virginia was much less afraid of everything now that she knew Bubba was dead. She never considered returning to River Springs, and she was excited and eager to see if her artwork could make it in New York City. She loved working on her creative projects and stayed up late at night to produce new inventory. She wanted to have plenty of things to display and sell for the gallery opening which was scheduled for the week before Christmas. The show was to be called "The Lost and Found."

Virginia was working on a one-of-a-kind piece called *Take Me Out.* It was a life-size sculpture of a woman who was sitting for an artist, and it was made entirely from various kinds of take-out plastic and Styrofoam containers. Virginia had scoured dumpsters throughout Hoboken and had brought the variety of containers back to the warehouse. She'd scrubbed the containers clean and carefully cut them and built them into a sculpture of a beautiful woman. She painted her "container woman" so that she looked incredibly real...like she was alive. This creation was the new, dramatic piece that was intended to shock and surprise everyone... even the gallery's owners. Virginia's creativity was taking off, and she was in a prolific phase of her artistic life.

Virginia was working late one night. She was trying to finish everything a week before the scheduled opening. The gallery wanted every piece on hand ahead of time so they could do all the setup just the way Virginia wanted it to be done. She had already delivered everything the gallery was expecting, but she'd had a last-minute inspiration that used plastic bags she'd found in dumpsters...to make people for her artwork. She'd bought a helium tank, and she was attempting to make balloons of different shapes and sizes out of the plastic bags. She would fill the long, narrow bags with helium, and these would be the arms and legs of her people. She wanted to create a child's birthday party scene with "people" sitting around a table. She dressed her "people" with colorful clothes from the Goodwill.

The table legs were made out of reclaimed wooden 2X4s. Virginia found some jagged pieces of plywood in a construction dumpster. She cut the plywood into a rectangular tabletop. She made the chairs that would go around the table out of the 2X4s and squares cut from the scrap of plywood. A birthday cake made of plastic bags with candles would be at the center of the table. The people in the scene would be made entirely out of : her balloon bags filled with helium. Four "people" would be seated at the table. There would be real balloons tied to the backs of the wooden chairs. As she worked, she'd found that too many of her plastic bags from the dumpster were split or had holes in them. They were not holding the helium.

Virginia had labored over a solution to her problem and felt she finally had a breakthrough. That's why she was working late at night to put her "people" together, paint them, dress them, and seat them at the birthday party table. She was alarmed when she heard someone fiddling with the lock that secured the person door into the warehouse. Virginia never used that door, and it was locked all the time. She had bought a motor scooter which she rode around downtown Hoboken to do her dumpster diving and gather her supplies. She opened and closed the overhead garage doors with an automatic opener when she came and went from the warehouse on her scooter. No one ever used the person door. Becky had changed the locks on all the doors before Virginia had moved in, so no one except Virginia and Becky had a key.

But someone was definitely trying to get into the warehouse. Virginia could not imagine who might be trying to break in, but her mind went immediately to the people who had supplied Bubba with his drugs. She had lived in fear that somehow the people higher up on the drug-dealing chain with which Bubba had become involved would find out about her and come after her. Sidney had assured her she was safe, but Virginia had continued to live with the fear of exactly what seemed to be happening to her at this very moment.

Virginia didn't own a gun, but years ago she had secretly taken some self-defense classes behind Bubba's back. She'd been afraid that she would one day have to defend herself against the man she had married. If the intruder, who was trying to break into the lock on the person door of the warehouse, had a gun, she would be finished. She thought about escaping to her condo and hiding there, but she knew whoever was looking for her would hunt her down there, too. She decided she would rather battle things out in the warehouse itself. She turned out all the lights in the warehouse to make it more difficult for the intruder to see.

Virginia did have some extra pieces of wood that she had left over from creating her artwork, and she grabbed a short piece of a 2X4. She stood by the person door, waiting for the unknown intruder to get in. The man who finally let himself into the warehouse was a short, dark, skinny man with black curly hair. He was not anyone Virginia had ever seen before. Virginia's eyes had become accustomed to the dark, so she could see the man when he broke into the warehouse. He could not see her. She hit him on the head with the 2x4 and brought him down. But she didn't hit him hard enough, and he scrambled back to his feet and went after her.

"I not think there be person here. I think warehouse be empty." It was almost an apology. The man spoke broken English and had an accent of some kind. He was not really a fighter. He didn't have a gun and went after Virginia with his fists. He swung his arms wildly and hit Virginia in the face. He struck again and knocked her to the ground. She twisted her knee when she went down, but she got right back up, ready to keep on fighting. Her self-defense training kicked in, and she made quick work of the little skinny guy. He'd been out-classed in the fighting department before he'd even started.

Virginia sat on him. "Who sent you here? Why did you break into my warehouse?"

"Nobody send me. I think warehouse is empty. I not think anybody is here. I just came for money. Some of money is left behind. They all dead but Vasily. Nobody know I'm alive. I just come for my share of Benjamin bills."

"If you are here for the drugs, I don't have anything to do with that."

"Drugs? I don't know with drugs. What is with drugs?"

Virginia knew she should call the police. This man had broken into her place. She didn't trust law enforcement because of her experiences in Arkansas with Bubba's cousin who was a deputy sheriff. She didn't know what to do with the man she had captured. She had her cell phone in her pocket and called her friend Becky. Becky would know what to do. Over the phone, Virginia told Becky everything that had happened with the break-in and the fight and what the man had said to her.

"I really don't think he has anything to do with Bubba or the drugs. He said he thought the warehouse would be empty."

Becky had her own opinion about what the man was doing there. "I think he's connected to the people who rented the warehouse and the condo before you moved in. They paid rent for the entire year, and then they left after less than two months — and they left in a big hurry in the middle of the night. I suspected they might be into counterfeiting money. I'll tell you sometime why I think that. I don't know why they left, but I was sure they were doing something illegal. For some reason, they must have been spooked and had to relocate. I don't know anything for sure about why they left, but I do feel like this is my fault."

"What am I going to do with this guy I'm sitting on? Yes, I am quite literally sitting on him to keep him from attacking me again."

"Are you hurt? Do you have anything you can tie him up with until I can get there?"

"I'm only hurt a little bit. He smacked me in the face, and he kicked my legs out from under me. Just about the same things Bubba used to do to me. Except Bubba didn't hit me in the face because he didn't want any outward signs to show other people what a bastard he was."

"I really think we should call 911, but I understand why you don't want to do that. I understand why you don't want to involve any official law enforcement people. That's okay with me, but we have to be sure this turkey doesn't come back to the warehouse. He didn't find what he wanted. He didn't get whatever it was he came for. If we just let him go, he might try to break in again. I will be there as fast as I can, but I'm almost an hour away. I'm going to send someone immediately, someone from New Jersey who is closer to you. He's a friend of mine. He will arrive ahead of me, and he will take the man away and deal with him. I'm coming to check on you and take a look at your injuries. You have a big night coming up this week. You have to look your best."

"Send your man and tell him to hurry. The person door at the side of the warehouse is wide open. Tell whoever it is to come in that way. I am sitting on this guy right inside the door."

Virginia had been distracted by the phone call with Becky. The man she had captured took advantage of her not paying attention. He pretended to be unconscious, and all of a sudden he summoned a burst of energy and freed himself from lying underneath Virginia. He threw her off his body and knocked her to the floor. He wasted no time making his way to the door he'd used to enter the warehouse, and he was gone. Virginia was nursing her wounds. She was glad he had disappeared but worried that he might come back. He didn't seem to have anything to do with Bubba or the people who Bubba had been hanging out with in the drug business.

Virginia groaned as her eye began to ache. Her legs were already showing where they'd been bruised in the fight. She hurt all over her entire body. There was no way she was ever going to look her best for the night of the gallery opening. The adrenalin surge she had summoned to fight the intruder had now faded, and she didn't have the energy to move. She lay on the floor, trying to recover enough to sit up and assess her injuries. She called Becky back to tell her the man she'd temporarily captured had escaped. There was no need to send anyone to deal with the intruder. The little man was gone.

Virginia examined her legs. When she tried to stand up, she had to grab hold of the wall for help. She knew she was in trouble and wondered if she would even be able to walk. When she finally worked up the courage to look at her face, she realized she was going to have a whopper of a shiner around her right eye. She would not look good on the opening night of her show. She was able to get herself into a chair. She was in pain and didn't want to move. She sat as still as she could at the table in the warehouse and waited for Becky.

Becky finally arrived with a first aid kit and some shopping bags. She examined Virginia's face and was relieved that the black eye was the only thing that would remain on her face as evidence of the attack. It was not a serious injury; it was just an ugly one. As she went to the freezer in the condo to get ice for Virginia's injuries, Becky made a note to herself to buy a beautiful eye patch for Virginia to wear to the gallery opening. The leg injuries were another story. Virginia was limping badly when she tried to walk, and she admitted that she was in considerable pain. Nothing was broken as far as Becky could tell. Except for the bruises and the very dramatic black eye, Virginia didn't really look that badly hurt. The skin on her legs wasn't broken, but Virginia was hobbling. It looked as if she would have to hobble for a while before her legs healed. Becky made another note to herself to buy a beautiful cane for Virginia to use at the gallery opening.

They applied ice to both injuries. Virginia was exhausted and just wanted to climb into bed and sleep. The intruder had arrived in the middle of the night, and it was now very early in the morning. Becky had brought clothes for Virginia to try on...clothes she'd bought for the artist to wear to the gallery opening. Even though it was the middle of the night, Becky was here and the clothes were here, so Virginia would try on the clothes.

"Fortunately, I picked leggings and a tunic top for you to wear rather than a dress. If I'd chosen the cute mini-dress, which I almost bought for you, it would have had to be returned. We have to hide those bruises on your legs. Artists almost always wear black to gallery openings. There is more than one reason for that, but mainly they wear black because it doesn't detract from the artwork."

"How do you know these things?" The talented but basically naïve artist from rural Arkansas was happy to be advised by the more sophisticated New Yorker.

"I have attended so many gallery openings…trust me. I know what I am talking about."

"I do trust you. What about my eye?"

"The swelling will have gone down in a few days, but you are going to have one heck of a shiner. And that's going to last for more than a week. I'm going to buy you a very sexy eyepatch to wear the night of the opening. Can you manage that? You will also be using a cane. You are going to need a cane anyway. But the eyepatch and the cane will create a certain mystique and make you even more intriguing than you already are. No one has ever seen you in person. No one who's going to be at the opening…including the owner of the gallery…knows what you look like. I'm really the only one who knows you here in the New York area. I've wanted to keep you a secret until the opening. That's one reason I always picked up your artwork and delivered it to the gallery myself. I didn't want anyone at the gallery to get even a glimpse of you until Saturday."

Becky paused and then decided to continue telling the rest of the story to Virginia. "You know, Sidney didn't even want you to show up in person at the gallery opening. When I told her that idea was out of the question, she insisted you had to wear a disguise, or at least a wig. I told her no. But she's going to get a little bit of what she wanted because the eye patch will hide part of your face. And the cane will be a distraction. But first we have to get the swelling down."

Becky pulled some clothes out of an expensive-looking shopping bag. She held up a soft and beautiful black cashmere outfit of leggings and a scoop neck tunic top. She gave the outfit to Virginia to try on. Both pieces fit perfectly. The scoop neck was a little too low cut for Virginia's tastes, but she loved the look otherwise. Becky pulled a shoebox out of a second shopping bag. "Black leather flats. I bought these before I knew you were going to be using a cane, but they are the latest thing. They are handmade and soft and just scream success. They cost more than all these other clothes put together. And, I'm loaning you my mother's gorgeous triple strand of pearls...just to wear for the night. I'm sorry you were attacked and got hurt. But I have to say, the eyepatch and the cane are going to make you unbelievably wonderful at your opening. The cane and the eyepatch will be a distraction, as the low-cut top will be. No one will be looking closely at your face. You look the part of a newly discovered and up-and-coming New York artist. You will wow them. You don't have to say a word. Just show up and limp around a bit. They will love you, and they will love your work."

Virginia was very sore and very tired. She was past ready to go back to bed. She loved the image Becky was creating for her, but she needed to rest after everything she'd been through. She promised to keep ice on her eye and on her leg. But both women knew that something had to be done immediately to permanently close the person door of the warehouse. Changing the locks had not been sufficient to keep out the intruder who had broken in that night. Becky knew people, and she would call that day for someone to install sturdy metal bars across the door. She wanted Virginia to be safe and to feel safe.

First thing the next morning, Becky made arrangements for the warehouse door to be secured. She texted Virginia that she would be returning to supervise the project. Becky was doing a great deal of driving back and forth from Manhattan to Hoboken. After the work on the warehouse door had been completed, she would be back once more before the day of the opening. She would be coming to pick up Virginia's newest surprise creation for the gallery opening. And of course, Becky was coming to Hoboken early on the day of the opening to do Virginia's makeup.

*W*hen Becky came to pick up Virginia at the warehouse in Hoboken on Saturday evening, she arrived in a long, black limousine. She wanted Virginia Delacroix to make a grand entrance at the gallery opening. Virginia was awed and a little frightened by the luxury and the expense of hiring a limousine. She was at heart still a young woman who had been until very recently living on a farm in Arkansas. She was still trying to build back her self-esteem after having been married to an abusive husband. She had accepted the expensive cashmere outfit and the outrageously expensive shoes Becky had bought for her to wear to the opening. But the arrival of the limousine seemed over the top. The driver even wore a limo driver's cap.

The limousine and driver waited in the warehouse outside the condo while Becky did Virginia's makeup and put the finishing touches on her outfit. The eyepatch completely covered the artist's black eye, and Virginia welcomed the cane which kept her from falling and eased the pain she was still feeling in her legs. When Virginia Delacroix was dressed and ready to leave for her big event, Becky took some photos with her phone and texted them to Sidney Richardson.

Sidney texted Becky:

```
Who is this? It can't be Ginny. She looks fab-
ulous and so sophisticated...like she's always
lived in New York City. Amazing. No one will
recognize her. Good work, Becky. Wish her the
best of luck this evening. S.
```

Becky sent a text back to Sidney:

```
This isn't Ginny. This is Virginia Delacroix,
artist extraordinaire, the hottest and most
creative new personality on the New York art
gallery scene.
```

Becky had kept Sidney up to date about what was happening with Virginia. She'd told Sidney about the break-in and about Virginia's injuries. So Sidney was not surprised to see the eyepatch or the cane. Becky had brought a black wool cape of her own for Virginia to wear to the special event in Soho. She knew Virginia didn't have a coat that was warm enough and, at the same time, elegant enough to wear in December. It was a week before Christmas, and snow was expected later that evening. Virginia and Becky climbed into the back of the limousine. Virginia wanted to pinch herself. She'd never ridden in a limousine before. She'd only seen limousines on television shows and in movies. She'd never actually seen one in person before. Now she was riding in the back of one, and someone else was driving. They were on their way.

The gallery opening was scheduled for 4-6 on Saturday evening. This gave the *New York Times* plenty of time for their art critic to file his story for their print edition of the Sunday paper. There would also be an online version. Most critics of all kinds filed online stories these days. Virginia and Becky arrived purposely late so Virginia could make a grand entrance. Becky was at her side. The limousine driver put her cap on the seat, handed the keys of the limousine to the valet, and assumed the role of bodyguard.

Both the driver/bodyguard and Becky were dressed in stylish black leather outfits, and they accompanied Virginia into the gallery. Becky was on one side of Virginia, and the limo driver was on the other side. They were there to lend a certain panache to Virginia's entrance, but they were also there to be sure she didn't fall. The upscale gallery was located in SoHo, an artsy neighborhood in New York City. Virginia did not know the differences in the various neighborhoods of New York City, so she did not fully realize at what a fancy place her artwork was being showcased.

The flurry of activity inside the gallery came to a halt as the three entered the packed throng of art lovers, rich people, and potential buyers. Everyone stared at the woman with the eyepatch and the cane. Someone began to clap, and then someone else shouted "Bravo!" They loved her. They loved her art. Virginia blushed and smiled and laughed at the applause, and she relaxed a little bit.

The three made the rounds of the gallery. The crowd watched. Virginia Delacroix choked and almost fainted when she saw the prices the gallery had put on her artwork. She looked at Becky with alarm in her eyes. Becky put her finger in front of her lips so Virginia wouldn't say anything. Becky whispered to Virginia that they would talk later.

Virginia's piece, *Take Me Out*, had its own small room. The sculpture of the plastic and Styrofoam woman looked wonderful in the room which had been painted especially for the opening and had just the right lighting to show off the sculpture. The piece had a sticker that said "SOLD" over the price tag. Virginia couldn't believe the piece had already been sold. She'd only just arrived. She wasn't that late. How had it been sold so quickly? When Virginia looked at the price the gallery had put on her work, she gasped out loud. The gallery had asked one hundred thousand dollars for Virginia's sculpture made from plastic and Styrofoam take-out containers. The amount the gallery had asked for the sculpture was stunning to Virginia. What was even more stunning to her was that someone had been willing to pay that much money to acquire Virginia's work of art.

"I think I'm going to be sick. I can't do this." Virginia was in shock at the prices her art objects were commanding. She felt lightheaded and as if she wasn't really there in her body. She was dissociating. "You're worth it, dear." Becky said. "I knew this would happen. So did Sidney. Congratulations. Enjoy it. You are a star. You are also hungry and thirsty. Let's walk by the buffet table. You can tell me what you like." She took Virginia by the arm and guided her past four tables of elaborate hors d'oeuvres.

"I don't eat raw fish. I got sick on it once and have never been able to eat it since." They turned away and didn't finish walking the length of the crowded and extravagant sushi bar. They went to the table where hot food was being served. "I think I could eat one of those little roast beef sandwiches. Who even knew they made buns that small? Yes, I love horseradish. And I love stuffed mushrooms…as long as they aren't stuffed with liver or with something else weird. Anything from that other table will be fine, too. I like all kinds of vegetables and fresh fruit." She paused to catch her breath. "I can't believe this is all for me." She didn't even look at the beautiful dessert table.

Someone brought a chair for Virginia to sit on. Becky knew Virginia didn't drink alcohol, so she brought her ginger ale in a champagne flute. It looked like Virginia was drinking champagne. The bodyguard, whose name Virginia didn't know, brought her a plate of food. Becky told Virginia to eat something. "Eat. You'll feel better if you raise your blood sugar." Becky was giving orders. She knew how to take care of this ingénue in the art world whose life had just changed dramatically.

The owner of the gallery came up to Virginia to congratulate her. He told her this was the most successful opening he had ever sponsored and praised her creativity and the precision with which she executed her work. He asked her what her inspiration had been to create these artistic miracles out of found objects. Virginia Delacroix was able to answer that question with complete honesty.

"I work with things that other people throw away. I dumpster dive. I like to recycle something nobody else wants into something I think is beautiful. It's what I do to help save the planet and at the same time express my own artistic soul." This was a quote for the ages. The art critics standing around watching Virginia all had her comments recorded on their phones.

Becky had told her not to talk too much at the opening. This would add to her mystique, the image of intrigue and mystery she was trying to convey. Becky had told her to try to disguise her voice a little…maybe with a fake British accent. They were both afraid her soft Arkansas drawl might give away her true origins. Virginia had adopted a somewhat British accent on top of her Southern accent. It was a delightful and unique brogue which no one would ever be able to pin down exactly. An art critic, who had never been to New Zealand, would write later in the evening that Virginia had an accent which definitely pegged her as being from New Zealand. Because no one in New York City had ever heard of her before, the critics believed she must have come from someplace exotic and very far away.

After Virginia had eaten something and said a few words, Becky told the gallery owner they had to leave. The owner protested and said he didn't want Virginia to miss out on the auctioning of her surprise piece, *Birthday Balloons*. It was also in its own special room, and the gallery owner said he expected it to be sold for a very high price. Virginia was beyond caring at this point. She was worn out. Her injuries were aching. She wanted to go back to her condo and lie down in her own bed. Becky was gracious and told the gallery owner that Virginia could not stay any longer. The bodyguard had the valet bring the limo to the gallery door, and they left.

Before they drove away from the gallery, Virginia tapped the driver and bodyguard on the shoulder. "I don't know your name, but you seem to be someone who is important to me. Who are you?"

The bodyguard laughed. "I'm your agent. My name is Susanna Craig. I'm a friend of Becky's, and we thought it would add to the mystery of your persona if you had an agent who was also a mystery. This limo is owned by my cousin Marvin who lives in Newark. It didn't cost us anything for the limousine…except for the gas. Marvin runs a limousine and sedan rental service. He insisted that I be the one to drive his limo. He wants to know all about the gallery opening…what they served to eat, how they liked your artwork, how much it was selling for, and all that sort of detail. That's what he gets in return for this freebie…all the details. Marvin was thrilled to lend this stretch limo to us for the evening."

Virginia was tired, but she laughed when Susanna told her the limo belonged to her cousin and that they'd had it all evening for free. She felt better knowing that no one had paid big bucks for the fancy ride. "And what does an agent do for me? Are you really an agent?"

"I'm an agent now…as of today. I teach art history at a private school on Long Island, and I also have an MBA. I'm doing this agent thing for fun. But if it becomes too much fun, I might quit my teaching job and become an agent full time. Don't worry. I'm just practicing on you. I'm not charging you anything to be your agent. Although after seeing what your artwork is selling for, I might decide to send you a bill." Susanna laughed. Virginia fell asleep in the limo on the way back to Hoboken. Becky roused her gently when they arrived at the warehouse.

Virginia thanked Susanna and Becky for all they'd done to make the evening memorable for her. The artist was overwhelmed and exhausted. The limo pulled into the warehouse, and Becky walked Virginia to her condo. Virginia promised to go right to bed and not stay up late working on her art. Apparently, every one of the pieces Virginia had displayed at the gallery opening had been sold. This sellout was a first for the gallery. Those who had not been able to buy what they wanted and those who wanted to buy more than they'd already bought, had left orders and deposits for more of Virginia's artwork.

Virginia glanced briefly at the list of orders. "Look at this. A Mrs. Gordon Westover wants ten of the plastic fork houses. She wants each one in a different color, and she is sending me paint chips with the colors she wants. Who would ever want ten of those?"

Becky knew fame could be intrusive and exhausting. She assured Virginia that she and Susanna, the new agent, were there to try to protect Virginia from all of the pressure and the unpleasantness. Becky told the tired and over-whelmed Virginia that she would be in touch with Sidney Richardson that night and would tell her about everything that had happened at the opening. Becky told Virginia to call her in the morning, and she would come over so they could debrief the previous evening's event. Becky would bring bagels for breakfast. Virginia was to call her when she woke up the next day…even if it was at two o'clock in the afternoon. Virginia remembered to return the triple strand of pearls that were on loan from Becky.

Virginia took off her black cashmere outfit, the very costly leather shoes, and the eyepatch. She fell into bed. She didn't even take time to brush her teeth or put on her nightgown. She was too tired and too flabbergasted by her new success. When she woke up in the middle of the night, because she heard noises she thought were coming from the warehouse, she wished she'd at least taken off her makeup and washed her face. She couldn't help but want to know what had awakened her. She threw on a bathrobe and made her way out into the warehouse. It sounded as if someone was inside the warehouse throwing things around or searching for something.

When she arrived in the warehouse, Virginia couldn't believe her eyes. She didn't see anyone, but someone had definitely been there. Whoever had broken into her workspace had pulled most of her supplies off the built-in shelves along the wall. Virginia was an organized person, and she kept her work materials meticulously sorted and inventoried. Her supplies and everything else was on the floor. The place was a mess. She was much too tired to deal with it all in the middle of the night. Who had invaded her space, and what in the world had they been trying to find?

Virginia sighed in frustration and began to pick up a few of the thousands of things that had been scattered all over the floor of her work area. She really wanted to sit down at one of the tables and cry. As she gathered her energy and leaned over to begin the cleanup, she was hit over the head with something very hard. She fell on her face and lay unconscious on the floor in the middle of the mess.

When Virginia regained consciousness, she found herself locked inside a very small closet. It was more of a niche in the brick wall than it was a real closet. If she'd been any bigger, she would not have been able to fit into the tiny space. As it was, she couldn't stretch out her legs or arms or sit up straight. Virginia suffered some from claustrophobia, and being stuffed into this cramped enclosure was putting her into a full-blown anxiety attack. Her head ached, and in the confined space, she had to almost dislocate her shoulder to reach behind her head. When she felt for the lump she knew would be on the back of her head, her fingers touched a wound that was streaming with blood. She realized she'd left her cell phone charging beside her bed. She couldn't call for help. She could barely breathe, and she was desperate to get out of this box, this awful claustrophobic place where she found herself.

It seemed like she had been imprisoned forever in the wall or whatever it was. After what seemed like a very long time, she thought she heard Becky's voice coming from somewhere. She screamed as loudly as she could, "Becky, Becky are you there? I'm here…closed up in the wall. Please find me and get me out of here. Somebody hit me over the head and closed me up in this little place. I have to get out. Please come and get me. Can you hear me?" When she heard nothing in reply to her screams and no one came to free her, she wondered if she had imagined hearing Becky's voice. Maybe she had been hallucinating. Maybe it was just wishful thinking that she thought someone had come to find her. Virginia slipped into unconsciousness again.

Becky had been exhausted, too, after the gallery opening festivities and the long trips driving back and forth from New York City to Hoboken. She'd put forth her best efforts to present Virginia Delacroix to the public and at the same time keep her cloaked in mystery. She did not want to reveal too much about the real person behind the image she'd created for Virginia. Many artists are reclusive and unconventional and shun the limelight. The new artist on the block, Virginia Delacroix, was one of these. She had made an impressive appearance at her gallery opening. Now she would retreat into her somewhat hermit-like and introverted artistic life style.

The art critic at the *New York Times* had begun his piece with Virginia's own quote: "I work with things that other people throw away...." It was a rave review. All the critics were singing her praises. Although she was delighted for Virginia's success, Becky felt like it was overkill. But clearly the art lovers of NYC had been hungry for somebody new to arrive on the scene. Virginia Delacroix was being lauded as "The Artist of Climate Change." Becky thought this was stretching things. Virginia might be the artist of recycling, but climate change... really? Becky bought extra copies of the newspaper to send to Sidney and to give to Virginia. She forwarded the online reviews of the showing to Virginia's phone and to Sidney's phone. It turned out that Birthday Balloons had brought close to a million dollars in the auction that had taken place after Becky and Virginia had left the gallery the night before. Even Becky, who was well aware of the excesses of those who lived in New York City, felt this amount that someone had paid for plastic bags and helium was obscene. Some people had more money than they knew what do to with. Some people had more money than they had common sense.

All in all she was thrilled with Virginia's success. She knew Virginia had struggled financially all of her life, and Becky was beyond thrilled that the young woman would never have to be poor again. Becky kept waiting to hear from Virginia. She'd anticipated that Virginia would be sleeping late and probably wouldn't call her before noon. But when she'd not heard anything from her by five in the afternoon and after repeated calls to the artist's cell phone had gone unanswered, Becky decided to drive to Hoboken to see if Virginia was all right.

ecky had her own garage door opener to allow her to drive her car into the warehouse. It was impossible to find any place to park on the street in this part of Hoboken, so she always drove directly into the warehouse to park. Virginia didn't have a car, so there was plenty of room for Becky's Mercedes. When she drove into Virginia's workspace the day after the gallery opening, Becky saw immediately that someone had ransacked the warehouse. Virginia wasn't anywhere to be seen. Becky quickly got out of her car and ran to the condo. She searched everywhere for Virginia. Becky looked in every closet and under the beds, but the artist was nowhere to be found.

Much later, it occurred to Becky that she should have been more concerned that the intruder who had trashed the warehouse might still be there somewhere. But of course, her first instinct had been to find Virginia. Virginia's bed was unmade. Becky knew Virginia made her bed religiously every morning. And Virginia's phone was charging beside her bed. Becky was terrified that the artist, who by now had also become her friend, had been kidnapped. No one was in the condo, and no one was in the warehouse. What had happened to Virginia?

Becky hated to involve law enforcement. She knew how skittish Virginia was about calling on the authorities for any reason. Becky understood and respected Virginia's fears, but this situation went beyond consideration for Virginia's distrust of the police. Virginia had disappeared. Becky called 911. While she waited for the police to arrive, Becky accessed the surveillance cameras she'd had installed inside and outside the warehouse. Becky had installed these security measures before Virginia had moved into the warehouse. Becky usually would have hesitated to view the surveillance videos because she didn't want to intrude on Virginia's privacy, but this was an emergency. Becky needed to find out what had happened.

As Becky watched the videos, she was shocked and terribly upset to see that the same man who had broken into the warehouse and attacked Virginia before the gallery opening was the same man who had again broken into the warehouse the night before and trashed it. The man was obviously looking for something, and he seemed determined to find it. Becky did not have any idea who this man was who had invaded Virginia's home and workplace, but she felt somewhat responsible. She'd suspected that the previous renters at the warehouse had been doing something illegal. She'd been delighted when they'd left in the middle of the night one night, months before their year-long rental agreement ran out. Becky suspected that this recent intruder was somehow connected to the previous occupant's gang of low life criminals.

The man in the video had to be the person who had done something with Virginia. Becky was frantic to find the young woman whose life had, only the night before, taken an enormous turn for the better. It seemed like Virginia just could not get a break from bad luck. She'd escaped from her life with Bubba, but now a new and persistent adversary had arrived to bedevil her. The intruder had broken into her place twice, and now he was gone.

Becky watched all the surveillance videos. They were motion activated. She saw the mystery man tear everything out of the shelves along the wall. He must have heard someone coming because all of a sudden, he hid. Then she saw Virginia appear in the warehouse in her bathrobe. Becky saw her bend over to begin to clean up the mess the intruder had made. She watched in horror as the intruder hit Virginia over the head with a crowbar. Blood began to flow from Virginia's head. Becky was gripped with fear when she saw how hard the man had struck her.

He let her lie on the floor for a while, bleeding and unconscious, as he continued to tear the place apart. Finally, he seemed to give up his search and dragged Virginia closer to the shelves that he'd just emptied. He stuck his arm deep into one of the shelves, and after a few seconds, a section of the shelving swung open. A small niche was revealed behind the shelves. The walls of the warehouse were brick and the space in the wall looked as if it might have once been part of a coal chute. The niche was empty, and it was very small.

The man dragged Virginia, who was now covered with blood, into the space and stuffed her into the crevice. He roughly folded her arms and legs to force her to fit into the small space in the wall. Becky cringed when she saw how brutal he had been with Virginia's unconscious body and when she saw how he'd bent and pushed her limbs in order to force her into the niche. Becky could not imagine how uncomfortable Virginia would be if she ever regained con-sciousness in that enclosed and claustrophobic place. But at least Becky now knew exactly where Virginia was.

The intruder had left the crowbar behind on the floor, and Becky grabbed it to begin to rescue Virginia. She was determined to tear the shelves apart with the crowbar if she had to. But Becky decided she would first try to open the shelves the way the bad man had opened them. She replayed the relevant section of the video and watched carefully which shelf he'd reached into. She suspected she would find some kind of mechanism, a button or a lever, inside the shelf that would open the shelves and reveal the hiding place. Becky reached her arm into the shelf she thought was the right one. Her hand found the lever, and she pulled on it. Sure enough, a section of shelving swung open, and there was poor Virginia stuffed into the open space in the wall and drenched in blood.

Becky did her best to be gentle and at the same time quickly free Virginia from her tiny prison. She lay the young woman on the floor of the warehouse and ran to her car to grab a blanket. She knelt down beside the artist. She spread the blanket over Virginia and then dialed 911 again to request an ambulance. As it turned out the ambulance arrived before the police arrived. Becky was determined to go to the ER with Virginia. She called 911 again and told the operator to put a hold on sending the police. Becky explained she was going to the hospital with her friend and that no one would be at the scene of the crime to let the police in. Becky promised to give law enforcement a full explanation after she made sure her friend was all right.

While they were in the ambulance on the way to the hos-pital, the EMTs were able to stop the bleeding on the back of

Virginia's head. Fortunately, once Virginia had been rendered unconscious, it didn't look as if the intruder had continued to attack her with the crowbar. He hadn't done anything else to hurt her, but he'd been terribly cruel about the way he'd handled her body as he stuffed her into the wall niche.

No one might ever know what his real motive was for why he'd sealed her up in the wall behind the shelves. He might have wanted her out of the way temporarily so he could continue his search for whatever he was looking for. He certainly knew, from the experience of his first break-in, that she had self-defense skills and could give him a run for his money in the fighting department. Or he may have imprisoned her in the wall hoping she would die there. Becky realized that, until the intruder was caught, Virginia would continue to be at risk. This very bad actor was not going to give up until he found what he was looking for. And whatever that was, he thought it was hidden someplace in the warehouse.

Becky knew Virginia didn't have any health insurance. When anyone arrives at the ER, the first thing the hospital always wants to see is insurance cards. Becky signed the papers promising to cover the costs of Virginia's care. The young doctor who saw Virginia had to shave off some of her hair before he could sew up the lacerations on the back of her head. She had thirteen stitches, and then she had an MRI to check for possible brain damage. She had a concussion, but the imaging studies didn't show any serious or permanent damage to her skull or brain. She would have a bad headache for several days, but the ER doctor promised she would be fine after a period of rest, recovery, and healing.

Becky wanted to take Virginia back to her own apartment in New York to recuperate. Becky felt strongly that Virginia would be safer if she stayed away from the warehouse...at least until the police found and arrested the man who kept breaking in there. But Virginia, who was now awake but foggy, insisted on returning to her condo in the warehouse. The place had become home to her, and in spite of the attacks that had happened there, she craved the comfort of her home. Becky reluctantly agreed to take Virginia back to the warehouse. Because she was the one who had rented the condo and the warehouse to Virginia, Becky felt responsible for what had happened to her.

The police showed up at the ER to question Virginia and Becky. The doctor wouldn't allow them to talk to Virginia until she said she was ready. But Becky was able to tell law enforcement everything they needed to know. She explained exactly what had happened…all about both break-ins. She was able to show the two detectives who questioned her everything from the surveillance videos on her phone. She showed them the videos, and then she sent the evidence of the break-ins and the attacks on Virginia to their cell phones. She promised to meet them back at the warehouse as soon as Virginia was cleared to leave the hospital.

After what seemed like hours waiting at the hospital and a lot of paperwork, Becky finally put Virginia and herself into an Uber. They were home in a few minutes, and Becky made sure that Virginia was comfortable. Virginia was not supposed to go to sleep for several hours because of the concussion. Becky wanted to call a nursing service and hire someone to care for Virginia, but she had long ago promised the frightened woman she would not bring anyone into Virginia's private space. After a few hours, Virginia would be allowed to go to sleep, but someone had to wake her every few hours and question her to be sure she knew her name and where she was. That someone was going to have to be

Becky. Becky was going to have to take care of Virginia on her own.

Virginia hardly ever left the warehouse and the condo. She had, until now, considered this to be her safe space. She ordered her groceries and everything else online and had it all delivered. She had the deliveries left with the pizza restaurant. Becky's friend who owned the place brought Virginia's groceries and other deliveries to her and left them outside the garage door of the warehouse. Through her extensive security camera system, Virginia was able to keep an eye on the arrival of the deliveries. As soon as Becky's friend from the pizza place left, Virginia retrieved her groceries or her medications or whatever else she'd had delivered. She was that determined not to allow anyone to come inside her warehouse, and she was equally determined that no one would see what she looked like. Becky hoped Virginia would begin to get over these obviously intense and inconvenient fears, but it seemed as if being comfortable around others was going to take Virginia considerably more time.

The police arrived with a team of crime scene investigators. They took hundreds of photographs and lifted hundreds of fingerprints. The appearance of law enforcement at the warehouse also violated Becky's promise to Virginia, but it could not be avoided. Virginia was resting in the bedroom of her condo and did not actually see how many people were going through her things and taking photos. They would have finished collecting evidence and would be gone before Virginia knew they'd been there. The police, of course, wanted to question Virginia, but they'd been warned off by the ER doctor. Becky was also determined to keep them away from Virginia. She knew Virginia would not be happy to have to talk to the police.

Becky told the police she had no idea what the intruder was looking for. He'd mumbled something about "the money" on the surveillance videos from the first break-in. His English was broken, or so it seemed from the few words he'd spoken. Becky had arranged for the condo and the warehouse to be thoroughly cleaned before Virginia moved in. Becky knew there was no money hidden anywhere. At least she didn't think there was. But she certainly had not known anything about the hidden niche in the wall. It occurred to her that maybe there was another niche somewhere that contained "the money."

Virginia needed to rest and take it easy. Becky knew if she left her alone, she would soon insist on coming to the warehouse to clean up after the ransacking by the intruder. As soon as the police and the crime scene people had finished their work, Becky called her emergency clean-up service to come at once and try to restore some order to Virginia's workspace. Becky had these cleaners on retainer. She and another real estate agent kept them busy cleaning their listings. Becky knew these people would come in the middle of night, if that was what was needed. They charged through the nose for the immediate and off-hours response, but Becky felt it was worth it to have them come to the warehouse to keep Virginia from attempting to clean it up herself. This was another intrusion from the outside that Virginia wouldn't like, but Becky intended to oversee their work. She knew everyone on the cleaning staff, and they too would be gone before Virginia was able to return to see the condition of the warehouse.

Explaining to the clean-up people was complicated. Many of the things that looked to them like trash to be thrown away were in fact Virginia's art supplies. Fortunately Virginia had labeled each shelf of the built-in wall unit. This made the cleaning process easier. The cleaning team could mostly figure out where to put things away. They were used to cleaning up places after fingerprints had been taken by the police. Dark smudges were left on everything, so the cleaners took care of that, too. Becky herself cleaned up Virginia's blood from the niche in the wall. The cleaning company people didn't need to know about the niche or the blood. At last, the warehouse was clean again. All traces of the intruder, including the blood, were gone. It wasn't exactly the way Virginia would have organized it, but it was a huge improvement over the mess the mystery intruder had left behind.

Becky made chicken broth with noodles for Virginia to eat. She made her cups of green tea with honey. She helped her with a shower and carefully washed the blood out of her hair without getting the bandages or her stitches wet. She put Virginia to bed after the danger period from the concussion had elapsed. After the cleaning people left, Becky slept in the guest room of the condo for what was left of the night. She hoped to be able to convince Virginia that she needed to hire some help, but she realized that was probably not going to happen.

The next morning, Becky was toasting the bagels she'd brought the day before. Becky had slept late, and Virginia slept even later. It had been a crazy and disturbing and exhausting twenty-four hours for both Virginia and Becky. Virginia made an appearance in the kitchen of the condo and sat at the table. Becky thought she looked terrible, but she didn't say that to Virginia. The artist looked like she had been in a serious fist fight. Her face was black and blue, and she had two black eyes from where she had fallen on her face after being hit with the crowbar. Her hair was a mess because whoever had put the stitches in her head and shaved her hair had been more interested in an immediate medical solution than in a cosmetic one. Becky made a note to herself to get Virginia to a hairdresser who might be able to repair some of the damage to Virginia's hairstyle.

"The most important thing is that you are okay. You were found in time, before you became too dehydrated or suffered too much from being forced into that tiny space." Becky could tell that Virginia's entire body was sore. She had used the cane to walk into the kitchen, and she was limping badly. When she sat at the kitchen table, Becky could see that she had bruises and small abrasions all over her legs. She imagined that Virginia's arms were similarly bruised and cut.

"I'm thankful I am still alive. You told me it was the same man who came back the second time, the same man who broke in and fought with me before the gallery opening. How do I know he won't come back a third time? He seems determined to find something he thinks is hidden here. And how did he get in the second time? He doesn't have a key or a garage door opener, and we had bars installed across that person door into the warehouse."

"He made his way in through that person door again. You can see how he cut through the metal bars. We are going to have to have that door completely walled closed. I will arrange it today." Becky turned her attention to her phone. Something had to be done about the door. New locks and metal bars were not keeping trouble out. She needed a construction crew and a brick mason to make the warehouse secure. And she needed them that day.

"I want to see the video footage from the surveillance cameras. I want to see what this man really looks like and what he did when he was here."

"Are you sure you want to see all of that? It's very disturbing. It was terribly upsetting for me to watch what happened. He tears the place apart. He bangs you on the head with a crowbar. Are you sure you want to see how he folded your unconscious body into the wall?"

"Yes, I definitely want to see everything there is to see. It will help me to understand what has happened to me, and maybe I will be able to figure out why this guy keeps coming back here."

They watched the surveillance videos together. Virginia was visibly shaken as she watched herself being attacked and her cherished workroom being destroyed. Seeing the destruction exhausted her, and after she'd eaten half a bagel and had a glass of orange juice, she went back to bed. Becky wondered if it had been a mistake to show Virginia the videos, but it was too late to undo that now. Becky wanted to talk to the police again. She wanted to know if they'd made any progress finding the man who'd done the damage to the warehouse and to Virginia.

Becky thought the intruder was acting on his own. At the back of her mind was always the fear that the men who'd gone into business with Bubba had decided to come after Virginia. But Becky didn't think the man who had broken into the warehouse was connected to the drug people. If the police could find this little man who kept coming back and breaking in and put him in jail, Becky thought Virginia would be safe. If it was the drug people who had been in league with Bubba and if they had found her here in Hoboken, Becky was worried that Virginia might never be safe again.

All of the excitement with Virginia and the intruder had taken more time than Becky had counted on. She was behind in dealing with her real estate business. Fortunately, she was able to put out some fires and finalize some deals using her phone. She knew she had to get back to work soon, but she also felt obligated to lend a hand to Virginia in her recovery. She cared about Virginia and wanted to help her. Becky also wanted to give a push to the law enforcement people who were supposed to be searching for the intruder. She needed to get back to New York City and her day job, but she didn't feel she could leave Virginia alone in the warehouse condo until the mystery man was caught and put in jail.

Becky knew that Virginia had not felt like eating much of anything after the attack. She'd tried hard to finish the cup of chicken broth and noodles Becky had fixed for her the day before, and she'd eaten only part of a bagel this morning. When Virginia had left the hospital, the ER doctor had impressed on Becky that their patient needed to consume as many fluids as she could and try to eat at least a little bit of something. Becky knew that Virginia loved tuna salad. Virginia always had a container of the tuna in her refrigerator…made by Virginia from her own special recipe. Becky made two tuna sandwiches with slices of whole grain bread she found in Virginia's freezer.

When Virginia was awake, Becky insisted she come to the kitchen to eat something. Becky made a pitcher of iced tea and filled two plates with sandwiches and potato chips. She sat with Virginia and also ate a tuna sandwich. She urged Virginia to eat, and after a lot of encouragement, she finished the entire sandwich. As they were sitting at the kitchen table, Becky's phone rang. It was one of the detectives who was on Virginia's case. Becky hoped to hear some good news. She put her phone on speaker and propped it up against the salt and pepper shakers on the kitchen table so Virginia could also hear what the officer had to say.

"Hello, detective. This is Becky. What good news do you have to tell me?"

"Actually, I do have good news for you. We have your guy. We arrested him today, and we've been questioning him intensively."

"How did you find him? Tell me everything."

"We already had him on our radar screen…in our local database of people we were looking for. His name, he says, is Agron Zogolli, and he's a small-time crook who makes a living from burglaries. He's homeless part of the time, and we knew where to look for him. We brought him in and showed him some of the video from the warehouse, the video you sent to us. When he saw we had him on camera…trashing the warehouse and then attacking your friend, he decided to cooperate and tell us what he knows. At least he says he's going to tell us what he knows."

"Congratulations on picking him up so quickly. I'm impressed. Are you going to be able to hold him in jail, and do you have a case against him that will keep him away from here for a long time?"

"We intend to throw the book at him, but you know how judges are these days. It's all about the bad guy's rights, and the heck with the rights of law-abiding citizens. I can't make you any promises, but we're going to do all we can to lock him up for as long as we can."

"So, what's the story? What's he looking for here in the warehouse? It must be something valuable because he's certainly been persistent about coming back and searching again and again."

"I'll tell you what we know so far. We're still questioning the guy and it's slow going. He's Albanian. His English isn't very good, or at least he is pretending it isn't very good. He speaks Russian better than he speaks English, but his Russian isn't that good either. He speaks a dialect of Albanian called, or we think it's called, Gheg. We are looking for someone we can trust who knows this Albanian dialect. It's not easy to find someone like that, as you can imagine. And, of course, this bad guy is in the country illegally."

Both Becky and Virginia listened closely to everything the detective was saying. Both were worried that because he was in the country illegally, the immigration people would take over and set him free to prey on the public...along with all the millions of other illegals who were supposedly waiting on some kind of legal proceedings that would never happen. Becky and Virginia worried that the Albanian guy would be back and breaking into the warehouse again, as soon as he was set free.

It was as if the detective had read their minds. "Don't worry, we're ignoring the fact that he's here illegally. We don't intend to let him go under any circumstances. We intend to charge him and put him in prison. He's got a lot of other charges against him...in addition to breaking into your place. But you gave us the incriminating videos that will convict him. So thank you very much for that. We have him now."

"Why this warehouse? And what's he looking for? It's important to know what he wants here. The current tenant won't be safe until we sort this all out."

"It's difficult to get the straight story from him. Either he really can't communicate very well, or he's dragging his feet. What we have found out so far is pretty confusing. He says he used to work at the warehouse. He was hired to clean up every evening after the day workers had gone home. He says there was a business there in the warehouse that printed money. Or we think that's what he said. He keeps talking about some valuable plates. We think he means plates that print money, but he talks about them like they are dinner plates, plates you eat off of. He says the plates have disappeared, but then he also says something about the money that has disappeared. So we are not sure exactly what has disappeared. He keeps coming back to the warehouse to try to find the money or 'the plates' or both."

Becky had always suspected that the previous tenants had been involved in something illegal, and she'd even suspected them of printing counterfeit currency. Things that had happened when the rental agreements were being signed had led her to believe that something illegal was going on. And the few things that had been left behind after the tenants had abandoned the warehouse led her to suspect counterfeiting. She knew that the man who had actually signed the rental agreement to live in the condo had never stayed there. She suspected that no one had actually ever lived in the condo. Whoever had rented the warehouse had used the kitchen and the bathrooms, but no one had used either of the bedrooms.

Fire department regulations were strict about how many people were allowed to occupy the condo and how many people were allowed to work in the warehouse. Becky had been suspicious and had gone back to check on the condo and the warehouse several times. The tenants would never allow her to come inside. She'd demanded to talk to the man who had signed the rental agreement and said he was going to live in the condo. But he had never been there when Becky wanted to see him. Or, that's what she was always told. He'd never been available to talk to Becky, and she'd never seen him again after he signed the rental agreement papers. She was delighted when this very sketchy group had left the premises.

The previous renters had taken mostly everything with them, but Becky had found ink spilled on the floor in several places. She'd found part of a box of official-looking paper leaning beside the trash can. The trash had been removed from the trash can, but it looked as if someone had forgotten about the box that was left beside it. When Becky examined the paper more closely, she'd decided it was the kind of paper used to print real U.S. money. When she found the paper, she'd considered calling the authorities, but the people who'd rented the place were gone.

Becky saved the paper and had her cleaning people come in to give the place a first-rate cleaning job. They'd been able to get some of the ink off the floor, but there were several visible stains left after they'd done their best. It was a warehouse. There were stains on the floor from lots of things. It didn't seem as if any of the recent tenants had really used the condo. These previous occupants had left their fancy coffeemaker behind, and they hadn't stolen any of the furniture. As far as Becky could tell, there wasn't anything missing from the condo. She counted the dishes in the cupboards and the flatware in the drawers. It seemed as if hardly anything in the condo had been used, and everything seemed to be where it should be.

Becky knew the next question that was coming. The detective asked, "So you were the real estate agent who took care of the rental agreement for the previous tenants? Did you suspect that they were into anything illegal? Like counterfeiting money?"

"Actually, I did suspect they were doing something illegal here. I could never get into the property to check if they were abiding by the fire regulations. I came by several times to talk to the guy who'd signed the paperwork to rent the place, and he was never here. I began to suspect something was wrong. Then one night the previous occupants just left in the middle of the night. They never told me they were leaving or told me anything at all. When they left, they didn't take anything that didn't belong to them…as far as I could tell. I did find some paper after they left. The paper looked to me like the kind that's used to print money, U.S. money. I saved the paper, and I'll get it to you. There wasn't anything else left behind when they abandoned the place. One day they were here, and the next day they were gone. I had the place cleaned and rented it to the current tenant. That's all I know."

"Please get that paper to us as soon as you can. And we'd like to see that rental agreement that was signed for the use of the condo and the warehouse. Do you happen to remember the name of the man who signed the papers, the one who said he'd be living in the condo?"

"He said his name was Kenneth McNulty. At the time, I was suspicious of him. I wondered if Kenneth McNulty was his real name, but he had a driver's license and a passport in that name. Both pieces of ID had his picture on them, so I had to accept the identification as being authentic."

The detective excused himself and went away from the phone for a few minutes. When he returned, he said he'd confirmed that Kenneth McNulty was the ordinary and common name that a man used who acted as a front for the Russian mafia. This front man was an American, and he rented properties, signed papers, and took care of business that Russian nationals would not be allowed to take care of. It seemed that no one knew what McNulty's real name was or anything about where he lived.

This information didn't surprise Becky. But she was alarmed that she had rented the warehouse and the condo to someone connected with the Russian mafia. She hoped they were gone now. But the Albanian guy wasn't gone, and he was a problem. If he was released from jail, he could turn into an even bigger problem.

"So you didn't find anything except the paper in the trash can? They didn't leave anything else behind?"

Becky knew the coffee maker was not suspicious, and she didn't think they had left anything else. "You know, this is not my condo or my warehouse. I mean, I don't own it. I manage it for the owner. I find renters for him. I have a good idea what furniture and pots and pans belong here, but I don't keep an inventory of everything that's here. I'm mostly concerned, when someone moves out of a property, that they haven't taken something that doesn't belong to them. I don't pay that much attention to what they've left behind. I call in a cleaning team that I use all the time, and they get rid of the trash and whatever stuff doesn't belong here. If the previous occupants have left any clothes or left behind something else of value, the cleaning people turn it over to me. I try to contact whoever had been renting the place, and I send their jacket, or their boots, or whatever back to them. These last people who rented the warehouse didn't leave anything behind except the paper...oh, and some ink stains on the floor."

"Okay. If you think of anything else, please get in touch immediately. We think we've found a translator who speaks this guy's Albanian dialect. After she's been able to spend some time with him, I hope to have more specifics...especially about what he's looking for at your client's property. From what you've told me, I guess it wouldn't be useful to talk to the owner of the warehouse. It sounds as if he's pretty much turned everything over to you."

"The owner doesn't know anything, I promise you. He has no idea who rents this space. He owns many properties. I handle quite a few of them for him. He is the ultimate absentee landlord. Don't waste your time talking to him. He doesn't know anything."

"We will be in touch after the translator has had a chance to talk to Agron...if that's really his name. Oh, how long ago did your cleaning people clean out the place...after the previous tenants left town?"

"The tenants left in September. I had the cleaners in during October. I will check to get the exact dates, if you want that."

"Never mind. That's a dead end, too. It won't help us to talk to the cleaning people either. We will be in touch, probably with more questions, after our translator has been able to question Agron." The call ended.

Virginia looked worn out from just listening to Becky's long phone call with the law enforcement people. After everything she'd been through, it was not surprising that she would tire easily. "I didn't learn much of anything I didn't already know. I suspect that all these people are using fake names. At least the police have the Albanian guy in custody...but for how long? I know he'll be coming back here as soon as he's out of jail. I wish I could figure out what he was looking for. If I knew what he wanted here, I'd just give it to him to make him go away and stay away."

Becky shared Virginia's concerns. "I worry that he'll be let out of jail, too. But we can't worry about that all the time. Do you want to come to the city with me and stay at my place? You know you are always welcome to do that."

"I refuse to allow that little pipsqueak to drive me out of my home. And I have work to do. I have orders to fill. I need to get back to making my artwork. I don't have the energy right now to do anything, but I am feeling a lot of pressure to get back to it. Besides loving what I do, there are all those orders from the night of the gallery opening. I've also received emails and texts on my phone from the gallery owner. He wants me to bring in samples of everything I make so he can set up a permanent collection. He says people can look at those pieces, and place orders. If I could get back to work, I could do all of that. I'm just so tired all the time. I need to stay here where my materials are, but I can't deal with that Agron guy coming back again and again. He could have killed me the last time he was here."

Becky didn't know what to do. She wanted Virginia to be safe, but she also knew the artist wanted to stay in her workspace and in her condo. Becky respected that. "Promise me you'll eat what I fix for you and promise me you will drink a lot of fluids. That will help you get back to feeling like yourself again. We will know more from the police after their translator has spent some time with the intruder. We'll just have to wait on that. Now, how about a big, thick steak medium rare with a big baked potato. And sour cream and mushrooms and some fresh asparagus. And how about a salad?"

Virginia laughed for the first time since she'd been attacked.

*T*he next morning, Virginia seemed greatly improved. She actually smiled when she drank her coffee and ate all of her toasted Asiago cheese and onion bagel with cream cheese. Becky was encouraged. After breakfast, Virginia got on her computer and placed a big order for more supplies. She knew she couldn't get out of the warehouse and go dumpster diving while she was barely able to walk. And Christmas was in just a few days. Virginia didn't have anyone to buy gifts for or to celebrate with, but before she'd been attacked the second time, she had planned to get a Christmas tree. Becky smiled to herself at the enthusiasm Virginia was beginning to exhibit. She volunteered to buy a Christmas tree for her friend.

When Becky returned with the box that contained the artificial tree, Virginia decided she wanted to put the tree in the kitchen of the condo. When she wasn't working on her art projects or sleeping, she spent most of her time in the kitchen. The tree came out of the box with hundreds of tiny white lights already on it. Becky had bought some boxes of ornaments, and the two women had fun laughing and doing their best to follow the directions that came with the tree about how to set it up. They finally had it securely upright and decorated, and when they plugged it in and lit it up, the tree from a box looked pretty good. Virginia was tired and had to take a nap after the Christmas tree excitement.

Later that afternoon, the detectives who were questioning Agron Zogolli, called Becky again with news. Becky had to wake Virginia so she could listen to the phone call. "Have you found out anything else that might be useful?" Becky got straight to the point.

"I think what we have is more questions than answers. Let me fill you in on what Mr. Zogolli has told us. Our translator has been able to get quite a bit of information from the man. He seems pleased that she can speak his Albanian dialect and is, for whatever reason, eager to talk to her and tell her all about it. Go figure. Apparently, there was an informant in the group that was printing the illegal one-hundred-dollar bills at the warehouse. Or, at least Vasily, the Russian guy who was in charge, believed there was an informant among his group of employees. He threatened the people who were working for him, and because of his paranoia, he began to behave erratically.

"Agron says that one day the printing press was turning out hundreds of sheets of what he calls 'Benjamin bills,' and the next day, the plates that were being used in the printing press had disappeared. Agron believes that Vasily, the Russian guy who was the boss of the counterfeiting operation, did something with the plates... like hid them somewhere. In any case, the plates were gone. The next step in the counterfeiting process, after the sheets of bills are printed on both sides, is cutting the sheets into individual bills. The money is printed in sheets of thirty-two bills, which means there are thirty-two bills printed on each sheet. The sheets have to be carefully and precisely cut into the individual bills." The detective stopped to see if he still had his audience.

"I know this might be more detail than you want to know, but it all seems to be important to what happened subsequently. There were stacks and stacks of the large sheets of bills that had to be cut. These were piled in the warehouse. After they are cut, the bills have to be counted and banded, in bundles of one hundred, in order to make them easier to handle. I know you've seen stacks of bills with the currency bands around them. I guess that most of the pieces of equipment this rogue group was using were pretty high quality. The printing press was top notch, and the plates they used to print the money were apparently the real thing. More on that later. They had the exact ink the Bureau of Printing and Engraving, the BPE, uses, and they had the right paper...stolen from the BPE facility in Ft. Worth, Texas, if you please. But the machine they were using to cut up the large sheets of 32 bills was not that new, and Agron says the cutting machine was always breaking down. The Russian guy, Vasily, went nuts when this kept happening. He decided there was not only an informant working for him but that someone was also sabotaging his cutting machine. He got totally paranoid and violent. Agron thought he might be using cocaine.

"One night, he completely lost it. Agron had come in to clean up, like he usually did. He was a little early, and the other workers were still there. Vasily was screaming at them and waving a gun around. When Agron saw the gun, he hid behind some of the equipment, so Vasily didn't know he was in the warehouse. That's why Agron didn't die that night along with everybody else. Vasily went berserk with the gun. He was screaming and turned into a crazy man…Agron's words. He went completely over the edge and shot all of his employees. Vasily killed four people. Agron watched all of this happen from his hiding place. After he'd killed his workers, Vasily wrapped each of the dead bodies in plastic and duct tape. He rolled the bodies up a ramp into the van. The van was the way the employees traveled to and from the warehouse for work every day. Vasily also used the van to take his boxes full of brand-new money away every night. There was a ramp at the back so the carts with the boxes of money could be rolled right into the back of the van. According to Agron, Vasily rolled the bodies up into the van using the ramp. After he'd loaded the bodies, Vasily drove the van away. Agron says he doesn't know what happened to the bodies. After Vasily drove off with the bodies in the van, Agron left the warehouse. All of the equipment was still there, and hundreds of sheets of uncut money were also still there. Vasily had left everything behind. Agron says he thought Vasily left everything behind in the warehouse because he was anxious to get rid of the bodies as soon as possible…as he should have been. There was a considerable amount of blood on the floor. Some of the money that had already been cut into individual bills and banded was also left there. That night, Agron was tempted to help himself to some of the packs of money, but he was afraid to take any of it. He was afraid of surveillance cameras, and he mainly just wanted to escape with his life.

"But after he'd left the scene of the crime and began to think about the money, he decided to go back to the warehouse and see if he could get some of the bills. The next night, he waited outside and listened for voices before he used his key to get into the person door of the warehouse. When he didn't hear anything, he finally worked up his nerve and went inside. The warehouse was completely cleared out. Everything was gone. There was no van. There were no machines. There was no money. There was no more blood on the floor. Someone had come in and completely cleared it all out. Everything that had to do with the counterfeiting operation had disappeared.

"Agron was furious that he had waited too long to try to get what he felt was his share. He hadn't been given his last paycheck, and now everyone had vanished. He knew he wasn't going to be paid. He didn't know if Vasily would be back or what had happened to him. He was terrified of Vasily anyway and didn't want to run into the Russian. Agron was frightened and decided to lay low for a while. He realized he was the only person who had worked in the warehouse who hadn't been shot…except for Vasily who had done the shooting. Agron was the only one of the employees who was still alive. He knew he was a loose end and decided he had to disappear. And he did that for a while. He stayed below the radar screen for as long as he could. But the possibility that he could find some of the money or find the plates that had been used to print the money finally got the better of him. He decided that something must have happened to Vasily. Vasily was out of the picture, and Agron still had his key to the warehouse. He made a decision to go back into the warehouse to try to find some of the money. He knew the plates were also valuable, but he was mostly interested in finding the already-printed money. He didn't know the locks to the doors of the warehouse had been changed and that someone else had rented the warehouse and the condo."

Becky wanted to be sure she'd been able to follow all the details of what the detective had said. "So everyone but Vasily and Agron is dead. And of course there is Kenneth or whoever he really is. He's not dead. Or maybe he's dead, too, and we just don't know it yet. Agron is looking for the money and/or the plates that print the money, and he thinks these are still at the warehouse. If anything of value is here, I wonder why Vasily hasn't come back to get it. What's happened to him?"

The detective interrupted Becky's thinking out loud. "I can probably answer that question for you. We think we know what has happened to Vasily. I've checked the dates, and a few days after he killed his own employees, we think Vasily himself was fished out of the Hudson river. We think the body we found is Vasily, but until we arrested Agron, we haven't had anybody who might be able to positively identify him. Of course, even if we are able to identify the body as Vasily, we will probably never know who killed him or exactly when he was killed and his body thrown into the river."

"One other thing." The detective continued. "I guess when he came back the night after the murders, Agron stuck his head into the kitchen of the condo and had a look around. He commented to our translator that he was sure that Vasily would be coming back to the warehouse because his 'precious coffee maker' was still there in the kitchen of the condo. Apparently, the coffee maker in question is expensive, and it was very important to Vasily. Agron said Vasily would never have left it behind. We think that's one reason Agron decided to hide out and stayed away from the warehouse for so long. Agron was afraid to take the chance that he might run into Vasily. He was sure that Vasily would be coming back to pick up his expensive coffee machine. Agron was sure that Vasily would want to take it with him."

Becky and Virginia looked at each other and almost giggled. They'd decided they also loved the coffee machine and didn't want to turn it over to the police as evidence.

The detective had more of the story to share with them. "When we heard about the BPE plates that supposedly were the real thing and the fact that the Russians were involved in all of this, lots of bells went off with the feds. They got involved and had quite a story to tell us. Many years ago, in 1990, a plate that printed the front side of one-hundred-dollar bills disappeared from the BPE in Washington, D.C. The people who'd lost the plate made up a number of stories about what happened to it, but the truth is that they never found it. They didn't know what had happened to it. Of course, the BPE didn't want to admit this. A couple of years after the plates went missing, an un-usual number of Benjamins began to show up in the former USSR. This was during the brief window when we were friends with the Russians. Yeltsin allowed our investigators to try to find out the source of these printed bills that were flooding the Russian economy. The U.S. federal authorities investigated and eventually found an abandoned printing press in Russia, near St. Petersburg. The place had been shut down by the time our guys found it. A few bills had been left behind, but the plates were gone. Interestingly, the plate the Russians used for the front of the bills was the real deal… stolen from the U.S. But the backs of the bills had been printed with an inferior plate which was not the genuine plate for the back of the one-hundred-dollar bill. The Russian counterfeiters only had the real thing for the front of the bill. But who looks at the back of the bill anyway? And of course the serial numbers on the bills were wrong."

The detective continued his story. "So the BPE didn't get its plate back, and it's been missing ever since the 1990s. The plate Vasily was using for the front of the bills could have been that very same plate. But Agron swears they also had 'the real thing' for the backs of these batches of bills that were being printed in the Hoboken warehouse. He said something about 'AI' and a 3D printer making a perfect plate. I don't think Agron knows what AI is or has ever seen a 3D printer. He says he overheard the men who were actually doing the printing of the bills talking about these things. He didn't really seem to have completely understood that part of the story. But Agron did say that apparently the only thing Vasily was worried about, the only thing that was not perfect on the bills, was the serial numbers.

"That's all I know so far. I will let you know if Agron is able to identify Vasily's body. The printing machine and the cutting machine and all the rest of it have disappeared. Agron thinks they were probably dumped at the bottom of the Hudson River along with Vasily's body and the other bodies. He has no idea, really. He's just speculating. He didn't have anything to do with getting rid of Vasily. We're convinced of that. Agron maintains that two plates and a coffee maker are still missing. But he probably doesn't really know anything about those things either. Any more questions?"

Becky spoke for herself and for Virginia. "Thanks for all of this. We will keep our eyes open for those plates. As I told you, I had the place cleaned out completely before I rented it to the current tenant, so I don't expect we will find anything. I think Vasily must have done something with the plates, and Agron is chasing ghosts. He's just wishing he had taken the money or the plates or both that first night and not waited. And he's wishing he hadn't been caught on video breaking in here…twice."

The detectives thanked Becky for her help with the case, and she thanked them for keeping her in the loop. Everybody hung up.

"How big are these plates that everybody keeps talking about?" Virginia was curious.

"I have no idea." Becky was thinking. "Why, do you think they are still here someplace? They couldn't be. I cleaned this place out completely. I admit I kept the coffee maker, but I didn't know that belonged to Vasily. I assumed it was here before those suspicious people rented the place and that it automatically came with the furnished rental. I have to admit, it seemed pretty high end compared to the other appliances the owner bought to furnish the kitchen. It makes great coffee."

"If one plate prints the fronts of 32 one-hundred-dollar bills, we can figure out how big the plate is. I don't know exactly how the bills are supposed to be configured on the plate, but maybe the plate is not really that huge. Maybe it is hidden here some place."

Becky was busy Googling information about BPE plates and the size of one-hundred-dollar bills. She made a few calculations and came up with some numbers. "The plate would be about 25.5 inches by 21 inches. It's made of steel and coated with chrome. It isn't very thick. In fact these plates are pretty thin. One of them weighs about twelve pounds. So that's not too big or too heavy to hide somewhere. But I had my people clean out all the closets, and then I checked everywhere to be sure all the previous people's stuff had been removed. The plates can't be here anywhere."

Virginia was thinking. "You don't have to stay with me tonight. I know you are behind in your real estate work. I'm forever grateful to you for saving my life and taking care of me these past few days. But I can manage on my own from now on. Since this Albanian guy is finally in custody, and it seems that everybody else has been dead for a while, I think I will be all right. I promise to eat and drink. I want to get back to my artwork. It's the best therapy for me. I will heal more quickly if I'm working on my projects."

Becky agreed that Virginia was able to manage on her own. Becky had scheduled a carpenter and a mason to come and seal up the person door on the warehouse once and for all. They were going to arrive within the hour. As soon as they had completed their work, Becky felt Virginia would be safe. She felt she could leave Virginia on her own at the warehouse. Becky packed up her few things and was looking forward to driving back to New York City.

Virginia woke up in the middle of the night. She'd had a dream about something important, but she couldn't quite remember what it was. She fell back asleep. When she woke the next morning, she remembered what she'd dreamed about, and she went to the closet of the condo's guest room.

When she'd first moved into the condo, Virginia had left pretty much everything in place that was already there. When Sidney Richardson had sent Virginia's things from Arkansas, she'd rearranged some furniture and put her own things out on the shelves and tables. She'd wanted to make the place her own, and she'd wanted to hang her own artwork on the walls. One thing she had really despised about the décor in the rented condo had been the two large framed prints that hung over the bed in the main bedroom. They were cheap prints of flowers, and the colors were not those that Virginia liked. The frames were thick and ugly. Mostly everything else in the condo was in good taste and suited Virginia. But the two ugly prints grated on her. She hated having them hanging over her bed. When Virginia's own things arrived from Arkansas, she took down the cheap prints. She hung four framed water colors that she loved over her bed. She carried the two framed uglies into the guest room and stored them in the back of the closet.

What she had remembered from her dream was about those two prints and how heavy they were. Both prints were framed with thick frames and were fairly large, but even so, they seemed terribly heavy for what they were. Virginia had been busy with other things and had not given any more thought to the weight of those prints until her dream last night. She pulled the paper and the tape off the backs of both of the framed prints. Sure enough, there were two metal engraving plates. These were the currency plates… back and front…for printing one-hundred-dollar bills. They'd been hidden in the frames behind the flower prints. Vasily must have framed them himself and hung them in plain sight where no one would ever think to look for them. Virginia called Becky and told her everything. Becky called the Hoboken detectives.

During the COVID epidemic, employment every-
where and at all levels was disrupted...along with
everything else in the world. The doorman who worked the
day shift at Rebecca Sells' New York City apartment house
had been employed there for years. He'd faithfully stayed on
the job during the epidemic, armed with masks and hand
sanitizer. After the worst of the COVID crisis had passed,
he was still there. He continued to open doors, call for taxis,
take in packages, screen visitors, and do everything else required of an excellent and experienced doorman in the city.

Because almost nobody likes to cover the night shifts, even
Becky's high-priced apartment house had run into trouble finding qualified people to handle the doorman's non-daytime shifts.
Management had gone through a number of doormen who had
stayed for a while and then left. It was one of these short-timer
employees who had signed for the certified mail when Sidney's
package which contained the questionable oil painting had
arrived at the apartment house addressed to Rebecca Sells.

The person who was working as the doorman on the evening shift when the package arrived had signed for it and put it in the mail room. This small room was just behind the front desk and was used as an office for the doorman and to temporarily store packages, mail, and other kinds of deliveries. It served as a lost and found as well as a place for residents to leave suitcases packed and ready for a quick getaway on Friday afternoon. The evening shift doorman did not pay much attention to the package and put it in the mail room without really thinking about it. He hadn't been on the job long enough to know for sure exactly who Rebecca Sells was. Because everyone ordered from Amazon these days, there were more and more packages delivered every day to the apartment house. The ever-increasing volume of deliveries from Amazon alone threatened to overwhelm the small mail room.

The night shift guy put Rebecca's package on top of a stack of other packages. Inevitably the stack of packages had fallen over, and the package addressed to Rebecca Sells slipped off the top of the pile and fell behind an old radiator that was no longer functioning. The building's long-time day-time doorman, who worked days and kept things organized and on track in his office, knew all of the building's tenants well. He never saw the package addressed to Rebecca.

Juanita had not wanted to keep bugging Sidney about the expert who was supposed to be examining her painting, and Sidney had not wanted to keep bugging her friend Becky about it. But when Sidney didn't hear from Becky that the package had arrived, she became concerned. She sent a couple of texts to Becky asking if she had received the box. Becky had been so busy dealing with Virginia's issues and the police, as well as trying to keep up with her own real estate business, finding the package from Sidney had taken a low place on her list of things to do. Becky made a couple of quick inquiries of the various doormen about a package that was supposed to have been sent to her.

As Becky began to get her life straightened out and organized again, she paid more attention to the missing package. She asked her day-shift doorman, who knew her well, if there were any packages for her languishing in the mail room. He checked everywhere and told her there was nothing for her that she'd not already picked up. She texted Sidney that she'd never received the painting. Sidney had insured it and sent it certified mail, so she knew someone had signed for the package when it was delivered. She'd received a notification postcard that the package had been delivered and signed for. The loss of the package could not be blamed on the USPS.

After some investigating, Sidney and Becky realized that a doorman who was now gone and no longer worked for Becky's apartment building had been the one who had signed for the package…several weeks earlier. Becky had never picked up the package, and now it was nowhere to be found. Sidney stressed to Becky that Juanita was very concerned about the painting that was missing. She had promised Juanita that an expert would examine the painting Juanita had rescued from the trash can. Becky said she would do everything she could to try to find the person who had signed for the package, but she was already running at full speed to try to catch up with her real estate business and the rest of her busy life. Looking for the lost package went on the back burner again.

Sidney didn't want to tell Juanita that the painting was missing, so she just told her it was still in New York City. She let Juanita assume the painting was being examined by the art expert and that the authentication process was taking more time than expected. Sidney felt terrible about not being completely up front with Juanita about the painting, but she held out hope that Becky would eventually be able to locate the missing painting.

It was not until the spring cleaners arrived in late February that the package was found behind the radiator in the mail room. The shipping box was covered with dust and dirt, but the address label was still attached. Becky finally took possession of the box and sent a text to Sidney that the lost package that contained the painting had been found. Sidney was greatly relieved, but the examination by an art expert had already been delayed by several months.

Becky knew all about the heist at the Isabella Stewart Gardner Museum that had occurred in 1990. She loved the artist Johannes Vermeer and had studied all of his works. When she finally unwrapped the package and really looked at the painting Sidney had sent, she was shocked. Seeing the Vermeer for the first time took her breath away. She sent a text to Sidney:

```
If I didn't know where this came from, I
might swear it was the real thing. I studied
this painting in college, and what you have
sent me is a very, very good copy. Yikes! I
hope it's not the stolen one, the real one.
Please tell me exactly where you found this
Vermeer copy. I am calling in top experts
to take a look at it. They will want all
the details about how you happened to have
it. I hope the FBI doesn't come knocking on
your door. I will do my best to keep your
name out of it. Thanks for putting me in
the middle of another kettle of complicated
fish. I still love you. Becky
```

When Sidney received the text from Becky, she also began to worry that maybe the painting was genuine and was one of the lost paintings from the Gardner Museum heist of the last century. Sidney didn't think the painting from the trash can could possibly be the real thing, but even a remote chance that it might be made her stomach turn over. What in the world would she tell Juanita? What in the world would she tell the FBI…if it came to that?

Sidney knew almost nothing about the man who'd lived in the cottage where the painting had been found. He had cleaned out most of his furniture and personal belongings before he'd been found dead beside the road. He'd either been an extreme minimalist or he had done an excellent job of getting rid of his things before he died. When Sidney and Juanita had gone into the cottage to clear it out for the women's shelter and get it ready to sell, there had not been much of anything left to get rid of. Sidney had already made arrangements with the women's shelter to buy the place. She didn't know exactly what she and Cameron would do with it, but she'd always loved the English cottage and was thrilled to have the chance to own it.

Sidney tried to find out as much as she could about Simon Maxwell, the man who'd owned the cottage and had lived there for quite a few years as an almost total recluse. The problem with researching his background was that he had never existed, or at least he was not in any public records or on the internet, until he'd purchased the cottage in River Springs. The cottage had been owned by an innocuous sounding LLC, which told Sidney nothing at all. Even after he'd moved to River Springs, Simon Maxwell was a ghost in terms of having any background or footprint on the internet or even in the town. Sidney decided he had to be hiding out from something and had assumed a new identity when he'd moved to River Springs. She wondered if he could have been in the federal witness protection program. A more likely explanation was that he was a true recluse, even a hermit. Because he had cleared out his house so completely, there were no papers or photos or other personal items left behind. There was not a single clue that might give anyone an idea about who Simon Maxwell really was.

Sidney asked Cameron to put his computer gurus on the case and try to find out anything they could about Simon Maxwell. It was an unusual name, but it was not a unique name. Even with the best computer researchers working on the issue, they could not find out anything about the man before he had arrived in River Springs. Their own local Simon Maxwell had not existed anywhere before he'd purchased and moved into the English cottage. The man seemed to be a genius at erasing his past. Sidney basically had nothing to tell Becky or Juanita or the FBI, if they ever came calling and asking questions about Simon Maxwell or the Vermeer. Sidney crossed her fingers that the experts Becky was using would find the painting was just a very, very nicely done forgery. It could be returned to Juanita, and she could hang it back up on her bedroom wall.

Sidney could not help but wonder how Simon Maxwell had happened to own such an excellent copy of the famous and infamous painting. Maxwell's body had been kept at the county morgue for a few weeks. When nobody came forward to claim him, it was assumed he had no family. His remains were cremated. This was the usual procedure for bodies which nobody claimed. Simon Maxwell had left no instructions about people to notify of his death or what was to be done with his body or his ashes after his death.

He'd had a small bank account at a local bank, and what was left in the account was paid to the county to cover the costs of his cremation. So in the end there was not even any DNA that could be tested to discover what Simon Maxwell's ethnic heritage had been.

Sidney was sad that apparently nobody at all had mourned this man's passing. She wondered if he had ever loved anyone or if anyone had ever loved him. She realized she would never know the answers to these questions. He remained a ghost... in life and in death.

The Reckoning

ARKANSAS

2024

Every community in the United States wants to keep illegal drugs away. But in fact, drugs are every-where…in cities, in the suburbs, in small towns, in rural communities, in high schools and colleges and universities. No place is completely drug free or can protect itself from the invasion of the illegal killers. The drug business thrives on and is driven by demand. Communities world-wide deal with this in different ways…from encouraging kids to "Just Say No" to giving away clean needles and free Narcan—and everything in between. Nalmefene Hydrochloride is the official name for the drug Narcan that is increasingly in the news and even now is advertised on television.

Legalizing hard drugs and treating addictions exclusively as a medical issue has met with mixed success in the European countries which have tried this approach. Those who take a hard line in the U.S. feel that failing to punish drug users and drug dealers enables the abuse and makes it worse. Rehab programs vary widely in their quality and in their effectiveness. In short, there are no very good solutions to the drug problem.

Deadly fentanyl's arrival on the drug scene has made everything worse. Fentanyl is so unpredictable and so dangerous. It is mixed with other drugs such as cocaine and heroin, and the user never knows exactly what he or she is ingesting. Agencies at every level, charged with keeping drugs from proliferating all over the country, are underfunded and understaffed. Some leaders in positions of power have even made ridiculous pronouncements and in fact truly believe that doing drugs is a "victimless crime." In spite of the utter foolishness of this point of view, communities continue to struggle to keep drug dealers out of their neighborhoods and to prevent more people from becoming addicts. Making drug busts and shutting down drug networks is still a goal and a priority for law enforcement.

Raymond Barstow was a retired FBI special agent. He had arrived in River Springs to do a favor for his friend, Cameron Richardson. This favor had led to Barstow's becoming involved in the local effort to deal with the drug business. Cameron had not wanted to take on this additional project. He already had way too many things on his plate. But Sidney had drawn him in to help her save someone she cared about. Sidney did not want to become involved as a crusader against the drug trade either. However, in trying to save Ginny Randolph, she had inevitably had to confront the consequences of the drug problem.

Now that Ginny Randolph had disappeared and Virginia Delacroix had been safely relocated, both Sidney and Cameron wanted to leave their minor involvement with drug dealers behind. But in fact, everyone in the country was already involved. There is not a person alive who does not know about a family who has tragically lost a loved one to illegal drugs. The irresponsible overprescribing of oxycodone coupled with fentanyl's popularity and widespread distribution have elevated the situation to an even more serious national crisis.

Although Raymond Barstow was retired and was no longer actively employed by the FBI, he'd become involved in the River Springs situation. He was an investigator. That aspect of his personality did not cease to exist because he had stopped going to work every day for the FBI. And he was a bulldog and could not let the problem go. Bubba Randolph was no longer among the living, but the people who had recruited Bubba to distribute their product in this rural area would soon find another dupe to replace Bubba and do their dirty work. That's the difficulty with drug enforcement. Officials work hard to shut down one network, knowing full well that because the demand is always there, another network will soon come together to take its place.

Barstow had taken Bubba Randolph's backpack and substituted powdered sugar for the packages of fentanyl. Barstow had replaced the backpack that was now full of powdered sugar in Bubba's hiding place under the bathroom sink at his house. Barstow's cameras inside the Randolph house had recorded two drug dealers' faces on video, and the FBI was looking for them. These efforts had been able to get a little bit of fentanyl off the street, a backpack full to be exact. The former FBI agent was pleased with himself for that accomplishment, but he knew his success would be short lived. What he really wanted was to find the source of the supply. This was the real gold to be mined in the investigation. He felt if he could find the two men whose faces he had on the security video, he might be able to get them to spill the beans and reveal who had hired them. Raymond Barstow wanted to put in prison the kingpins who had brought fentanyl to this part of idyllic and beautiful rural Arkansas.

Barstow knew that when the dealers who had employed Bubba discovered the backpack contained sugar rather than fentanyl, there would be trouble. The volume of lost drugs and the money involved were too great to allow this much product to just disappear. The drugs had to be somewhere. Someone had to be held accountable. Someone had to pay. Barstow intended to watch carefully what happened when the inevitable trouble began. Who in the community would be punished for the disappearance of the backpack's contents?

Ideally, Barstow would have liked to put Ginny Randolph out there as a target to draw the drug dealers in. She really had messed with the backpack and the distribution chain of Bubba's drug dealing. But Ginny was gone. Barstow had no idea where she was. He suspected that Sidney Richardson had something to do with Ginny's disappearance, but he knew Sidney was not and would not be talking. And he had promised the Richardsons that he would do everything he could to divert attention and blame away from Ginny's involvement with this situation. She was untouchable… in theory because of his promise to Cameron as well as in practice. Barstow would have to catch his bad guys without being able to use Ginny as bait.

Raymond Barstow waited. And then he waited some more. It was surprising to him that no one had turned up dead as a result of the backpack full of drugs going missing. Did those who had retrieved Bubba's backpack not yet know their fentanyl had turned into sugar? Barstow could not believe that those who controlled the network would write off the loss of the fentanyl as collateral damage or as a business expense. Something had to happen.

Oddly enough, it was a remark that Juanita made to Sidney that set off a chain of events that gave Barstow his best and only clue. Sidney and Juanita had discussed the death of Ginny's husband in the river behind the Richardson's house. Both women accepted that it had been Bubba's drug use that had led him to stumble down the embankment, hit his bead, and fall face first into the Little Red River. Everyone who knew about the security video footage from the Richardson's property knew that Bubba was dead. But Juanita innocently asked Sidney why no one had pressured law enforcement to try to find his body. She could not understand why his family had not made more of a fuss about his death in the river and his disappearance. Didn't they want to find his body so he could have a proper burial?

"Bubba doesn't really have any family." Sidney was hoping to explain to Juanita why no one seemed to care that Bubba was dead and gone.

"What about the deputy sheriff that always protected him? Wasn't he part of Bubba's family? You and Mr. Richardson were always talking about how no one could touch Bubba or report him to the authorities because he had a relative in the sheriff's office that was protecting him."

Sidney realized that Juanita had an excellent point. Why had Bubba's cousin or nephew or whoever he was, never come forward and demanded that the sheriff's office look for Bubba? Sidney hated to bring up with Virginia anything about Bubba or anything about what had happened to him. Sidney knew that being reminded of Bubba was painful for Virginia. But Sidney was curious and sent a text to Virginia with some questions:

```
Sorry to bring up the uncomfortable past. But
what is the name of Bubba's relative who is or
```

was a deputy sheriff and protected Bubba from
ever being investigated or arrested? He didn't
come forward or demand, to my knowledge, any
search for Bubba's body after he died in the
river. I find this somewhat odd — that he
would not have wanted to find Bubba. Were
they close? Why did this relative of Bubba's
want to keep anyone from filing a complaint
against him? Tell me what you know. Thanks. I
hear your artwork is a huge hit in New York
City. I knew it would be. Congratulations.
Wishing you continued success. Sidney

It was a few days before Sidney heard back from Virginia.

Hi Sidney, Yes, I am busy, busy, busy making
art to sell. It's so much fun to create my
pieces and also fun to have money coming in.
To answer your questions, Bubba's cousin is
Eugene Randolph. Bubba always called him Gene.
They grew up together. They were almost exactly
the same age. Bubba's parents raised Gene from
the time he was a newborn. When Gene was just
a few weeks old, his mother ran away and left
him with her boyfriend. The boyfriend couldn't
cope and gave the baby to Bubba's parents. I'm
not sure, but I think Bubba's parents eventually legally adopted Gene. The two boys were
like brothers although they are actually only
second or third cousins. The two became even
closer, if that was possible, when Bubba's parents passed away. After the boys grew up, Bubba
had lunch every day with Gene at the diner in
Rosewell. My husband never missed his lunch

date with Gene unless he was incredibly sick
with something. However, Bubba and Gene fell
out when Bubba began using fentanyl. Once I
overheard Gene blowing out Bubba over the drug
use. He said Bubba was putting everything at
risk by becoming a user. He told Bubba that
"things were not going to end well." And of
course now we know they didn't... end well.
Gene never liked me, and we never really talked
to each other. Gene was probably the only person who believed Bubba when he said I was the
one who stole his backpack. And of course, I
was gone before Bubba fell into the river and
died. That's all I know. Best to you and Cameron and a BIG HI to Georgio at the Old Mill.

Sidney read and reread the text from Virginia. She also
read between the lines, the things that Virginia hadn't bothered to say. Gene had become angry with Bubba when he'd
started *using* fentanyl, not when he'd started as a drug dealer.
It was not until Bubba had begun using the product he was
selling that Gene had become upset with him. Gene had
said Bubba was "putting everything at risk by becoming a
user." This gave Sidney an idea about who might have been
supplying Bubba with the drugs in the first place.

Sidney knew that Raymond Barstow wasn't making much
progress in his investigation to find out who had been supplying
Bubba Randolph. And Sidney suspected that Barstow had not
entirely given up on the idea of using Ginny Randolph to draw
out the higher ups in the drug chain. Sidney decided to have a talk
with Barstow and tell him about deputy sheriff Eugene Randolph's
close relationship with Bubba. She knew law enforcement people
were reluctant to believe that one of their own might have gone

over to the dark side, but everyone knew it happened. Sidney was going to suggest that Raymond Barstow take a hard look at Gene Randolph...and leave Virginia Delacroix alone.

It all happened on the same day, and the case began to break. Something had floated to the surface of the lake. Two fishermen in a cabin cruiser had spotted it bobbing in the water. Because of its size and shape, they suspected it might be a body. They didn't want to touch it and called in the authorities to deal with whatever it turned out to be. If whoever put the body in the lake had hoped it would rest forever at the bottom, sleeping with the fishes, they'd done a poor job of it. When the body wrapped in plastic and duct tape was hauled to the dock, it wasn't difficult to figure out who it was.

Although the corpse had been in the water for many weeks, it was not a surprise to find Bubba Randolph in the plastic wrap. The fish had done a pretty good job on his face, but there was no doubt about the identity of the man who had floated up from the depths. An autopsy was ordered to be done on the corpse.

When he heard that Bubba's body had been recovered from the nearby lake, Bart went to the marina to see who else was there and who might show a particular interest in the recovery of the corpse. It wasn't every day that a body was discovered in the lake and arrived wrapped in plastic at the local marina. Of course, a crowd of looky-loos had gathered to try to catch a glimpse of what was going on. The locals had known Bubba all of his life. Most realized he'd become a drug user and had died an ignominious death. But they couldn't stay away. Hanging around the marina in hopes of finding who was curious about the body had not worked out for Raymond Barstow. Because everybody was interested in the body and everybody was curious, it was another dead end for the retired FBI guy.

On the same day, two suspicious-looking characters, who were not known locally in River Springs, turned up dead, sprawled out in a public park. They both had gunshot wounds to their heads. Even though the cause of death was obvious to all, an autopsy was ordered to be done on both corpses. The local coroner, who almost never had anything to do, was all of a sudden in the hot seat. Bodies were piling up. The county coroner had been elected to his position. He had no medical training. He could pronounce people dead, and that was not particularly difficult to do in these three cases. The body that had been in the water for more than three months was definitely dead. Likewise, the two men with gunshot wounds to their heads were definitely dead. The bodies of the two dead thugs were taken away by the FBI. Bubba's body was sent to the medical examiner in Little Rock.

Before the remains were taken away, Raymond Barstow was notified about the two dead men in the public park. He confirmed that they were the ones he'd been looking for. They were the same two men who had recovered the backpack full of powdered sugar from Bubba's hiding place underneath his bathroom sink.

Barstow had wanted to find these two alive. He had intended to have them arrested and grilled for information about who employed them. These men were the key to Barstow's investigation...the men who would lead him to the higher ups who were running the Arkansas drug network. Barstow was furious that someone had beat him to these potential stool pigeons and killed them. Now they would never be able to tell anybody anything. Barstow figured that whoever was running these guys must have become convinced that they were the ones who had substituted the powdered sugar for the fentanyl in the backpack. That mistaken assumption had sealed their fates.

Bart had known someone would eventually pay the price for the disappearance of the drugs. He'd realized from the beginning that the two men he had recorded on the security videos from Bubba's house were just low-level operatives like Bubba was. He had hoped these two he'd planned to threaten and force to squeal on their employers would not be the ones punished for losing the drugs. But he should have known they'd be the ones who would be suspected and blamed when the drugs were never found. He was back to square one.

Then Barstow received a call from Sidney Richardson. He knew he had to tread carefully with Sidney because she was so protective of Ginny Randolph. But this time, Sidney had not called with a scolding or a warning to stay away from Ginny. Sidney wanted to meet with Barstow. She said she had some ideas about the direction his investigation ought to take. Barstow was surprised that Sidney would want to help him out, but he figured she was doing him a good deed partly to keep him from involving Ginny Randolph. He could not involve Ginny anyway as he had no idea where she was.

When she met with Bart, the retired FBI friend of Cameron's, Sidney explained to him about the close relationship between Bubba Randolph and Deputy Sheriff Gene Randolph. She told Bart that, in spite of their close family ties, they'd had a falling out. Sidney never mentioned Virginia Delacroix's part in disclosing the information about their disagreement. Sidney explained to Bart that it was not until Bubba had begun *using* the fentanyl that Gene had become angry with him. Sidney told Bart she thought Gene Randolph might be an important link in the drug chain that could lead to the higher ups in the fentanyl network that was trying to establish itself in rural Arkansas.

Because Gene Randolph was a deputy sheriff, Raymond Barstow knew he had to be extra careful with his investigation. He had so little to go on to begin with, he almost dropped the entire thing when Sidney suggested that Gene Randolph was involved. Bart didn't want to deal with the complications that would inevitably result from an investigation of the local constabulary. He groaned and moaned about the only lead he had in the case. But the bulldog inside him urged him to push on and continue investigating. His quest for answers drove him forward and would not allow him to throw in the towel.

Raymond Barstow, of course, did not know if anyone else in the county sheriff's department was involved with the drug network. He didn't know if he could trust anybody. He wanted to be able to track Gene Randolph around the clock, but it was not easy to tail a law enforcement officer, even for a short period of time. Law enforcement people have been trained to be able to pick up on whether or not they are being followed and watched...whether in person or in a vehicle.

Bart was able to convince his former boss, who was still an active special agent with the FBI, that the local county sheriff's department might be involved in the growing drug presence in the area. Bart was able to talk the FBI into assigning a special agent to work with the sheriff's department. This special agent arrived in River Springs as a consultant and liaison to assist with the investigation, but in fact, she would also be spying on Gene Randolph. No one outside the FBI would know anything about that part of her assignment.

The special agent liaison was able to put a tracker on Gene's personal vehicle as well as on the car he used when he was working for the sheriff. The agent also took a risk and added software to Gene's personal cell phone that would allow the FBI to see everything he did with the phone…who he called and texted and what he did and where he went every day. Putting the tracker on Gene's car and installing the special software on his phone had been made easier because Gene was not paying attention to what was going on around him. It had not been easy for Raymond Barstow to put all of these pieces in place, but he'd kept at it until he'd done everything that was possible. Now all they had to do was wait to see if and when Gene Randolph made contact with the drug network.

After Bubba's death, Gene had been told to lay low for a while. Because of his close association with Bubba, Gene's controllers were concerned he might come under suspicion. Until his cousin's death, he'd been their untouchable and pristine sleeper inside the local law enforcement structure. Those who were running Gene Randolph wanted to keep it that way.

When two men were found shot to death in a local park, Gene Randolph was put in a difficult position. He could no longer stay uninvolved. He was part of the investigation that the sheriff's office was doing to find who had killed the men. Although Gene knew exactly who the two men were and what they did, he had to pretend he didn't know anything about them.

In fact, a kingpin who told Gene what to do and had hired the two men to go into Bubba's house to search for the backpack had no idea who had killed their people. Gene's controllers swore that they'd not been responsible for the killings in the park. Gene believed them. No one knew who had killed the two. Because of what these two men did, the murders had to be related to dealing drugs, but whoever had actually done the killing remained a mystery.

Because of all these unknowns, Gene Randolph was even more spooked about investigating the murders. He was treading a narrow path between his employment as a sheriff's deputy and his much more lucrative job as a part of the drug network. This tightrope that he was required to walk caused him a great deal of anxiety. He was preoccupied with not messing up on either job and he neglected to keep an eye on who was keeping an eye on him.

Raymond Barstow's break came when Gene was off duty and made a trip to an abandoned farm that was located in a remote part of the county. Bart picked up on the fact that Gene had traveled to the farm because he saw it on his phone app. The tracker on Eugene Randolph's personal vehicle had done its job. Bart suspected that this trip to the farm was not a part of anything connected to Gene's work as a law enforcement officer. This unexplained behavior was what Bart had been hoping for and watching for, and he followed Gene Randolph on his phone as the deputy's personal vehicle turned off the main highway and traveled down a dirt road to the abandoned Denken farm.

Everybody who lived in the area of River Springs knew about the Denken farm, but it was so remote and such a poor homestead that no one ever thought about it. The last elderly owner had died years earlier. He'd not had any heirs, and he'd had no will. The farm didn't have any mortgage on it, so a bank was not involved. When no one paid the property taxes, technically the property had reverted to the county tax assessor's office.

Because the place was so far removed from anything and had no good access road, it had not been auctioned off for unpaid taxes, as these properties usually were. The tax office had not held a sale because they knew no one would buy the place. In addition to its inaccessibility, it had rocky soil, and nothing would grow there. The house on the property had burned down two decades earlier, but there was a small barn still standing that had fallen into disrepair. The roof of the barn had collapsed, and subsequently, most of the building itself had fallen down. It wasn't worth salvaging the wood or anything else from the old barn.

One day there might be a buyer for the property, but until that day arrived, no one ever cared about the place or went there. The Denken farm was deserted. Hardly anyone remembered that it was even there. It was the perfect place for making fentanyl.

Until recently, most fentanyl had been made abroad, usually in Mexico, from chemicals imported from India and China. It was relatively easy to get the necessary ingredients into Mexico and relatively easy to manufacture the drug there. The more difficult part was smuggling the product across the border into the United States. Drug dealers had proven to be exceptionally clever at finding ways to smuggle drugs across the border. Drones, tunnels, and mini-submarines were the latest innovations for getting drugs into the U. S. It was a constant contest between drug dealers and law enforcement as to who would get ahead in the game. It seemed that the drug dealers were more ingenious in the ways they found to get their fentanyl into the United States. It seemed as if law enforcement was always one step behind and struggling to catch up.

The most recent trend in the fentanyl trade was to make the drugs inside the United States. This completely avoided the issue of bringing the drugs across the border. Fentanyl manufacturing centers were being set up in remote and secret locations throughout the U.S. Not all the fentanyl factories were in rural areas. Some were located in urban centers, but the even more likely places for these drug factories were the upper-middle-class residential suburban neighborhood rentals that no one paid much attention to. One of these suburban drug houses had recently been discovered and closed down in Tucson, Arizona.

The Tucson operation had become suspicious because so many packages from China and other places in Asia were being sent to the house. Law enforcement watched the comings and goings at the expensive home and finally raided it. The good guys had been able to shut down the Tucson location, but there were so many other similar facilities that had not yet been found. This shift to domestic production had occurred because, for some reason, it seemed to have become easier to bring the ingredients for fentanyl into the U.S. than it was to smuggle the already-made drugs across the border. Drug dealers had learned from their mistakes. They had the ingredients to make their fentanyl sent from abroad to a variety of places in different towns and in different states.

Deliveries were made to the Denken farm at night. When Raymond Barstow arrived at ten o'clock in the morning, there was no one anywhere in the area to see what happened there. Barstow wasn't a local, so he'd never heard of the Denken farm. When he'd seen that Gene Randolph had visited this farm in the middle of nowhere in his off hours, Barstow decided to investigate. He had a feeling he would find something there. He also knew he had no business going there on his own, without backup and without authorization. But he was still an investigator in his heart and soul, even without his badge. He set out to find what had been so interesting to Deputy Gene Randolph at the map coordinates where he had visited.

Barstow drove his truck to the farm. The place looked abandoned. The barn was totally unusable. Nothing was going on in the barn. Without a roof, the rain poured in and flooded the dirt floor. The barn's floor was a sea of mud. Barstow might have given up and decided there was nothing at all to find there at the Denken farm, that it was a false alarm, and that he'd been mistaken. But there had been a rain storm the night before, and there were tracks, freshly made impressions in the mud from some kind of a heavy truck in the dirt road leading to the barn. Something had very recently either been delivered here or picked up here. Or maybe both.

There didn't seem to be anybody on the property that morning. Barstow decided to take a chance and take a look around. He was already out here at the farm and didn't really want to make another trip. There was one corner of the dilapidated barnthat still had a piece of a roof over it. The floor of the barn was dirt and mud, so he didn't think there would be a lower level or any way to access a basement. The barn wasn't locked or secured in any way, so Barstow walked in and headed for the corner that was protected from the weather. He slogged through the muddy floor to get to the one dry corner. He was happy he'd worn his boots.

Raymond Barstow carefully examined all the remnants of the collapsed barn. He had the feeling there was something important here, but for the life of him, he couldn't find what it was. He couldn't find anything. He searched the inside of the barn again, and then he walked around the outside of the barn. There were quite a few pieces of discarded farm equipment spread around on the ground behind the barn, but nothing struck him as being unusual or out of place. Barstow was about to call it a day and leave the farm. He did not want to be anywhere around if and when the drug people showed up for work or if and when Gene Randolph, deputy sheriff, made another visit. He walked over to a tractor seat that was upright but sitting on the ground. The rest of the tractor was nowhere in sight, but the seat looked fairly comfortable. Barstow decided he was going to sit down for five minutes to clear his head and allow himself to think things over.

When he approached the tractor seat, he realized it was totally clean on the top. How could that be? The tractor seat, which had been separated for years from the tractor where it used to be, was old and rusted and full of dried grass, cobwebs, and muck underneath. But the cracked black leather on the top was clean. In spite of the recent rain, with all the birds and animals that had to be living around the abandoned barn, there was no way the tractor seat could possibly be as pristine as it was. Barstow examined the tractor seat more closely. When he pulled on it in a certain way, all of a sudden, an opening in the ground near the backside of the barn appeared as if by magic. The entrance was so well concealed that Barstow never would have found it if he hadn't pulled on the tractor seat.

Barstow saw a primitive wooden staircase that went from the opening in the ground behind the barn down into someplace dark below. He knew he'd found it…whatever it was. No one would go to this much trouble to conceal an entrance or to design such a complex way of opening it unless there was something valuable to be found in the underground hiding place. He didn't think there was anyone currently in the subterranean compound because it was completely dark down there. He activated the flashlight on his cell phone. It wasn't much light, but it was something. He drew his gun in case there was anyone unexpectedly at work in the space at the bottom of the wooden stairs.

He climbed down carefully but quickly. He found himself in the middle of a fentanyl laboratory. This was where the wickedness was made, and there was an unbelievable amount of it. When Barstow got to the bottom of the stairs, his cell phone's flashlight allowed him to see shelves and shelves packed with plastic bags of fentanyl tablets. If this fentanyl was of any strength at all, the volume of product stored here could kill many thousands of people. Barstow was in shock at how many fentanyl tablets he'd found.

He walked into the next underground room and found the place where the fentanyl pills were made. This was a massive operation. Machines lined the walls. There were five automatic machines that pressed the fentanyl powder into tablets. Ingredients for the deadly mix were in bags and boxes on wheeled metal carts. Raymond Barstow knew he'd discovered the motherlode. He began to take photos with his cell phone. He photographed the machines and the shelves of ingredients. He took shots of the room where all of the equipment and supplies were stored. He took photos with his phone, as fast as he could, of the many hundreds of bags of already packaged tablets.

Barstow realized what he had to do, and he had to do it fast. He didn't know exactly how long he'd been inside the drug-making facility, but he knew it had been too long. He clambered back up the wooden stairs. He took several quick photos of the tractor seat, the staircase, and the entrance in the ground. On his way to his truck, he turned around and shot a few pictures of the dilapidated barn. He wanted to document everything before he destroyed it all.

Because he'd often found himself in places where there were no gas stations, when he'd been a special agent, Bart had always traveled with two ten-gallon containers of extra gasoline. This was not the safest thing to do, but even after he retired he still kept extra gasoline in his truck. It saved him from running out of gas at inconvenient times and places. It made him feel secure. Because he was former military as well as a former FBI special agent, Barstow also kept a small amount of Semtex, some fuses, a timer, and a few grenades in his truck. The Semtex was old and so were the grenades. Bart didn't know if they would still work.

He lugged the containers of gasoline to the wooden stairs and struggled to get them to the bottom without dropping them. He poured the gasoline mostly over the already man-ufactured fentanyl tablets. When he thought how many lives would be destroyed by this amount of product if it ever made its way to the street, he decided this was the priority that needed to be obliterated. He set up the fuses and the Semtex in the room with the machines. He knew it would be touch and go for him to be able to get himself safely out of the un-derground bunker after he'd started the fire. He hoped that taking these chances and putting himself in danger would result in reducing it all to nothing but ashes.

He was working against the clock and up against the fear that the people who were employees in this fentanyl lab would return at any minute. He'd done a patchwork job, but he hoped it would be sufficient. He would like to have burned it all with the workers inside, but that was too much to wish for. He set the timer on the fuses. He dropped some matches into the puddles of gasoline. Flames were al-ready licking at his heels as he raced to make his way back up the rickety wooden staircase. He pulled the pins from the grenades and tossed them back down into the hole in the ground. He left the entrance to the underground drug lab open. He wanted the fire he'd started to have plenty of oxygen to keep it going. He ran to his truck. He was going to make it.

Bart's heart sank when he saw a sheriff's car approaching the barn on the dirt road. He could see that Gene Randolph was driving and that the deputy was alone. Barstow had a split second to make a decision. He raised his gun as the sheriff's car passed him on the dirt road. Bart took his best shot at the driver's head but did not stay around to see the driver lose control of the vehicle. The deputy sheriff's car careened into the barn. Barstow was taking a chance by not checking to make sure that Randolph was dead. Randolph was a witness and could identify Barstow's truck as having been in the vicinity of the drug barn at the time it was, hopefully, destroyed by fire. Raymond Barstow was primarily interested in making a surreptitious and very quick escape from the scene.

The retired FBI agent had not had time to think about the consequences of his actions. He was no longer an FBI special agent. What he had done, both starting the fire and shooting Gene Randolph, were completely against the law. If he'd still been employed by the FBI, he would have had to handle everything very differently. He would have had to arrest Gene Randolph and hope he didn't make bail and disappear. Who knows what would have happened at a homegrown trial with a home-cooked judge.

If he'd done things by the book, Bart would have had to secure the remote drug manufacturing site and hope the people who ran it didn't clear it all out before the crime scene techs could arrive and do their thing. Bart knew the drug people would have been able to save at least part of their fentanyl stash if he hadn't acted as he did. He had decided on the spur of the moment that he couldn't allow any of those things to happen. He had been rash and impulsive. He had broken the law, and he wasn't sorry. Maybe his gasoline and explosives wouldn't even work. Maybe there would not be any fire. It had all happened so fast, and his efforts to destroy the fentanyl lab had been reckless and by the seat of his pants, using only what he had on hand.

Driving back to his hotel room, he was operating on automatic. Every morning when he left his room, he packed his duffle bag with all of his belongings. He was always prepared to leave at a moment's notice. Cameron Richardson had initially rented the motel room for his friend when Raymond Barstow first came to town. Cameron had rented the place for a month, not knowing exactly how long it would take to sort out the situation with Bubba and his backpack.

Then Bart had become obsessed with finding Bubba's suppliers. He'd kept the motel room and paid by the month. It was cheaper that way. He came and went. He stayed in the room sporadically. He drove back and forth between River Springs and his home in Fayetteville. The people who ran the motel and the housekeeping staff were used to his sometimes being there and sometimes not being there. His room was paid for through the end of January. He didn't want anyone to think he was checking out today.

He was lucky that he was able to avoid seeing anyone when he let himself into his room, grabbed his bag, and returned to his truck. He drove as fast as he could away from River Springs. Raymond Barstow was on his way home to Fayetteville. It was more than a three-hour drive. He had finished his work in River Springs once and for all and did not intend to return any time soon. He was going to pretend he'd been at home in Fayetteville all day — that he'd never been in River Springs that morning and that he'd never ever made a visit to the Denken Farm. If he had been successful, no one would ever know who had taken things into their own hands and wiped out the massive drug manufacturing and storage facility at the remote Arkansas farm.

He hoped the gasoline and the grenades and the Semtex had done their job. He didn't look back at the horizon to try to see if there were any flames or smoke. He kept driving northwest. He would know soon enough if his fire had actually started and how much of the drug lab it had destroyed. He would find out about the chances he had taken when he listened to the evening news. Everyone had thought the drugs were coming by way of Memphis. No one had ever imagined that the Denken farm in rural Arkansas was in fact fentanyl central.

34

Cameron and Sidney were relaxing in front of a fire when he heard the familiar bing and checked his phone. He knew Sidney would be interested in what he'd just read on his phone. "I just received a text from Bart. He says he's giving up on the drug dealing case and going back to Fayetteville for good. He says he's exhausted all the leads he had, and there's nothing more for him to pursue. He says to thank you for your help with the lead on Gene Randolph. He hopes the FBI agent who was assigned as the liaison to the sheriff's department will eventually be able to get the goods on Gene. But Bart's out of it, or so he says. I'm actually kind of shocked he's not keeping at this. I thought he would follow it through to the end and actually solve it. He's such a bulldog about his cases. But he's retired now. Without any real power any more, I think it's been frustrating for him to try to run down these drug suppliers. He was operating on this one in kind of a no man's land. He gave it his best shot."

Sidney thought this text from Bart was good news. "If he really means to give it up, I have to say I'm relieved. I was always afraid he would intentionally or unintentionally bring Ginny's name into this. I've held my breath all these months, hoping that wouldn't happen. I hope he's really going back into retirement for good."

They decided not to watch the news that night. The news had become so depressing that, even Cameron, who always wanted to know the latest about everything, sometimes took a night off.

They heard about the fire and the explosions at the Denken farm soon enough. It was the top news story on all the Little Rock TV stations for days. Sidney's and Cameron's cell phones exploded with story after story about the remote and little-known farm outside of River Springs. At first the story was just about the emergency responders, about all the fire trucks and firemen from everywhere that had descended on the Denken farm to try to put out the massive blaze. Everyone wondered what in the world could have started such a conflagration at the abandoned homestead. The next thing on the news was no more news. There seemed to be a muzzle on what was happening with the investigation of the fire.

There was also a story about a local sheriff's deputy who had responded to the fire. That was the assumption…that the law enforcement officer had been responding to the fire. Or at least it was the story that had been given out to the press. Authorities said a deputy sheriff had died when his car lost control and ran into the abandoned barn on the Denken farm. The report said that the county sheriff's vehicle had been mostly consumed by the fire when the first responders arrived on the scene. Because of the resulting condition of the vehicle, it was impossible to determine if the deputy sheriff's car accident had happened before the fire started or as a result of the massive fire. There was no mention that anything other than the car crash had contributed to the deputy's death.

The press demanded to know the name of the deputy who had died in the car crash at the scene of the fire. At first the sheriff's office refused to reveal the name of the deputy who had died. The reason given was that the next of kin had not been located and had not yet been notified of the death. Eventually and inevitably, the name of Eugene Randolph leaked to the public. The press also wanted to know what had caused the car accident that had killed the sheriff's deputy, but there had been no explanation given out about that. The sheriff's department wasn't saying much at all about the deputy who had crashed his car and died.

Sidney and Cameron wondered why nothing much was being said about the deputy who had lost his life at the scene of the fire. The sheriff's department might have been expected to make a hero out of the man. The Richardsons figured that something about Eugene Randolph's complicity in the drug dealing and his connection with the fentanyl lab must have come to light for the local law enforcement agency, the sheriff's department, not to make a big deal out of the deputy's death. Whatever had been discovered was being held back from the public. If the truth ever came out, they figured it might cause unwanted embarrassment for the sheriff's department.

Finally the story came out about the fentanyl lab. The FBI, the DEA, and the various other feds who were involved would like to have kept it all under wraps. But the story was too sensational and too big to keep quiet. The media was all over every detail. The bottom line was that the underground fentanyl manufacturing and storage facility had been completely destroyed. No one had been working in the drug lab at the time it was set on fire, so there had been no loss of life. There was nothing in the news about who had been operating the fentanyl lab. It was impossible to know if the lack of information was because law enforcement didn't know who was behind the drug manufacturing or because investigators had been able to keep a lid on that part of what had happened.

Cameron had connections everywhere. He hadn't been able to learn much more from his connections other than what had been on the news, what everybody knew. From the little his sources had been able to tell him, the federal agencies, who were sorting through the few ashes that remained in the destroyed underground lab at the Denken farm, knew pretty much nothing at all about who had set up the lab, who had been running it, or who had destroyed it.

The people who had worked there had disappeared into the woodwork or into the woods or someplace. They were long gone, as far as the federal agents were able to determine. Cameron hated to hear this, as he worried that whoever was responsible for bringing drugs to Arkansas would soon set up their evil activities someplace else. He especially didn't want them to set up a new facility in his state, but he didn't want these evildoers making drugs anywhere in the country. That was wishful thinking, of course. With the money that could be made selling fentanyl, new drug-making facilities would unfortunately be appearing in every state.

Cameron was thankful somebody had destroyed the operation at the Denken farm. He was certain that farm's remote location was one place which would never again be used as a drug laboratory. Whoever the person or persons were who had been responsible for starting the fire and setting off the explosions that obliterated the lab also remained a mystery to investigators. There was nothing remaining after the fire that might lead the authorities to either the people who had been running the drug facility or to the people who had destroyed it. There were no clues left to follow.

Cameron did hear there was a rumor that the deputy sheriff who had been at the Denken Farm had been shot several times in the face. That was what had caused him to crash the car into the abandoned barn. This information had not been released to the public and was unconfirmed. The truth was being closely held by the local authorities. Cameron sensed that there was a massive cover-up going on regarding this part of the story. No confirmation was ever given about anything when this issue was brought up at a news conference.

Sidney and Cameron had suspected all along that it must have been Gene Randolph who had died at the Denken farm. His name had been leaked by the press, but the sheriff's office had not officially confirmed that it was Gene Randolph who had died. As far as the Richardsons knew, Gene was the only member of the sheriff's department who would have known about the existence of the fentanyl lab. Several weeks after the destruction of the lab, the sheriff's department quietly announced that Deputy Eugene Randolph was deceased and had "died in the line of duty." Sidney was disgusted that the "line of duty" thing had been included in the announcement. It made Gene sound almost like a hero, which he certainly was not.

Sidney and Cameron would probably never know the whole story, but the fact that the announcement of Gene's death had been delayed and had been so quietly and minimally reported, led them to believe that the truth about

Eugene Randolph's connections to the drug network must have been uncovered. The department was saving face by not revealing Gene's involvement with the crimes.

Raymond Barstow closely followed every detail that was in the news about what had happened in River Springs. His fellow FBI agents who had known how involved Bart had been in the case had wondered why he'd decided to throw in the towel and go home to Fayetteville for good. A few might have briefly suspected that Bart had something to do with the destruction of the fentanyl lab. Bart kind of had an alibi. Nobody bothered to ask, but if they had, he would have told them he'd been in Fayetteville all day. But everyone was happy the place was no longer in operation. Whoever had done the deed had done the world a favor. If any of his former colleagues really thought Raymond Barstow had anything to do with the fire, they never said anything to anyone about their suspicions.

Another aspect of the case that would never be solved was the mystery of who had sent to the FBI nearly one hundred photos of the drug facility at the Denken farm. What was fascinating about these photos was that they'd all been taken *before* the facility had burned. The authorities suspected that whoever had destroyed the drug factory had taken the photos before starting the fire. The FBI wondered if one of the people who worked at the fentanyl facility had gone rogue and decided to photograph what was happening at the farm. It was almost as if whoever had taken all these cell phone pictures had wanted to document what he or she was intending to obliterate. The photos had been sent from a burner phone to an FBI hotline via an email account that no longer existed. Neither the phone nor the email could be traced.

From time to time, Raymond Barstow felt like he wanted to tell Cameron Richardson what he had done. Cameron had been the person who'd called him in on the drug situation in River Springs. At first Bart had not wanted to become involved, but once he started investigating, he was hooked and couldn't let go. Raymond Barstow knew his friend Cameron Richardson well. He knew Cameron was a straight arrow and a law-and-order kind of guy. He knew Cameron was undoubtedly delighted that the drug lab had been burned, but Bart also knew he could never tell Cameron that he'd been the one who had actually destroyed it.

Raymond Barstow realized that he could never tell anyone that he was the perpetrator of two very high profile and dramatic criminal acts. He had shot and killed a law enforcement officer. The man had been a crooked, drug-dealing deputy sheriff, but Bart had been judge, jury, and executioner. He had destroyed a drug-making facility that might have yielded clues about the network that was manufacturing fentanyl. The retired FBI special agent would have to live alone with whatever guilt he might feel as well as with whatever pride and satisfaction he might feel for having taken the law into his own hands and acted. He would focus on fly fishing in his retirement. He would probably visit River Springs from time to time, but he could never mention his secret role in ending the madness there.

It had been months since Sidney had sent Juanita's painting to Becky Sells in New York City. After the package had finally been found behind the radiator in the mail room of her apartment house, Becky had turned the painting over to the experts at Sotheby's. There was an art historian and restoration specialist on their staff that Becky trusted. She knew she would get an expert and honest evaluation of the artwork, and she knew the painting would be returned to her without a huge delay. Becky had considered sending the painting to the Metropolitan Museum of Art. She was certain the well-known museum's experts would be able to determine if the painting was a copy, but she also knew it might be years before the Met returned the painting to her... even if they determined that it was a copy.

Becky knew the painting had to be a copy, but it had looked incredibly well-done to her amateur and inexpert eye. Once in a while Sidney would ask her what was going on with the Vermeer copy. Becky could only tell her to be patient. Sidney in turn would tell Juanita to be patient, that these things took time, that the very best experts were being consulted.

What Becky didn't know was that her expert at Sotheby's had been stumped by the Vermeer painting. The person at Sotheby's with whom Becky had shared the painting had promised to keep the existence of the excellent copy a closely guarded secret. They both realized what a sensation would be created in the press, in the art world, and in the public, if word slipped out that one of the paintings had turned up from the infamous 1990 robbery in Boston. Or, if anyone even suspected that one of the paintings in question *might have turned up.* Even if the painting was determined to be copy, there would be a storm of interest generated. Becky and her expert both wanted to avoid this kind of attention at all costs.

The Sotheby's expert had done chemical tests on the paint and on the canvas. She had done x-rays on the piece. She had done every possible test on what was believed to be a copy of Vermeer's *The Concert,* and the expert was still unable to say with complete certainty that it was a copy.

The stakes were incredibly high. If this was not a copy and was the real thing, it would be the first piece, and only piece to date, to be recovered from the 1990 robbery at the Isabella Stewart Gardner Museum, the first and only painting to see the light of day. The results of the analysis of this Vermeer painting could mean the recovery of a work of art that alone was worth many millions of dollars. If this painting was determined not to be a copy, new investigations into everything would be ignited. If this painting was the genuine Vermeer from the heist, what had happened to the other paintings and other items that had been stolen in

1990? It was a momentous responsibility to be tasked with determining the authenticity of the painting.

The Sotheby's employee had reluctantly decided to consult with the appropriate expert at the Metropolitan Museum of Art. Sotheby's expert would not allow the artwork to leave the premises of the auction house, but the Met had been accommodated and had been able to examine the painting. All of this had been accomplished under conditions of continued total secrecy. After a delay of several months, the verdict was finally in. The auction house and the museum had agreed at last that the painting was indeed a copy. It was a very good copy to be sure. It was almost a perfect copy, but it was a copy just the same.

Their joint decision had ultimately rested on the condition of the canvas that had been used to make the copy. The canvas had been used before. It had been carefully cleaned before the new paint had been applied, but it had not been cleaned perfectly. The painting itself had been flawless. Whoever had done the forgery had been a genius. There was much discussion about whether or not AI might have been used to paint the copy. It was so perfectly done, the experts could not imagine that a human hand had been responsible for this amazing but almost certainly fake work of art.

Becky's expert at Sotheby's had a client who collected forgeries, fakes, and copies of famous works of art. He was very rich, and he owned hundreds of pieces, none of which were genuine. The eccentric billionaire was willing to pay high prices for the works he bought for his collection, but the works had to be certifiably not created by the original artist. The collector was adamant about this. The Sotheby's expert knew her client would be willing to pay a very large sum of money for the Vermeer copy. It had taken months to determine that it was a copy... it was that good. And, it was beautifully done, in and of its own right. The original that had been stolen from the Gardner Museum had been darkened by age and by deteriorating varnish. The copy was bright and probably closely resembled the original painting. It now looked much as it might have looked in the seventeenth century when it was fresh from Vermeer's studio.

When her expert at Sotheby's mentioned to Becky that she might have a buyer for the Vermeer copy, Becky wanted to know how much the client would be willing to pay. Becky didn't feel she could go to Sidney's friend and employee Juanita and ask her to give up her painting without being able to quote a price. Because of the notoriety of the original painting, the burglary, and the provenance of the circumstances that surrounded both the original and the copy, the art expert told Becky she felt her client would be willing to pay Juanita two million dollars for the copy.

This amount of money would change Juanita's life completely. Even after paying a significant amount in federal and state income taxes, Juanita would never have to work another day in her life. She would be rich, a millionaire. Becky passed the information along to Sidney. Juanita was greatly relieved that her copy of *The Concert* was not the original that had been stolen from the Boston Museum so many years earlier. Sidney assured Juanita repeatedly that the painting was really hers.

If Juanita had not retrieved the Vermeer copy from the trash can, it would now be moldering away in the local landfill, lying beneath piles of coffee grounds and grapefruit rinds and other garbage... gone forever from anyone's view. Juanita had saved it by rescuing it from the garbage can and putting it in her bedroom. The only other claim on the ownership of the painting might be from the people who had bought the cottage from the women's shelter. And the new owners were, of course, Sidney and Cameron Richardson. Juanita and Sidney had a good laugh about that.

Sidney and Juanita had a heart-to-heart talk about the possibility of Juanita selling the painting. Juanita was stunned, as Sidney had been, with the offer of millions for the painting. With such an extraordinary offer on the table, everyone expected that Juanita would of course opt to sell the fake Vermeer...without a moment's hesitation. Juanita, however, liked her life as it was. She was an intelligent, wise, and well-grounded woman. She wanted to think things over before she agreed to sell the painting.

The Return

BOSTON

2024

Epilogue

Maximillian Sobrille had made very careful preparations for handing over to the Isabella Stewart Gardner Museum the masterpieces he had painted. He claimed in his letter that the copies he was "returning" were the original works of art. In addition to the ten copies he had created, Maximillian was also returning the actual bronze eagle finial that had sat atop a flagpole that held a silk flag from Napoleon's First Regiment of the Imperial Guard; the actual ten-inch-tall Shang dynasty bronze beaker or gu which was by far the oldest of the stolen objects; and the actual 1.75-inch by 2-inch medallion etching, a miniature self-portrait by Rembrandt, *Portrait of the Artist as a Young Man*. These three pieces had been stolen from the museum in 1990. They were the very same pieces that had been stolen nearly thirty-five years earlier. Maximillian felt that returning these three original artifacts which were the real thing, with his five paintings and five drawings, would lend credence to the belief that the copies were also the real thing.

When he realized that he was nearing the end of his life, Maximillian had hired a lawyer. Maximillian had used an assumed name when he'd hired the lawyer. Using his computer, he had conducted his business with the lawyer and made the arrangements for the return of the paintings to the Isabella Stewart

Gardner Museum. Maximillian and his attorney never met in person. Maximillian had paid the man generously and in advance for the work the man was to do...mostly after Maximillian died. The attorney who was handling it all knew nothing about his client's connection to the Isabella Stewart Gardner Museum's lost treasures. He did not know that the letters he had in his possession had anything to do with the Gardner Museum. He only knew that he was to conduct business on behalf of his client after the client's death.

There were three envelopes and two letters of explanations and instructions. The first and most important letter was the one that Maximillian had composed to send to the Gardner Museum explaining how he had come into possession of their stolen artwork. The story he told them was only partly true. Maximillian explained that the masterpieces he'd found had been in terrible shape after many years of being stored under extremely poor conditions. Without any attention to climate control, they had been neglected and forgotten for all those years. Maximillian explained that he was an art restorer and had restored the five paintings and the five drawings to the best of his ability. He explained that he wished to remain anonymous, even after his death.

His letter also explained why he had not wanted to return the artwork until after he had died. He had not wanted the notoriety that he knew would arise as a result of his being the person who had found the stolen works of art, restored them, and returned them to the Gardner. He knew that if he were alive when the artwork from the heist was returned, he would be at the center of a storm of publicity, controversy, and questions. He'd wanted to avoid all of that, so he had decided to wait until after his death to return the artwork to the museum.

In his letter, Maximillian gave the museum the location of the climate-controlled storage unit where the stolen artwork could be found. He had also enclosed in the letter two keys that would open the lock that secured the door to the unit. He sealed this letter, addressed to the Isabella Stewart Gardner Museum, and put it inside another envelope.

This second envelope contained, in addition to Maximillian's letter to the Gardner Museum, instructions to his attorney. These instructions told the attorney to send the enclosed letter by certified mail to the Isabella Stewart Gardner Museum. Someone at the museum would have to sign for the letter. This would be proof that the letter had been delivered and received. This second envelope addressed to Maximillian's attorney was in turn put inside a third and larger envelope that said on the outside, "Only To Be Opened ONE YEAR After My Death." Maximillian was covering all the bases.

Maximillian's agreement with his attorney was that the artist would send a text to the attorney once a year on a certain date to verify that he was still alive. Maximillian had purchased a pre-paid cellular phone to send this yearly text to the law office in Boston. He used the phone exclusively for this once-a-year texting task. Maximillian always sent the text to the attorney on the occasion of the anniversary of the Gardner Museum heist, but of course the attorney had no way of knowing this detail.

If the attorney did not receive the text on the scheduled date, March 18th, he would know that his mystery client had died. The attorney's instructions were that he was to wait one year from the date of the missed text message. These instructions were also spelled out clearly on the outside of the largest envelope in the attorney's care. After waiting the prescribed one year, the attorney was to open the outside envelope and follow the instructions inside.

When the attorney in Boston did not received the yearly text in March of 2024, he knew his client had died. He knew the client was elderly and in poor health. The attorney had promised to follow the client's directions exactly. He would wait one year, as directed, and he would open the first envelope in March of 2025. The second envelope was inside the first, and the attorney would find that this second envelope was addressed to him. Inside the second envelope, along with his instructions, he would find the third envelope addressed to the Isabella Stewart Gardner Museum. As he had promised, he would send it as directed by certified mail. The attorney knew nothing about his client. He would not know what was in the letter addressed to the Gardner Museum. He had been well-paid for this responsibility to his now-deceased client.

After Maximillian's attorney had sent the letter to the Isabella Stewart Gardner Museum, his work was done.

WHEN DID I GROW OLD?

When did I grow old?
    It is now so still around me.
    When did all the noise turn to quiet?
    The cacophony of busyness that engulfed me
        for so many years, has subsided.

When did I grow old?
    Did it happen slowly as the years passed by?
    Did it happen as I filled my time with immediacy...
        moving from one crisis to the next?
    Did it happen all of a sudden when I found I had to use
        a cane to get up and down the steps?

When did I grow old?
    Did I fill those years that passed with goodness and giving
        and love?
    Did I spend too many days in anger and hoping for retaliation
        for things in life that didn't go my way?
    Did I spend too many hours organizing and cleaning and
        worrying about my material possessions?
    How much time did I spend shopping? Sorting out
        my closet?

When did I grow old?
    Was it when I learned that I was deaf in one ear
        and there was no help for that?
    Was it when I realized there were so few days ahead
        and so many already gone?
    Was it when I accepted that I would die?

When did I grow old?
>Was it a gradual process as the hairs on my head
>>one by one turned white?
>Or did it happen overnight? And what night was that?
>Was it when I became a grandmother?

When did I grow old?
>Did I spend this precious time I have been given
>To make a difference?
>To make the world a better place?

When did I grow old?
>Is it today when I know that however this life was spent,
>>it cannot be respent?
>It was what it was…
>Full of imperfections and mistakes and trying hard
>>and often struggling and falling short
>And full of joy and good luck.

When did I grow old?
I just don't know.
Or, maybe I'm not old yet.

MTT 5–7–2014

Author's Note

It is my fondest hope that one day all the artwork that was stolen from the Isabella Stewart Gardner Museum in 1990 will find its way home to where it belongs. Because there has never been a credible sighting of the artwork since it disappeared, and because law enforcement, in spite of herculean efforts, has never been able to find anything, I fear that these lost treasures may never be found.

My story, *Going Home*, is fiction, and I hope it will not turn out to be true. However, it is puzzling that no one has ever seen these works of art again. The statute of limitations has run out on the crime. Those who stole the artwork will not be prosecuted. There is a huge monetary reward for information that leads to the return of the stolen masterpieces. Why not return the artwork so that the world can once again appreciate what has been kept from our eyes for far too long?

Henrietta Alten West

ABOUT THE COVER:

After the robbery at the Isabella Stewart Gardner Museum in 1990, a decision was made to hang empty frames on the walls where the stolen paintings had previously been hung. The empty frames hang on the walls of the museum to this day. The cover of *Going Home* echoes this tribute to the stolen artwork.

COMPLETE BIOGRAPHIES
of the
REUNION CHRONICLES
MYSTERIES CHARACTERS

MAIN CHARACTERS

The following extensive biographies are those of the characters who appear in all of the Reunion Chronicles Mysteries. These include Richard and Elizabeth Carpenter, Gretchen and Bailey MacDermott, Tyler Merriman, Cameron and Sidney Richardson, Matthew and Isabelle Ritter, and J.D. and Olivia Steele. ***Going Home*** is the sixth book in this series.

In the previous four books, I included these extensive biographies in the text of the manuscript. For readers who had read all the books in the series, rereading these lengthy descriptions of the characters became tedious and annoying. I have received many suggestions about to how to give readers background on the characters but not put these biographies in the story itself. I decided to include the complete biographies at the end of the book, but not to include them within the pages of the manuscript. Hopefully, the action will flow better without these interruptions. But following is everything new readers need to know about the main characters in the series.

H.A.W.

ELIZABETH AND RICHARD CARPENTER

When Elizabeth Emerson was a senior at Smith College in Northampton, Massachusetts, the CIA was actively recruiting from the Ivy League men's schools and from the Seven Sisters women's colleges. The spy agency had decided women had good brains after all and made good analysts. The CIA was especially interested in hiring economics majors because they'd found that people who understood economics had analytical minds, were able to process information in a systematic way, and could reach conclusions and solve problems. The CIA was not looking for covert operatives when they interviewed the college seniors. They were not hiring women to wear the classic fedora and trench coat spy outfit, lean against a lamppost in rainy, post-war Vienna, and wait for a rendezvous with a Russian double agent. The CIA wanted desk jockeys.

Elizabeth, an economics major, was of the duck-and-cover generation and had lived in the shadow of the Cold War all her life. She was intrigued by the pitch from the CIA and decided to look into what would be required for her to pursue a career with The Agency. She went to the initial meeting on the Smith campus and then made the trip to Boston with three other women from her college class. In Boston, the four were given a battery of tests, designed to evaluate their abilities to do the work the CIA would require of them. This was the first step in the application process. Those who passed the initial tests would be given more tests, some interviews, and then perhaps the offer of a job in Washington, D.C.

Elizabeth scored "off the charts" in the inductive reasoning part of the testing. Only one other person in CIA recruitment history had ever scored higher than she did in this one very important area, critical to the kind of work the CIA needed done. Although she had never realized it before, Elizabeth was told she could read and evaluate vast amounts of material in an incredibly short period of time and come up with an accurate analysis and conclusion. The testing people made a big deal over her, and this embarrassed the somewhat introverted Elizabeth. They singled her out, and she didn't like it. Since she'd never known she had this special skill, she wasn't that impressed with herself. She wondered what all the fuss was about.

Elizabeth had been seriously dating a graduate of Princeton who was now a first-year medical student at Tulane. Elizabeth was in love, and she thought Richard Carpenter was, too. It was 1966, and women married young. It was early in the women's liberation movement. Not all women, even very well-educated ones, had careers. Many became housewives and mothers. Elizabeth had always been very independent, but she couldn't imagine her life without Richard. Richard was not enthusiastic about her pursuing a career with the CIA. He didn't really understand that she wouldn't be in any danger, sitting in an office in Langley, Virginia, reading newspapers and looking at data sets. He wanted her with him in New Orleans, although he'd not yet asked her to marry him.

When he did pop the question, Elizabeth said yes. They would be married that summer. The CIA was disappointed when Elizabeth turned down their offer of a position as an analyst. They pulled out all the stops and harassed her mercilessly for the remainder of her senior year. They played the "serving your country" card and everything else they could think of. Elizabeth did not waiver, and she and Richard were married in August. She got a job teaching in the New Orleans public schools, and the CIA became a distant memory. But the CIA kept its eyes on her, and years later when she decided to change careers, they welcomed her with open arms.

After she left New Orleans, Elizabeth went to graduate school. After spending two years on the faculty at the University of Texas at El Paso, she took a position teaching economics and economic history at a small college in Maryland. She was pressured to change a grade so that a failing student could become a "C" student. The student, who had not put forth any effort whatsoever in her class, had to have a "C" in order to maintain his eligibility to play basketball for the college team. The academic dean leaned on and threatened Elizabeth. Because she was only a part-time professor, the dean told her she could easily be fired from her position, if she didn't do as she was told and change the grade. Elizabeth refused to knuckle under to the threats and gave the student a "D." He had barely made the "D" and had just escaped failing her class by the skin of his teeth. After she'd turned in her grades, someone went to the registrar's office and changed the student's grade to a "C." The young man never missed a step or a dribble on the basketball court because of his failing academic work. Learning and getting an education had proven to be an afterthought, or given no thought at all, when it came to qualifying for a sports team.

Elizabeth thought she could hang on to her job, but she decided she did not want to be a part of the rotten system any more. She'd always known academia was fraught with politics, corrupted by competition to get ahead of one's colleagues, and filled with bloated and narcissistic egos. She decided life was short, and she didn't have to play the stupid games required to succeed in the university arena. She didn't want to be around the grasping and ambitious meanies any more.

She decided to take a job that she'd been offered years earlier. She made some phone calls and began the difficult task of hiring babysitters, drivers, and a housekeeper. She made complicated arrangements for her duties at home to be taken care of when she was gone. She began to build her cover story, that she was taking a research position at the Wharton School in Philadelphia. It was a three-hour commute one-way to her new job, and she would be away from home a couple of nights a week, sometimes more. It was a big commitment, but her new boss was willing to work with her to maintain the illusion of the imaginary job she supposedly had at the University of Pennsylvania. She was a valuable commodity, and the CIA helped her manage her home duties and her cover position in Philadelphia, as she committed to the more dangerous job she'd really been hired to do.

Most of her work was in Virginia, using the skills she'd demonstrated when the CIA had wanted to hire her years earlier. Occasionally she had to make trips overseas. None of her family or friends ever doubted for a minute that she was working at the Wharton School. They thought it was odd that she was gone from home so much, but by now, two of her children were away at boarding school in New England. Only one daughter was still at home. No one, not even Richard Carpenter, was allowed to know what Elizabeth did when she was out of town.

It was a rocky period in the Carpenters' marriage. Richard was consumed with his work as head of the surgical pathology department and clinical laboratory at the local hospital. He participated in the children's activities whenever he could, but he was pretty much oblivious to Elizabeth's needs at this time in their lives. He was angry that she wasn't around all the time, as she had always been before, but he was so preoccupied with his own career, he only noticed she wasn't there when something went wrong.

Richard Carpenter had risen to the top of his career and was the main partner in his pathology group, Richard Carpenter, M.D., P.A. He had done his internship and residency at the University of Pennsylvania, and during those years he'd had an opportunity to work with Philadelphia's medical examiner. In addition to spending his days accompanying the Chief Medical Examiner, Richard had done moonlighting for the medical examiner's office to earn extra money. The young doctor became a skilled and convincing expert witness. He was a favorite with prosecutors because juries loved his boyish looks and earnest, honest voice. When he was on the witness stand, members of the jury believed everything Richard Carpenter, M.D. had to say. If he gave evidence against someone in a murder trial, that person was always convicted. Vance Stillinger, M.D. was the Philadelphia Medical Examiner, and Richard Carpenter M.D. became his golden boy.

Carpenter's testimony had sent a number of very bad guys to prison. The child molesters, murderers, drug dealers, and drivers who had committed serial DUIs all should have known it was their own behavior that had caused them to be convicted. But bad boys and girls always want to find someone other than themselves to blame. Carpenter became a lightning rod for their anger, and some wanted to blame the blonde, cherub-faced scientist who had so convincingly swayed the juries that had convicted them. Occasionally, a defendant would shake his fist at Carpenter when he was on the witness stand.

Once a man stood up and shouted threats at Carpenter after he'd given his expert witness testimony. The defendant, who had been resoundingly drunk when he'd crossed the highway's median strip and run headlong into a van full of children, said Carpenter had misrepresented his blood alcohol level. The driver of the van and four of the children had died, and the defendant was sent to prison. The drunk vowed that when he got out of jail, he would hunt down Carpenter and kill him and his family.

Elizabeth Carpenter had just come home from the hospital after giving birth to the Carpenters' second child. Law enforcement took the threats against Carpenter and his family seriously, and until the convicted criminal was sentenced and safely locked away, the police kept a guard on Carpenter's rented house in the Philadelphia suburbs. Elizabeth wondered who would be there in a few years to watch out for her family when the man was released from prison.

Stillinger tried to convince his protégé to stay in Philadelphia and become a forensic pathologist, but Carpenter owed Uncle Sam two years of his life, serving in the U.S. Army. Furthermore, Carpenter had educational debts and needed and wanted to earn some money. He wanted more income than the salary of an urban medical examiner would pay him, and he didn't want to live in a city. The Army sent Carpenter to William Beaumont Army Medical Center in Texas for two years, and from there, Carpenter took a position at a hospital in a small town in Maryland where he built a successful pathology practice. He still testified as an expert witness, but the threats that had come his way when he was at the Philadelphia Medical Examiner's Office were long-forgotten. The question was, had the men he'd helped send to prison forgotten him?

When Elizabeth reached the age of seventy, she began to write mystery novels. An avid reader, she'd read thousands, probably tens of thousands, of mystery stories over the years.

She began with Nancy Drew and moved on to Agatha Christie and everybody else. Of all the careers she's had in her life, being an author of mystery novels is her favorite.

GRETCHEN AND BAILEY MACDERMOTT

Bailey MacDermott graduated with an engineering degree from the University of Arkansas. He was hired by IBM directly out of college, and because of his outgoing personality and gift for gab, he quickly became one of Big Blue's best salesmen in his region. But Bailey was an independent guy, and he felt as if he was being smothered in the corporate world. He'd been selling computer systems to the oil industry, to help them with payroll and inventory and to keep track of where their oil was coming from and where it was going. Bailey let a couple of his clients know he was interested in making a change, and within a few weeks he had a job offer from a major oil company. He submitted his resignation at IBM and left his job in Chicago. Houston was calling, and Bailey was ready to conquer the oil business and earn some big money. Soon he was flying back and forth from Houston to the oil-rich kingdoms in the Middle East. Before long, he knew the countries and who the movers and shakers were in the world's wealthiest oil-producing nations.

When the Shah of Iran fell, the world, and especially the Middle East, was turned upside down. Previously ignored actors on the world's political and economic scene were on the march, and a few days after the hostages in Iran were taken, the U.S. Department of Defense was knocking on Bailey's door. He was a patriot and agreed to work with the DIA, one of the pentagon's spy agencies.

At first, he just met with Americans in Riyadh and other Arab capitals. He carried the packages and papers these agents asked him to take back with him when he flew home to the U.S. Then he was asked to meet with foreign nationals and accompany them to safe houses. Once, in Lebanon, he had to rescue an American who was in desperate shape, running from Hezbollah, and suffering from serious gunshot wounds in his lower leg and thigh. Bailey drove the man to the airport in his rental car and slipped him aboard the oil company's plane. Bailey's assignments became more and more complex and more and more dangerous. He told himself he was doing all of this because he was helping to fight terrorism, but he also loved the rush he got from taking risks.

After a particularly harrowing mission, Bailey had to take some time off from his regular job with the oil company and from his special work for the DIA. He spent a month recuperating in Paris. He slept late and ate well. He also met and fell in love with an American woman he met at the Rodin Museum. Bailey had gone there to learn more about the sculpture. Marianna Archer was at the museum posing for magazine photographs. She was a gorgeous redhead who earned her living as a highly-paid fashion model. She was doing a photoshoot for an American fashion magazine and was dressed in very tight stretch stirrup pants, enormous earrings, and a sexy faux suede off-the-shoulder top. Bailey stumbled into the room where Marianna had her arms draped around *The Thinker*. That day Bailey completely missed seeing Rodin's most famous work of art, but he couldn't take his eyes off Marianna as she pranced and posed around the naked man made out of bronze.

It was the 1980s and Bailey MacDermott decided he had been a bachelor long enough. Marianna was a lonely ex-pat living in France, and she quickly succumbed to Bailey's warm and friendly personality. They spent a lot of time at her apartment getting acquainted, and before Bailey's month of vacation was over, the two were married. It was probably a mistake for them to marry, even under the best of circumstances. The complexity of their work lives and the travel both of their jobs required meant they spent a lot of time apart. Their time together was frenetic, and they never had a chance to really get to know each other.

What Bailey didn't know about Marianna was that she was manic-depressive, a mental illness that has since been renamed "bipolar 1 disorder." If she stayed on her meds, Marianna was mostly fine and a lot of fun. When she went off her meds, all bets were off. When they returned to the U.S., she realized she was pregnant. Bailey and Marianna's son was born in Houston, and Bailey was beside himself with joy. Marianna, on the other hand, lapsed into postpartum depression and a serious depressive phase of her mental illness. She reached the point where she didn't want to get out of bed at all.

Bailey and Marianna eventually divorced. She ceded custody of their son to Bailey, but Bailey was juggling too many things. He told the DOD he wasn't able to work for them anymore, and he quit his job working for the oil company because he didn't want to travel all the time. He began dealing in oil futures and was incredibly successful in this field. He made a lot of money, but the best part of his life at this time was that once he settled down in Dallas, he was able to make a home for himself and his son.

Before he met Gretchen, rumors flew that he had married again in haste twice and then quickly divorced twice! He didn't like to talk about what had happened in his love life during this period, and no one wanted to ask. It was clearly a painful subject for Bailey.

Gretchen Johanssen technically worked in human resources, but she was one of those people who was so competent that, wherever she worked, she eventually took over running much more than the HR department. She was petite and fit, and her good looks and style attracted attention. Once you got to know Gretchen and once you had worked with her for a while, because of her extraordinary competence, you forgot how small she was. Her abilities and her organizational skills belied her size, and she took on a significant presence in any room where she worked or spoke.

Gretchen had married twice and had two wonderful sons. She adopted and raised a foster daughter. Her daughter was still in graduate school, but after her second divorce and after her sons were launched, one into the military and the other to college, Gretchen decided to take a job with an international financial group. She had always wanted to travel and was excited to be sent to run the HR department at her company's office in Zurich.

As always happened when Gretchen arrived on the scene, her ability to get things accomplished was immediately recognized, and she took on more and more responsibilities, above and beyond her HR duties. She always attracted attention at a board meetings. When she made an outstanding presentation to a group of international businessmen, the head of one of Switzerland's wealthiest and most secretive banks noticed her. He wanted to date her and wanted to hire her to work for him. He offered her a salary three times what she was earning in her current job. She agreed to take the lucrative position as his special advisor, but she never mixed business and romance.

The Swiss banker was smart enough to agree to her terms, and Gretchen spent several years making top-level decisions in the arcane world of Swiss banking and international finance. She became fluent in German. She met arms dealers, heads of state, assassins, movie stars, Russians and Saudis, and people she was sure were mafia figures or drug dealers or both. She helped her employers invest their clients' riches. She knew the identities of many who had secret money and needed to conceal it.

When one of her ex-husbands was murdered, Gretchen returned to the United States. Her son, who was a Navy Seal, was involved in an almost-fatal car accident, and Gretchen wanted to spend time with him, helping him heal and boosting his spirits as he recovered. She was an accomplished corporate operator, but she was first and foremost a mother. It was while her son was recovering the use of his legs at a rehabilitation center in Texas that Gretchen met Bailey.

Bailey volunteered at the VA hospital where Gretchen's son was going for physical therapy. Bailey still made deals of all kinds. He had branched out from oil futures into commercial real estate, and it seemed that whatever he touched turned to gold. Volunteering to work with military personnel who were trying to get back on their feet was Bailey's way of giving back. He loved his work, but he loved working with the disabled vets even more. He spent time with Gretchen's son on an almost daily basis, and it was the young Navy Seal who introduced Bailey MacDermott to his mother.

Bailey and Gretchen had both been burned in the marriage department. Neither one was looking for a spouse. Each of them was happy living alone, but as they spent more and more time in each other's company, they realized how much they loved each other and wanted to spend the rest of their lives together.

Gretchen had taken a job with a company in Dallas, and in no time, she had, as she always did, made herself indispensable to her new company. She was the kind of employee who quickly became critical to the organization. When she mentioned the possibility of retirement, she was offered a large bonus to stay on for two more years. At the end of those two years, when the subject of retirement came up again, she was offered an even larger bonus, if she would just stay on a little longer. She might never retire because she was making too much money just by mentioning the word "retirement."

Bailey had moved into doing deals in international real estate, and this new clientele sometimes presented challenges. There were language barriers, although most people involved in the upper echelons of the business world spoke English. There were cultural differences, especially when it came to determining what was legal and ethical and what was not. Most of his clients were legitimate buyers who actually wanted to own a warehouse in Hong Kong or Mexico or an apartment building in Singapore. But a few clients who contacted Bailey were interested in buying real estate for the purposes of laundering money.

The schemes the money launderers devised were complicated and slick. Bailey found himself involved in a couple of these transactions before he caught on to what was happening. When he realized what these faux buyers were up to, he had to say no. He refused to participate in any money laundering intrigue. More than once, a disappointed money launderer had threatened Bailey's life. Bailey loved the rush and the risk of doing high-flying business transactions, but he definitely did not enjoy having a loaded gun pressed against his head. When one of these crooks tracked him to his home and threatened him, Bailey and Gretchen had to move to a different house. Bailey learned to be more discreet, but it was impossible for him to give up the thrill of making a deal. Now he was always wary when he took on a new client. In his early seventies, he was a vital and busy wheeler-dealer in the financial world.

TYLER MERRIMAN

Tyler Merriman was a high school football star. The Air Force Academy recruited Tyler to play football, and he played for one year before he was sidelined by a shoulder injury. Tyler stayed on and graduated. He subsequently earned an MBA from Stanford. He became a pilot for the United States Air Force and spent ten years flying military missions for the USA. He never talked about the years he'd spent in the USAF, but his closest friends speculated that he was flying the Lockheed SR-71, "the Blackbird" spy plane that supposedly had the capability to see the numbers and letters on the license plate of a car parked in Red Square. When anyone came right out and asked him if he'd flown the Blackbird, Tyler would hum a few bars of the Beatles' song of the same name and smile his enigmatic smile. If he had flown the Blackbird, he would have been able to see everything and everybody from way up there. But he would never tell.

Tyler had married, briefly, when he was in the military, but his wife was young and somewhat spoiled. She resented the time Tyler spent away from home, and they divorced when they'd been married for less than two years. Tyler moved to Northern California after he left the Air Force. He built a commercial real estate empire and became a wealthy man. Tyler dated well-known and glamorous women — movie actresses, anchorwomen who appeared on national television, and female politicos. He was very good looking and a much sought-after bachelor, but he successfully avoided the altar for decades after his first marriage ended.

Tyler Merriman had been smart and lucky in his business dealings, and he was a consummate athlete. He bought a condominium in Telluride, Colorado so he could ski for several months in the winter. Because he was such a skilled and outstanding performer on the slopes, it wasn't long before he was hired as a ski instructor. His time was his own, and he arranged his schedule so he could spend most of the winter in Telluride. He found he loved teaching others to ski. Tyler had his own plane and flew around the country to check on his commercial real estate empire. He hiked and biked and ran, and he even sometimes played squash when he couldn't be outdoors. Tyler was a very active guy. He decided he wanted to be closer to his condominium in Telluride and eventually relocated from California to Colorado.

Tyler had been attending the reunions for years and looked forward to seeing his old friends and their wives and girl-friends. He'd never brought a date or a partner to one of the events until he'd met Lilleth Dubois when he was in his early seventies. They had a long-term relationship, and Lilleth had attended several of the Camp Shoemaker reunions. Tyler wasn't sharing the details of their breakup, and no one was asking any questions. But Lilleth and Tyler were no longer a couple, and Lilleth would not be attending any more reunions. Tyler was still athletic and energetic. He was still a force on the ski slopes and in other demanding athletic arenas. Who knew what the future might hold in terms of romance for Tyler Merriman?

Tyler recently moved from Colorado to a wonderful property in Fayetteville, Arkansas. He lives beside the White River. He has great neighbors. In the past year, he has had a series of surgeries that will allow him to continue his active lifestyle. He had now officially become the Bionic Man.

SIDNEY AND CAMERON RICHARDSON

Cameron Richardson had always loved to build things. From the time he was a child, he'd been taking things apart and putting them back together again. He loved to tinker. He loved to invent. He liked to change something, even just a little bit, to make it work better. That was the way his mind worked. There were stories of the rockets he and a friend had constructed launched; they were just in junior high school at the time. There were stories of gunpowder explosions in the woods and the resulting craters in the ground. Of course he would study science when he entered the small, exclusive southern college. He transferred to a university with an engineering program for his last two years, and upon graduation, he was immediately recruited by IBM.

Mastering the technology of computers opened up a whole new world to Cameron, and it wasn't long before he was out on his own, inventing and tinkering and making things better. He built an innovative and tremendously successful computer empire. Then he built a second revolutionary electronics enterprise. The man lived to challenge the status quo, and his head was always in the future.

Cameron's businesses dealt with enormous amounts of data, and thanks to computers, this data could be accessed relatively easily. It made him millions. It was inevitable that the U.S. federal government would, from time to time, come asking for help with something. Cameron was a straight shooter, a good guy. He was an entrepreneur of the first order, but he was also honest through and through his character and soul. He would not knowingly do something that was illegal or wrong. Sometimes he helped out the feds, and sometimes he didn't. He knew how to say no, even to Uncle Sam. When he said yes, it was never for his own gain but because he felt a patriotic duty to lend his expertise. He helped crack the cell phones that led to the arrests of terrorists. He helped out whenever he felt it was the right thing to do. He didn't want his part in any of these operations to become public, but there were some people who knew he had been instrumental in tracking down and gathering evidence on the bad guys. The question was, did any of the bad guys know that Cameron Richardson had helped to finger them and put them away?

There was no question about it. Cameron had information on everybody and everything. He didn't use it for nefarious purposes, but he did have it. Anybody who knew what his companies were all about knew he had the goods, and the bads. Anyone who has achieved the level of success that Cameron had, and anyone who has made the hard decisions about everything, including personnel, has acquired some enemies along the way. Because Cameron was a fair and benevolent boss, he'd made fewer enemies than most, but he had appropriately fired the dead wood that unfortunately but inevitably turned up, from time to time, among his employees. He'd made some people angry. He was cavalier about his own security, but his second wife Sidney worried about him.

Cameron had married for the first time when he was just out of college, and he'd married a woman several years older than himself. His friends had been puzzled about the union that, to those on the outside, seemed unusual. Were these two well-matched? Did they have anything at all in common? The guys loved their buddy and accepted his marital decision. Sometimes, love is strange. The marriage produced two children but eventually came to an end. The failure of the marriage wasn't anybody's fault.

After being a bachelor for a few years, Cameron met the love of his life. He had made his fortune and his reputation, and he finally had the time to invest in a relationship. Sidney Putnam insisted on it. She let Cameron know that, to make their marriage work, he needed to listen to what was important to her and spend time with her. He was wildly in love with Sidney, but she refused to marry him until he learned that she would be an equal partner in their marriage. She was not a back seat kind of woman.

Sidney's first marriage had also ended in divorce. She had one son, to whom she was devoted, and she'd been able to remain friends with her first husband, her son's father. Most people can't achieve this almost impossible feat, but Sidney had people skills that most people don't. Sidney had been the runner-up in her state's beauty pageant for the Miss America contest. She'd always had the looks, but more importantly, she had the smarts — of all kinds.

Sidney's most outstanding way of being smart was her gift for reading people. Her uncanny ability to know when someone was lying was an asset when she worked as a consultant for the Texas Department of Criminal Justice. She was the prosecutor's secret weapon. She consulted on jury selections and sat in on law enforcement interviews with suspects and witnesses. She was never wrong in her assessments. She didn't necessarily tell the authorities what they wanted to hear. She told the truth. And sometimes, nobody wanted to hear the truth. Sidney demanded that her assistance in criminal cases remain confidential, but she was almost too good to be true. Eventually, what she could do leaked out beyond the walls of the justice department, and she knew being exposed could put her in danger.

Her ability to vet people was invaluable to Sidney when she started her own business. As a single parent, she needed to support herself and her son. With her business, You Are Home, she identified a need that existed and built a business that responded to that need. Her first clients were corporations that frequently moved their employees from place to place. Corporations arranged to move their employee's household goods and paid for the packing and moving and unpacking. The gap in these employee benefits came when the wife, and it usually was the wife back in the day, had to put it all away and set up the new household. The husband, and it usually was the husband back in the day, was off doing his corporate thing, and the wife was at home with the kids, trying to find a place to put their stuff in the new kitchen and the unfamiliar closets.

Sidney's company was hired to come in and put their household goods away where they belonged. Her well-trained employees would organize the kitchen, at the housewife's direction, but with suggestions from the experts about the best kitchen logistics to make it fully functional. They put shelf paper in the drawers and on the shelves. They put away everybody's clothes—organizing, folding, and hanging everything in the most efficient and easy-to-access way. You Are Home would arrange for a room to be painted and would bring in other professionals to position furniture to its best advantage and hang art work. Sidney was good at this, and she taught her carefully-selected employees to be good at it, too. She charged high prices for her services, but there was a huge demand for what she was selling. Her company grew rapidly. She was a very successful entrepreneur in her own right when she literally ran into Cameron Richardson in a restaurant.

It was an expensive steak house in Fort Worth, and Sidney was there having lunch and closing a deal with a corporate client. It was summer, and she was dressed in a stunning white designer linen dress. She had a white cashmere cardigan sweater over her shoulders because the air conditioning was turned up so high in the steak house, to counter the July Texas heat. She got up to go to the ladies' room, and a tall, good-looking man didn't see her making her way through the tables in the dark, wood-paneled restaurant. The man pushed back his chair and stood up from his table with a large glass of iced tea in his hand. He ran straight into Sidney and spilled the entire glass of tea all over her dress, cashmere sweater, and expensive white high-heeled shoes. They were both stunned. He looked into the bright and beautiful eyes of the woman whose clothes he'd just ruined and couldn't turn away. To say it was love at first sight on his part would probably be the truth. She was angry that her outfit had been spoiled, but Cameron Richardson was so gracious about sending a car to drive her home to change her clothes. He insisted on paying for dry cleaning and replaced the clothes that could not be saved. Sidney had to soften her annoyance.

She had no idea who Cameron Richardson was, and they'd had several dates before Sidney fully grasped the extent of Cameron's wealth and success. Sidney was not looking for a relationship of any kind at this point in her life. She had a business to run and a child to raise. She was incredibly busy. But Cameron always went after what he wanted, and he usually got it. He went after Sidney like nothing he'd ever gone after in his life. Cameron pulled out all the stops to court the independent and strong-willed Sidney Putnam. The more she got to know him, the more she realized that Cameron was not only a success. He was also a kind and caring human being. She finally had to admit to herself that she'd fallen in love with the man.

Sidney and Cameron's latest project is building a world class resort in River Springs, Arkansas. It's a work in progress and Cameron is loving every minute of developing this remarkable venue. Sidney has discovered talent among the women of River Springs and has founded the Women's Work Collective.

ISABELLE AND MATTHEW RITTER

They met in New Orleans when he was a fourth-year medical student at Tulane and she was a freshman at Newcomb College. They both had roots in Tennessee, albeit at different ends of that very long state. Their first few dates had long-term relationship written all over them. Isabelle Blackstone was considerably younger than Matthew Ritter, but he was committed to being eternally young and worked out every day to stay that way. They made a handsome couple. Isabelle was blonde and beautiful, and Matthew knew she was the one. He was in love, but he wasn't ready to settle down. He had places to go and people to see. He had an internship and a residency to do, and he had signed up to fulfill his obligations to his country by spending two years working for the United States Public Health Service. She had just finished her freshman year in college. Matthew was moving on to California for his internship, the next chapter in the long quest to become a urologist. Would Isabelle go with him or would she stay in New Orleans?

In the end, she decided he was worth it. She would transfer to UCLA and complete her undergraduate studies there. Her parents were not happy when their nineteen-year-old daughter told them she wanted to leave Newcomb College and move to California to complete her degree, but they trusted her and agreed to pay her tuition in California. She was an excellent student and worked hard to graduate with a dual degree in psychology and sociology. Isabelle and Matthew married after Isabelle finished her undergraduate studies, and they moved to the Phoenix area where Matthew served his two years in the Public Health Service, working on what was then called an Indian Reservation. While they lived near Phoenix, Isabelle earned a master's degree in clinical psychology at Arizona

State University, and she later opened her own counseling practice in Palm Springs, the same year Matthew joined a thriving urology group in that California city.

The professional corporation Matthew Ritter joined was the leading group of urologists in Southern California. Movie actors and other famous people from Los Angeles drove to Palm Springs for medical care, especially when they had an embarrassing problem they didn't want anyone in L.A. to know about. Matthew was bound by the Hippocratic Oath and the covenant of professional confidentiality not to talk about his patients. And he never did. He kept many confidences about highly-placed people in all walks of life. As well as the Hollywood crowd, he treated wealthy businessmen and politicians, including two governors of Western states, several United States senators, and assorted congressmen and judges. His group was known for its medical expertise as well as for its discretion. Matthew knew many scandalous things, secrets quite a few famous people hoped he would carry to his grave. He would, but did they all trust that he would always abide by his commitment to confidentiality?

Isabelle likewise knew her clients' secrets. She was an effective therapist and a warm and caring human being. Her patients loved her. She had a successful practice within a year of hanging out her shingle and had to begin hiring additional counselors to join her. There was a lot of money in Palm Springs. There were also some very large egos in residence, a not unexpected circumstance. The very successful wanted to live, vacation, and retire in this golf course mecca that was reputed to have more sunny days than any other place in the United States. There was a great deal of infidelity, and many people came to her with problems that were associated with their addictions to drugs and alcohol. There was domestic abuse, and women, who did not want to be seen in public with a black eye or a broken arm, left Beverly Hills to hide out and seek counseling in Palm Springs. Isabelle listened and dispensed advice to the rich and famous.

Isabelle was sometimes called to testify in court, something she hated to do. She didn't like to break a confidence, but she was legally bound to respond to a subpoena to appear in court and to testify honestly when questioned under oath. She had almost been called to testify in the extraordinarily high-profile murder trial that involved a very famous football player and his second wife. Everyone knew the athlete had been beating up his wife on a regular basis. He'd finally killed her and was on trial for murder. Thankfully, Isabelle hadn't had to testify in that case. But there were other cases where her testimony had resulted in an unstable parent being denied custody of their child in a divorce. She had received direct and very personal threats as a result of some of these court cases.

Isabelle had struggled to work, at least part-time, while she raised the couple's two children. She had household and babysitting help, and she spent as much time in her office as she could. She knew she needed the stimulation of doing her own thing while dealing with diaper changes, wiping down counters, making endless peanut butter and jelly sandwiches, and driving her children to their after-school activities and numerous sports events. When her children graduated from high school, Isabelle realized she was burned out being a clinical psychologist, and she began to look for a new and less stressful career.

She found her next identity as an interior designer and owner of an elegant high-end shop that sold European antiques, lamps, and other wonderfully beautiful and expensive accessories for the home. Isabelle's store, Blackstone White, immediately became everybody's favorite place to find the perfect piece to make a room both interesting and classy.

What Isabelle had not expected was the extent to which being an interior designer and a store owner would call on her skills as a therapist. People came into the store to talk and sometimes to cry. Her clients had a great deal of money, but they did not always have much happiness or contentment. Isabelle was a good listener. She was patient and kind. People she barely knew poured out their hearts to her. If a husband was laundering money, his wife might express her disgust or her fear about his activities to Isabelle. If a boyfriend was involved in the drug trade, the girlfriend would confide in Isabelle. There were plenty of mafioso living in Palm Springs.

Isabelle sometimes helped a client disappear. It started with a woman who was a prolific shopper and regular customer of Isabelle's. The woman came into the store one day, terrified that her husband had sent his henchmen to kill her. She begged Isabelle to allow her to hide in the storage room at the back of Blackstone White. Isabell trusted her gut and helped the woman lie down, well concealed, behind a pallet of oriental rugs. Sure enough, two greasy looking tough guys with tattoos all over their arms arrived at the store, and without asking, searched high and low for the gangster's wife. Isabelle was frightened, but she was also angry. The mobsters were unable to find Isabelle's client, and as soon as they'd left, Isabelle called the police and reported the two for bursting into her store, turning everything topsy-turvy, and searching her property without her permission. She knew nothing would come of the police report she'd filed, but felt she had done the right thing.

Isabelle hid the frightened woman in her own home for several days and then drove her to Mexico. The woman had a secret bank account in L.A. and hoped to start a new life south of the border. The incident had been terrifying, but Isabelle had found a new calling. She was now an interior designer, store owner, and rescuer of the abused. It was a lot to take on, and Isabelle often asked herself if she had merely traded one stressful job for another even more stressful job.

The interior design part of her business was booming. Isabelle had excellent taste. Everybody wanted her help to design the addition to their house; consult with them about the space planning in their new kitchen; and do the paint, curtains, and new furniture in the family room renovation. She had more business than she could handle. She spent a lot of time in clients' homes and often drew on her counseling skills to settle disputes within their families. The husband, who was paying the bill for the redecorating project, didn't like white walls. The wife, who would be spending most of her waking hours in the room, wanted only white walls. He dug in his heels. She refused to talk about it. The interior designer/marriage counselor came to the rescue and brought a compromise and reconciliation. Isabelle often wondered how interior designers without experience in clinical counseling were ever able to accomplish anything.

Isabelle saw and heard many things she never wanted to see or hear. She kept her secrets, but she sometimes wondered if an angry father, who had been denied access to his children because of his mental illness, would remember her court testimony and come after her. She worried that the women she'd helped disappear would be found. Would the assistance Isabelle had given to rescue and hide these victims be exposed? Would an angry abuser come after her?

OLIVIA AND J.D. STEELE

J.D. Steele had been an athlete and a scholar in high school before he matriculated at the University of Oklahoma. He was handsome and outgoing as well as smart. He joined a fraternity and dated many women, but he also managed to make good grades, at least good enough for him to be admitted to the University of Oklahoma College of Law after he finished his four undergraduate years. After law school, J.D. fulfilled his obligation to Uncle Sam and was stationed in El Paso, Texas with the JAG Corps. J.D. had always wanted to be a prosecutor. He had a strong sense of right and wrong and wanted to help make sure the bad guys were found guilty and put in jail. He would devote twenty-five years of his life to this cause, and he became a legend in Tulsa legal circles. His specialty was trying the most complex and difficult criminal cases, including murder, rape, and drug cases. He was a relentless defender of justice and a dispenser of appropriate punishment. He was always prepared and performed brilliantly in front of the jury. J.D. seemed to thrive on convicting the worst of the worst, and he could count the cases he'd ever lost on one hand!

J.D. and his first wife were married just after they'd finished college. They were both very young, and neither of them was ready for marriage. The two had almost nothing in common, and after less than a year, they realized their union had been a mistake. They had no children and few assets, so their divorce was relatively amicable. They remained friends.

After his divorce, J.D. became one of Tulsa's most eligible bachelors and was quite the man-about-town for a few years until he met Signa Karlsson. It was a love match, and they married and had twins, a boy and a girl. Signa had her pilot's license and loved to fly. Both of their children had graduated from college when Signa was killed in a plane crash. She was a passenger in a friend's private plane. J.D. was devastated and terribly angry. He was convinced that if

Signa had been flying the plane, there would not have been an accident. He didn't handle his enormous grief well and vowed never to marry again. He resigned abruptly from his job as an assistant district attorney, abandoned his beautiful Art Deco mansion without even cleaning out the refrigerator, told no one except his grown children goodbye, and left the country for French Polynesia.

This was where J.D.'s life and marital history became murky. Some say he married again on the rebound ... two times! But no one is really sure whether he ever married again at all, or if he did, whether it was once, twice, three or even four times. Rumors flew, and J.D. wasn't talking about it. It didn't matter. J.D. never went back to Tulsa, and his house was sold. He eventually returned to the United States, and with the money he had saved, combined with an inheritance from his now-deceased, well-to-do parents, he bought a trucking company. The company's headquarters were in Missouri, and J.D. bought a condo in St. Louis.

He'd never thought he would enjoy anything as much as he'd enjoyed being a prosecuting attorney, but he found he loved running his own transportation empire. He was good at logistics and good with people, and RRD Trucking made him ten times more money than he'd ever dreamed he would make in his lifetime. He bought a cattle ranch. J.D. liked to travel to Washington, D.C. to lobby his legislators in person about transportation issues. It was on one of these trips to the nation's capital that he met Olivia Barrow Simmons.

Olivia Barrow had been a cheerleader and her high school's homecoming queen. She was beautiful and outgoing. She was the prettiest and the most popular girl in her school, and she was also very smart. After graduating from the University of North Carolina with a degree in mathematics, Olivia moved to Washington, D.C. where she shared an apartment with three other young women. Olivia had landed a job as a cypher specialist at the National Security Agency, so she wasn't able to talk to anybody about what she did at work.

Because Olivia was so attractive and had such a winsome personality, the NSA quickly identified her as a person who could represent the agency at Congressional hearings and other official public events. She always had all the answers, and although she would rather have been spending her time working on the complicated puzzles, mathematical constructs, and computer coding she loved, she was happy to be the pretty face of the No Such Agency. It was during one of her appearances before the Senate Select Committee on Intelligence that she was introduced to Bradford Simmons, the youngest man ever to be elected to the United States Senate. He was from Colorado, and he had a reputation as a womanizer.

Once he'd laid eyes on Olivia, he had to have her. She was young and vulnerable and flattered that a United States Senator wanted to date her. The women with whom she shared her apartment were envious and urged her to continue going out with Bradford. Olivia was eventually persuaded by the young senator's attentions, and within eighteen months, they were married. Olivia was devoted to her work and insisted on keeping her job at the NSA. Olivia and Bradford had three children, and Olivia chose to stay married to the senator until all three had graduated from college. Simmons had continued his womanizing behavior all during their miserable marriage, and Olivia had finally had all she could stand of the ridiculously handsome and adulterous cad. She divorced him.

Olivia vowed she would never marry again, and she focused her life on her children, her grandchildren, and the career she loved. Olivia had a very high security clearance and was a valuable employee at the NSA. Nobody could ever know exactly what she did, but whatever it was, she was very, very good at it. She knew lots of secrets about everything and everybody, but she was a person of the highest integrity. No one ever worried that she would suffer from "loose lips."

Many eligible bachelors in the nation's capital wanted to date her, but she was done with men ... or so she said. Even in her late fifties, she was a beauty. She was a fascinating conversationalist, and everyone, men and women, wanted to sit next to her at dinner. It was at one such dinner party, hosted by her best friend, that Olivia was seated next to J.D. Steele. The two hit it off immediately and were roaring with laughter before the main course was served. The hostess, who had known Olivia for decades, had thought J.D. and Olivia would appreciate each other's company, but she'd greatly underestimated the enormous amount of fun they would have together. For Olivia and for J.D., there was nobody else at the party.

They were inseparable from that night on. J.D. bought a townhouse in Georgetown and courted the woman who had swept him off his feet. He had never expected to fall in love like this so late in life, but he adored Olivia and didn't want to be away from her. Olivia was just as shocked to find herself head over heels in love with J.D. She liked men, but after her disastrous marriage, she wanted nothing more to do with romance. But these two were a match that was destined to be. They had such a good time in one another's company. Each of them had a wonderful sense of humor, and they could always make the other one laugh. Even their very skeptical grown children had to admit it was a beautiful thing to behold.

It was Olivia's idea to move closer to where J.D.'s business had its headquarters. The couple bought a house in St. Louis. She hated to leave her job at the NSA, but it was time to retire. Because Olivia insisted on spending one week out of every month near her children and grandchildren, who all lived in the Northern Virginia, Maryland, D.C. area, they kept the townhouse in the District. This was fine with J.D., and he usually came East with her. They traveled and enjoyed their lives. In spite of love and compatibility, Olivia was skeptical about marriage for many years. She didn't see why it was necessary. J.D. finally convinced Olivia that being married would not be the end of their romance, and they tied the knot when they were both in their late 60s.

Olivia Steele passed away in November of the previous year after an incredibly courageous fight to live. Everyone who knew her had loved this special woman. She was beautiful, brilliant, brave, kind, fun, and funny. She personified every good thing you could imagine in a human being. It had been less than a year since Olivia died, and J.D. was inconsolable. He was making a valiant attempt to keep on keeping on.

Acknowledgments

Heartfelt thanks to my readers and editors. I couldn't have done this without you. Thank you to the photographer who always makes me look good, Andrea Burns, and to Jamie Tipton at Open Heart Designs. Jamie puts it all together for me. I am nothing without Jamie. Thank you to friends and fans who have encouraged me to continue writing.

About the Author

A *former actress and singer,* **HENRIETTA ALTEN WEST** *has lived all over the United States and has traveled all over the world. She writes poetry, songs (words and music), screenplays, historical fiction, spy thrillers, books for young people, and mysteries. She always wanted to be Nancy Drew but ended up being Carolyn Keene.*

More Books By
Henrietta Alten West

I Have a Photograph
Book #1 in the The Reunion Chronicles Mysteries

Old friends gather in Bar Harbor for a reunion. They've made it to age seventy-five this year and are ready for a party. Who knew that their annual celebration of camaraderie, food and wine, laughter, and memories would turn into an adventure of murder and revenge?

Released 2019, 277 pages   Paperback ISBN: 9781953082930
Hardcover ISBN: 9781953082947   ebook ISBN: 9781953082923

Preserve Your Memories
Book #2 in the The Reunion Chronicles Mysteries

After surviving the previous fall's harrowing adventure in Maine, the Camp Shoemaker group of friends has gathered at the fabulous Penmoor Resort in Colorado Springs. In this sequel to *I Have A Photograph*, unanswered questions are addressed, and complex Russian connections become clear.

Released 2020, 362 pages   Paperback ISBN: 9781953082015
Hardcover ISBN: 9781953082008   ebook ISBN: 9781953082022

When Times Get Rough
Book #3 in the The Reunion Chronicles Mysteries

In spite of the COVID pandemic, the Camp Shoemaker yearly reunion was being held in Paso Robles, California at the elegant Albergo Inn. Kidnapping and torture were on the program. The group once again rallied to save a fellow guest at the Albergo and a physician whistleblower from Hong Kong who had been targeted by Chinese Communist agents operating inside the U.S. Then these seniors had to scramble to save the lives of two of their own.

Released 2021, 352 pages   Paperback ISBN: 9781953082077
Hardcover ISBN: 9781953082060   ebook ISBN: 9781953082084

More on following page...

A FORTRESS STEEP AND MIGHTY
Book #4 in the The Reunion Chronicles Mysteries

The Cold War is hot again. The audacious plot to assassinate a powerful world leader will keep you on the edge of your seat. Bogged down in an endless war, will Russia's Hitleresque president decide to use nuclear weapons to achieve his objectives? Forces are at work to bring him down. The world holds its collective breath as the threat of global annihilation looms. This thriller, the fourth book in the Reunion Chronicles Mysteries series, reaches into the future with an outrageously bold plan.

Released 2022, 378 pages
Hardcover ISBN: 9781953082183

Paperback ISBN: 9781953082190
ebook ISBN: 9781953082206

THE WELLS OF SILENCE
Book #5 in the The Reunion Chronicles Mysteries

Set in present-day Arizona with WWII-era flashbacks to Poland and the Soviet Union, the story weaves themes of fentanyl trafficking, domestic abuse, and the Katyn Forest massacre into a riveting adventure of escape and revenge. The cover-up of atrocities is stunning, and the woman married to the grandson of Stalin's henchman must fake her death to escape his threats to kill her.

Released 2023, 418 pages
Hardcover ISBN: 9781953082244

Paperback ISBN: 9781953082251
ebook ISBN: 9781953082268

Available in print and ebook online everywhere books are sold.

MORE FROM
LLOURETTIA GATES BOOKS

CAROLINA DANFORD WRIGHT

Old School Rules
Book #1 in the *The Granny Avengers Series*

Marfa Lights Out
Book #2 in the *The Granny Avengers Series*

MARGARET TURNER TAYLOR

www.margaretttaylorwrites.com

BOOKS FOR ADULTS

Traveling Through the Valley
of the Shadow of Death

I Will Fear No Evil

Russian Fingers

Do You Know Who I Am?

BOOKS FOR YOUNG PEOPLE

Secret in the Sand
Baseball Diamonds
Train Traffic
The Quilt Code
The Eyes of My Mind

Available in print and ebook
online everywhere books are sold.

Printed in the USA
CPSIA information can be obtained
at www.ICGtesting.com
JSHW011918270724
67075JS00003B/3/J

9 781953 082305